THE ENDING LEGACY

THE RAVEN QUEEN

LINDSEY POGUE   **LINDSEY SPARKS**

The Raven Queen
By Lindsey Sparks and Lindsey Pogue

Editing by Holly Hill Mangin
Fresh as a Daisy Editing

Cover Design by Deranged Doctor Designs

L2 Books
101 W. American Canyon Rd. Ste. 508-262
American Canyon, CA 94503

978-1949485271

To the best readers a couple of authors could ever ask for…

We started this adventure together in 2012 with a crazy idea to write a book about the end of the world, never dreaming it would burgeon an epic journey for both of us.

What began as a story about two friends, separated by thousands of miles during a viral outbreak, turned into a beloved series. It introduced us to the most voracious, supportive, and loving readers. Even now—dozens of books later—you Endingers have shown us so much love and support, helping us live our life-long dreams of being authors. There is no amount of gratitude or heartfelt words that can describe what that means to us.

Even now, Dani and Zoe's story lives on in The Ending Legacy, this new series in The Ending World that we never would have written, if not for you.

From the bottom of our giddy author hearts, we thank you, Endingers, for everything.

The Lindseys

THE ENDING WORLD

Maryland: Dr. Anna Cartwright discovers a base pair on a specific strand of DNA estimated to be present in a little over 10 percent of the human population. It holds the genetic key to accessing never-before-seen mental and physical abilities. She reads an article about gene therapy and sets out to conduct human trials.

1978

In a second round of trials, Dr. Anna Cartwright's colleague, Gregory Herodson, asks her to administer the gene therapy to him. Once developed, Herodson begins honing his Ability, using Anna to amplify it, and starts putting his plan and mind-controlled army into place for the Great Transformation.

1988

Colorado Springs: Gregory Herodson, now a General, takes Anna away from her family, threatening the lives of her family if she ever disobeys him. Anna changes her name to Dr. Wesley, and becomes the General's plaything and greatest weapon.

Nevada: PANBO BIOTECH implements the Fulfillment Study (also known as the Program), which attracts candidates through solicitation and then alters their DNA. If the subject carries the Pandora strand they develop special abilities, if they don't carry the strand they get very sick and either go mad or die.

1990

The Colony: General Herodson makes Dr. Wesley create a modified influenza virus, nearly universally contagious and designed to take advantage of the weakened immune systems of the non-P-strand carriers. They release the Virus on the general population.

2012

United States: People begin getting sick with an unknown flu that is spreading rapidly, deaths are being reported. The Center for Disease Control start quarantining people based on whether or not they've had H1N1.

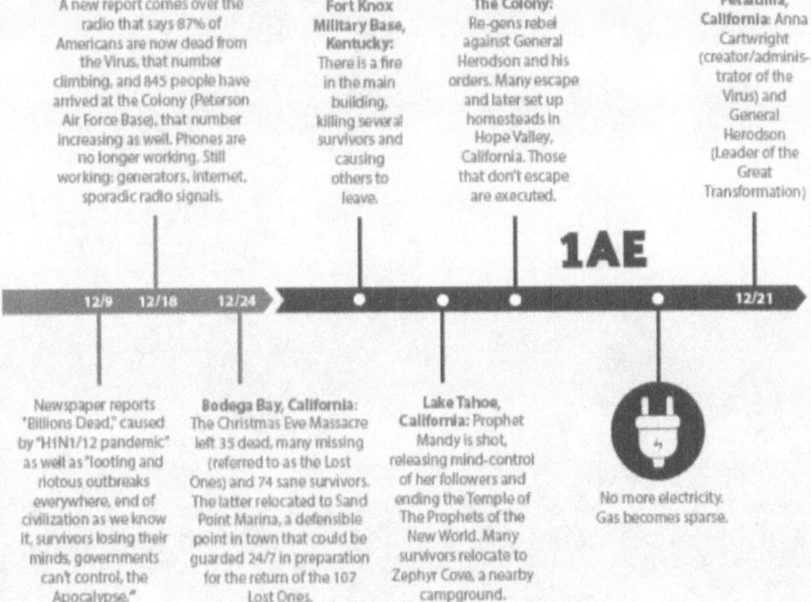

A new report comes over the radio that says 87% of Americans are now dead from the Virus, that number climbing, and 845 people have arrived at the Colony (Peterson Air Force Base), that number increasing as well. Phones are no longer working. Still working: generators, internet, sporadic radio signals.

Fort Knox Military Base, Kentucky: There is a fire in the main building, killing several survivors and causing others to leave.

The Colony: Re-gens rebel against General Herodson and his orders. Many escape and later set up homesteads in Hope Valley, California. Those that don't escape are executed.

Petaluma, California: Anna Cartwright (creator/administrator of the Virus) and General Herodson (Leader of the Great Transformation)

1AE

12/9   12/18   12/24   12/21

Newspaper reports "Billions Dead," caused by "H1N1/12 pandemic" as well as "looting and riotous outbreaks everywhere, end of civilization as we know it, survivors losing their minds, governments can't control, the Apocalypse."

Bodega Bay, California: The Christmas Eve Massacre left 35 dead, many missing (referred to as the Lost Ones) and 74 sane survivors. The latter relocated to Sand Point Marina, a defensible point in town that could be guarded 24/7 in preparation for the return of the 107 Lost Ones.

Lake Tahoe, California: Prophet Mandy is shot, releasing mind-control of her followers and ending the Temple of The Prophets of the New World. Many survivors relocate to Zephyr Cove, a nearby campground.

No more electricity. Gas becomes sparse.

CRESCENT KINGDOM
ZENIA
HOPE VALLEY
FALLEN WOOD
MANTIS
SHADOW DISTRICT
SIERRA KINGDOM
CORVO CITY
CORVO KINGDOM
OUTERLANDS
NOCTEM
PEARSONVILLE
SHOSHONE
MORRO CITY
KINGDOM OF ANGELS
ARCADIA
THE SEVEN KINGDOMS

THE PATRONS

BECCA ORACLES	**ZOE** EMPATHS
SAM SENSORS	**DANI** TELEPATHS
CAMILLE MOVERS	**JASON** GAUGES
JAKE HEALERS	**CARLOS** ELEMENTALS
FORBIDDEN CONTROLLERS	**MASE** SUPERS

I

FIN

Sometimes, I could feel the soft curve of her cheek in my palm and the warmth of her skin against mine. Sometimes, I could still taste her lips and smell the lavender in her black, curly hair, silky between my fingers.

But her form and features were a mirage, like so many things in the desert, blurred and undefined, and the memory of her was just as fluid. It evaded me when all I wanted was to see her, hoping that if I did, she would stop haunting me when I closed my eyes.

Del was one more ghost from my past. One more regret.

Blinking, I stared up at the cave ceiling. Scant morning light seeped in from the wooden door, illuminating the cool stone walls that were both a reverie and a cursed, daily reminder of my naive childhood hope.

Remembering the woman I'd found comfort in last night, I looked to my left, the cot beside me surprisingly empty. Exhaling, I rubbed my hands over my face. Another night of vague dreams and restless sleep, followed by another day in the desert.

I sat up, and the earth was cold against my bare feet as they hit the dusty ground. I wondered how many new folks we'd have by the end of the week.

"Sir?" came a chipper voice from outside. I groaned and stared at my closed door as Callon's footsteps crunched closer. "Are you up yet, *sir*?" He called me that to rankle me, and it worked.

Elbows on my knees, I waited for my best friend to dare to open the door.

"Oh, *sirrr*," Callon sang.

"What?" I growled.

"You wouldn't happen to have company in there, would you?" he asked with a smile in his voice.

I tugged on my pants. "Why? That's never stopped you from interrupting me before." I took three steps to the door and opened it, meeting Callon's gleeful brown gaze. "It's too early for you to be so . . . annoying," I grumbled.

He smirked, his teasing grin one I'd counted on many times over the past ten years and half-heartedly despised for as equally long. His dark eyebrows danced over his slightly slanted eyes as he peered over my shoulder, surveying my quarters. "I didn't want to intrude," he said insincerely.

"Since when?" I muttered and met Tick's coyote gaze from her burlap bed outside my door. Her tawny, fluffy tail thumped languidly as she stretched in a patch of morning sunlight.

"I saw you leave the fire last night with the new girl," Callon explained and stepped inside.

I grabbed my boots beside my bed.

"The tall one," he whispered, leaning in conspiratorially. Callon's gaze swept my quarters again—over the rickety table, the carved-out shelf in the cliff wall, my unmade cot and the trunk of clothes at the end of my cot—everything with a thin layer of sand covering it.

"You think she's hiding somewhere?" I asked dryly, lacing my last boot.

"No, but it seems she got the drop on you," Callon mused. "She left before you could and before the sun rose, even. Someone must have tipped her off to your usual ways."

Callon was an amazing tracker and one of our strongest human Telepaths—he could communicate with familiar minds from miles away—but he was also a pain in my ass most of the time. I would never change that about him, except for most mornings.

"Are you finished yet?" I asked and rose to my feet. "Because you only prattle on like this when you're procrastinating." Needing to wash the night away, I splashed water on my face from the bowl on the table. It was chilled from the cold night, and I reveled in it.

"I'll admit," Callon conceded as I wiped my face dry. "I was sussing out your mood."

"By making it worse?" I retorted, and when Callon's silence lingered, I peered over my shoulder at him. He was suddenly very sober, which was un-Callonlike. "What is it?" I turned to face him. "Is it Dylon? Has he gotten worse?" One of our newest arrivals had a sick son, and we weren't sure if he would make it. It was likely the result of a weak constitution and the stress of so much travel as they fled their home in the north. The journey through the desert wasn't easy.

Callon's expression was cautious as he shook his head. "Not Dylon," he hedged. "Some, uh . . . uninvited guests arrived in the night." He held up his hand as my body tensed, my stomach dropping instantly.

"And you're only *just* telling me this?" I bit out.

"There was no point in saying anything until we knew what was going on, Fin," he said defensively. "We have twenty pairs of eyes and ears on them. I wanted more intel before I, um—" He glanced at my cot again. "Disturbed you."

I stiffened, and I glared at him. "That's not for you to decide," I gritted out, and any ease and comfort I'd found last night evaporated. I rubbed my forehead instead of shoving Callon against the wall for assuming *anything* was more important than the safety of the 1,012 people who relied on us to keep them safe. "Who is it? And how many are there?"

"A small team set up camp in the Rainbow Hills. About two dozen of them."

"From?" I held my breath.

Callon blinked at me before finally answering. "No one knows for certain yet—the men carry no banners—"

"Then they're mercenaries."

"Aye, and they have Ferals for slaves." Callon watched my reaction carefully as his words settled in. It could have been because he knew Ferals killed my parents when I was young or that it was a ballsy move to enslave Ferals, people who, by no fault of their own, were more animal than human. Who were wild and unpredictable. Or so most would say.

"It has to be King Eduart," I said through clenched teeth. "Only Sierra Kingdom would have the hubris to think that was a good idea."

"It could be Eduart's ally," Callon added carefully. "The Corvo Kingdom."

Unbidden, my mind drifted to the princess, and I realized then why Callon hadn't wanted to tell me. But we said nothing about it.

"Who's got their senses on the mercs?" I asked, knowing it could have been any of the fifteen perimeter teams who watched our borders and telepathically communicated with Callon, the lead of all safeguarding measures.

"Lyra," he reported with a dip of his chin. He knew in that, at least, I would feel slightly more at ease. She was new to the team, but she was fiercely dedicated and alert, and her hyper-senses made her an invaluable asset to the security of this place.

I grabbed a T-shirt from the trunk by my cot and absently sniffed it. It smelled clean, even if it didn't look like it. "Have the mercs made contact?"

"No contact. In fact, Lyra doesn't think they know we're here."

I frowned in confusion. "Then they aren't here for us."

Callon shook his head. "No, which is why we wanted to wait to see what they were going to do."

"And?" I impatiently tugged my shirt over my head and snatched my tan headscarf from the table. "What are they doing?"

"Digging for something."

My frown deepened. "Digging?" I deadpanned. That both surprised and unnerved me as I stepped out into the cool morning.

Tick popped up, and I bent to scratch her behind the ears, her left leg twitching as I hit the perfect spot.

"There's nothing out there to dig for," I thought aloud.

"Which is why it's more unsettling than usual," Callon added.

Mentally, I surveyed the valley, taking stock of what mercs could possibly be here for, if not for us. Aside from scant vegetation, old bones, rocks, and metals in the volcanic earth, there wasn't much else.

Shaking my head, I peered out at our camp that covered the desert floor nearly as far as I could see. There was nothing to find here. That's why we'd chosen it years ago. When we first fled to the old mining dwellings carved in the cliffs, they were shelter enough to keep what few of us there were hidden from the blistering summer temperatures. It was a place to rest, not a place to live. Now, though, it was a refuge—more than that, it was a proper settlement, a hodgepodge of wood cabins and tents that surrounded the mudbrick buildings storing our food and providing shade for the people to work in. Tanners, farmers, blacksmiths, doctors—our camp had become a proper town in all the ways that mattered, and now, potential danger had found us again.

As Callon and I wove our way through camp toward the stables, woodsmoke tickled my nose, and distant chatter met my ears. "They're digging in the Rainbow Hills?" I clarified. The settlement was bustling as if it were already mid-day, people making use of the cool morning before the sun grew too hot and we all retreated into the shade again until nightfall.

"Yes. At the fork in the canyon."

Some people nodded in greeting as we passed, likely wondering where we were hurrying off to, so I tried to smile with forced reassurance. But most were too busy cleaning laundry, dredging and filtering water from the wells, or tending to the gardens to notice us.

Stride unwavering, I looked at Callon, my mind sifting through the possible reasons the hills would be of any interest to outsiders. "It must be for the metals in the soil." I wrapped my scarf loosely around my head and face. The sun was already warming my skin, and though I'd grown used to the heat, the sun remained relentless. I had the farmer's tan and freckles to prove it.

Callon shrugged. "Yeah, maybe metals. Lyra wasn't certain the last time I checked in, and I've been too busy harassing you to ask her again."

Dusty's gray and white spotted head bounced up as we strode into the adobe stable. It smelled of damp clay and manure, and a few other horses looked out to greet us. With limited resources, we had only the horses we needed, but they were necessary with such a vast landscape to patrol and our numbers growing every day.

Instinctively, my mind connected with his, and a featherlight tickle brushed the back of my mind. "Time for a ride, buddy," I murmured, and I barely unlatched the gate before he nudged it open the rest of the way and walked into the sunlight that filtered through the windows. Dusty's tall frame took up the entire aisle, and his hooves clomped over the stony earth as he made his way through the entrance and into the blue-sky morning.

Callon rubbed his hand over the mustang's face, leaning into him like they were old friends. "Lyra said our uninvited guests only have a few guards. Do you want me to get Taggart and the rest of the team prepped for a visit?"

"No." I hoisted myself onto Dusty's bare back and glanced again at the tent city stretched before us. These people came here for sanctuary, and I wasn't ready to cause a stir. "Not yet. I want to know more first."

Resting my palm on Dusty's neck, I closed my eyes. *To the Rainbow Hills.* It was a single thought but all I needed to get Dusty walking in that direction. "Tell Lyra I'm coming," I called to Callon over my shoulder.

"Done!" he answered. "I'll just wait here then!"

Callon disappeared as we headed toward the horizon. Dusty and I trotted at a fast clip, as Tick loped over to join us. Together, the three of us made our way into the rugged mountains bordering the western edge of our settlement, Dusty's long strides eating up the desert floor as we rode with the morning breeze.

Along the way, I sifted through Tick's mind, but having been at the Badwater Basin hunting shrew and rattlesnake all night, the coyote knew nothing that would help me discern what the hell these people were doing so far east of the Seven Kingdoms. The desert lands, unlivable and desolate at best, were nothing compared to their lush forests.

The farther we rode, the more the landscape changed, barren in some places and remarkably dangerous and otherworldly in others. Though our village was a thousand people strong, with more coming every week, we'd found a peaceful existence in Death Valley over the years. Especially with our powers to better serve us.

The Elementals could manipulate the soil for crops, control fire for cooking and warmth on cold, cruel nights, and find under-ground water sources to keep us, our animals, and our gardens hydrated. Telekinesis and enhanced strength, speed, and senses came in handy with daily chores and helping the patrol teams. And Telepaths, well, they were invaluable for communication between outposts in an expansive place like this, where security in our hidden oasis was paramount.

We'd found a way to live out here, away from the unrest of the Seven Kingdoms, and it worked. Even if it never quite felt like Fallen Wood—like home.

What home? I had to remind myself it hadn't been home in a very long time. The memories were as painful as they were precious, and as much as I hated dwelling on the past, I couldn't stop myself from missing it, either.

I told myself this bout of nostalgia was because Jake had been abroad for so long this time, searching for whatever it was he never seemed to find. Being the last of his kind—an original changed during the Turn and celebrated by so many as the Patron of Healers—Jake was always wandering and restless. He was always searching, but for what, I was never certain. And I missed the only family I had left. That was only part of my reminiscing thoughts, though.

I missed my sister. Had Autumn survived Queen Corisande's attack on our village, she would have been thirty-eight yesterday. More than that, had I killed the Corvo queen when I was in the castle ten years ago looking for Jake, she never would have been able to go back on her word and slaughter my people.

Bottom line, had Jake and I been there when it happened, we might've stopped the siege on our village, and my sister might still have been alive. Instead, now we were out here, living off lands too brutal to be claimed, with the treacherous Sierra mountains stretching between us and the trading ports and outposts we needed to better survive.

Sensing my darkening mood, Dusty rode harder and faster, as if he, too, wished to outrun my memories. And as soon as the eroded Rainbow Hills glinted into view, we slowed, Tick, Dusty, and my human eyes scouring the rocky canyon for unwanted attention as we approached.

Tick trotted ahead in search of Lyra, sniffing as she scaled the smooth rockface to the hiding post. Through Tick's eyes, I could see Lyra and Martin, her scouting partner, crouched in the shadows of the outer cliff as Tick crested a boulder. Everything was so crisp and clear through the eyes of a coyote, even if our mental connection made my senses tingle a little.

Absently, I dismounted Dusty, prepared to follow Tick.

When Lyra saw the coyote, she nodded in greeting and gave me the signal that our visitors were a klick south. Nulling myself so that any probing minds wouldn't sense me, I left Dusty in a patch of shade in the foothills and began to climb.

"They arrived in the middle of the night," Lyra said as I crawled into place beside her. Her blue eyes were fixed on the scene below.

I nodded. "Callon reported no banners."

"No, none. And out of the two dozen of them, most are enslaved."

I peered down into the shadows of the rugged valley, the greens, blues, and purples of the metallic soils shimmering in the rising sun as I took in the sight of our intruders working below. I hated that they were here, bold and brazen as ever. Whatever the mercs' reasons were for coming, it had to be important to have driven them to no-man's-land.

"They started at sunrise," Martin offered gravely. "So far, they've kept to the lower valley."

"Any idea what they are digging for yet?" I squinted, seeing only a glimpse of what Lyra's enhanced vision and hearing could glean. She was the eyes and ears I relied on most that patrolled the perimeters of our band of castaways and refugees. "Hematite?" I asked. "Manganese?"

Lyra shook her head. "I'm not certain, but they need samples for someone in the Sierra Kingdom," she said, confirming what I'd feared. "But that man, right there—" Lyra pointed to a guy in brown garb who stood no bigger than my thumb in the distance. Though she could see every minute detail and twitch of our visitor's mouth from here, to me, he looked like nothing more than an insect I wanted to smash between my fingers.

"He doesn't know who he's working for," she explained. "Only that he's been ordered to collect samples and return by the full moon if he wishes to receive his coin."

Martin handed me his binoculars, and as my eyes adjusted, an emaciated Feral came into view, his hair shaggy and as long as his beard. He moved like a beaten animal, only going through the motions he knew would get him food and water at some point.

I eyed the three guards patrolling the tops of the hills behind them. The man in the brown cape had disappeared into the single tent they'd set up in the flattest part of the valley.

"Why so many wagons?" I asked. There were far more than they needed to transport the Ferals.

"They need enough of each soil color to fill one of them," Lyra explained. "They should be finished before nightfall." She stared at me. Her dark blue eyes glinted in the sunlight, and I knew that look. It was the same one I'd seen the day I found her and her ailing father, half-starved and hiding in one of our outposts. An all too familiar weight hung in the air. *Fear.* "From here, they're headed to Mantis."

Dread needled its way into my shoulders, and I peered down at their temporary camp. "I was afraid you'd say that." Nothing good ever came from the Sierra capital.

"If we go," Lyra started—she clearly knew what I was thinking —"getting in will be one thing. But getting out . . ." She huffed derisively.

The Sierra Kingdom was known for its armies, and King Eduart was known for taking resources and tech from everywhere he could—more than what he needed to protect his lands against the Ferals and anyone else who would think to encroach on his territory. His kingdom was as vast as it was dangerous, with his military spread throughout, patrolling every border and town. No village was untapped or untaxed, nor were they free of constant military occupation and perpetual mistreatment. I hated King Eduart almost as much as I loathed Corvo's Queen Corisande.

"No good ever came from that king's plans," Martin said, mirroring my thoughts. He shrugged. "Maybe it has something to do with a new weapon?"

"Maybe, but whatever it is," Lyra said, "Corvo is likely involved too."

Despite how hard Princess Delphinia had tried to convince me the queen had changed her tyrannical ways ten years ago, and despite her promise to leave us alone, the queen had done what, in my heart, I had known she would do—exterminate my entire village.

I'd been the idealistic idiot who thought that after all that transpired between Del and me, of all the lies we'd uncovered and the truces that were made, we'd secured at least a temporary safety for my people. But I'd been deathly wrong, and my village—my sister —had paid the price.

Did Del know what had happened and how bad things were? Was she still fighting for good? A part of me had to believe she was still the rebel princess I remembered. But then, I wasn't as young and idealistic as I once was, so I doubted she was either. By marrying into King Eduart's family, Del had aligned herself with the Sierra Kingdom, combining the reach of both their realms.

So, no, I wasn't sure what to think about Princess Delphinia. Not anymore.

I looked at Martin. "Stay here and stay sharp. If anything changes, alert Callon immediately."

Martin nodded, he and Lyra looking at me for additional orders.

"I'm sending Tick out to sniff around, see what she can discover. We need to learn all we can before they head out again. If they've come once, they'll likely come again, and next time, they won't be collecting samples." I nodded to Lyra. "You, come with me."

I squinted out at the workers below, already sheening with sweat. The longer I thought about it, the more my resentment and anger grabbed hold of me. I was tired of anticipating the enemy, of running from the Corvo queen—from all the kingdoms that ruled with greed and fear.

But I knew living this life was an endless battle for freedom, for the right to live, and I would fight that battle until my dying breath. It was what my ancestors—my direct ancestors Dani and Jason—had to do centuries ago, alongside Jake, Zoe, Becca, and so many others after the virus spread. Together they learned to survive what was left of the world warped by Ability-amped chaos and to protect those they loved. And it was Becca, Jake's sister and the Oracle who prophesied it would come to this, who helped give them a fighting chance.

Meeting Lyra's expectant gaze, I knew what had to be done. Fighting to survive was in my blood and what Jake had been training me for, even if it felt like I'd been treading water for the last twenty-nine years.

"What's the plan then, boss?" Lyra asked.

I pushed off the boulder. "Whether it's on behalf of Corvo or King Eduart is acting alone, we have to know what they are searching for. If that means following them back to Mantis, then that's exactly what we'll do."

2

DEL

"In addition to his usual debauchery, Alastor has been meeting with an inordinate number of dignitaries in Mantis," Garath said, his voice a gentle rumble from across the breakfast table. "From the Seven Kingdoms, and from elsewhere."

I continued to gaze out the sitting-room window, staring at the Tower of Solitude as I trailed a fingertip back and forth over the two-inch-long pink scar on the back of my wrist. The forbidding stone tower stood all alone on that tiny island near the eastern edge of the moat, and a lone castle guard stationed at the door at the tower's base was just visible through the thinning morning fog.

No matter how hard I racked my brain, I couldn't recall who was imprisoned in the tower. Someone, obviously, or there wouldn't have been a guard stationed at the door. But *who*?

"My eyes in Mantis suggest Maylar may have been among the visitors," Garath added.

My focus snapped to Garath. His amber eyes were glassy and slightly bloodshot, like he had been up late into the night. That, on top of his several days' worth of stubble, made him appear positively roguish. A fleeting thought crossed my mind, prodding me to tease him about his usual nocturnal activities and his current lady-of-the-month, but I didn't have the energy for it.

Garath wasn't the only one who had been up most of the night, though my lost sleep stemmed from far less pleasant roots. Liam's tenth birthday was approaching, when he would be tested and officially placed in his Ability Class. It should have been simple in his case, little more than ceremony, since both of his parents descended from pure Empath lines. But his strong thread of telepathy told a different hereditary story.

There was no question that I was Liam's mother. His paternity, however, was another matter entirely. Which meant the kingdom would finally know the truth I had kept hidden all this time.

And Liam's life would be in grave danger.

I shook my head, dispelling the troublesome thoughts. "Maylar *may* have been among the visitors?" I said, repeating Garath's words back to him to confirm I had heard him right. I raised my eyebrows.

Garath nodded solemnly.

Dread coiled in my gut. Calling Maylar a snake would have been cruel—to snakes. He was snake excrement, always sniveling and scurrying around. Mother had dismissed him from his post as spymaster nearly a decade ago. I found out after the fact that she had intended to assassinate him since he knew too many of the kingdom's secrets, but Mother's attempts failed, and he escaped. We had heard whispers of him every few years since, but there was nothing concrete enough to track him down.

"But you're not certain?" I clarified. I wondered if Mother had already heard, if she had already directed her people to follow the trail.

"No," Garath said. "We're not certain."

I narrowed my eyes. "And these other dignitaries, the ones from *elsewhere*," I said. "Are you suggesting they came from *outside* the Seven Kingdoms?"

I couldn't remember the last time we had hosted an emissary

from beyond the borders of the Seven Kingdoms within the walls of Corvo City. The western border of the allied kingdoms was an ocean as far as the eye could see, and a vast desert bordered the east. So far as I could recall, the last outsiders who had stayed in Castle Corvo had been from the Evergreen Nation, the strange land far to the north of the Seven Kingdoms, where Abilities were outlawed. How they functioned on old-world tech in place of Ability-run amenities was beyond me.

Mother had diplomats stationed in all the richest foreign lands, of course. After all, the Corvo Kingdom was the trade center of the Seven Kingdoms, making our kingdom the wealthiest and most well-connected because of our ports. Still, most of the negotiating was done via our diplomats in those distant places.

I glanced at Hills, the diminutive general of the Corvo army. She tensed the corners of her mouth and lowered her chin in confirmation that Alastor had, in fact, been meeting with dignitaries from outside the Seven Kingdoms.

"Hmmm . . ." I leaned forward, tapping the tip of my index finger on the oak table. We had long since pushed our breakfast plates away, leaving them clustered together in the center of the table. I stared into the last dregs of tea in my mug, counting the specs of tea leaves that had settled at the bottom and stood out against the cream-colored ceramic.

"Which kingdoms has he been meeting with specifically?" I asked, my finger continuing to tap.

"Crescent and Zenia." Garath settled back in his chair, his leather armor creaking as he crossed his arms over his broad chest. "I'm still waiting on intel to identify the origin of the outsiders and to confirm Maylar's identity."

"Maybe it's some of those desert people we've been hearing whispers about?" I said, thinking out loud. "This supposed *Ghost King* and his followers?"

Rumor placed them somewhere on the fringes of the Seven Kingdoms, but I had yet to hear any concrete evidence that they actually existed. None of the southern kingdoms had the military resources or manpower to spare on scouting so far beyond their borders with the Sierra Kingdom openly readying for war from their fortress in Mantis. So long as I kept Alastor and his father, King Eduart, happy, Corvo City wasn't in immediate danger. Their forces freely moved across our kingdom's borders but not with Corvo City as their target. King Eduart wanted control of our ports, but at the moment, he seemed content with using Alastor to ensure the Sierra Kingdom had a say in our trade relations. Which meant his sights were turned to the other kingdoms bordering us, and they all lived in constant fear of invasion.

"Where did all this happen?" I looked up from the lukewarm tea. "Ironwood Keep?"

Garath shook his head. "A tavern in Mantis."

Which meant either King Eduart didn't know about Alastor's secret meetings, or he knew but wanted the rest of us to think he wasn't involved in whatever Alastor was plotting. I considered reaching out to the Sierra king through one of Garath's people to feel him out, but the relationship between our two kingdoms was increasingly tense, hanging by the ever-thinning thread that was my marriage.

What a joke. I might have laughed if I wasn't so miserable.

I sat back in my seat, setting my forearms flat against the arms of my chair, and returned to staring out the window. "What's that bastard up to?" I muttered.

Sid, perched on the back of my chair, snapped his beak upon hearing me utter my favorite nickname for my husband. The raven, with me since I was a baby, as was tradition among the Corvo royal line, was my most loyal companion and greatest champion.

I raised one hand to stroke the puffed-out black feathers on his neck.

"We'll know soon enough," Garath said ominously.

I looked at him, my stomach twisting into knots. "He's returning?" I asked, once again tracing the scar on my wrist. It was Alastor's most recent *gift*.

Garath's heavy stare told me his answer before his words confirmed it. "It looks that way," he finally said. "A raven arrived this morning carrying word of travel preparations at his mistress's estate."

Which meant I needed to make my own preparations, to steel myself to welcome my dastardly husband back into my home. Back into my bed.

I tensed instinctively. Even thinking about Alastor's cruel hands on my body made my skin crawl. But it had to be done. I needed an heir. A *female* heir, as was the Corvo way.

And until I had one, my claim on the Corvo throne would be increasingly precarious. But if I could just bear a girl and prove to the other kingdoms that the Corvo line was still stable, my position would strengthen tenfold in the eyes of the other rulers, and King Eduart would back off, feeling more secure in his hold over my kingdom once he had a granddaughter destined to sit on the Corvo throne. At least, that's what I kept telling myself.

The only upside to having to try for a legitimate heir with Alastor was that the instant his skin touched mine, I could skim his mind for some of his carefully guarded secrets. We were both Empaths, both powerful in our own ways, but when our skin was touching, my ability to dig into his mind far overpowered any attempts he might make to keep me out. I couldn't see everything, but I could usually catch enough of a glimpse of his schemes to stay a few steps ahead of him.

He knew it too, which was why he filled his mind with thoughts of all his other women while he was with me. Of the myriad of ways he enjoyed breaking them. Of the times he went too far. Of how desperately he wanted to hurt me, just as he hurt them. It turned my stomach, more often than not, leaving me vomiting in the washroom after we were together.

But I would experience that revulsion a hundred times over so long as it continued to keep me apprised of his duplicitous ways. So long as it continued to reveal the ever-narrowing path I needed to walk to keep his father from invading Corvo City and ripping away my waning power once and for all.

So long as it continued to show me how to keep my son safe.

"Who's in the tower?" I asked, purposely changing the subject.

Hills cleared her throat. "The queen caught wind of an enterprising pharmacist quietly peddling a synthetic healing elixir to some of the noble families."

I sat up straighter, my attention snapping to Hills. Her gray-streaked dark hair was pulled back and bound at her nape, further sharpening her angular features. "Does it work?" I asked, hope surging.

A synthetic elixir would fix *everything*. It would eradicate the wasting sickness plaguing our nobles, whose desire to preserve Class purity had made them vulnerable to the congenital ailment. To the other kingdoms, we appeared to be dying a slow death, but if we could show that the wasting sickness was no longer an issue, we would be seen as strong again, no longer the tempting, low-hanging fruit King Eduart had his heart set on claiming.

The wasting sickness had first emerged among the pure, inbred elite of Corvo City several decades ago, but recent reports suggested it was branching out to the murkier bloodlines of lowborn people throughout the Corvo Kingdom—and possibly elsewhere. It was hard to say for sure, as many of the symptoms were similar to those of strix addiction, and the drug ran rampant throughout the mixed-class commoners of not only the Corvo Kingdom but throughout the Seven Kingdoms. We had yet to receive reports of the wasting sickness appearing outside our borders, but I was holding out hope that it would—if only to take the target off our backs.

But a cure, even more than a female heir, would strengthen our kingdom's position—*my* position. Maybe, just *maybe*, it would be the key that unlocked the cage of my marriage. It would *free* me.

Hills's brow furrowed, and she shook her head. "It's a sham," she said. "Just an opiate in a corn starch solution with some glitter added to replicate the iridescent shimmer of the true healing elixir."

My shoulders slumped, the hope within me fizzling out.

For ten years, we had been searching for a cure to the wasting sickness that didn't involve harvesting blood from a stable of captive Healers. We could produce *some* of the true elixir from the few who volunteered their blood, but the production quantity wasn't even a thousandth of what it had been when those same Healers had been Mother's slaves. It's not that I approved of her methods—slavery, forced breeding, and what essentially amounted to daily torture—but watching the rapid deterioration of the Corvo Kingdom now that we were *without* ready access to the healing elixir had helped me to understand her reasoning. Desperation would drive even the noblest queen down a corrupt path.

"What does Mother plan on doing with the prisoner?" I asked, returning my attention to the tower. The fact that the pharmacist had been imprisoned in the tower *at all* suggested she meant to make an example of them.

"I haven't the faintest idea," Hills admitted. "Perhaps you should pay her a visit. I hear she's bedridden again today."

I sighed, nodding slowly. I wasn't due to meet with the ailing queen, my mother, until tomorrow, but digging into the situation surrounding the prisoner would provide a much-needed distraction while I awaited my despised husband's return.

"Are we done?" I asked, glancing at both of my trusted advisors. The simmering hatred for my husband burning in Garath's eyes hit too close to home, and I slid my chair back like I was preparing to stand. "I should get cleaned up if I am to visit Mother."

"Just one other thing," Hills said, frowning. "I considered not mentioning it, but . . . " She hesitated.

"What is it?" I asked, surprised to see my no-nonsense general second-guessing herself.

"The Ferals," she finally said. "Our rangers stationed in the east have been receiving reports from the outlying villages of organized attacks on small farms and hunting camps."

My eyebrows rose. "That's impossible." I laughed under my breath and shook my head. "Ferals don't organize. It's probably just Sierra soldiers." Their occupying forces had camps all along our eastern border, and they were often just as brutish as Ferals.

Hills raised one shoulder. "I sent a special team out to investigate. It could be nothing."

I sighed and pinched the bridge of my nose. "Or it could be *something*."

The Ferals—the descendants of the people who had devolved three hundred years ago during the Turn, when the same virus that gifted my ancestors their superhuman gifts *tore away* the humanity from theirs—had been a thorn in our kingdom's side since before I was born. Despite our best efforts to eradicate them from our forested wildlands, they were still often sighted around the smaller villages, especially those nearer the Sierra Kingdom's ever-encroaching border.

At least King Eduart had a much larger Feral problem to deal with in his territory.

I wondered if we could use that to our advantage. Even if the Ferals weren't truly organizing, perhaps we could plant evidence that corroborated the reports—just enough to pull King Eduart's focus away from our kingdom long enough for us to regroup and formulate a plan to regain our independence. If he would just pull back his occupying forces and remove his implied threat to invade Corvo City should I displease him—or his son—there was a chance we would be able to actually fight back.

I have given my husband many gifts over the ten years we've been married, to appease him and his father both. But if King Eduart were to focus his military efforts on the Ferals, it might *finally* be time to give Alastor the one gift he actually deserved. An accident. The kind he wouldn't recover from.

"Nyx is coming," Garath warned, sensing the youthful raven a few seconds before she swooped in through the open window.

Nyx flew around the sitting room before landing on Sid's vacant stand in the corner. Nyx—short for Onyx—has been Liam's faithful companion since the day of his birth, just as Sid has been mine. If she was here, then Liam wasn't far behind.

Sid's talons clicked on the chairback behind me as he fluffed his wings. The younger raven's dramatic window entrances always ruffled his feathers, probably because he had injured his left wing a few years ago, making him far less agile in tight spaces.

Right on cue, the door to my private quarters burst open, and Liam barreled into the sitting room, the gangly nine-year-old closely followed by the last remaining member of my inner circle. Prim, proper, and pretty, Adasia strode in, her blond braid pulled over her shoulder and her long, lavender skirts swishing. Ada was deceptively dangerous, hiding her ferocity behind a ladylike veneer.

She had impressive combat skills, and as a Gauge, she could amplify or nullify the gifts of those around her. I kept her close to Liam to increase the strength of his empathy to a level befitting the son of two powerful Empaths—and to block any searching minds from sensing the other facet of my son's Ability. The progeny of two pure Empath lines absolutely should not have *also* been able to talk to animals in their mind.

If anyone outside my trusted inner circle knew Liam was also a Telepath, they would suspect my secret, and the truth would get back to Alastor. The second he realized Liam wasn't his son, Alastor would throw Liam in the Tower of Solitude and use him to force me into officially handing over the kingdom to him as soon as Mother was gone. The Corvo Dynasty would be dead, destroyed by the mistakes I had made as a young, idealistic fool.

"I found it, Mom!" Liam exclaimed, skidding to a halt beside the table and placing a palm-sized stone on the polished oak surface. His auburn hair was wild and unruly, as usual.

The glossy face of the stone displayed a painted raven the size of my thumbnail. The stone had been hidden somewhere within the castle—by Garath this time. To Liam, it was a game that just so happened to force him to exercise his empathy, but the rest of us saw it for the potentially life-saving training it truly was.

Not only would strengthening his ability to delve into the minds of others protect him from potential threats, but the stronger his Empath gifts appeared, the more secure our secret. If we could increase his empathy until it overpowered his telepathy *before* his tenth birthday, he would qualify as an Empath during his testing. At least then, *one* of my problems would be solved.

"Garath hid it really well, too," Liam said. His green eyes shone like emeralds when he was excited, like he was now, and he turned his wide grin toward Garath. "Tell her. Tell her where you hid it." Liam returned his attention to me. "You'll never guess, Mom."

I glanced at the smudge of white powder dusting his cheekbone and pursed my lips to suppress a smile.

"The flour canister in the kitchen," Garath said, nodding slowly. He studied Liam under raised eyebrows.

"You don't say," I said, the corners of my mouth rising.

Garath shrugged one shoulder. "It was a good spot."

"Tell your mother the rest," Ada said, joining us. She perched on the sofa nearby and adjusted the layers of her skirt, then folded her hands together on her lap.

I would never understand her preference for the long, cumbersome dresses favored by the ladies of the elite houses, but Ada called the dresses her *armor*. I only ever swapped out my leather-reinforced tunics and leggings for dresses when ceremony required it, and even then, I did so grudgingly.

Liam flashed me a boastful smirk. "I found it all by myself. Ada didn't help me *at all*."

At that revelation, I was the one raising my eyebrows. I looked at Garath. "Could you feel him rooting around in your mind?"

Garath shook his head, then let out a muffled laugh. "Which is a little terrifying. I'll have to strengthen my mental shields around the princeling."

I beamed at my son. "Well done, Liam!" I said, standing and wrapping him up in a tight hug. "I'm so proud of you." I squeezed him until he squirmed in my embrace, then let him go.

"I'll take that," Hills said, snatching the raven stone off the table and heading for the door. "I've got the perfect spot in mind," she tossed over her shoulder. "You'll never find it." She grinned wolfishly, and then she pulled the door open and left the room, shutting the door firmly behind her.

"My clever boy," I said, reaching out to smooth down Liam's unruly curls. There was another smudge of flour on his neck beneath his ear. I wiped it away with my thumb before he could swat my hand. "Go with Ada and get cleaned up. I'll meet you down in the courtyard for our morning rounds."

It was good for him to see and assist the people who served the castle. It helped strengthen the bond between us all. Besides, I refused to raise a son who had been handed everything. Even if Liam would never rule the Corvo Kingdom—only a female could carry on the Corvo line—he would always have privilege and power. I would not let him abuse that power. He would *never* end up like the man he believed to be his father.

Liam followed Ada toward the door but paused in the middle of the sitting room and turned back toward me. "Can we go for a ride around the grounds again—like yesterday?"

I had about a million things to do, especially with the threat of Alastor returning soon, visiting Mother chief among them. But when Liam turned those hope-filled green eyes on me, I couldn't resist giving in, despite the tightness in my chest that appeared every time I thought about Liam venturing over the bridge that crossed the moat, even if only to explore the castle grounds beyond. This was an unkind world, more so for a boy believed to be the son of a man whom the masses feared only slightly more than they despised.

I glanced at Garath, hoping he was available. I really did want to go, but only if we had adequate protection. When I was on horseback, galloping across a meadow, or leaping a fallen tree, it was the only time I felt truly free. I could shift my training session with Hills to the evening. Sparring before bed usually led to unsettled nights for me, but I hadn't had a restful night in so long that one more wouldn't make much of a difference.

Garath dipped his chin, confirming he could make room in his schedule to join us.

"All right," I said, forcing an easy laugh. "We'll go for a ride after lunch." I made a shooing motion. "Now go! Clean up!"

Nyx launched herself off the raven stand as Ada opened the door. She swooped across the room and careened through the doorway ahead of the pair.

My smile slipped as soon as the door latched, and the trembling set in. I turned my back to Garath, closed my eyes, and hugged my middle. If Alastor didn't kill me, this anxiety would. One day, it would suffocate me.

Wood scratched against wood as Garath pushed his chair back. He stood, his footsteps marking his approach behind me, and rested a heavy hand on my shoulder. "You can't keep this up forever, Del," he said, keeping his voice hushed to ensure his words were private, even to anyone with Ability-enhanced hearing. "My offer still stands."

I shook my head, then inhaled a deep breath, releasing it slowly through my nose. "We can't kill Alastor," I whispered. "Not yet."

If I let Garath kill my husband, I would replace one demon with another, and King Eduart was far more calculating and ruthless than his son. He wouldn't be interested in playing power games with me like Alastor so enjoyed. He would invade. He would slaughter. He would destroy.

Liam and I would have no choice but to run. To hide. And that was if we managed to escape Corvo City with our lives in the first place.

"You could go to *him*," Garath said. "Live a different life—*your own* life."

His words reminded me of something Fin had said during that single, blissful night ten years ago when I had dared to dream of what it might have been like to run away. To be free for the first time in my life. If I closed my eyes, I could still hear the crackle of the bonfire, still feel the waves of warmth.

Fin's voice whispered through my mind, *"Don't you deserve to have a life of your own? To choose your own path?"*

"How?" I asked Garath, choking on something that was a cross between a laugh and a sob. There was nothing I wanted more than to run away, to take Liam and flee from the dangers and responsibilities that had plagued me my whole life, but it was impossible. "I don't know where he is. I don't even know if he's still alive."

With a heavy sigh, Garath pulled me close and wrapped his arms around me. He tucked his chin over the top of my head and held me, letting his strength seep into me while I collapsed under the mounting weight of my burdens. I could be weak now, with him.

To the rest of the world, I had to be strong. Hard. Cold.

I had to be the Corvo heir, just as Mother had taught me to be.

3

FIN

For two days, Lyra, Callon, and I followed the merc envoy through the forest toward Mantis. Their wagon of rocks and soil samples was heavy, keeping us at a slow pace as we lingered a few miles behind on horseback, out of sight. We were there for reconnaissance, not to make ourselves known, so using my Ability, I nulled us and used Tick and the other forest animals' eyes to see what we couldn't.

We'd learned little more about the mercs and what they were up to than what Lyra had already gleaned from them in the desert, but we knew they were being paid an exorbitant amount by way of a messenger. A messenger whom they were scheduled to meet in the Silver Bow Inn at the edge of the city tonight, when the full moon was at its peak.

By the time we neared the capital, the sun was already setting, which meant once we were inside, we could move about the streets in darkness with more ease. Still, we stopped, needing to leave the horses and Tick behind. The last thing I wanted was all of us locked inside the city walls should something happen; going in was always the easy part, but if the Mantis officials took any interest in us—specifically in me—it would be far harder to leave.

"I can't wait to sink my teeth into a lamb shank," Callon murmured as he grabbed an apple from his saddlebag. He patted his horse's rump, shooing him to the brook to drink, and draped his cloak around his shoulders. Callon's eyes glittered as he smiled to himself, lost in daydreams. "Or maybe I'll find one of those kabobs, the ones with the caramelized dressing." He groaned and licked his lips. "The markets here are famous for their spiced pork —" He kissed his fingers. "It's the best I've had in the Seven Kingdoms."

Lyra stared at him, incredulous, as she untied her cloak and sack from her horse's saddle. "Didn't you *just* finish the last of our jerky? Now you're eating an apple while lusting after your next meal."

Callon bit a hunk out of the fruit and shrugged. "So?"

I loosened Dusty's saddle and the bags tied to him, so he could relax a little while we were gone.

"*So?*" Lyra mimicked in a deep, flippant voice. "Do you ever stop thinking about food?"

Callon made a point to contemplate her question, then shrugged again. "Not really. Just ask my ma. She says it's a good thing I work for Fin, or we'd be indebted to him even more for all the food I consume."

Dusty nudged me goodbye and walked over to the water with the other horses.

"You don't work *for* me," I reiterated for the dozenth time, but Callon ignored me and continued.

"Besides, this"—Callon tossed his apple up, catching it with a wink—"is for the road. In case I need the energy."

Lyra rolled her eyes and clasped her cloak around her shoulders.

"If you two are ready," I prompted, knowing I'd be standing there until midnight listening to them bicker back and forth if we didn't get moving. I tugged a hat over my head to hide my hair, ensured our weapons were stored out of sight since we couldn't take them with us, and we headed for Mantis.

My steps were heavy and adamant as we made our way through the forest to the thick walls of the city. They sparkled in the waning daylight, but it was more ominous than beautiful. Mantis reminded me of a poisonous flower, a beautiful and blooming city luring its victims closer. Protection. Wealth. Comfort. It boasted all those things, but the citizens and visitors of Mantis—all the Sierra Kingdom, for that matter—weren't given such graces for free. And I hated that we were walking into the city, knowing that once we were in, we were at the mercy of King Eduart's goodwill and generosity, traits he wasn't particularly known for.

Callon snorted about something, and Lyra hit him with one of the empty sacks we planned to fill with provisions while we were there. "Do you ever take *anything* seriously?" she hissed.

"Of course." Callon tossed his finished apple core behind us. Tick smelled it and then continued to hang back, scoping out the area for any danger. "Do *you* ever smile?" he countered. "It doesn't hurt, you know?" Lyra glared at him, and Callon threw up his hands in defense. "I'm just saying, you should work those smile muscles a little more before they atrophy."

"You should shut your mouth more. You might actually get a woman that way."

He laughed. "Touché." And that earned a small, victorious smile from Lyra.

I couldn't help but chuckle watching them. Even if they acted as if they didn't get along, Callon had risked his life for Lyra on multiple occasions, and she for him.

Only months ago, after she'd arrived, he'd pulled her off a ledge when she'd slipped during a bandit attack at a trading post in Noctem, the kingdom southwest of here. And Lyra relied on Callon more than any of the men or women on our monitoring and scouting teams, trusting him the most. Because as silly and immature as Callon could be, he never screwed around with people's safety. He'd been with me for years and seen too much death to find any humor in that.

Still, if Callon could find humor in just about everything, Lyra could always find the danger or stupidity in it, and their clashing personalities made for a few laughs and lighthearted moments that we were in short supply of these days.

The long missions, the trading trips, and the nights around the campfire were more pleasurable with them around, and despite my sour moods, I was grateful for them.

They continued bickering until the Mantis gates came into view. Then we all sobered.

Guards lined the stone parapets and flanked the barred portcullis. And as I assessed what we were walking into, I hoped that what should be a straightforward recon would be fruitful and go off without a hitch. I knew better than that, though. Callon said I was cynical and pessimistic, but I was realistic, and we needed to stay on our guard. Especially in this place.

"Explore all you want," I told them under my breath. "But keep a low profile and make sure you're back at the inn before midnight. I'll stick to the outskirts of the city." With only a handful of hours until the meeting at the inn, less could go wrong, and I was grateful for that, at least.

"Why the outskirts?" Lyra whispered, should any prying senses start probing. "Don't you want to scout all that you can? We're allowed in Mantis, right?"

"Aw, you're cute," Callon whispered, unable to resist. That earned him a huff from her and another eye roll. "*We* are allowed in the city," he clarified, pointing between the two of them. "But Fin here has a target on his back, and that moppy, red hair of his is hard to forget, no matter how haggard he's looking these days."

"You're hilarious," I muttered, but despite my smile, Lyra frowned.

"Fin's been around a while," Callon explained, and I braced

myself for some theatrically embellished account of a scrape I'd likely forgotten. "He's quite the rebel—his hair ain't that color for nothing, you know. He's got a fire in him that's gotten him into a few tight spots over the years."

Lyra's eyes widened minutely. "I never thought *you* to be reckless." There was as much awe as there was reproach in her voice.

I smirked at that. "I'll be the first to admit I belong on no pedestal."

"He keeps it under wraps now that he has to set a good example and all." Callon sobered a little. "But trust me, someone will recognize him if he's not careful."

"That's enough," I told them as we neared the gate, our bags and sacks slung over our shoulders to fill with market goods, like anyone from outer lands coming for a routine trade would do. I lifted the hood over my hat for extra precaution and continued inside.

The air was buzzing with chatter and commotion once past the gate, and I felt my muscles tense in preparation for the next few hours. In and out—that's all we needed to do. We had hundreds of people relying on us back at the settlement, and we couldn't afford any missteps.

I thought about Callon's mom's missing eye from the Feral attack she survived as a young woman and how her hands shook from nerve damage, making it harder for her to work in the garden every morning. Callon was her only light left in this life, and without him, she had nothing. I thought about Lyra's father, hunting and skinning his kills to help put clothes on our backs and food in our bellies. They were both waiting for us back in Shoshone and relying on *me* to bring their children home, safe.

In and out. I breathed as I thought the words, exhaling the ever-present knot tightening my shoulders. We only had to last the night and could leave at dawn when the gates opened again.

The guards patted us down, and after a few grunts, they nodded for us to be on our way. The sun was setting behind Ironwood Keep, casting the city in evening shadows. Men and women wearing red robes moved along the streets, the colored attire marking them as Elementals as they expertly flicked their flames to light the torch lamps lining the alleyways.

Lyra paused, taking in the sight before her. Watching her, I could almost appreciate Mantis as if I was seeing it for the first time. Almost. Having lived off the land most of her life, moving from one settlement to another after being run out by soldiers and Ferals, Lyra had never been to a city like this one.

She peered up and down the flagstone streets. Stretched out before us, on the top of the mountain and surrounded by a forest of pine trees, was Ironwood Keep, a granite monstrosity that lorded over the city below. The roads wound their way up the foothills like riverbeds, carving out a cliff face. They stopped at the city's inner walls, dividing the castle grounds from the rest of us.

Callon's eyes lingered on the Communication Dome, its rounded glass ceiling rising above the townhomes in the distance. He knew as well as I did that Mantis liked to collect powerful Telepaths for their communication efforts across the kingdoms, and I could practically feel the chills raking over him as he tore his gaze away.

"I don't think I'll ever get used to seeing that place," he muttered.

Lyra glanced at both of us.

"Just keep to the city streets," I told him. "And don't draw any attention to yourself. I'll null us as much as I can." While most people only had one power, like Lyra and Callon, there were some of us with a stronger, purer lineage and two Abilities, a combination of our ancestors, like I had. I could null others' powers like Jason and had animal telepathy like Dani, my great-great-grandparents. "We'll be fine," I reassured them, and with a warning glance at Callon, I focused on our surroundings again.

Mantis was much like any other capital within the Seven Kingdoms, congested and bustling, but the buildings were uniform, and the streets were clean. Guards were posted on nearly every corner, which was strange, yet I wasn't entirely surprised either. This place wasn't feared for no reason. There were as many laws to follow as there were creative punishments for breaking them.

The streets were teeming with people. Some men and women rode vehicles powered by Elemental slaves with metal collars on their necks, boasting wealth and status. Other traders hauled their goods in creaking, hand-drawn wooden carts. There were robotic and whittled toys, herbs and paints and scarves. Traders and merchants bartered with customers, and children ran through the alleyways, some playing while others haggled for coin.

The old world met the new as we made our way deeper into the city. Ancient artifacts filled crates and bins. Some contraptions I'd seen before, like handheld communication devices with cracked and shattered screens, were obsolete but a part of history for which collectors paid exorbitant amounts. There were booths displaying handmade jewelry, with rings made from old keys that would never open anything again, and boxes of photos long forgotten but fascinating nonetheless. There were food booths, which caught Callon's eye, and there were furs, silks, and woolen blankets hung from clothing lines.

Wide-eyed, Lyra took it all in.

"A bushel of sage, my lady?"

I glanced over at Lyra.

A young girl with blonde braids, a dirty but tailored red dress, and matching torn stockings stood in front of Lyra, offering her herbs with a wide smile. "It will chase the evil spirits away and bless your stayrooms during your visit. It's only a quarter-piece, miss."

Lyra opened her mouth to say something, but I shook my head at the girl, knowing what scheme she was playing. "I can smell the hawthorn from here," I told her.

The girl's open, smiling expression dropped. She no longer looked young and innocent but twice her age and thwarted. She scowled at me, but just as quickly, she locked eyes with her next victim, her smile returning as she hurried away.

"Hawthorn?" Lyra asked, her brow pinched in question. "Was she trying to kill me?"

"Only sedate you," I explained. "They follow you to your stay-room, wait for you to light the 'sage' before you pass out, then they rob you blind."

Lyra's mouth hung slightly open. "But . . . There are guards everywhere. Why would they even try such a thing?"

Callon snorted. "Guards are in on the take," he grumbled. "And probably the king as well," he added under his breath.

"I need a moment," I told them, stepping off to the side by a milliner's shop while I searched for a pair of willing bird eyes above to help me locate the Silver Bow Inn.

Vaguely, I could hear Lyra and Callon talking, but I was too busy scouring everything through hawk eyes, looking for our midnight meeting place. There was no short supply of taverns and inns, and my hawk gaze narrowed on the signs and banners as I flew over the darkening city.

Finally, I spotted the inn nestled between a brothel and a dye caster a few blocks away.

And that's when I saw it. In the upper city, the blue, up-lit holograms stood tall and ostentatious at the inner gates of the keep. They cycled through images and tributes to the king and other members of the royal family.

First, King Eduart and Queen Tam, with their sour-faced expressions, as if they were too good to even pose for their own portraits.

The three princes followed, though only one posed with his princess.

Hawk landed on a finial atop the castle wall, and I stared at the couple in the next image.

Princess Delphinia and Prince Alastor.

Del. Princess. Tough Stuff. Heir of the Corvo Kingdom. A

frozen picture of the girl I once knew beamed at me in a black and silver gown fit for a queen. Her dark curls were gathered atop her head, her silver and black-feathered crown gleaming in the uplighting that brightened her dark features. She was just as striking as I remembered.

Beside Del stood her pale husband, whose auburn hair was combed away from his grim face. He looked equally disapproving and cruel. But it was the boy that my hawk eyes lingered on the longest.

Del had a child, something I'd known for years, but to see it was gutting. She was not only a princess; she was a wife. A mother.

Meanwhile, I was much the same. Still living off the land. Still fighting to survive for only a semblance of peace. It was at that moment I realized I hadn't changed at all. Not really. Yet seeing her up there as she was made all that had transpired in the past ten years feel more real. More lonely.

"Did you hear that, Fin?" Lyra asked, and I felt her hand on my arm.

Blinking myself from the hawk's mind, I swallowed thickly.

"Fin!" she hissed, shaking me.

I glowered at her. "What?"

She pointed to the man walking toward us, his eyes scanning the onset of a crowd. His words drifted in and out of my ears as I gathered my bearings again. He looked like a priest from the old world, with a black cloak and a cap on his head. His gray beard was long, his teeth crooked, and his eyes were wide and fervent.

"Beware the prophecy!" he boomed. "The kingdom will fall if we don't repent. If we don't sacrifice! If we don't give back to the king and queen, who—"

"What's he talking about?" I whispered so low only she would hear. I watched the crowd thicken around him. Their faces were fearful as they gripped pamphlets in their hands and clutched them to their chests.

Lyra shook her head, her eyes fixed on the old man. "Listen."

"At dawn, we meet at the King's Church in Prior Square. We pray for the royal family. We pray for all our souls and future selves, for if we do not uncover and destroy the destructive force hidden under the earth in Death Valley, we will all perish!"

"What?" I blurted. Frowning, I scanned the square, noticing for the first time what rhetoric was plastered on posters and holograms projected on the sides of buildings: *Join the king's army. Save the kingdom.*

"Fin," Callon hedged conversationally. "This wouldn't be something you've heard of by any chance, would it? Something Jake told you about—one of his sister's old prophecies he loves so much?" Callon was being sarcastic. Jake loathed Becca's prophecies. Her predictions had upended the lives of everyone he loved centuries ago, and I was beginning to understand why he resented them so much. They always came at a heavy price.

I shook my head, my heart racing as I processed how bad this was. *Uncover and destroy the destructive force hidden under the earth in Death Valley.* Our Death Valley, where we lived?

"That's why they were digging," I realized aloud. "They think their salvation is in the ground."

"What if it is?" Lyra asked.

"Then everyone is in danger," I said brusquely and ran my hand over my face. *Fuck.* "Whatever fear they're spreading, and whatever they're trying to find, more of them will come to Death Valley, that's for certain." *And it will be an army.* I didn't say that part aloud, but by the way Callon and Lyra were looking at me, they already knew.

"What do you want us to do?" Callon asked. "We have to get back—to get organized. But we still need to confirm who's behind this. I mean, the answer seems obvious, but if it's Eduart, why hide it?" He shook his head.

Realizing my hood had fallen, I pulled it over my hat again with more force than was necessary, and I glanced around, ensuring we hadn't caught anyone's attention. "We go on as planned," I told them. "We see what happens at the meeting tonight. I'll do some reconnaissance at the pub, where minds are plied with ale and tongues are looser. See what you can learn on the street. We need to know what else they're fearmongering here, and get all the intel we can. I want an estimate of how many soldiers might be coming and when."

"At least they no longer have the element of surprise," Callon offered, shedding light on the silver lining, though it felt like only a scant glimmer in the looming darkness ahead. "We can prepare for this."

The three of us were quiet as our situation settled in.

"Did you find the inn?" Lyra asked.

"Uh, yeah. It's three blocks down." I cleared my throat, the image I had seen of Del projected onto the palace walls flashing to mind. "I'll secure us a room for the night and meet you there."

Callon and Lyra nodded, and without a word, I made my way toward the pub I saw next to the inn to see what else I could find out and to grab a much-needed drink.

The three of us hadn't been tucked in the corner of the inn's tavern room for more than a handful of minutes, ale in our mugs and Lyra's senses open and probing, before the merc we'd been following strode into the Silver Bow Inn. He maneuvered around tables of drunken patrons and over to a bench on the other side of the room where a nondescript man with a brown hood pulled up over his head was already sitting. They made no gestures in greeting and simply sat across from one another.

Lyra listened while Callon and I counted our breaths in suspended anticipation. Callon rubbed his stomach, full from too much stew and bread, and I took another hearty gulp of ale.

My head was light, having downed two pints already, just enough to take the edge off. Other than the prophecy, we'd unearthed no other concerns, for which I was grateful. King Eduart was raising additional men and women for his army, intent on going to the desert lands, and that was plenty for us to be worried about for now.

We had people who could fight, warriors and others capable and willing to give their lives for the greater good. But that they would have to at all was as disheartening as it was enraging. They'd already been forced from their homelands, all of them seeking refuge in the outerlands because they'd lost everything else.

Now, I would have to return to tell them they needed to prepare themselves to fight again and perhaps die in the process.

"Do you think the prophecy is real?" Callon asked in Lyra's silence.

"I don't know," I admitted. "Regardless, they are using it to build a bigger army, one that will be at our doorstep, probably within a matter of months. We have no choice but to be ready for them."

More silence hung between us as Lyra listened. Callon took another swig from his mug, his fingers tapping on the table. "What are they saying, Lyra?" he hissed. "The suspense is killing me." He took another sip of his ale and looked at me. "I don't think she knows how this works, Fin. She has to relay the information, not just—"

"Shut up," Lyra bit out. "They haven't said how, exactly, but—" Lyra took a sip of her ale to wet her lips, staring at her mug as she focused on their conversation. "Corvo's definitely involved."

Callon straightened as I stared at Lyra, unblinking. It took all the focus I had to register her words—to mull them around and let them root—because that was the last thing I'd wanted her to say.

I cleared my throat. "What else are they saying?"

Lyra's face was a mask of consternation as she continued to listen. "He says his master wants half of the samples taken to Corvo . . . To a temple . . . a temple on an island."

Alcatraz.

Callon gasped, and my blood ran cold as chills prickled over my skin.

"Isn't that where they were harvesting Healer blood?" he asked.

I nodded, reluctant to believe it was all circling back to where it started in the first place.

"He's telling them they have to leave tomorrow so they can get to the city before the equinox." Lyra shook her head, rolling her eyes and completely oblivious to the gravity of her words. "God, they're superstitious bastards."

"So . . . we have to go to Corvo," Callon said, his gaze burrowing a hole through me.

I hadn't stepped foot inside the Corvo Kingdom in ten years, not since the massacre in my village that sent us on the trek for refuge. Corvo was the last place I wanted to be—the only place I swore I'd never return. But . . .

"We have to know what they're doing on that island," I said to no one in particular. And I knew what that meant. As much as it twisted me up inside, my path was glaringly clear.

"Fin," Callon said cautiously. "Are you sure? I mean, I know you can do this, but—" He grabbed my shoulder. "Maybe you should think about it."

Lyra glanced between us, knowing very little of my past with the Corvo princess. But Del's mother was up to something like always. I would find out what it was. "I have to go," I told him. There was no other choice.

Callon filled my mug to the brim and slid it closer to me. The ale sloshed over the side, and I gladly grabbed the handle, gulping the entire contents down. Then, with a heaving breath, I ran the back of my hand over my mouth, and Callon poured me another.

Despite the time that had passed, seeing Del would not be easy. But I refused to believe she would intentionally put my people and me in harm's way or that she would knowingly sit by while her mother used that damned island for her schemes again. I *had* to believe that.

I gulped down half of my ale and stared at Callon and Lyra. Both of them watched me with concern.

"You should get some rest," I said curtly. "We leave at first light."

4

DEL

My steps echoed down the shadowed corridor like the dreadful ticking of a clock. I was in no mood to sit and speak with Mother, to bear witness to her accelerated deterioration. But it had to be done.

We were closer than ever before, she and I, thanks to the weekly empathic check-ins that forced near-absolute honesty between us—it had taken all my effort and focus to conceal the truth about Liam's paternity—and it seemed a cruel twist of fate that she would be taken from me soon. Now, when I had finally come to know her, to trust her, to seek her council. How unfair that the same circumstances that had breathed life back into our relationship were also killing her.

I paused at the door to Mother's private chambers. A guard stood on either side of the doorway, their gazes weighing a thousand pounds each. I slowly drew air into my lungs, reinforcing my resolve to enter her rooms.

After blowing out the deep breath, I nodded to Saira, the dark-skinned, bright-eyed guard on the right. She was from a long line of royal guards, like Garath, and she was absolutely devoted not only to the kingdom but to our family. She stepped toward the doorway and pushed the door open, entering the dark sitting room ahead of me. The waning flames in the fireplace cast flickering shadows across the dark wood furnishings. I wrinkled my nose. Even out here, the scent of sickness tainted the air.

"Thank you, Saira," I murmured.

She bowed her head and retreated out to the corridor. The door clicked shut behind me as I rounded the back of the sofa and crossed the sitting room, and I glanced over my shoulder to make sure I was alone.

When I reached the doorway to Mother's bedroom, I paused on the threshold, my heart lodged in my throat.

Mother lay in her bed, flat on her back, still as death. Her long white hair had been wound into a thin braid that disappeared under the covers, but her arms were on top of the blankets, her frail hands folded over her middle, her veins clearly visible through her transparent, crepe paper skin.

I stared at her chest in the dim illumination from the lamp on her nightstand, waiting for it to rise, too long uncertain if it moved at all. The golden tint to the lamplight told me either Donis or Clover was the electric Elemental on duty tonight, powering the castle's electricity.

Mother's eyelashes fluttered suddenly, and her eyes drifted open. A terrible weight lifted off my chest.

"Del?" Mother said, her voice raspy where it had once been resonant. Her rheumy stare searched the room before latching onto me in the doorway. She squinted, then smiled. "It *is* you."

Groaning, she rolled part of the way onto her side and stretched her arm toward the bedside table, her fingers reaching for her eyeglasses but falling short.

I rushed forward, retrieving her glasses off the nightstand and handing them to her, then helped her lean forward so I could add a couple of pillows behind her back to prop her comfortably in a sitting position. The physical contact between us sent images flitting through my mind, too fleeting and indistinct to understand. But her emotions were clear enough—sorrow, longing, regret.

And above all else, fear. Fear for herself and what she might soon find in the hereafter, and fear for the kingdom she would leave behind.

"I thought you were coming tomorrow," Mother said, watching me as I turned away to fetch the chair in the corner and move it closer to the side of the bed. "Or are you worried I won't make it that long?"

I set the chair down and stared at her hard. "That's not funny," I said, rounding the chair to sit.

She chuckled, but the laughter quickly transformed into a deep, rattling cough.

I waited until she had regained her breath and handed her the glass of water from the nightstand. "The cough is worse again?"

She nodded, raising the cup with one shaking hand. The hand tremors were one of the first telltale signs of the wasting sickness. She closed the fingers of her other hand tightly around the silver raven pendant she had worn for as long as I could remember. She looked so unsteady that I reached out to help her lift the water to her lips. When she finished drinking, I set the glass back down on the table.

"A small dose of the elixir would eradicate the pneumonia," I reminded her. And it would knock back the progression of the wasting sickness a little.

Mother sighed, and even that rattled the fluid in her lungs. "Perhaps, but then what? In another week, it will be some other ailment." This was how it always was in the end stage of the wasting sickness. The body was so weakened that every cold became a deadly illness. "No," she went on. "We need to continue rationing doses to those with less severe cases, and we will reserve the rest for the labs. It would be wasted on me."

I sat back in my chair and crossed my arms over my chest, huffing out my displeasure. "How long do you have, then?"

"A few days," she said. "Perhaps a week."

I clenched my jaw, my focus shifting past her to a painting of two women walking through a grain field hanging on the far wall. I had memorized the description on the bronze placard attached to the bottom of the frame long ago: *Zoe Annabell Cartwright, Patron of the Empaths, and Rebecca Marie Vaughn, Patron of the Oracles*. It was a common enough image in the iconography of the Temple of the Seven Kingdoms, but this was an unusually lifelike and vivid depiction of the two women.

Zoe's dark hair, fair complexion, and keen aquamarine stare reminded me so much of how Mother had looked a decade ago, before the wasting sickness reclaimed her stolen youth and beauty, that I wondered if there might just be some truth to her claims that the Corvo line was descended from Zoe herself. I had my father's darker coloring, so it was harder to make the comparison to myself directly.

I released a silent, bitter laugh. What did it matter? The Temple of the Seven Kingdoms was a sham. The Patrons weren't gods. They had just been ordinary people trying to survive during extraordinary circumstances. They had lived through the Turn, and their momentous actions during the viral outbreak that transformed the world inevitably shaped the Seven Kingdoms into what it was. Only history and the Temple's ever-evolving scriptures had warped them into something godlike.

"You're in a sour mood," Mother noted, still clutching her pendant. She had been doing that more and more frequently, as if it were a holy object, linking her to the Patrons themselves. "Alastor must be on his way back."

My lip curled at the thought of my husband, but I said, "It's not that." My arms relaxed as the next breath left my body, and I leaned forward, resting my elbows on my knees and scrubbing my hands over my weary face. "It's Liam," I confessed.

Mother's stare sharpened, and it was as though she had shed

years right before my eyes. "What exactly is troubling you about my grandson?"

I lowered my hands and swallowed roughly, hesitating. Reconsidering. Doubting myself and the wisdom of finally sharing this secret with her. But the brief spark of hope from his empathic triumph this morning had been snuffed out by what I had witnessed during our ride.

I closed my eyelids, needing the visual shield from her penetrating stare. "Alastor is not Liam's father," I confessed.

Silence hung in the space between us, and my heartbeat became deafening to my ears.

Until Mother let out a bark of laughter that set off another round of coughing.

My eyes snapped open, and I waited for her to settle once more.

"Oh, Del," she said, her chest still quaking with aftershocks of the coughing fit. "That is the best news I've heard in years."

My mouth fell open, and I slowly shook my head.

"That would explain his Ability to communicate with animals," she said, shocking me with the revelation that she had already known he was more than just an Empath. "Who is the father, then? A Telepath, obviously, but who?" Mother mused aloud. "Garath?"

Before I could respond, she answered for me. "No, that doesn't fit with Liam's coloring. Those green eyes and that auburn hair . . . " She narrowed her gaze, pursing her lips.

I saw it the moment she connected the dots to the events of ten years ago. To the day I learned what she and Maylar had been up to, imprisoning and harvesting blood from Healers to create an elixir to keep the inbred elite of our kingdom alive. The same elixir had allowed Mother to extend her lifespan decades beyond what was natural. And the same elixir had caused a rebound effect within her body, resulting in her rapid decline over the past decade since she finally stopped dosing herself.

Ten years ago, we could have passed for sisters. Now, she appeared old enough to be my great-grandmother.

"It was *that boy*," she said, her eyes unfocusing as she recalled the confrontation in her study. "The meddlesome Telepath who helped you steal Jake away from me."

"We didn't *steal* Jake," I snapped. "You were holding him prisoner, Mother. You were torturing him. Your own ancestor. One of the *Patrons*." I scoffed, disgusted by her past actions. "We *freed* him."

She had captured Jake ten years ago, the only Patron who still lived, thanks to his Healer blood making him essentially immortal. She had intended to use him as she had the hundreds of other Healers she and Maylar had imprisoned, forcibly taking their blood to process into their precious healing elixir. She hadn't planned on my interference.

"You know," she said, ignoring my correction. "When you chose Alastor as your consort, I remember thinking you had a type." She smiled to herself. "Big men with red hair."

I frowned, seeing Fin in my mind's eye. He had been on the taller side, his body honed by a life of hard work and survival with his people in the wildlands to the north, but he had been nowhere near as large as Alastor.

"His magnitude was more in his presence than in his physical size," Mother said, picking up on my train of thought.

My mental shields had slipped, and she had plucked the thoughts right out of my mind. I slammed my walls back down, locking her out of my head.

"That's why you fought me when I advised you to pick another suitor as your consort," Mother mused. "I thought infatuation had blinded you to Alastor's cruel nature, but you needed him to disguise your indiscretion. He was the closest in appearance to Liam's father."

The fight left me, and my shoulders sagged. Earlier today, during my ride around the castle grounds with Liam, he had proudly introduced me to each of the animals whose paths we crossed, even telling me many of their life stories.

"Liam's telepathy is overshadowing his empathy," I told Mother. "When he is tested on his birthday, I have little doubt that he will be classified as a Telepath, and then Alastor will know the truth."

"Then I guess you have your deadline," Mother said resolutely.

My stomach lurched. "My deadline for what?" I asked evenly.

Mother's thin lips twisted into a sly smile, deepening her many wrinkles. "Don't play the fool, daughter. You're smarter than that." She paused, letting the implication sink in. She was talking about killing Alastor. "Will *you* do it? Or will Garath take care of it for you?"

I straightened in my chair, my heart beating faster.

"He will kill you, Del," Mother said. "He will kill you and Liam, both." A statement. A fact. "The instant Alastor realizes Liam is not his blood, both of your fates will be sealed, if only to contain the truth of his inadequacy from his own father."

My chin trembled, my eyes filling with tears. My heart leaden and sank into my stomach.

"Liam's existence threatens Alastor's claim to the Sierra throne," Mother continued. "You have borne a healthy child—one healthy child—but not *Alastor's* child. After all the failed pregnancies conceived by Alastor, his father will see him for the unqualified heir he truly is. He is incapable of fulfilling a regent's most basic, essential duty—producing an heir of his own. If the truth gets out that the fertility issues plaguing your union are almost certainly born of his defective seed, he will lose *everything*, Del. He will silence every single person who knows."

I swallowed the rising panic. "But if he kills me, he loses his hold on the Corvo Kingdom."

Mother released a breathy laugh, then cleared her throat loudly. "It's not quite as simple as that." She offered me a sad smile. "Your death leaves the Corvo throne vacant. The nobles will fight over it like starving dogs, and I have little doubt that Alastor will take advantage of that power struggle. One way or another, he and his father will have our kingdom and our ports."

I stared at Mother in disbelief. "What are you saying?" I shook my head. "That it's a lost cause? That I should take Liam and run?" It was impossible not to think back to what Garath had said that morning. "I would be abandoning the kingdom to a monster. The Corvo Dynasty would be over. Your legacy . . ."

Mother's focus drifted past me to the window and the view of the moonlit sea and the starry sky. "It was over before you were ever born," she murmured. "But at least if you run, you and Liam will be alive." Her lips quivered. "The two of you will be my legacy."

I shook my head again, more firmly this time. "I'm not ready to give up just yet. There may be another way," I said before filling her in on the reports of organized Feral attacks and my idea about playing those up to distract King Eduart.

I sat in silence, watching Mother's carefully guarded expression as she considered my proposed plan. "It's not a bad idea." She angled her head to the side. "It would take time—far more time than I have left. You must be patient and subtle, or Eduart will catch wind of the subterfuge."

"I can do that," I assured her. "I can be subtle. And if it doesn't work, Liam and I will leave before his birthday." Before his ill-fated testing.

Mother was quiet, her stare assessing. "In the meantime, there is one other thing you will need to do to make this work," Mother said.

I raised my eyebrows, a silent question.

"You will need to have a child, Del," she said. "*Another* child. A successful pregnancy will divert Alastor's attention from Liam and bolster his reputation with his father—both are essential while you lay your trap. It wasn't hyperbole when I said you would need to be patient. This plan will stretch beyond Liam's birthday."

I was already shaking my head before she finished speaking. "I've been trying to bear Alastor's child for ten years," I reminded her. "Dozens of pregnancies—all ending the same way. Alastor and I *can't* have a baby together."

Mother's eyes twinkled, and the corners of her mouth tensed. "I never said Alastor needed to be the father. He only needs to *believe* the child is his."

I opened my mouth, then shut it again and leaned back in my chair.

"Garath would—"

"Garath and I aren't—" I took a steadying breath, reorganizing my response before speaking again. "I don't want to put him in that position. He's the head of my personal guard and is always with me. He would have to be around his child every day but never be acknowledged as the father. It would be unfair, and worse, it would be cruel."

Mother guffawed. "Garath is more of a father to Liam than either Alastor or that red-haired rebel has ever been, and it would be no different for his own child, regardless of what the rest of the world believed." She inhaled a faintly gurgling breath. "He is a good man, and those are increasingly hard to find." She raised her hand and tapped her temple with two fingertips. "Trust me, I know. And he is absolutely devoted to you. That man would walk off a cliff if he believed doing so would save your life. Besides, there has been no trace of the wasting sickness in his family." She nodded definitively. "It should be Garath."

My chin trembled at the thought of approaching Garath with this request. He was my best friend. My most trusted confidant. He was strong and handsome, and he truly was like a father to Liam, but he wasn't . . . we weren't . . . *I* didn't feel that way about him. After so many years with Alastor, I wasn't sure I could feel that way about anyone.

I knew she was right. Garath would do it. But in the end, it would wound him deeply.

I captured Mother's hand and lowered my mental shields, allowing her to see the secret history I shared with Garath. I needed her to know exactly what she was asking me to do.

When I first learned I was pregnant with Liam, I had attempted to seduce Garath into eloping with me to disguise my indiscretion. But Garath had seen through me, and once he coerced the truth from me, he convinced me to tell Fin—to give my baby's father a chance to *be* the father. We had made plans to meet at the summer solstice festival, but Fin never showed up. I was two months along, and I was scared—and desperately in need of a husband to preserve the perceived purity of my child's bloodline.

Once again, I had turned to Garath. He had pledged his life to me but refused to marry me, knowing my heart lay elsewhere. He had claimed he feared he would end up falling in love with me, and the knowledge that I loved another would eat away at his devotion until he grew too bitter to fulfill his sworn duty. In the end, he had said, it would kill him.

He hadn't liked my choice of Alastor for consort any more than Mother had, but none of the other available suitors had red hair or green eyes, like Fin, which meant the ruse would be pointless should the child emerge resembling its father. I had been foolishly determined to make my marriage and family appear legitimate, so much so, that I had been blind to just how *unlike* Fin Alastor truly was. Too late, I discovered the rotten core hidden beneath his charming exterior.

I had bled so heavily after Alastor's rough consummation of our marriage that I felt certain I had lost the baby. Garath had been prepared to end Alastor's life then, but two weeks later, I felt the first flutters of movement within me, and for the time being, Alastor's life had been spared.

"Enough," Mother said, withdrawing her hand. Tears streaked her heavily lined cheeks, and she wiped them away with one hand. "This changes nothing. If you wish to preserve your relationship with Garath, gather Liam and leave Corvo City now—tonight. If you wish to fight for the kingdom and follow through with the Ferals plan, then you must commit to this course, Delphinia, wholly and completely." She suppressed a cough. "Or you will surely fail."

Her shoulders hunched, her chest jerked with the most violent coughing fit I had witnessed yet. Blood splattered her hand and sprayed on the sheets. All of this talking was taking its toll on her body.

"I'll fetch Dr. Robins," I said, standing abruptly and rushing out of the room.

As I raced down the corridor, Mother's words echoed in my bones, leaving me feeling hollowed out and incapable of making a decision. A decade ago, I had cursed her for her ability to make ruthless decisions with an ice-cold heart. But after all these years, I finally understood.

She had sacrificed the few—the Healers—to save a kingdom. She had made the tough call, time and again, so nobody else would have to do it. She couldn't trust anybody else *to* do it, certainly not her tender-hearted, idealistic heir.

And now she was dying, leaving the fate of the kingdom in my hands.

All my youthful idealism had fled the moment the midwife set Liam on my chest. The world had crumbled and reformed around a new focal point—my son. Nothing else mattered as much as Liam and my desperate need to keep him safe. To protect him.

Motherhood had made me ruthless where my son was concerned. My marriage had hardened my heart, surrounding it with walls of iron and ice. Giving up hope of ever seeing Fin again had taught me about sacrifice, and each lost pregnancy strengthened my will to survive, press on, and persevere.

I could make the hard decisions now. I could be the heir Mother needed.

But was it enough to fool a greedy king? Was it enough to save a dying kingdom? Was it enough to protect my son? Was *I* enough?

5

FIN

Tick was curled beside me, her tail twitching against my side as she dreamed, stirring me awake. The tree shadows played across my face as I blinked my eyes open to a misty morning. Inwardly, I smiled. The greenery was one of many things I missed about these lands. The rich valleys, falling waters, and rugged mountains teeming with life, unlike the arid expanse of the desert. These were woods I could get lost in, woods that felt like home.

My friends. My sister. Fallen Wood wasn't only the final resting place of my family, but the Patrons as well. I understood Jake's restlessness—part of it, at least. When you are damn near immortal, you lose everything you love at one point or another, and all Jake had left of his past he had been forced to leave behind after Queen Corisande's attack. Fallen Wood was home to his sister Becca's final resting place. He'd had to watch her die twice in his lifetime—once because of the virus and then later in life, after she'd been reborn an Oracle. Then, there was the love of his life. His Zoe. The people of the Seven Kingdoms may have worshipped them all like gods, but to Jake, they were ghosts from his past, and when he and I had to leave their graves and our home behind, we'd lost all we'd had left.

Fleetingly, I thought of Beast, my best friend and faithful companion. It had been three years since the grouchy cougar had walked away from me to find his eternal sleep somewhere. Other than Jake, he had been all that remained of the old parts of my life.

Folding my arm under my head, I inhaled a deep breath, filling my lungs. In two days, I would be closer to that past than I'd been in ten years, and it loomed on the horizon as much as it beckoned me.

Tick's wet nose brushed my cheek, her tongue licking my scruffy face, making me smile.

With a yawn, she stretched out beside me, her bushy tail thumping as I rubbed her belly. "Good morning," I muttered.

Even if I hadn't raised her from a pup, Tick was my companion in every way. A familiar mind and steadfast friendship, more connected to me than any human. I'd been able to communicate with animals my whole life, but only a few had ever felt so entwined with me. Tick and I didn't need words. She was simply there. Always. Close enough to reach with my cerebral fingers and never too far away for a belly rub and head scratch.

Like me, she preferred her solitude, though, so I basked in her nearness this morning. Though I typically ran from the silence—tried to drown it out and push it away—it was a welcomed sense of peace when Tick was with me.

I rubbed behind her ear, earning her reliable leg twitch when I found just the right spot.

Above the sound of her tail thumping, indiscernible whispers met my ears from the fire pit across camp. Callon and Lyra were awake, and I strained to listen.

"—grew up in the wildlands beyond Corvo City. Fin met the princess when he went to find Jake, and she helped them get out of the city."

"I heard stories about it," Lyra said softly. "They wanted Jake's blood for some magic elixir. And the queen was using his Ability to keep herself young and healthy—typical for the Corvo Kingdom, really, since all they care about is purity."

"Yeah, well, while Fin and Jake were in Zenia rescuing me and my ma, the queen went back on her word. The truce was broken, and their village in Fallen Wood was slaughtered. The four of us returned to nearly everyone dead, Fin's sister included."

"The Extermination," Lyra breathed. "I didn't realize that was Fin's village."

I squeezed my eyes shut to the onslaught of memories, shuttering away the carnage and utter heartbreak. The stench of the scorched forest. The image of toppled cabins and dead bodies left in bloody heaps for Jake and me to find. After getting him away from Corvo and the queen's torture, and then the massacre of all the family we had left, Jake was never the same. But I guessed three hundred years' worth of survivor's guilt would do that to a man.

I swallowed the regret, guilt, and hatred I tried to keep buried. I needed to be strong for the people who came to us for protection, and I had to be strong for Jake, too.

How many months had he been gone now? Five? Six? I considered the baleful days to come, knowing he wouldn't be here to help us.

"If we go to Corvo," Callon said thoughtfully. "If this is all part of the queen's plan—"

"You think?"

"Either way, if Fin sees the princess after everything that's happened—" Callon huffed a breath. "I don't know what will happen to him."

Clearing my throat, I sat up. I couldn't take it anymore. I glanced at Callon and Lyra by the fire as I climbed to my feet. Tick stood, stretching beside me. "Is the envoy on the move?" I asked, rolling up my bed mat.

Lyra set her mug on the tree stump beside her. "Um, no.

Nothing yet."

"We should pack up—be ready to head out as soon as they are."

"Sounds good," Lyra said, but neither of them moved. In fact, I could feel their eyes on me as I gathered what few things I'd used last night.

"What?" I said gruffly, tightening the knot on my pack.

"I was thinking," Callon started, brushing his hands off as he walked over. "Maybe going back to Corvo City isn't necessary."

My brow furrowed. "Of course it is. That's where the envoy is heading."

"But what if you sent a raven in your place?"

My hands stilled, and I looked at him.

"Hear me out." Callon held up his palms. "What if you sent word to Del and had her meet you somewhere? That might be safer than going into the city, especially since we don't know whether the queen is after you."

"No," I said, shaking my head. "What if someone sees the raven or learns of our meeting? It needs to be a surprise visit, and I want to be there—for Del to see me—so I can weigh the truth in her eyes."

"You're assuming you'll even get to see her, Fin," Lyra countered. "What if the queen has guards waiting for you? What if she knows it's you in the desert, and this is one of her schemes?"

As much as I hated Queen Corisande, it was hard to fathom her caring much about what I did. The queen had what she wanted. Del was still by her side. She'd even helped her mother forge the most powerful alliance possible within the Seven Kingdoms. And her mother had already exacted her vengeance and killed my people.

"The queen probably assumes I'm dead with the rest of my family and has no reason to come after me again." I shook my head, almost certain it was true. "This isn't personal. Not this time. And I am no threat to the queen."

Twigs snapped beneath my boots as I strode to Dusty, basking in the morning sunlight. "She wouldn't waste her energy and resources on me. This has *secret agenda* written all over it, just like her bloodletting from before . . . I just have to put the pieces together."

Reticent as they were, Lyra and Callon tended to their own bed rolls before saddling their horses.

"Besides," I added. "We'll be dressed as Sierra soldiers going into the city. They won't know it's me." I ran my hand down Dusty's gray forehead. He nipped at my shirt, coaxing me to give him an apple as payment for riding all day again. I shoved his head away playfully and heaved his saddle onto his back. "All right, bud. Be patient."

"About the uniforms," Callon started, flipping his dagger from blade to hilt. "Will we have Sierra blood on our hands by the time we're done? Or are we knocking them out in their sleep?"

I cinched Dusty's saddle and reached into my pack for an apple. "I guess that depends on how it goes over the next two days, but either way, we have to wait until we're close to the city. Assuming the envoy is communicating telepathically with their point person, we can't give their contact lead time to come snooping around when the men fail to check in." If I wasn't mistaken, Callon looked disappointed by that, and my eyebrow arched of its own accord. "Why? Are you getting restless already?"

Callon tucked his bedroll under his arm. "I've got all this pent-up energy and did all that training before we left. And all we've done is eat and walk—"

"That's all *you've* been doing," Lyra interjected, making Callon grin with a nod of truth.

I couldn't help myself. I reached for Callon as he walked past and wrapped him in a headlock.

"Son of a bitch," Callon grunted.

"You want to expel some energy?" I asked with a chuckle.

"That's a dick move, Finlay!"

I laughed louder and let him go, both of us breaking off into a defensive stance as we stared at one another, waiting for the other to strike. "Let's do this," I told him and took a step forward.

Callon jabbed me in the abs before I knocked his feet from under him, and he landed on the ground. He was fast, though, more agile than me as I caught my breath from his sucker punch, and he jumped back onto his feet before I could blink.

"Oh, I'm coming for you, Fin," he warned, and as we blocked each other's jabs and roundhouses, I reveled in a moment of levity. Lyra goaded us both as she finished saddling her mare, and I realized I missed our morning grappling sessions and the comfort of routine.

"Guys—they're under attack!" Lyra blurted as I locked Callon in an armbar.

I released him, and we both straightened, our chests heaving and my pulse pounding in my ears.

"What?" Callon gasped, cinching his gun belt around him. "Attack?"

"Ferals!" she called.

I holstered my shotgun into the strap on my back and grabbed my bow and quiver as Dusty clomped over. I jumped onto his back. *The men in the woods,* I told Tick. *Danger.* I pictured the envoy we'd been following, and with a mixture of thoughts and urgency, I sent Tick ahead to scope out whatever was happening until we could get there.

Within seconds, Callon and Lyra fell into step beside me, and we made our way through the forest.

I didn't push Dusty too hard or too fast. I wanted to know what we were up against or if we even needed to get involved at all. Assuming the Ferals prevailed, the envoy dying at their hands was to our advantage. No one would question what happened to the mercs or why.

As the three of us rode through riverbeds and wove around the thick bases of the redwood trees, I connected with Tick, who was jetting through the brush.

I'd always had a strange hesitation when it came to killing Ferals. I knew I should fear and hate them for murdering my parents and for the havoc they'd wreaked on many of the lives around me. But was it murder when all a person knew was base instinct and a primal need to protect their kin? Their territory? Or to attack out of fear? I wouldn't shoot a territorial bear if I ventured too close to her den unless I was forced to. That's what Ferals were—humans reduced to creatures, and the connection I'd always had with the animals wouldn't let me hate them, not entirely.

Tick stopped in the dense ferns near the boulders surrounding the guards' camp. A small pack of Ferals ravaged the place, attacking the soldiers with spears and axes, but it wasn't the number of them that gave me pause. Two Ferals sat on horseback, removed from the fight.

I'd never seen a Feral on horseback, let alone removed from the group, watching the others fight as the woman and girl were, as if they were merely observing.

The guards were heavily armed, but they'd been caught unawares, their movements frantic and disjointed, unlike the Ferals.

I frowned, watching through Tick's eyes with a strange sense of awe. While some Ferals were injured or dead, the others weren't crazed and desperate, like wild animals ravaging a meal. Instead, they worked together like a wolf pack as they cornered a guard, allowing one Feral man to lunge forward, striking the fatal blow.

I felt Lyra and Callon's nearness but could only hear the gurgling cries and savage snarls around the bend. "Wait," I rasped, pulling Dusty to a stop in a thicket of trees. I wasn't ready to make us known. "They're coordinating," I explained, barely registering my own voice.

"The envoy?" Callon asked telepathically.

I shook my head, watching the woman on horseback. Her clothes were tattered, as most Ferals' were, and her black hair was long and unkempt. There was nothing significantly different about her other than the fact she kept herself separate, unwilling to join the fight.

Only when she nudged her horse toward the ravaged camp did I realize the fighting was over and the Ferals had won.

Disconnecting from Tick's mind, I motioned for Callon and Lyra to follow me.

"You're sure about this?" Callon asked silently.

"I'm sure we need those uniforms before the Ferals take them, or we're screwed. That's our way into the city."

I glanced at Lyra. She gripped the hilts of her knives sheathed beside her gun, her eyes wide and waiting for whatever came next. Everyone hated the Ferals. They were unpredictable and acted out of desperation most of the time. Now that they seemed to be organizing, I didn't know what to expect. Still, whether it was an inexplicable feeling of guilt about the lot they'd been dealt in life or my hatred of slaughter, having seen too much of it over the years, it didn't feel right to ambush them and draw blood. They'd killed our enemy, after all.

I looked at Callon, afraid to speak aloud in case the Ferals would hear us. *"Maybe I should go alone,"* I said silently again. *"They outnumber us—"*

"No. We all go," Callon insisted.

"We have no fight with them," I told him, glancing over my shoulder. *"They are killing our enemy. Not us."*

"Yet." Callon's jaw ticked. *"They aren't killing us yet."*

My eyes hardened on him. *"We don't hurt them unless we have to. And if they don't take the uniforms, there's no reason to disturb them."*

We stared one another down, but Callon finally dipped his chin with a sigh. I nodded for him to fill Lyra in, and I connected with Tick again, watching the Ferals through her eyes.

The woman on the horse peered around, assessing the carnage before dismounting in the center of it. She grunted at the young girl, still sitting on her horse on the outskirts. Since the girl didn't move, I assumed she was told to stay put.

The Feral woman passed the beds that hadn't been rolled and the smoking fire that had gone out in the night. Outwardly, there was nothing to mark her as a leader, save for her horse and her posture, a bit more assured than the others.

The longer I watched her, the more convinced I was that she knew the members of the envoy would be asleep, that their stumbling upon the guards wasn't luck at all but planned.

More grunts were exchanged as the surviving Ferals riffled through the envoy's saddle packs. They tasted their food and smelled their garb, picking through anything that smelled or looked appealing to them and disregarding the rest.

The leader walked over to the cart loaded with soil from the desert and lifted the blanket covering it. She eyed the crates of rainbow rocks, then aggressively searched through the glass vials of different colored soils. She made inaudible sounds and waved her arms around, and even if I didn't know what she was saying exactly, it seemed she wanted them to take everything.

I hadn't realized I'd dismounted Dusty and was walking closer until I blinked, seeing the Feral through my own eyes beyond the trees. Instantly, the woman's blue eyes were latched onto me.

There was a gurgle to my left, followed by a scathing scream, and before I knew what I was doing, I raised my bow and shot an arrow through the neck of an injured guard who had grabbed a handful of a Feral woman's hair. He let go, and she gasped and scrambled away as he fell back with a final breath.

Chest heaving and bow still raised, I looked at the Feral leader. Her chest was heaving, too, her eyes wide and assessing me. Easing my stance, I lifted my hands, bow unaimed, and hoped she understood I was not there to harm them.

The longer the woman stared at me, her blue eyes boring into mine, the more I believed she did.

I stared back at her, thinking about a day in the ruins outside of

Corvo City years ago, when another Feral woman had Beast in a cage, prepared to skewer him for her evening meal. I'd been able to communicate with that woman like I could with animals. It was different and difficult, straining my mind in a way that had debilitated me for hours after. But I'd done it.

The leader's head twitched, her eyes darting behind me as Lyra and Callon stepped into view. "Hey," I said calmly. "We won't hurt you." I raised my hands and bow higher. I wasn't ready to completely divest myself of my weapon yet.

Though the woman snarled and her lip curled with distrust, she didn't attack us, nor did her people.

"Fin," Callon warned silently. *"What are we doing, exactly?"*

"Just wait," I breathed, and gaze unwavering on the woman, I thought about each and every time I'd fought a guard or against the kingdoms. I made a conscious effort to think about my own fear and hatred and about the people I loved dying because of men like these, lying on the forest floor in dead heaps.

My sister in a bloody heap among dozens of others—children included—and my utter guilt and sorrow.

My best friends with holes in their stomachs from laser warfare.

The woman's eyes widened as she saw my thoughts, probably only flickers of them, but it was enough. She straightened, looking half panicked but more confused than anything. And curious.

I pointed to the guard nearest me, then gestured to my clothes. Her head tilted, much like Tick's did when she was watching a gopher hole, and I risked breaking the silence between us again. "We won't hurt you," I repeated, even if she didn't understand.

Slowly, I walked over to one of the dead guards, and while the Feral woman watched, unmoving and intent, I removed the dead man's pauldrons and helmet.

The woman continued to observe me for what felt like a thousand heartbeats until, finally, I had undressed one of the guards and slowly walked the uniform back to Callon.

"Are you trying to give me a heart attack?" he said, taking the armor from me.

I laughed in my head. *"Apparently, I'm trying to give myself one, too."*

The woman looked between Callon and me as if she sensed something between us, which made me all the more curious about what was happening between my mind and the Feral leader's.

I pointed to another dead guard, and this time the woman's head jerked slightly, as if she was giving me permission. And that's how it went for minutes that felt precariously long and thrilling at the same time.

When I had the three uniforms we needed, I took a step back, realizing our horses had walked up behind us at some point, coming to our aid should we need it.

The Ferals around the woman grew restless, their heads whipping from her to me and back again, waiting for direction. I'd never seen anything like it—never knew it was possible for Ferals to be anything other than one-track minded, acting out of fear, instinct, and necessity alone.

But this . . . This was something else. Something new.

"Thank you," I said, staring into her blue eyes. I couldn't tell if she was closer to thirty or fifty, with her hair hanging in her face and her cheeks covered in dirt. As I took another step backward, I willed her to say something. To converse with words, but none came.

Slowly, I climbed onto Dusty's back, trying not to make any sudden movements that would crack this ice-thin truce between us.

The Ferals were silent, making no moves against us as the three of us turned our horses, nudging them into a run, and got the hell out of there.

"Holy shit!" Callon's voice was breathy, even in my head. *"Did that just happen?"*

"Yeah," I said aloud, taking a deep breath. "It did."

6

DEL

"It's your call," Hills said, her voice hushed to keep her words from reaching the ears of the doctor waiting in Mother's sitting room.

From my position on the window seat, I stared past Hills to Mother's bed. She hadn't opened her eyes for three days. This morning was the critical point of prognosis. At least, those had been the doctor's words. If she hadn't awakened by then, she likely never would.

All night and all morning I sat at her bedside. Not once had she stirred.

Garath lowered himself to his knees on the floor before me and captured one of my hands in both of his. "Del? I know this is a difficult time, but we need to know what you want to do."

I dragged my focus to him, to his amber eyes. Sympathy softened his hard features, and his stubble was scruffier than usual with a couple of extra days' worth of growth.

"Do you want our rangers to start staging Feral attacks?" Garath asked.

My attention drifted past him once more to Mother's still, dying form. She would have said yes. She would have argued that the lives lost in the staged attacks were necessary sacrifices to save the kingdom. A few dead now to save tens of thousands later. She wouldn't even have hesitated before agreeing.

I turned my head toward Sid perched on the windowsill and the view of the grounds beyond the moat, unable to face that hard truth. The fruit trees in the orchard were awash with blossoms ranging from snow white to vivid pink, and the verdant hedges in the maze bordering the northern edge of the orchard appeared faded by the bright afternoon sunlight.

I shook my head. I couldn't do it. I couldn't damn innocent people. There had to be another way.

"They can stage Feral attacks at existing attack sites," I said, my voice weak, and once again looked at Hills. "But no new attacks. No new deaths."

Mother had said I would need to commit fully if this plan were to work, and I was prepared to do it. But I was committed to doing it my way—without throwing away the lives of innocents. I may not have been crowned yet, but I was the queen regent of the Corvo Kingdom, and if I wanted to retain the people's loyalty through the trying times that lay ahead, my reign needed to be built on a platform of honor and trust from the very beginning. From this moment.

"Very well," Hills said, her tone flat. "We'll focus on planting reports of organized Feral attacks for now." She bowed stiffly, then turned and strode away.

I watched her leave the room. "She doesn't agree with my decision."

"She's not queen," Garath said, rising only to lower himself down to sit beside me on the window seat.

My attention drifted over Mother, then Garath, and landed on the window. From my vantage point, I could see the entire western portion of the city as well as the wildlands across the strait to the north, beyond the water glittering in the afternoon sunlight. Fin's wildlands. His people had abandoned their settlement concealed within those coastal woods nearly a decade ago, but part of me still believed that if I stared hard enough, if I searched long enough, I would find him out there.

"I'm not queen, either," I reminded Garath, glancing at him sidelong. "Not yet." Not until Mother was gone. Dead. Not until I was crowned.

I drew in a deep breath and exhaled slowly, hoping to release some of the dreadful anticipation knotting my gut. It wouldn't be long now.

"I need to think," I said, standing abruptly.

Sid stirred on the windowsill, fluffing his feathers to prepare for flight. He hopped closer to me, then spread his wings and flapped once, propelling himself toward me.

I held out my arm so he could land. His talons dug into the bracers on my forearms and caught on the ridges of hard leather sewn into the upper portion of my tunic sleeves as he climbed my arm to take his usual position on my reinforced shoulder.

Garath rose as well. "A walk around the grounds?"

I shook my head and looked at Garath, offering him a pitiful excuse for a smile. "I don't want to go too far from her," I said, glancing at Mother's bed. "Besides, Alastor could return any day now." I never liked to stray far from Liam when that man was potentially nearby.

"Come with me," Garath said, starting for the doorway to the sitting room, his leather armor creaking with each step. "I know just the place."

I stared after Garath, thinking I didn't deserve him. Not when, for five days, I had been withholding from him the essential role *he* would play in this delicate, complicated plan to save the kingdom.

Garath stopped in the doorway and looked back at me. He cast such an imposing figure that part of me believed he truly could shield me from all harm. I grasped that illusion tightly, holding it close as I followed him out of Mother's bedroom.

I peered around Mother's study from the wingback chair at her desk. Walls of packed bookshelves surrounded me, and beneath the scent of woodsmoke from the fireplace, my nose detected the hint of vanilla that was ever-present in this room. It was the books. Mother explained once when I asked her about the faint but distinctive scent. Many were ancient, from before the Turn, and apparently, as the paper bound within their covers aged, it released the familiar, sweet notes of vanilla.

Garath had taken up a post at the door, positioning himself between me and the most likely source of threats. And Sid dozed on the mantel, his beak tucked against his wing, soaking up the heat drifting up from the fireplace below him.

The surface of Mother's desk was barren, as usual, the scuffed expanse of oak on full display. How many of the Corvo queens had sat in this exact spot, planning and plotting? How many awful decisions had they made in the name of protecting their kingdom? How many would have ordered the rangers to stage additional Feral attacks?

Was I making a mistake by holding back? Would doing the "right" thing result in disastrous consequences?

I reached for the handle to the desk's top drawer, unsurprised it didn't budge when I pulled. Mother had kept her desk locked for as long as I could remember.

I withdrew a pair of decorative hair pins from my low bun and leaned forward, fitting the pins into the lock. It had been ages since I last picked a lock, and I was rusty, taking far longer than I should have. But after a couple of minutes, the lock clicked, releasing the drawer.

I glanced at Garath. He was watching me, the corners of his mouth tensed like he was suppressing his amusement at my unqueen-like behavior.

My attention drifted back down to the drawer as I pulled it

open, and my brow furrowed. I wasn't sure what I had expected, but not this. Not an assortment of mundane desk supplies and writing utensils.

Frowning, I pulled the drawer open as far as it would go. It stopped short at roughly the halfway point. I fished out the pens, scissors, and other supplies, setting everything on top of the desk. Then, I felt around the drawer, searching for a false bottom or back panel, but nothing unusual was found. There was no obvious reason why it had been locked. It was just a drawer.

I shut it and moved on. The next drawer down was filled with a half dozen thin, leather-bound books. Ledgers, it turned out. I would need to look through those more closely, but not today. I returned the ledgers to the drawer after briefly skimming through each and moved on to the next drawer.

This one was filled with loose sheets of paper. I leafed through them and found reports on many things relating to the kingdom, from the dangerous to the mundane.

The bottom drawer was filled with manila file folders, each folder labeled in Mother's slanted hand with the name of a location within the Seven Kingdoms, most within Corvo Kingdom.

I pulled out a folder labeled *Alcatraz*. That forbidding island was where Mother and Maylar had held the captive Healers prisoner. It was the place where everything had changed. The folder was fairly full, and when I opened it, I thought I might find information on the elixir, the Healers who had been held against their will, or possibly even a report on Fin's and my infiltration of the elixir operation all those years ago. I had *not* expected to find a sketched portrait of Fin staring back at me atop the stack of papers, his face looking exactly as I remembered him.

My breath hitched, and my chest tightened, constricting my lungs. I traced the strong lines of his face with gentle fingertips. He had grown fuzzy and indistinct in my mind's eye, but my memories of him sharpened into pristine focus as I studied the drawing. It was so incredibly lifelike.

I could see Liam in his eyes and the shape of his lips. And this was merely a pencil sketch. Though Liam was still just a boy, I could see how much more he would grow to resemble his father in the years to come.

Hands trembling, I folded the sketch, then folded it again and tucked it into the side pocket of my tunic.

I felt a little light-headed as I skimmed through the rest of the documents in the folder, then peeked into the other folders, but all I found were more reports, along with some more sketches—of people and places I didn't recognize. I shut the bottom drawer and settled back in the chair, thrown off balance by the unexpected encounter with an image of the man I had given my heart and body to so long ago. My stare lingered on the top drawer, my thoughts returning to its refusal to open as far as the three drawers beneath it, not to mention the fact that it had been locked at all when the only items within were utterly inconsequential.

Straightening, I pulled the top drawer open again, tugging harder than before. If I pulled it all the way out, maybe I would find something hidden behind it.

But it still wouldn't budge.

I reached into the drawer, feeling the underside of the desk's top to figure out what the back of the drawer was catching on. Maybe a protruding screw or nail. The desk was ancient, after all. Perhaps it was in need of repairs.

My fingers brushed over something hard and rectangular. Something shaped very much like a book. Or, rather, a metal pocket screwed into the underside of the desk *holding* a book.

Heart beating faster, I slid the concealed book free and set it on the desk. It was leather-bound and worn but not ancient, like so many of the books in the study. The raven insignia that had represented the Corvo Dynasty since its inception two centuries ago was stamped onto the front cover.

Breath held, I opened the book. The first page was blank, but the second was filled with Mother's familiar slanted handwriting.

The top of the page was labeled _Corvo City Marina, 276-279AE_. Beneath the underlined label, Mother had listed a series of letters and numbers. It appeared to be some sort of code.

RMV - 25AE - 177

DIF - 178AE - 23

SHF - 236AE - 79

KSD - 143AE - 34

The first list filled nearly two columns. The second, labeled _Shadow District, 281-282AE_, had only a few of those coded entries listed. I leafed through the book, surprised when the dates on the page titles moved past the present year and into the future, then flipped back to one of the earlier entries:

Corvo City, 285 AE

RMV - 23AE - 7

TLR - 264AE - 314

RSD - 225AE - 13

JNN - 116AE - 56

I skimmed over the four lines beneath the heading again and again. The trio of letters at the beginning of each coded line made me think they were the initials of a person's name. Obviously, the first set of numbers were years, with AE standing for _After the Ending._ The Patrons had established the dating system to delineate the time before the Turn from the time after. But the second set of numbers . . .

Brow furrowed, I shook my head.

Someone knocked on the door, and my attention snapped up to Garath.

His eyes locked with mine, and he drew the pistol from his hip holster before reaching out to pull the door open.

Saira, one of Mother's personal guards, bowed her head. When she straightened, her expression was grim. "Doctor Robins sent me to fetch Princess Delphinia," she told Garath.

Cold washed over me, and I closed my eyes, shutting the mysterious book. I inched the heavy chair backward and stood, hugging the book to my chest, using it to shield my heart as I marched out of the study and down the corridor to watch Mother die.

7

FIN

I stood at the window of our room at the Drunken Stag Inn, peering out at the torchlit city. Corvo City might've been everything I'd remembered, or perhaps it was greatly changed, but I wouldn't have known either way. My gaze was fixed in only one direction. My body was a humming, thrumming bundle of nerves I couldn't shake.

"I think he's finally lost it," Callon whispered under his breath.

"Why?" Lyra murmured.

"He's too quiet."

"He's always this quiet."

"Yeah, but—"

"I can hear you, you know," I said, tugging down the steel, black chest plate of the Mantis guard uniform. It was too restrictive, and the leather pauldrons were too tight around my shoulders. The uniform was too small and suffocating, and even in the cool evening, my forehead beaded with sweat.

I ran my fingers through my hair. I'd worn a dozen disguises, but this . . . this was different. The castle glowed through the mist, a daunting beacon in the heart of the city, taunting me.

Now was the time, under cover of the foggy night, to sneak into the castle unseen. My owl friend had scoped it out, ensuring Del's suite was lit up, that someone was within.

"Fin," Callon said, and when I looked at him, his expression was one of concern and fatigue. We'd been on the road for days, the three of us wrought with anticipation at every step, even if it was for different reasons. "How will you get to her?" he asked. "The castle is heavily guarded."

"I know the castle well enough," I told them, meeting Lyra's eyes first, then Callon's. "I'll take the route she showed me last time."

"And if the route is blocked or guarded?"

"It won't be."

"But what if it is?" Lyra hedged.

"Then I'll pose as one of the guards," I said hotly and began to pace. "Del's married to a Sierra prince, isn't she? I'm sure that place is teeming with Sierra guards, which is exactly what I look like." I tugged at the snug bracers tied around my forearms. "Mostly. And once I'm in the castle, there are passages in the walls. I'll go directly to Del's suite and wait for her if I have to."

"And . . ." Lyra hedged.

I shrugged. "And what?"

"And if those aren't her rooms anymore? Or if she's with her husband? One look at you, and he'll know you aren't one of his men."

I paused, my footsteps faltering only slightly before I started pacing again. I hadn't thought about her being with Prince Alastor when I confronted her. Not really. In my mind, Del was still . . . Del, littering her floor with unworn clothes to make it look like she hadn't snuck out for the night, or Del hiding in her bathtub so her mother wouldn't know she was covered in cobwebs from sneaking through the tunnels, wouldn't smell the sea air clinging to her after hours of late-night rowing.

To me, the princess was still the Del who would sneak out of the castle to save an innocent man and risk everything to do what was right. Who would help me if I asked her to because she knew she could—that she *should*.

But I couldn't help the flood of uncertainty as I considered Callon's fears. *Had* she moved to another wing of the castle? *Would* I find her with her husband? My hands clenched at my sides.

With the owl only able to see light through the shuttered window, there was no way to know what I might walk into, and the endless possibilities had me second-guessing the entire plan.

Callon and Lyra sat on one of the cots, ale mugs gripped in their hands, watching me in silence.

I'd had two days to come to terms with this moment, and I thought I had, but it wasn't a stranger with a pistol I would find at the other end of this. It wasn't a shadowed figure or a man with menace in his eyes who I could fight and kill, knowing it was for the greater good. If all went according to plan, I would be face to face with Del before the sun rose, and I wasn't sure I could bear what I might discover.

"Fin," Callon rasped. "Take a deep breath, man. You're stressing me out."

I ran my fingers through my hair again, glaring at the wall of pitted plaster.

"What if you're found out?" Lyra asked more softly.

Callon glared at her. "He's not likely to calm down if you keep asking him questions like that, now, is he?" he gritted out.

But Lyra ignored him, calculated and pragmatic as always. "What if Callon checks in with you and you need our help?" She glanced around our dilapidated room at the cracks inching up the walls. "There's only so much we can do from so far away. We should go with you. That way, we're closer in case you need us."

I shook my head. Unless they were inside the castle with me, there was little they could do to help. "You can come as close as the castle walls, but you can't go inside. I won't risk you being captured. Someone needs to make it back to Shoshone to warn our people. Besides, I'm less likely to be found if I'm alone."

Lyra looked me up and down, and I rolled my eyes. I knew what she saw. A big guy like me wouldn't go unnoticed easily. "Just trust me," I said as I began pacing again.

"You want me to trust you?" Lyra scoffed. She stopped me and gripped my shoulders as she turned me to face her. "Then pull yourself together." Her deep blue eyes hardened on me, lingering and seeing more than I probably wanted her to, but I didn't want to hide from her. From them.

"Look," she said, exhaling a heavy breath. "I don't pretend to know what you went through before I met you, Fin, but this isn't you. Whatever this princess did to you, it's in the past. That's what this is about, isn't it? You need to be here *now*. You have hundreds of people to protect in the present. People who have a sense of peace they've never even dared to hope for because of your efforts. And now the Sierra soldiers are likely coming for our settlement within a few weeks' time, so you have to figure this out."

I blinked at her. "Wow, nice pep talk."

"Well," she shrugged. "You've held it together for what, ten years? Don't fall apart now. We'll need a leader when we get back." Lyra pointed out the window. "If that princess is the only way to figure this out, then get in, get your answers, and get out so we can move on. What's the worst that could happen?"

Callon opened his mouth, but Lyra waved her hand to silence him. "Don't answer that." She sighed, her eyes searching mine again. "Del is the *only* reason we didn't go back right away. So, see this through."

My shoulders squared as I imagined myself through Lyra's eyes. A pathetic, weak mess of a man still hung up on his boyish crush and still angry for betrayals I wasn't sure I had any business holding Del accountable for, even if I wanted to. I was angry for circumstances that wouldn't change unless I pushed it all aside again and did something about it.

"I know you, Fin," Callon said, rising from the cot. He gave me a sidelong look as he handed me his mug of ale. "This isn't just about seeing Del. She left a mark on you, sure, but you're stronger than that. What are you really afraid of?"

That I dared to hope. Realization dawned on me at that moment. A single childish hope that not everything had changed. "I'm afraid I'm wrong, and Del's not the same person I knew, and —" I hesitated. "And I don't want to hate her."

Lyra frowned. "I thought all of this brooding was because you sort of already *did* hate her."

Callon looked at her like she was daft. "Don't you know? There's a fine line between love and hate."

I ran my fingers through my hair. Was that what this was? Love or hate? It was hard to name anything in between. "I've convinced myself that Del's been a victim in all of this, like me," I explained. "Or that she was ignorant of all the horrible things that have been going on. And tonight, I'll learn the truth."

"Then tonight," Lyra said, brushing my hair from my eyes, "you'll get the answers you need, so you can move on. For real this time."

"Now," Callon drawled and licked the pad of his thumb. He moved to wipe something off my cheek like his mother always did.

I elbowed him. "Quit."

"What? You look like a wreck. You *are* going to talk to a princess."

"As if I need the reminder," I grumbled, unable to resist a grin. And with Lyra and Callon standing before me, utter loyalty in their eyes and determination set in their shoulders, I knew what we had to do.

8

DEL

Mother approached death as she approached life—with an iron will and a refusal to surrender. It had taken her over a day to give in. To finally let go.

But even she couldn't hold out forever.

She was gone.

After clasping her frail fingers for so many hours, it felt strange to be empty-handed. I wandered the halls of Castle Corvo, aimlessly crisscrossing and retracing my path, Sid on my shoulder and Garath trailing behind me. The only consolation was that Alastor had yet to return. For the time being, I was free of his cruel comments and snide sneers.

But there was only one way I would be free of him forever.

At some point, I noticed my feet ached from walking for so long, so I meandered back toward my private chambers, pausing to check on Liam in his neighboring rooms. He was sound asleep in his bed.

I already knew I wouldn't be able to sleep, not even after sitting up with Mother all night, listening to her rattling breaths grow shallower and less frequent. She had fallen into a pattern of taking several shallow, labored breaths, then nothing for longer and longer periods of time. More than once, I had sat, waiting as one minute passed, then another, wondering if another breath would ever come.

Eventually, it didn't.

The wine cabinet tucked into the corner of my sitting room would provide the oblivion I desperately needed. I rarely overindulged, usually only on the nights I had to *be* with Alastor. I always approached our marriage bed stone-sober, but it was afterward that I sought solace in the bottle, when Alastor sauntered out of the bedroom I only ever visited for our requisite couplings, and I retreated to the comfort of my own rooms.

As soon as I entered my private sitting room, I flipped one of the switches by the door to turn on the single overhead light above the fireplace. I wasn't in the mood for bright places right now, not when my heart had been darkened by the events of the past day.

Sid launched from my shoulder and glided across the sitting room to land on the windowsill by the breakfast table, where Garath, Hills, and I took so many of our morning meetings. He hopped sideways along the sill, gazing out at the moonlit grounds far below.

I headed for the wine cabinet in the corner near the fireplace, pulled out two bottles of red and a corkscrew, and crossed to the window to set the wine bottles on the table.

"Drink with me?" I asked Garath, turning partway to look at him.

Garath stood in front of the door in his usual guard stance, no sign of standing down.

"Macy and Zion are out there," I said, pointing toward the door behind him with my chin. "You trust them to guard me when I'm asleep. Drinking is no different."

Garath studied me for a long moment. "Alastor might return tonight."

I snorted derisively. "I don't want to drink with Alastor."

"Del . . . " Garath's broad shoulders and stiff posture relaxed some, enough that I knew I had won. "You know what I mean."

Standing beside the table, I grabbed one of the bottles and twisted the corkscrew into the cork. "I'll command you if I have to. My first official order as queen could be to make you drink with me."

The corner of Garath's mouth twitched. "You haven't been crowned yet."

"Touché." I raised my eyebrows as I leveraged the cork free. "Maybe I'll beg you, then." I lowered my chin, smiling coyly. "I bet you'd like that. *Me*, begging you."

Garath clenched his jaw, his expression going cold. "I know you're hurting right now, so I'm going to pretend you didn't just say that."

My cheeks heated, and my chin trembled. Tears welled and spilled over the brims of my eyelids in record time, and I set the wine bottle down on the table. "I'm sorry," I said, my chest convulsing with barely suppressed sobs. "I'm so sorry." I covered my face with my hands, hiding from him.

Garath's heavy steps marked his passage across the room—not toward me but the wine cabinet. I heard the clink of crystal and peeked through my fingers to see him approaching with two wine goblets. "I will drink with you, but I will not get drunk with you." Standing beside me, he set the crystal down on the table and filled each glass about three-quarters of the way full with deep-red wine. "Not when *he* could walk through that door at any moment."

Slowly, I lowered my hands and leaned back against the edge of the table, accepting the goblet of wine when Garath offered it to me. I took a sip, then another, reinforcing my confidence with the alcohol.

"I'm going to ask you to do something," I said, taking one more drink before setting the goblet beside me on the table. For a long time, I stared down into the wine's gleaming surface, such a deep crimson that it looked like blood in the dim light. Finally, I raised my gaze, meeting Garath's. "And this time I *will* beg you if I have to."

His throat bobbed. "You need only ask," he said, his voice softer than usual.

I licked my lips, then cleared my throat, hating myself for what I was about to ask of him. "As you and Hills are aware," I said, barely above a whisper, "the Ferals plan will take some time to set up effectively." I took a deep breath, bolstering my courage before barreling onward. "If King Eduart isn't invested enough in fighting the Ferals for us to dispatch Alastor before Liam's testing—" My voice faltered, my chest constricting as fear for my child's life threatened to suffocate me.

"I would never let that cretin lay a hand on Liam," Garath swore. He would kill Alastor first. That much was clear.

"I know," I said, swallowing roughly and nodding. "I know that; I do, but—" I sighed. "But then we would have to run, and the kingdom would be lost." I reclaimed my goblet and gulped enough wine to nearly choke. "There would be a way, however, to appease Alastor," I said, my voice strained. I cleared my throat. "A way to redirect his focus away from Liam, so we wouldn't *have* to dispatch him quite so early in the timeline." I stared down at my goblet. "We would redirect his focus *away* from Liam, and *onto* another child."

I risked a peek at Garath's face, but his shadowed expression gave nothing away.

"I know I can't give you everything you need," I said in a rush. "I know I can't *be* everything you want, but you're my best friend, Garath. You're the only person I can trust with this."

"What exactly are you asking of me?" Garath said, finally speaking. "To father a child with you and then hand it over to Alastor? Because that is something I cannot do."

"No!" I said, shaking my head frantically. "We would *take care of him* before the child was born. I will swear that to you. But Liam's birthday is barely six months away, and if Alastor doesn't have proof of his viability as an heir to the Sierra throne by then . . ."

Garath drew in a slow, deep breath, then held it in his lungs long enough to drag my gaze back to his face. To his burning amber eyes. He set his wine goblet on the table, then took mine and set it down as well. He sidestepped to stand in front of me and raised one hand, tilting my face upward with gentle fingertips. His eyes searched mine.

"You know I could never refuse you anything," he said, dipping his head lower until his breath caressed my lips. "But if this is what you need from me, I have a price."

My heart was suddenly galloping. "What price?" I asked.

The corner of his mouth lifted, and his eyes sparkled with promise. "That you let me remind you that pleasure can be found in another's touch, not just pain."

My belly gave a little flip-flop. An ember of desire sparked to life within me, something I thought impossible after being with Alastor for so long. "You drive a hard bargain," I said, my voice breathy.

Garath smirked. "You have no idea, *princess*." His mouth touched mine in the softest, tenderest of kisses.

I parted my lips, surprised to find I wanted him to deepen the kiss. That spark of desire ignited hope within me that maybe, one day, I *could* grow to love Garath in the way he deserved.

But he pulled back instead. "Let me know when it's time, and—"

A commotion out in the corridor had our heads whipping toward the door.

"My wife, *the queen*, is in mourning. I need to comfort her," Alastor boomed, his sneer audible through the door. He was back. And worse yet, he was in one of his *moods*. "Let me pass, or I will force my way through." A moment later, he said, "Have it your way."

"Reinforce your shields," I hissed, then backed away from Garath.

I heard a loud thump on the other side of the door.

Alastor could be extremely dangerous if allowed to penetrate one's mental barriers. And it was not only because he could easily pluck any surface thoughts or feelings from his target's mind. As befit his war-loving kingdom, King Eduart had taught all of his sons to weaponize their empathy. Alastor could strike out with a focused lash of his will that would drop any target with an unguarded mind. All he needed was the opening created by a moment of eye contact.

My stare remained locked on the door as I felt my way around the table to my usual chair. I pulled the chair out with shaking hands and sat. I couldn't handle this right now. I couldn't handle *him*.

Garath stepped in front of me, facing the door, shielding me with his body.

The door burst open, and Macy slumped backward into the sitting room, unconscious. She cracked her head on the hardwood floor hard enough for me to think she would need a doctor. Alastor had hit her with a blast of his will. No doubt Zion was down as well.

But all concern for my guards evaporated when Alastor stepped into the room.

With Liam.

My stomach twisted, and my heart lodged in my throat.

"Hello, *wife*," Alastor said harshly, his face twisted into his trademark sneer. His ruddy skin told me he must have been drinking during the last leg of his journey back to Corvo City. He pushed Liam into the room ahead of him.

Liam's toe caught on the edge of the area rug, and he stumbled forward, landing on his hands and knees on the hard floor.

I burst out of my chair and rushed to my son, helping him up and wrapping a sheltering arm around his shoulders. His whole body trembled, his fear and rage resonating in my bones.

I backed Liam away from Alastor, hatred raging through my veins. I knew how tonight would end. I would have to lie with my husband one more time—but it would be the last time. That knowledge would make it so much easier to stomach than all the other times that had come before.

"Take Liam to Ada's room," I told Garath, angling my son toward my most trusted guard without ever taking my eyes off the man looming in the doorway. "I'll meet you there shortly."

Garath lingered for a moment, torn between getting Liam safely away from Alastor and staying with me. I understood his dilemma. I wanted Garath to stay, as well. I didn't *want* to be alone with Alastor right now. But I *needed* to know my son was safe.

"No, Mom!" Liam protested. "I won't leave you."

"Go," I commanded.

Garath didn't hesitate again, curving a protective arm around Liam's shoulders. I released my son reluctantly and watched as Garath pulled him toward the doorway, toward Alastor, stopping when my asshole of a husband remained stubbornly in place, blocking the way out.

I held my breath, my hand pressed against my belly to quiet the anxiety writhing in my gut.

After an extended stare down, Alastor stepped aside, waving his arm and bending his neck in a mocking bow.

Liam resisted as Garath pulled him from the room, but he gave in when he noticed my pleading expression. As soon as they were out of sight, I could breathe a little easier.

I straightened my spine and pushed back my shoulders, holding my head as high as if I already wore the crown. "What do you want?"

"To comfort you, of course," Alastor said, stalking forward. The dangerous glint in his eyes told me he was here to pick a fight, to blow off some steam.

It took a conscious effort to stand my ground. I could handle myself in a fight. Hills had been training me since I was a girl, but Alastor's skill matched my own, and his size gave him the advantage.

"I'm not in the mood for your brand of comfort," I said, keeping my voice even. Arguing with him would only rile him up further.

Alastor's haughty expression transformed into one of mock innocence. "Oh?" He glanced at the two goblets on the table, and his eyebrows rose. "Do you prefer *Garath's* brand of comfort?" He was close enough now that I could smell the liquor wafting off him. There was also the hint of something musty, like mildew, as if he had recently spent enough time in a damp, underground place for the scent to cling to his clothes.

"It's not like that, Alastor," I said calmly. I hated being around him when he was drunk. One wrong move, one wrong word, and I would set him off.

He stopped to stand in front of me and leaned in until his nose nearly touched mine. "I heard a rumor while I was away," he whispered. "Can you guess what it was?"

I angled my face away from him but couldn't escape his fetid breath. "I haven't the faintest idea."

"That Liam's not my son." He gripped my jaw in one hand and jerked my face back toward his. "That you were whoring around and got yourself into a bit of trouble before we married. Is he Garath's bastard?"

I forced out a bitter bark of laughter when what I really wanted to do was scream in terror and run away. "Don't be ridiculous," I said. "Liam looks just like you." At least, his coloring was the same.

Alastor's cheeks twitched with the ghost of a smile. "Yes, well . . . " His gaze dropped to my lips. "You can't blame me for being jealous."

My stomach turned.

"Take off your pants, wife," Alastor ordered. "I need to plant my seed."

"My mother just died," I said, wrenching free of his hold and backing away. "I'm not in the mood." I sidestepped to walk around him. "Now let me go to our son."

Alastor shifted to block my path.

Sid rustled his feathers on the windowsill, preparing to launch himself into the air.

When I attempted to evade Alastor again, he mirrored my movement, and a cruel smile twisted his lips. "You're not going anywhere."

9

FIN

Everything was a frenzy of rapid heartbeats and chaotic thoughts between leaving my friends at the outer wall, creeping through the hidden escape tunnel Del had taken me through a decade ago, swimming under the castle bridge, and making my way through the torchlit courtyard to the servants' entrance dripping wet. Every part of me was hyperaware, and my nerve endings were on the highest alert. Nulling myself was one thing, but it wasn't as easy to hide myself in the shadows as it had been ten years ago.

Thankfully, the foggy night helped, and the animal senses around me alerted me to the guards stationed within the castle walls. But still, there was a disquiet in the air. Humans were on edge and distracted. Strange as the atmosphere was, there was little time to think about it and even less time to waste.

Calling on a feline mind within the castle, I found one of the servants' quarter's cats willing to provide eyes into the oversized kitchen before I walked through the servants' door. I'd expected there would be a handful of staff still cleaning after a day of meals and duties, but it was empty.

As I stepped inside, greeted by my black furry friend, I noticed trays of partially touched food—fruit, cheeses, and meats that had barely been eaten. Decanters and dirtied goblets were discarded on the counters as if they'd been hastily forgotten.

Hearing footsteps coming down the corridor, I dipped into the pantry, where I remembered there was a concealed door that would lead me into the secret passageways of the castle. Right toward Del.

I stared at the lamb shanks hanging from the ceiling for a beat, and a pang of longing filled my chest. The last time I was here, Beast was with me, and our clandestine night in Castle Corvo was one of the most pleasantly surprising adventures we'd had together.

Clearing my throat, I opened the hidden door in the wall and climbed into the secret corridor. Bursts of light filtered through the darkness from hidden openings in the wall, illuminating the path enough to see, and I made haste toward Del's wing of the castle.

The pathway was narrower than I remembered, my shoulders nearly brushing both walls, but my steps were careful. Like any other time I was tracking in the forest, I made no noise for someone to notice me.

Weaving my way through the labyrinth was a bit of a haze but one I navigated well enough. After all, I'd only ever been in this castle once before, and it wasn't an experience I would ever forget. Instead of years, it seemed like only months since I took in the garish decor and unnerving artwork of my ancestors hanging on the walls. It was so eerie; it remained unblemished in my memory.

The closer I drew to the castle's east wing, the sweatier my palms became and the more chaotic my thoughts were. As soon as I reached the back of what I hoped was the giant portrait of Dani, I knew I was close.

Left to my own senses to guide me, and perhaps a bit of luck, I popped the painting open as quietly and slowly as I could and peered through the crack, looking for movement and listening for voices. I heard a squawking bird in the distance. Then the sound tapered away.

Pushing the portrait open farther, I poked my head out to find the hallway was clear, and I hurried down the corridor toward Del's old rooms. With each step, I told myself this needed to happen, that I needed closure from Del as much as I needed answers for my people and to ensure their safety.

The squawking started again, louder and closer this time, and the hair rose on the back of my neck. A familiar sound. A frantic sound. *A raven.* Dread pooled in my belly as I connected with the bird's mind to see a red-faced Del struggling beneath a hulking male figure. Sid swept low, his beak snapping at her attacker's back.

I heard Del's garbled pleas and shrieks from down the hall, cutting into me like a blade shredding through my heart. I sped to her chambers, nearly tripping over two unconscious guards outside her rooms.

More cries met my ears. Then the man's curses as Sid attacked him again. I barreled through the open door and the sitting room into Del's bedchamber, where the man pinned her down on the bed, one hand gripped tight around her throat. She hit and scratched at the man's arm and face, bucking against him as he pulled at her pants, trying to tear off her clothes.

All I saw was red. All I could feel was rage and desperation as my steps swallowed the distance to Del.

"You will do your duty," the man gritted out.

Before I realized what I was doing, I was behind him, wrapping my arm around his neck. I wrenched him off her and refused to let go.

The force of his body colliding with mine sent us stumbling backward into the wall, my head hitting it with a crack. But I'd unsheathed the knife from my belt and impaled it into the man's neck before I could feel any pain.

His gurgling was music to my ears, but only when I felt his hot blood on my hands could I catch my breath. The man's body went slack, and I instantly let go, staring at him as he fell to the floor with a heavy thud.

My heart dropped. My ragged breath ceased when I got my first good look at his face. *Prince Alastor?*

Sid croaked, and the bed creaked, reminding me Del was in the room. I spun around to face her.

Her face was horror stricken. Her mouth hung open as she propped herself up on an elbow and stared down at her husband's body, one dainty hand curled around her throat. Her chest heaved, tears stained her cheeks, and her hair fell in black tangles around her shoulders. Her clothes were rumpled and torn, her neck already bruising from his hold on her, and any remorse I began to feel vanished, replaced with the need to kill her husband all over again.

"Del," I breathed, my heart breaking to see her like this. She gaped at him as I stepped over Alastor's body. "Del," I said again.

Her umber gaze snapped to me as I reached for her, and she shrank away. My heart plummeted, and dropping my hand, I clenched it at my side.

"Fin," she rasped, shaking her head. "What have you done?"

IO

DEL

"Fin?" I lay on my back on the bed, propped up on one elbow, the fingers of one hand curled protectively around my aching neck.

Sid huddled close to me, his head and beak resting on my arm.

I shook my head, breathing hard. This couldn't be happening. *He* couldn't be here. Alastor couldn't be *dying*. I was dreaming. Trapped in a nightmare.

For years, I had longed for two things—to see Fin again and to be free of my wretched husband. Suddenly, I had both. My wishes had come true. But at what cost? Alastor lay on the floor, gurgling his last breaths. He had been my tormentor for so long, but in a perverse way, he had also been my kingdom's protector—the only thing holding his father at bay.

I tore my stare away from my dying husband to look at my rescuer. At my kingdom's executioner.

Fin was barely recognizable as an older version of the young man I had known all those years ago. He was broader, harder, and rougher than before. He loomed over me, wearing the armor of a Sierra soldier, his hair hanging around his head in damp waves, and the knife grasped in his hand still dripping with Alastor's blood. If not for his eyes—the exact shape and shade of green as Liam's—I might not have recognized him.

"What have you done?" I rasped.

Fin clenched and unclenched his jaw, his nostrils flaring with his next breath. "He was *choking* you."

"He wouldn't have killed me," I said, averting my gaze to watch the pool of blood beneath Alastor's body slowly creep across the hardwood floor. I let out a short, hollow laugh. "At least, he never did before." I rubbed my tender neck, shame at revealing as much to Fin making my cheeks burn.

"Del . . . " Fin moved closer, kneeling on the floor in front of me.

My chin trembled, tears welling in my eyes. I focused on my unlaced pants, attempting to piece together some of my shattered dignity, but Alastor's rough attempt to undress me had torn several of the loops, leaving the ties nothing to latch onto. A tear glided down my cheek as I shifted the bottom part of my tunic to better cover myself.

At the sound of footsteps pounding up the corridor to my rooms, Fin stood abruptly, brandishing his bloody knife and angling his body between the doorway and me. My heart was suddenly hammering, the panic lacing my blood making my veins vibrate.

Whoever was coming would see the unconscious guards, then Alastor's body, then Fin in his no doubt stolen Sierra armor, holding a bloody knife. It *looked* like he intended to harm *me*, too. If it was Garath who approached, he would see only the armor and the blood, and he would shoot Fin without a second thought.

I couldn't let that happen. I couldn't lose Fin like that. Not when he had only just crashed back into my life.

Sid launched into the air as I scrambled off the bed. I stepped in front of Fin a fraction of a second before Garath appeared in the doorway, pistol drawn and finger on the trigger. He aimed at me initially but quickly shifted higher, targeting the man looming behind me.

"Garath," I said, my voice low and even, and I raised my hands. "Put the gun down. The danger has passed." I glanced down at Alastor's body.

Sid glided around the room, then landed on top of the headboard.

Garath's gaze swept from my dead husband to my neck, then beyond me to Fin and his knife, before returning to the mess on the floor. "Damn it," he said, lowering his gun. He did not, however, tuck it back into the holster on his hip. "I really wanted to be the one to end him."

"Then why didn't you?" Fin bit out, accusation dripping from every word.

I realized at that moment that Fin saw me as a victim, as someone needing to be saved. He didn't understand. He couldn't see that putting up with Alastor was my way to protect my kingdom—and my son.

Our son.

Garath looked at Fin, his stare assessing. I watched him scan Fin's armor, then his hair—obviously a brighter red than Liam's auburn, even when wet, but with the same floppy curl—then his face, lingering on his eyes. I saw the moment recognition struck, causing the slightest hitch of Garath's eyebrows.

My bedroom was spacious, but with all the aggression and testosterone these two big men were throwing off, it felt cramped. Needing space, I stepped off to the side, away from Alastor's body, so I could see both Garath and Fin.

I straightened my shoulders, held my head higher, and leveled a cool stare on Fin. "Garath let Alastor live on *my* orders."

Fin narrowed his eyes.

"Alastor liked to use the threat of invasion to keep me *compliant*," I explained. "Now that he's dead, his father, King

Eduart, won't hesitate to take Corvo City and through it, the kingdom."

I shifted my attention to Garath. "Liam?"

This Alastor situation was enough of a mess. The last thing I needed was for my son to stumble in, see the man he believed to be his father dead on the floor, killed by a stranger who just so happened to be his true father.

"With Ada in her chambers," Garath confirmed.

"Good." I nodded to myself. "Go to them—and take Sid. Make sure they stay put while we take care of this." I glanced down at Alastor. "We'll meet you there when we're done. I need to see my son."

Garath eyed Fin, clearly questioning the wisdom of letting Fin see Liam. "Are you certain?"

Fin had already witnessed my greatest shame. I couldn't stand the idea of him thinking I had *chosen* to be with Alastor for any reason beyond desperation. He would know the truth, and I would erase the pity from his gaze. Even if he didn't believe my words when I told him Liam was his son, he would have to be a fool to deny the evidence seen with his own eyes. And Fin was no fool.

"Yes," I told Garath.

"Very well." Garath bowed his head. "Everything you need is already up in the north turret."

"I know, I know," I said, nodding. "Beneath the false bottom in the ammo box under the Gatling gun."

Garath nodded once, his stare lingering on Fin for a long moment before he turned away and strode across the sitting room.

I glanced at the raven perched on the headboard. "Sid, go with Garath."

Sid cawed, then spread his wings as he launched off the bed.

"Oh, and Garath?" I called, stepping into the doorway to the sitting room after Sid passed through.

Garath stopped two steps from the corridor and looked back at me, leaning away as Sid flew past him.

"Can you drag Zion in here? I'll need to . . . " I raised one hand and wiggled my fingers toward my temple, indicating that I intended to tap into the lesser-known facet of my empathic gifts.

"Of course," Garath said, bending over and hooking his hands under Zion's armpits.

I inhaled deeply, steadying my fluttering nerves before planting my hands on my hips and turning back to Fin, half expecting to discover I had been mistaken and he was someone else entirely. Half expecting him to have vanished.

But he was still there, and he was still Fin, as impossible as it seemed. And he looked as flabbergasted as I felt, but we didn't have time for explanations right now.

"Move the body to the rug over there, please," I said, pointing to the antique rug with a swirling pattern of red, orange, and gold covering the hardwood floor in front of the fireplace. "I'll be right back."

Without waiting to see if he would comply, I hurried into the sitting room. I nodded my thanks to Garath a moment before he pulled the door shut, then knelt beside Macy, brushing her auburn hair out of the way and touching my fingertips to her temples. I closed my eyes and reached out with my empathic gifts. I dove into her head, searching her unconscious mind for the memory of Alastor's arrival.

I found it quickly, only slightly jumbled by what I assumed to be a concussion from when her head had struck the floor, and slapped an illusory memory over the top of it, one of me coaxing both her and Zion into the sitting room to drink with me. The false memory would fade one day, years from now. But by then, hopefully, it wouldn't matter.

Once I was finished with Macy, I scooted over to Zion and did the same to him. My head spun as I pulled out of his mind and sat back on my heels. Altering peoples' memories always sapped my gifts, and right now, after sitting up all night and day with Mother, I was already exhausted.

I took a few slow, deep breaths, regathering my strength, then opened my eyes and stood. I hurried back to the bedroom, pleased to find Fin had not only moved Alastor's body to the rug, but he had anticipated my intentions and rolled the body up in the rug as well.

"I tied his jacket around his neck to help contain the bleeding, too," Fin said, standing and dry-washing his hands.

My breath caught in my sore throat, and my heart thudded. I had known Fin was still in the bedroom, of course, but I hadn't been prepared to see him again.

"I assumed this is all so we can move the body." Fin shrugged his broad shoulders. "Figured you didn't want to drip a trail of blood through your castle."

I swallowed roughly and nodded. Realizing I was staring, I looked at the gleaming crimson pool on the hardwood floor and the smears marking Fin's path to the rolled rug. "We need to clean this up first," I said, my voice thready.

Macy and Zion would wake eventually, and the evidence of what had really happened here needed to be gone by then, or their false memories would destabilize, letting the truth shine through.

I rushed into the adjoining bathroom and crossed to the walk-in closet at the far end of the room to retrieve a stack of towels. I would have to hide the mess for now and burn it all later.

Fin was quiet as we knelt together on the hardwood floor of my bedroom and mopped up my dead husband's blood. His frequent glances reminded me he had come here for a reason that had nothing to do with killing Alastor. I had little doubt that when this was all over, I would find out exactly what had driven him back to Corvo City, pushing him to risk his life by sneaking into the castle. Either I was imagining things, or he was purposely staying out of arm's reach from me, like he believed I planned to lunge at him and take his secrets without permission, having done it to him before.

After I changed my clothes, and after Fin moved Macy and

Zion to the sofa to sleep off their supposed wild night of drinking with the grieving princess, we finally left my private chambers. I led the way up the vacant hallway to the painting of Dani, the Patron of Telepaths, and her German Shepherd, Jack. Fin followed close behind me, the rolled rug containing Alastor's body slung across his shoulders.

We slipped into the hidden corridors that snaked throughout the castle, Fin moving sideways to fit his awkward burden through the narrow passageways, and wound our way through the warren of tunnels toward the stairway to the north turret.

"We're almost there," I told him in a hushed whisper once we had emerged from the walls and started climbing the spiral staircase leading up to the top of the battlement.

Fin was breathing hard by the time I opened the door to the turret, and sweat beaded on his brow, dripping down his temples and making strands of his drying hair stick to the back of his neck.

"Can you unwrap the body?" I asked, taking a few steps, then pausing to turn part way back toward Fin. "I need to, um—" When my eyes met his, my heart stuttered yet again, and the words died on my tongue.

He was *really* here. His presence rattled me to the core of my being.

Why was he here? Where had he been all these years? What happened to him and his people? Why had they abandoned their village in the wooded wildlands to the north? Why had he abandoned *me*?

Oblivious to my rapid unraveling, Fin unceremoniously dropped his burden. The rug and body hit the stone floor with an audible crunch.

The sound of breaking bones shook me out of my momentary trance, and I cleared my throat. "This'll just take a moment."

I rushed across the turret platform and dropped to my knees in front of the ammo box tucked beneath the Gatling gun. Hands suddenly trembling, I fumbled with the box's latch for a few seconds before freeing it and lifting the lid. I hurriedly removed the bullets, setting them on the floor beside me, then lifted the false metal bottom and pulled out the sealed bottle of whiskey resting on its side and the forged note from a physician "confirming" Alastor was sterile.

I returned everything but the bottle and note to the box, arranging the ammo exactly as I had found it, and shut the lid. Tearing the seal off the bottle, I stood and hurried back toward Fin and the unwrapped body. The jacket that had been tied around Alastor's neck lay piled in a bloody heap on one corner of the rug.

I yanked the cork free and dumped about half of the liquor onto Alastor's body, spreading it around to soak into his clothes. When the pungent odor of whiskey was strong enough to make me crinkle my nose, I stopped, lifted the bottle to my lips, and took a long pull.

The whiskey burned my throat, and I coughed as I choked it down. Wiping my mouth with the back of my hand, I offered the bottle to Fin.

"Maybe later," he said with a shake of his head. He planted his hands on his hips and stared down at Alastor's liquor-soaked body. "He's going over the edge?"

I nodded, crouching down to tuck the forged doctor's note into Alastor's inner coat pocket. "Drop him head first," I suggested, standing. "To disguise the knife wound."

Fin's gaze was heavy, assessing. "You really hated him." It wasn't a question.

"Since the day I met him," I said, raising the bottle to take another drink.

I felt lighter all of a sudden. I wasn't sure if it was the alcohol already tingling through my blood or the relief I felt at realizing I would never have to grin and bear it through another day of being Alastor's wife.

"Then why—" Fin narrowed his eyes and shook his head

slowly, like he couldn't figure me out. "Why did you marry him? For the alliance?"

"With the Sierra Kingdom?" I guffawed. "No. Definitely not." I glanced down at Alastor's body. "Are you going to toss him over the edge, or do I need to drag him?"

Fin ignored my question, his stare burning into me. "Then why, Del? Why him?"

"I'll tell you as soon as you get rid of the body," I said, pointing down at Alastor with my chin.

With a huff of impatience, Fin crouched and hoisted the big man's body over his shoulder. He carried Alastor to the low wall, where he perched him on the edge to get the angle just right, before letting go.

I held my breath as the body fell, waiting. The sound of it hitting the ground made my stomach turn, and I barely suppressed a gag.

Fin marched across the turret to stand before me. "Why did you marry him?" he asked again, his stare burning into me.

My stomach knotted, my heart suddenly hammering. Unable to look at Fin while I confessed my secret, I turned away, hugging my middle and peering out into the foggy night. "*Because*, of all my suitors, he looked the most like you," I admitted quietly. "Which meant he would most closely resemble the baby."

Fin was quiet for so long that I had to glance at him to ensure he was still there. But I couldn't stand looking at him for long.

"The *baby*?" he finally said.

I lowered my eyelids, setting free a fresh string of tears. "Liam isn't Alastor's son," I whispered. "He's *yours*."

II

FIN

"Why did you marry him?" I pressed. The Del I knew wouldn't have condemned herself to a life of abusive misery if it wasn't for a grave reason. I feared the answer but needed to understand all the same.

She turned her back to me. "*Because*," she whispered, "of all my suitors, he looked the most like you."

The admission was so unexpected. I frowned, confused.

"Which meant," she continued, "he would most closely resemble the baby."

I wasn't sure how many heartbeats it took me to process her words, but their meaning seemed to settle into place impossibly slow, their immensity pounding with each racing thud of my pulse in my ears until a single word boomed so deafening, it was all I could focus on. "The *baby*?"

"Liam isn't Alastor's son. He's yours." Del finally faced me, and her umber eyes met mine, shimmering with fresh tears.

I swallowed the growing lump in my throat, my skin tingling with sweat all over again. I'd been with Del just once, yet everything I'd felt that night haunted me every time I closed my eyes since.

My surprise when she'd come into my bedroom, clicking the door shut behind her.

The gentle plea in her touch and yearning in her eyes.

The feel of her soft skin and the unspoken goodbye I knew would follow.

But it was the smell of her hair, lingering on my pillow for days after, that haunted me the most. It reminded me she was a princess, and I was only Fin, an orphan and outcast.

And yet there we stood, the truth she'd been keeping from me for over a decade hanging between us. "All of this time, you've said nothing."

"I couldn't find you!" Del said, wiping a tear from her cheek.

My heart plummeted as realization dawned on me. "That's why your mother attacked us," I gritted out. "It all makes so much sense now." I tugged my fingers through my hair and began to pace, all the pieces falling together. "She already hated me—we'd freed Jake and uncovered so many of her secrets. Then a baby . . ." I shook my head again. "Of course, she would attack us if—"

"*Attack* you? Mother couldn't have—" Del paused, shaking her head. "She never lifted a finger against you or your people. I would have known," she said adamantly. Her defensiveness, when she knew more than anyone how horrible her mother was, shredded the last of my patience.

"Then why did she attack my village, Del, if not for her empty truce?"

"I—" Del blinked, her mouth open as if the words danced on the tip of her tongue.

Her surprise was comforting, at least, and I stepped closer. "If your mother didn't order the attack, then who did? And if not for the truth of this child, then why? We had no armies. We had nothing worth anything but my family's legacy."

I could see the shock in Del's eyes and maybe a shimmer of sympathy—or perhaps it was doubt—but her expression hardened as she took a step back. "It must have been Maylar, Mother's advisor, and—" Again, Del shook her surprise away, only this time, her brow furrowed in its place. "I'm sorry, Fin. I really am. But we can't do this right now. We have to go before Alastor's body is found."

That I unwittingly killed King Eduart's son, consort to the Corvo heir, only fueled my utter disbelief that this could get any more complicated. And turning on my feet, I marched over to the soiled rug and jacket. "I'm assuming you've thought of a place to hide these in all your plans?" I said, rolling the blood-stained evidence and loading it onto my shoulder again.

Del nodded, furtively glancing around to ensure nothing was overtly out of place as I headed back toward the winding staircase. We descended with only our footsteps echoing in our silence. My mind was too full, my body coiled with too much tension.

When we were in the hidden passageway again, I followed Del to a dingy alcove in an offshoot of the walls where a forgotten chandelier rested, broken and covered in years' worth of cobwebs.

"No one comes here," Del explained. "I can burn them later." She glanced down the corridor. "Liam is likely sleeping," she said quietly, nodding for me to follow her. "But I'll take you to see him. Then—" She glanced back at me. "You should go until all of this gets sorted."

A very small part of me was happy to flee—to wake up—because none of this felt real. But I couldn't deny my growing desperation to stay, either. For Del. For the boy. *Liam,* I reminded myself.

That was all we said to one another as I discarded the carpet roll and quickly followed her through a corridor that opened to a linen closet.

As we stepped into another hallway, the gravity of all that had transpired in the past two hours didn't evade my muddled brain, but that Del was leading me to my son overshadowed everything. Each step grew heavier than the last, and when we eventually made it to the closed door, separating me from my son, I almost couldn't breathe.

My body was humming with too much adrenaline, too much anger and confusion. All I could do was stare at the door.

Del reached for the handle, about to turn it, but hesitated. "No matter what you think," she said, her voice a strange, quiet salve in the silence. She dropped her arm to her side as her eyes met mine. Sincerity gleamed back at me in the ocher glow of the hall. "It couldn't have been my mother who attacked you. I've been monitoring her mind for years. I would have known. I would have stopped her. And even if she had done it—which she didn't—it wouldn't have been because of Liam. She didn't even know the truth until recently."

I lifted my chin. "And I suppose you're going to tell me she isn't behind the rhetoric being spread about the new prophecy, either. That she doesn't know what's going on in her own city and has nothing to do with the troops targeting my people *again*."

Del frowned and opened her mouth to speak when I felt a tingle in my mind and raised my hand to stop her.

"Fin?" Callon's voice sparked to life. *"Are you all right? You haven't checked in."*

"I'm in the castle," I told him. *"There have been a few . . . complications."*

"But you're all right?" he asked again, and I rubbed my temple.

"Peachy."

"Did you find Del?"

"Yes," I said and stared at the closed door. *"But I need a moment."*

"We're outside the east wall."

"Fin?" Del asked carefully, her voice closer.

When I looked at her, she was inches away, studying me. "My friends are checking in," I explained. "They're waiting outside the walls."

"Feline?" she said, a lilt of nostalgia lightening her voice.

I gave Del a sad smile. "Human. Beast is gone."

"Oh." She wrung her hands. "I'm sorry to hear that." Del's dark eyes lingered on me, swimming with uncertainty, and I hated the awkwardness between us. I hated that I felt like I barely knew her.

With a sigh, Del rubbed her hands over her face. "Is that why you're here? Because you thought my mother was moving against you?"

"I'm here," I said carefully, "because the prophecy King Eduart is spewing to his people is directly tied to your kingdom—we followed the envoy that was digging near my settlement all the way here. So if your mother isn't involved, it's happening right under her nose." I glanced at the door again, realizing I would never have known the truth of who was on the other side of it if I'd never come. Jaw clenched, I met Del's gaze. "Someone in Corvo is conspiring with the Sierra Kingdom, and they are coming for my lands."

Though it felt like the desert lands were ours, the truth was, they belonged to no one. We had no legal claim over them. My people lived there because no one else dared to. It was supposed to be safe. And now even that was being threatened.

"Mother is dead, Fin," Del said brusquely. "This isn't her doing."

That was . . . unexpected, and yet, I remembered hearing a rumor years ago that the queen was unwell.

"I'm sorry," I said, surprising myself, and I looked away. Even if the queen was horrible, I couldn't imagine juggling a dying mother, an abusive husband, and an ailing kingdom was easy. *And a child,* I reminded myself.

Sighing, I scratched the scruff on my face. "If your mother's not behind the damn prophecy, then who, Del? Would Alastor contrive something like this?" After seeing what he had done to her, and knowing how ruthless and power hungry his father was, I wouldn't have been surprised if Alastor had been plotting something behind his wife's back. And by the look on Del's face, she wouldn't have been surprised either.

"It's possible he was," she admitted, rubbing her forehead. "But if Alastor has been scheming with his father, and now Alastor is *dead*, then we're in even more danger than I thought. Which means, the only thing that matters now is what Alastor's father will do." The look of censure in Del's eyes chafed a little.

I leaned in slightly, acutely aware I probably smelled as bad as I looked from swimming the moat and lugging a dead body across the castle. "I didn't know it was him until after he was already dying," I told her. "But even if I had realized who he was, I can't say I would have reacted much differently. He was choking you."

Del waved my growing irritation away. "It's done now, but the fact remains—he was all that stood between my family's rule and his father taking over the Corvo Kingdom."

As Del reached for the door again, I gently clasped her wrist. A tingle I hadn't felt in years shot through me, and we both stared at my fingers on her skin. Clearing my throat, I pulled away.

"We have to go to Alcatraz, Del. We have to know what's going on in there. Because, whatever it is, it's why the troops are coming for our land."

"What land?" she asked, then before I could answer, added, "What's the prophecy?"

"*Uncover and destroy the destructive force hidden under the earth in Death Valley,*" I recited, lowering my voice even more. Uttering it aloud felt like I was giving it credence when I knew there was none.

"Death Valley?" Del's eyes went wide. "You live in the desert?"

I nodded. "Mercenaries showed up a week or so ago and excavated soil samples. We followed them to Mantis, then here—well, Alcatraz, technically, where the order originated. That's all I know."

The door opened, and Garath stood in the doorway. He looked between us as if wondering if we planned on coming in. As his eyes shifted between Del and me, he stepped aside for us to enter the sitting room.

All I could do was stare at the boy sleeping on a couch by a low-burning fire. At his rumpled auburn hair and the way his arms wrapped around his pillow in his sleep.

"Are you all right, my lady?" A younger, fairer woman stepped into view and draped a blanket over the boy. As we stepped into the room, the woman's eyes widened on Del, assessing the bruising on her neck that would not be easily hidden. The woman gasped and rushed over.

"I'm fine, Ada. Thank you." Waving Ada's concern away, Del hurried to her son, Ada trailing behind her. Del was careful not to wake him as she crouched and rested her hand on his cheek. Leaning in, she kissed his temple.

I stared between Del, the mother of *my* son, and Liam. *The prince.*

His face was scrunched against the velvet pillow, and while I knew Del would never lie to me about such a thing, I wished I could see him more clearly in the dim glow of the fire because this didn't feel real. None of it did, and suddenly, I regretted not taking in the image of Liam projected by the hologram in Mantis more closely.

A blood-curdling scream pierced the night air outside the window, stirring me from my haze. And with renewed apprehension, I looked at Del. Our reverie was over.

"You should go now," she said, rising to her feet. She eyed my dirty soldier uniform up and down. "You'll draw more attention if you stay—attention we don't need at the moment."

The longer I lingered, the less I wanted to leave; I still had so many questions, and there was still so much to say. So much to know. But Del was right.

I looked at Liam again, then met the hard gaze Garath leveled on me.

"Fin," Del said, resting her hand on my arm. "You must go. Now."

"Will you be okay?" I asked. It seemed a stupid question, knowing how much she'd been through over the years. Still, it felt wrong to walk away—all of this felt so incredibly wrong.

"I'll be fine. Now go, please. You know how to get out?"

I nodded.

"Good. Stay out of sight. We'll figure out the rest as soon as we can. I promise."

With three adamant gazes boring through me, I dipped my chin. It was all I could do to make myself turn and go, but I knew my presence would only cause Del more trouble. And with a final look at her glaring guard, I turned and left the princess I had longed to see again—and our son—behind.

12

DEL

"Just give me the word, and I will gladly evict those entitled Sierra pricks," Hills said, one elbow propped on the mantel. Embers glowed in the fireplace behind her legs, the last remnants of the fire she had started to drive the early morning chill from the room when we first convened our emergency meeting well over an hour ago.

Backlit by the pale-gray light of dawn, Garath stood by the window, scanning the misty castle grounds beyond the moat. Every time he glanced my way, shadows darkened his eyes. It was impossible not to suspect Fin was the one casting those shadows.

In the adjoining bedroom, Ada and the ravens watched over Liam, who was fast asleep on my bed.

I paced back and forth from the table by the window on one side of the sitting room to the pair of tall bookcases against the opposite wall. I paused in front of the narrow altar table wedged between the bookcases, holding the tall gray votive candle I burned every Friday night in honor of Zoe, the Patron of the Empaths. Her portrait hung on the wall above the candle, and a huge landscape painting spread over the top of the bookcases, portraying the Battle of Hope Valley.

Even now, even knowing Zoe wasn't a goddess, I felt the urge to pluck a match from the jar beside the candle and light her votive. To pray to my Patron for guidance, as the Temple of the Seven Kingdoms had taught me to do.

I turned and headed back toward the window. Turned again and headed back toward the bookcases and altar. Over and over, back and forth, I paced, working through the potential ramifications of our next actions.

King Eduart would have received word of Alastor's death by now. If we cleared Alastor's people out of the castle and grounds, would it cast suspicion upon us? Upon *me*? Currently, Alastor's death was believed to be a suicide, and the bloody evidence had been destroyed, but would King Eduart view my eviction of his subjects as proof of foul play? Would he see it as something planned or as a reaction to Alastor's sudden and unexpected death?

There was no love lost between King Eduart and me. He was under no misconceptions that I *liked* having his people stationed inside the castle. And in the absence of Alastor's protection, Eduart would expect me to prepare for an invasion. So, letting his people—the enemy now more than ever—stay within the castle walls would be illogical, suggesting guilt on my part.

"Get rid of them," I said decisively.

Garath tore his stare away from the window to look at me. His slow nod—and Hills's wicked, eager grin—convinced me this was the right call.

"I want them gone," I added, turning to head back toward the altar. "All of them. By the noontime bell." I raised one hand to my mouth to chew on my thumbnail. "We'll reconvene then to begin preparations for the invasion. I don't want any of Eduart's people catching wind of our plans and relaying them to him."

"Understood." Hills bowed her head, her chin-length, salt-and-pepper hair swinging forward with the motion. "I would also suggest vetting our own people," she said. "To ensure the Sierra scourge has been eradicated completely. I wouldn't put it past King Eduart to make an attempt on your life—or Liam's—in order to throw the kingdom into further chaos. And if they've turned any of our own people, that would be the quickest and easiest means to accomplish the task."

My stomach knotted at even the possibility of anyone sending an assassin after my son.

"You could disguise it as 'checking in' with the people during this trying time." Hills angled her head to the side. "They did just lose their queen, after all . . . "

Having worried my thumbnail to the quick, I switched to chewing my index fingernail. "Good thinking. Clear everyone out of the castle—and I mean *everyone*—and I'll begin empathic interviews at the gate this afternoon. That way, we can be absolutely certain that every single person who crosses the bridge and enters the castle is loyal to us."

Again, Hills bowed her head. "It will be done."

I continued my pacing. "We'll need to move up the coronation. We no longer have months to prepare, and the people will need more stability than a queen regent can offer during the coming time of war."

"It should be on the equinox," Garath said, his voice a low rumble. "To mark a new beginning for the kingdom."

My eyebrows rose. "But that's this Friday—in just four days." How would we possibly prepare in time? Pythia Salma, who would be leading the coronation ceremony as head of the Temple of the Seven Kingdoms, was *not* going to be pleased about such an accelerated timeline.

The corner of Garath's mouth tensed, then hitched upward. "It *is* this Friday, which means it's also a sabbath. You could incorporate your coronation into the candle-lighting ceremony. Many of our people will see this as significant—the Patrons blessing your coming reign." Garath laughed under his breath. "Considering the timing of it all, I'm half-tempted to agree with them."

My lips spread into a slow, knowing smile. "Garath, you're a genius."

His expression was pleased, but the shadows in his eyes remained. We had a lot to talk about in the coming days. Personal matters. Much had changed now that Alastor was dead and Fin was back.

Fin *was back*.

I still didn't believe it—that the gruff man who had ended Alastor's putrid life was the same man who had taken such pleasure in teasing me all those years ago. *Tough stuff*. That was what he used to call me. I considered how he must have seen me now. Not so tough anymore. He wasn't the only one who had changed.

I recalled Mother's words when we first learned Fin's village had been abandoned. My heartbreak had been clear to her, even without the use of her empathic Abilities.

"I knew something like this would happen," she had said. "There's a reason we call them *Ghosts*—they can vanish in the blink of an eye."

But Mother had been wrong about Fin and his people. Again, I wondered what he had been through over the past decade. He had said his village was attacked. Was that why he had all but vanished? He had blamed Mother—potentially blamed *me*? I felt sick to my stomach knowing he might've thought me capable of such wretched duplicity.

It had to have been Maylar. I had pressured Mother to dismiss him shortly after I returned from my brief visit to Fin's village, the one that had resulted in me being with child. Maylar had not been pleased with being stripped of his position at court. He must have found someone else to leech power from and convinced them to attack Fin's village. Three birds with one stone. Revenge against Mother, Fin, and me—the three people he had likely blamed for ruining his life.

I shook my head, dispelling those thoughts. I didn't have time to dwell on the past right now, not when we were on the brink of war and the fate of my kingdom was at stake. I needed to focus on the present situation. This war would bring the fighting to Corvo City—likely to Castle Corvo. It would endanger Liam's life.

We could still run. Give it all up and flee. Fin was here in the city. We could leave with him, follow him to the desert. Liam could get to know his true father, someone he could admire and learn from.

When I reached the altar table, I stopped and stared into Zoe's piercing aquamarine eyes. She *wasn't* a goddess like the Temple proclaimed and so many of my people believed. But she had survived during the Turn centuries ago and made an impression on the world. The impact of her and her people's lives and actions spanned the two-and-a-half centuries separating us, shaping *my* people's daily lives.

I plucked a match from the jar and swiped it over the stone striker. A flame burst to life at the tip of the match, and I touched it to the votive's wick, waiting for the candle to light, then blew out the match.

Again, I looked at Zoe, studying her features. Strong, beautiful, wise, fierce. Dani was the Patron usually favored by mothers seeking guidance and protection for their children, but Zoe had been a mother, too. One who had faced fertility issues and other maternal struggles. Many forgot that.

I closed my eyes, imagining what Zoe would have done in my place. Would she have stayed and defended her people, or would she have run, protecting her family?

I lifted my lids and peered up at the sprawling battle scene stretching across the canvas above the bookcases. Zoe, Dani, Jason, Jake, and all the other Patrons were there, fighting for their home near a gleaming metal tree on the grassy hillside and in the blood-soaked valley below it. For their people. They had stood their ground.

I read the polished bronze plaque affixed to the bottom of the elaborate, gilded frame.

Always remember the fallen and be aware of their lasting foot-prints on our lives.

The quote was attributed to Becca, the Patron of Oracles. She was Jake's sister and one of the first people to develop the Ability to foresee snippets of the future after surviving the virus that caused the Turn. My focus caught and lingered on her name: Rebecca Marie Vaughn.

RMV

"Patrons preserve me," I breathed.

Turning, I rushed into the bedroom and fetched the small, leather-bound book I had taken from Mother's study from atop the nightstand, then returned to the sitting room. I opened the book as I hurried back to the painting, flipping past the blank page at the beginning to see the first encoded list.

RMV - 25AE - 177

DIF - 178AE - 23

SHF - 236AE - 79

"They're the initials of Oracles," I whispered to myself.

Which meant the dates likely marked when the relevant prophecy had been recorded, and the other number probably referred to a specific prophecy listed in that particular Oracle's book of foretellings.

"It's an index," I muttered.

I tore my focus away from the book and stared up at the sprawling painting once more, at the depiction of a battle that had claimed so many lives. It had changed the world, setting my ancestors on a course that led to me facing this decision right now.

Stand and fight.

Or run and hide.

There was a prophecy in play right now, driving King Eduart's actions. And it was likely behind Alastor's sneaking around, as well. Was there a chance I could use Mother's index of prophecies to my advantage? Could I beat Eduart at his own game? Could *I* use his prized prophecy to find some way to win this war—to rid ourselves of the threat posed by the Sierra Kingdom—that didn't include fighting *at all*?

"Del?" Garath asked, his quiet footsteps marking his approach behind me. "What is it?"

I snapped the book shut, my heart suddenly racing. "I have an idea," I said, glancing at him over my shoulder. "I need to go to Mother's study."

He shook his head. "You need to rest. You haven't slept in days."

But the adrenaline surging through my veins wouldn't allow for sleep. "In a bit," I told him, offering him a quick, closed-mouth smile. "I just have to check on something first."

13

FIN

"Fin," Callon said, stepping into my room at the tavern. "I know you've got a lot on your mind, and with good reason, but if you're not going to sleep or eat, will you at least drink? You've been sitting at that table, spinning that same gold piece so much, you've worn a hole in the wood." Callon widened his stance and crossed his arms over his broad chest. "We'll have to pay for that, you know. Same as the line you've worn into the rug." He shrugged and waved that one away. "Maybe not the rug. It was threadbare anyway."

I spun the coin again, staring blankly at it revolving round and round as my thoughts swirled with it.

"Fin." Callon stepped closer and squeezed my shoulder.

Finally, I looked at him. "I shouldn't have left," I said. I hadn't realized how hard it would be to wait, wondering what the hell happened after. I knew Del had her inner circle, and they'd kept her safe this long. Still, not knowing if she was okay after every-thing that had happened—not knowing if *Liam* was okay—was almost more than I could bear.

"You had no other choice," Callon said. "You'd be no good to any of us if you got caught. I'm sure you're wanted for one thing or another in these parts, aside from the latest Alastor mishap." He glanced out the dirt-stained window toward the castle. "Besides, it's what Del wanted you to do. You can't argue with a princess and win."

I almost smirked. "True."

"Look—" Callon braced his fists on the table in front of me. "All I'm saying is you should drink or do *something* to take the edge off. You're wound so tight, Lyra's senses are going haywire around you. Even *she's* downstairs drinking."

I leaned my forearms on the table and spun the gold coin again. "I need a clear head."

"Fine then, I'll go drink for the both of us. Maybe bring you some stew or braised lamb. Maybe some fresh bread with just a *little bit* of butter spread over the top." He groaned, and I looked at him, my eyebrow raised.

"Yeah, yeah. I'm going." Callon shoved my shoulder playfully, but his hand lingered. "Tell me if you need anything?"

I met his gaze with a grateful nod. I might not have been a talker like Callon, but that didn't mean I didn't appreciate him being there with me. "You're a good friend, Cal."

He flashed me a toothy smile. "I know." With a wink, Callon turned for the door. "You know," he started and gripped the doorway. "Just because you can't be in the castle doesn't mean you can't *be there.*"

The furrow in my brow deepened, but only because I hadn't thought of it myself. With sudden purpose, I sat up straighter.

Callon's grin widened, and he tapped the side of his head. "It comes in handy once in a while." And with that, he left me unattended with my thoughts.

Callon was right. I didn't have to be in the castle walls to know what was happening.

Walking over to my cot, I laid back, the frame creaking under my weight. Two weeks ago, I woke up in my dust-layered quarters in the desert, but it already felt like a lifetime ago.

Rubbing the exhaustion from my face, I crossed my ankles and closed my eyes. Exhaling a heavy breath, I searched for a soaring mind to nudge my way into.

I'd never understood exactly how my Ability worked, only that the fainter the tingle of an animal's mind, the farther away it was. So, reaching my cerebral fingers toward the castle, I searched for willing vessels, jumping from the animal minds in the lower estates toward the garden.

With no one I cared to see in sight, I continued mind-hopping until, finally, I found a murder of crows in the castle courtyard and settled into one.

My mind sharpened to focus. I was perched at the top of a eucalyptus tree, the centerpiece of a cobblestone mosaic rising from the middle of the compound. The walls of the ramparts surrounding me gleamed in the daylight, and muttering filled my ears as I tried to concentrate amid the onslaught of heightened sounds and senses.

Del stood at the mouth of the drawbridge, Garath standing sentry at her side. A line of her subjects stretched before her, but I couldn't look away from Del.

No longer dressed in her shirt and trousers, Del was a vision of black and looked every bit the part of a grieving queen regent. Her onyx, high-collar robe flared over the bruising on her neck and cascaded down, covering an understated, silver-embossed gown that matched her royal pendant. For all of her youthful rebellion, Del had the stature and grace of a queen as she greeted her subjects one by one.

She was the epitome of cool confidence. A reassuring vision with her shoulders back, her expression soft yet composed as she took a man's weathered hands in hers, uttering reassurances about the future of the Corvo Kingdom in the wake of her mother's death.

You would never know she'd been victimized last night or that we'd staged the death of her piece of shit husband, who had obviously tormented her over the years. Then again, I doubted Del saw herself as a victim. Watching her as she was now, the incoming queen, I realized the only person she might truly have needed saving from was herself. For all of her sacrifices, Del was a mother, a determined one, who would battle *any* foe to keep Liam safe and suffer any consequence in the wake of that determination. But at what cost to herself?

Hearing a child's voice on the terrace, I pivoted on my perch and peered over at Liam, reading a book on a castle balcony facing the courtyard, a raven friend of his own hopping along the stone beside him. Ada sat nearby, mending something with thread and needle in the shade of the honeysuckle vines.

But the rest of the world fell away as I stared at the boy. Liam. My son.

He looked older in the light of day, with bright, shrewd eyes, a roman nose, and a calm demeanor I hadn't expected. "When will Mother be finished?" he asked, gazing down at Del by the gate.

"Soon," Ada promised, peering at him over her needlework. "Be patient, young prince."

"Can we at least visit the gardens?"

"Your mother wants us to stay close, so we will wait until her duties are finished." Ada winked at him. "Only a little while longer," she added more softly, and though Liam huffed a sigh, he didn't complain again.

His raven friend waddled closer on the railing, picking at his sleeve playfully. Liam's lightly bronzed cheek rounded with a grin. He had his mother's nose, but as his eyes twinkled in the sunlight, I felt it—his mind. It tingled as he peered up at me. Not at the other crows perched on the surrounding branches, but right at *me*.

My heart lodged in my throat, and I held my breath. His mind was pulsing and probing, and I dared to fly closer to him.

As we assessed one another, I landed on a eucalyptus branch outstretched in his direction. The more I stared at him, the more I wondered how I hadn't seen the similarity between us the few times I'd seen images of him before.

Assuming Liam knew nothing about me, I wasn't sure what to do, so I waited, letting him make the next move.

"You're different," he said quietly, and crossing his arms on the terrace, he leaned forward, his head quirked to the side. "You don't feel like Garath feels in my mind."

I tilted my head to mirror his, making him smile, and I melted a little more inside.

"*What are you?*" he silently asked me.

I swallowed thickly. "*A friend.*" It was all I could think to communicate.

"*Your mind feels funny.*" He scrunched his nose, the most adorable thing I'd ever seen, and my chest cinched.

"I don't know, but this stinks of Maylar, just as Del said." My mind stirred at the words, breaking the bond between Liam and me, and I peered down into the courtyard. The older woman from last night had pulled Garath aside as Del continued consoling her subjects.

Del was methodical as she murmured reassurances to a young woman, squeezing the woman's hands in her own just like she had done with the others. I knew at that moment what Del was doing.

In touching everyone, she could peek into their minds and suss out the surrounding dangers. Even if the idea of Del touching me, seeing all I had done and become over the years, made me itchy in my own skin, it was clever. But then, Del had always been clever.

"You haven't found him?" Garath asked the woman and glanced in Del's direction, ensuring she was still standing there.

"Not beyond the potential sighting in Mantis. He's not in *this* kingdom, which means he'll be more difficult to find."

"A cunning snake like Maylar could be hiding anywhere," Garath muttered in agreement, and I remembered Maylar at the queen's side all those years ago, a wraithlike man with eyes that gleamed unnervingly.

"We'll keep looking," the woman continued. "But until we find him, we have to be diligent. If Maylar's behind the spreading mania of this prophecy business, he's been at his scheming for a while. There's no telling what he's planning to do next."

Though I was glad Del was taking the prophecy I'd shared with her seriously, the fact that they couldn't find the man they thought was responsible was less comforting. Because they were right. I knew some of the worst who frequented the Shadow District, this kingdom's underground city of debauchery, rife with illegal goods and empty promises. And whatever toxic rhetoric was spreading felt far more threatening than anyone down there, and I feared the endgame would be the most dangerous yet.

It dawned on me that even if Del's people weren't familiar with the underground veins that ran through and between kingdoms, I was. And turning back to Liam, still watching me far too acutely, I sidestepped closer.

"Goodbye, for now," I told him, though I could have sat with my son all day, watching the way his curious mind saw the world—how he saw *me*.

Liam reached out, and I hopped closer. He stroked my feathered head with the crook of his finger and smiled. *"Goodbye."*

And with an unbearable ache in my heart, I left the crow's mind, intent on collecting a few favors I was owed.

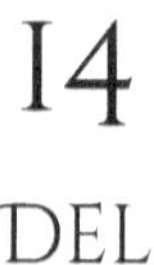

14

DEL

Feeling rejuvenated, I opened my eyes and rolled onto my back.

After the empathic interviews, I had crashed—hard. I had fallen into my bed in the late afternoon, intending only to nap for a few hours before continuing my research in Mother's study.

But the golden light streaming in through the trio of windows on the northeast-facing wall of my bedroom and the trilling birdsong filling the room told me I had slept through the night.

I heaved a sigh and stared up at the ceiling. Garath, the liar, hadn't awakened me as he had promised. Was this the first time he had shirked a command of mine?

I sat up and scooted out of bed, quickly washing up in the bathroom and donning a fresh pair of black leather leggings and a soft, slate-gray tunic lined with black leather on the shoulders and arms and embroidered with gleaming silver vines along the collar. I tamed my mussed curls with a few handfuls of water and some hair balm, then tied my hair back in a low bun. When, barely ten minutes after waking, I emerged from my chambers with Sid perched on my shoulder, I was not surprised to find Garath posted with a pair of guards in the corridor outside my sitting-room door.

Standing in the doorway, I nodded a greeting to the guards, Macy and Saira, then turned my attention to Garath. "You were supposed to wake me," I said pointedly. I planted my hands on my hips, and Sid shuffled closer to my neck.

Garath turned to face me with his arms crossed over his chest. "You needed the rest."

I narrowed my eyes to a gentle glare. "You are such a mother hen."

The corners of Garath's mouth tensed in the precursor to a frown as he studied me. "It is my sworn duty to protect you." He nodded his head to the side. "Sometimes that even means protecting you from yourself."

I bristled, and Sid, sensing my darkening mood, fidgeted with his wings. Without another word, I stalked into the corridor and past Garath. He fell in step behind me, the guards behind him.

I entered the neighboring suite belonging to Liam, passing by the pair of guards posted there, and popped my head through the doorway to the bedroom. Ada sat in the armchair by the unlit fireplace, reading a book, but Liam was still asleep.

Yesterday had been difficult for him, as well. He was confused about Alastor's death, convinced he should have felt sad, having just lost the man he believed to be his father, but instead feeling only relief. Not relief that he would never have to face Alastor's anger again, but that his father would never hurt his mother again.

Even thinking about the conflict I had sensed within Liam when I skimmed his mind the previous afternoon—something I rarely did but had felt compelled to do, considering the circumstances—brought tears to my eyes. Liam had *wished* Alastor dead. He had fantasized about interceding on my behalf. On being my defender, and I hated that I had been unable to shield him from all the conflict and discord in my marriage. I hated that *I* had brought Alastor into our lives at all.

But it was over now, I reminded myself. Alastor was gone, and it was time to move on. To face the greater threat: Alastor's father.

Ada looked up from her book. When she saw me in the doorway, she closed the book and stood, setting it down on the seat of the armchair and smoothing down the front of her long, periwinkle skirt before crossing to follow me into the sitting room.

"I'm so sorry," I told her, stopping by the window and turning to face her. "I meant to sleep in here last night, but I only just woke up, and—"

Ada waved my apology away. "It was no trouble at all, my lady."

"*Please*, just call me Del," I said for the thousandth time.

A sweet smile curved Ada's lips. "I could no sooner call a fish a bird," she replied.

I huffed out a breathy laugh. Ada was just as strong-willed as Garath. How had I ended up surrounded by such stubborn people?

"Would you like me to bring Liam to you when he wakes?" Ada asked.

I nodded. "I'll be in Mother's—in *the* study," I informed her. "Liam can take his breakfast in there with me."

I wanted to keep him close. We may have ensured everyone within the castle's walls was loyal, but threats could still sneak in from outside, as Fin had proved. Until we had secured peace, I planned on keeping Liam nearby at all times.

"As you wish," Ada said, bowing her head.

I reached out, grasping her arm. "Thank you."

With a flash of a smile, I released her, turned away, and headed back to the corridor, where Garath and the four guards waited. Garath, Macy, and Saira followed me up the hallways to a set of stairs that carried us down to the floor below, then through another corridor to the double doors leading to Mother's study.

I paused at the doors, waited as Garath unlocked and opened them, then crossed the threshold, hurrying toward the desk at the far end of the room. Garath remained behind to seal the two of us in while Macy and Saira took up posts out in the corridor.

Sitting in the armchair, I retrieved the little leather-bound book I had replaced in its concealed pocket inside the top desk drawer the previous morning. I set the index of prophecies on the desk and opened the cover. I had already carefully searched through the book and used a torn slip of paper to mark each page that, according to its heading, included the current year—295 AE—in its relevant date range. I had marked seventeen pages. That was as far as I had made it in my research before being called away to attend to more urgent matters.

The first page I had marked was labeled *Seven Kingdoms, 289-297 AE* and had a list of eight prophecies indexed below the heading, all from different Oracles, according to the initials.

Pointer finger tapping on the open page, I raised my head and scanned the walls of packed bookshelves surrounding me. Mother and I had become much closer over the past decade, but her study remained a relatively mysterious place to me. I didn't even know how she organized her books. This was hardly the type of thing I ever would have thought to skim from her mind during our weekly empathic exchanges.

Was a section of the study devoted to the Oracles' books of foretellings? I hoped so because tens of thousands of books lined the walls, and it would take me days to sort through them all.

I didn't have days to spare on something that *might* help with the coming war when an invasion by the Sierra Kingdom was *definitely* on the horizon. We had already received word of King Eduart's troops mobilizing within our borders. He had long been dead set on controlling our ports, and now that Alastor was dead, Eduart had lost his foothold in the trade arena. Soon, he would attempt to invade Corvo City. It wasn't a question of *if* but of *when*.

I needed to be out rallying the people who were already so beaten down by the wasting sickness. I needed to be at Hills's side, directing our military preparations and bolstering the city's defenses. I needed to be readying for the coronation, reaching out to our allies, and doing a million other things besides locking myself away in Mother's study.

But I had delegated those tasks to Hills, buying myself a little more time to follow a trail my gut told me was relevant to the current situation, even if no hard evidence corroborated my hunch. Time was precious, and I was wasting it sitting at the desk, second-guessing myself.

I stood and approached the bookcase bordering the left side of the window overlooking the bay. A quick skim revealed that these shelves were filled with books of history, the top few devoted to ancient tomes from the time before the Turn, the bottom filled with books recording more recent events, and the lowest shelf filled with blank books of various bindings and sizes. I grabbed a thin notebook bound with a soft, black leather cover to record my findings—assuming I had any—then moved on.

The next bookcase to the left contained biographies and memoirs. The next, books on political philosophy and military strategy. As I moved away from the window and toward the door, I left nonfiction behind, finding myself facing shelves filled with all manner of fiction titles, from mystery to fantasy to romance and every genre in between.

The opposite side of the room continued my journey through the extensive collection of fiction books. Had these been Mother's, or had one of her predecessors enjoyed escaping into imaginary worlds and fictional lives? Later, when the kingdom wasn't under the threat of an imminent invasion, I would come back to explore these shelves. Mother was gone, but I looked forward to getting to know her better through her books.

About halfway down the wall of bookcases on the right side of the room, the collection switched back to nonfiction, with books on mythology and religion, followed by a bookcase devoted to texts focused on science and technology. I searched bookcase after bookcase without coming across a single book of fore-tellings, and I was already thinking about where else Mother might have stashed the relevant books as I approached the last bookcase, the one bordering the right side of the window behind the desk.

And there they were, arranged in alphabetical order by the Oracles' first names.

I laughed, my shoulders relaxing as the knot of anxiety loosened in my gut. This may not have been a colossal waste of time, after all.

I had pulled what I believed to be all the relevant books for the first page I had marked in the prophecy index and was just settling into the armchair at the desk when someone knocked on the door. I looked up as Garath opened the door and let Liam and Ada into the study, followed by Neris and Tamal, two of the kitchen workers, who each carried a tray of food.

Liam ran across the room and around the desk, throwing himself into my arms. His lanky body trembled, and I held him close, rocking him gently as I rubbed his back. No matter how hard I tried to stay out of his head, it was impossible for my empathic gifts not to pick up on some of his feelings when his emotions were so raw and intense. Two of the most significant people in his life—one loved and one hated—had died on the same day. He was reeling, his mind instinctively preparing for more loss.

Despite Ada's many reassurances that I hadn't come to his chambers the previous night, as I had promised, because I had been exhausted and had fallen asleep in my own bed, Liam had feared he would never see me again. That I, too, would vanish from his life, and he would be alone.

My heart ached to tell him about Fin, to let him know he still had a father, but I wasn't sure if Fin *wanted* to be known. Garath and I had discussed visiting Fin's inn before nightfall. I made a mental note to prioritize talking about Liam and figuring out exactly what kind of relationship Fin wanted with his son—if he wanted any relationship at all.

Neris, plump and middle aged, set her tray down on the corner of the desk, lifting the teapot to fill a mug for me. I nodded my thanks over Liam's hair, and she turned away to head back to the door, where Tamal awaited her.

I loosened my arms and pulled away, cradling Liam's face in my hands. The last remnants of baby fat still filled out his cheeks, but I could already see him changing as adolescence crept closer. My little boy was growing up so fast. I felt as though I would go to sleep one night soon, and when I woke, he would be grown. He wouldn't need me any longer, not as he did now, and then *I* would be the one who was alone.

I cleared my throat, blinking back the threat of tears and forcing a shaky smile.

Liam's chin trembled, responding to the visual evidence of my own troubled heart.

"All will be well, my sweet boy." I wiped away the silent tears that streaked down his cheeks with a sweep of my thumbs. "Why don't you go eat your breakfast?" I said, glancing toward the low table in front of the sofa, where Tamal had placed the tray loaded with food and tea for both Liam and Ada.

Ada already sat on the sofa, arranging the two plates of food, cups, silverware, and teapots.

"*Then* you can pick a book to read," I offered.

Liam's glassy eyes lit up, and he stared around in wonder. "*Any* book?"

I grinned at him, knowing he would pick something from the fiction shelves. Something filled with discovery and adventure. "*Any* book."

His lips spread into a broad smile, and he turned and raced back to the sofa.

I watched him for a moment, pleased to see he had a good appetite despite his troubled heart. So long as he was still eating and sleeping all right, I didn't want to enlist the services of a Gauge who specialized in emotional siphoning to drain his excess anxiety.

I turned my attention back to my prophecy research. It took almost a half hour, but I finally found and recorded all the prophecies noted on the first bookmarked page of the index. Some were pages long, composed of incoherent and nonsensical ramblings, while others were a single line, so vague they could have related to almost anything, even to Fin's prophecy: *Uncover and destroy the destructive force hidden under the earth in Death Valley.* But none specifically mentioned Death Valley, a destructive force, or anything concealed or hidden underground.

With a sigh, I dismissed this first tagged entry as irrelevant and stood to return the books of foretellings to the bookcase before moving on to the next marked page in the index. It was going to be a *long* morning.

In midafternoon, I sat up straighter and squeezed my bleary eyes shut for a long moment before rereading the line marked as prophecy #76 in the book of foretellings attributed to Callum James Campbell. Lunch trays had come and gone, and Liam dozed on the sofa while Ada read, curled up in an armchair by the dormant fireplace. I was researching the ninth page of indexed prophecies I had marked in Mother's book, and my brain was fatigued from the mental gymnastics I had been performing in an attempt to make sense of the endless riddles.

Uncover and destroy the destructive force hidden under the earth in Death Valley.

"I found it," I breathed, sitting up straighter. I laughed softly, looking up to meet Garath's ever-watchful stare.

He only had a vague idea of what I was searching for, but he smiled back at me anyway.

I returned my attention to Callum's book of foretellings, skimming over the page. The lines directly preceding and following had been marked with #75 and #77, suggesting they were completely unique and unrelated prophecies.

I flipped back to the book's title page. It had been printed only thirteen years ago, and the brief biography at the beginning implied that Callum, a citizen of the Noctem Kingdom directly to the south of us, had still lived at the time of printing. Perhaps if we could track him down, he could expound on his prophecy. If *we* could get our hands on the destructive force mentioned in the prophecy before King Eduart, perhaps we could use whatever it was to stave off the war.

I quickly jotted down what I had found in my notebook, then moved on to the next prophecy listed in the index.

One by one, the seven will fall until only one remains.

The *seven* mentioned in the prophecy had to be the seven allied kingdoms. I was unsure of how Mother had linked these prophecies together, but if she knew of such prophecies, did others? I thought of King Eduart. If he had copies of the same books of foretellings and made the same connections between prophecies as Mother had, it was no wonder he was hellbent on fulfilling the first prophecy in this index entry. He wanted *his* kingdom to be the *one* named in the second prophecy.

I sat back in my chair, my stare going distant. This new prophecy was like a missing puzzle piece falling into place. It went a long way toward explaining why Eduart was behaving so aggressively toward not just the Corvo Kingdom but all of them.

Assuming Eduart truly had made the same connections Mother had, I couldn't help but wonder if he had done so himself or if he had received privileged leaked information from someone within Mother's trusted circle. And if he *had* received such assistance, there wasn't a doubt in my mind who delivered the information: Maylar.

Every rotten discovery seemed to point back to that cretin. I gritted my teeth, forcing myself to refocus on the task at hand. There was one more prophecy to find and record.

The last prophecy was attributed to RMV—Rebecca Marie

Vaughn, a.k.a. Becca, the Patron of the Oracles. My heart beat faster, a combination of anticipation and nerves. As I learned during my research, she'd had as many fragmented prophecies, cutting off mid-sentence, as clear and thorough ones.

I quickly found prophecy #256 in Becca's book of foretellings, my eyes devouring the page until I found it at the bottom.

When purity kills and the last raven falls, look to the dreamwalker for guidance. The cure will . . .

I turned the page, but the first line started with the heading of a new prophecy—#257. Of course—*of course*—the indexed prophecy was one of those fragmented in Mother's copy of Becca's book of foretellings.

"Damn it!" I hissed, sitting back in my chair. I stared at the books strewn across the desk, frustrated at reaching this dead end.

And to have the prophecy mention a cure—the very thing that could spread peace and unity among the people and strengthen the kingdom. What a horrible tease and a colossal disappointment.

I stood and approached the window behind the desk. The wooded wildlands that Fin had called home for so long stretched out across the strait toward the northern horizon. Perhaps this wasn't necessarily a dead end but a signpost directing my search elsewhere. What if I could track down the rest of Becca's prophecies—the rest of *this* prophecy?

My focus drifted closer to the city beyond the walls surrounding the castle grounds. Fin was down there, likely locked away in his room at the *Drunken Stag*. And it just so happened that Fin had been raised by Jake, the only remaining Patron who still lived. The only person alive who had actually *known* Becca. Better yet, she was his *sister*. If *anyone* knew where to find the original copies of her prophecies, it would be him.

I turned away from the window, snatched my notebook off the desk, and strode across the study, making my way over to Garath, who still stood in front of the doors. "We need to go into the city come nightfall," I told him. "To talk to Fin."

Garath glanced past me, looking at Liam's slumbering form.

"Not about that." I held up the notebook, grasping it tightly in both hands. "I've found something, and I think it could change *everything.*"

15

FIN

It would take Callon and Lyra most of the day to find Stone, the keeper of secrets, in the Shadow District across the bay. But it was necessary if I was going to collect the favor he owed me.

I searched for Liam in the courtyard while I waited, but I failed to find him anywhere within the castle walls where I might be able to see him again. None of Del's entourage was outside, and when I called upon my housecat and bird friends, there was no sign of them in her wing of the castle either.

Once again, I was left to stew alone in my room, unable to leave while my friends were sailing across the bay and Del was going about her duties.

Without knowing what was going on back home or what had come of Prince Alastor's death, I stewed with only my worries to accompany me. It was impossible not to feel like I was locked in a jail cell, rotting away.

Eventually, I couldn't stand it any longer. Sitting against the wall, I closed my eyes and sought out my ferret friend, accompanying Callon and Lyra on their journey in my stead. It took a moment to find the familiar tingle of his mind so far away, but within milliseconds, I could see the dark tunnels Callon and Lyra walked through in the bowels of the underground city.

I skittered to Lyra's other shoulder, looking at Callon and then at her, so they knew I was there.

"Oh, good. I thought you were going to miss all the fun," Callon muttered as his gaze darted around. He wasn't a fan of the underbelly, neither of us were.

Lyra patted my head. "You're so cute like this, Fin," she said mockingly.

I scowled at her, though it probably looked like no more than a blink, making her smile.

They continued down the cement halls of what had once been part of Oakland, a city long gone and forgotten. Though I couldn't be there in person, my ferret paws clung to Lyra's shoulder as she and Callon headed deeper into the underground metropolis.

As they stepped into the junction where the old sewers met, the new city burst into view, a blaring light in a colorful maze of holograms, hovels, and ivy-lined alleyways that made up the bustling world of the Shadow District hidden in the old zoo. The jeering grew louder in the distance, and the scent of sin more pungent.

"Holy hell," Lyra said, holding the back of her hand to her nose.

The cloyingly sweet stench of the latest synthetic drug to saturate the Seven Kingdoms, strix, hung in the air and clung to the cement walls like vines, hitting me like a punch to the face. I buried my ferret face in the collar of her vest. In animal form, I had an inkling of what Lyra's hyper-senses detected daily, and I didn't envy her for it.

"Don't worry," Callon told her. "You'll get used to it."

"Easy for you to say," she grumbled, and they scanned the vendors lining the alleyways as we hurried through the crowded city.

People hailing from all kingdoms wandered the streets, some

on stilts, hoping to make some extra coin, others without legs, driving electric bikes and holding out their hands for spare change.

Skinned rodents hung from bamboo poles, and the cooked meat glistened in the humming, flickering black-bulbed lighting that glowed throughout the merchant tents as we passed. Bizarre animals hissed from cages, and hats made with exotic feathers hung from posts and poles, pelts strung up and displayed for exorbitant amounts of coin alongside them. Vendors levitated their wares, and Elementals flashed their fire tricks, hoping to catch onlookers' attention.

My eyes fixed on a woman in a kiosk, spinning cones of glowing purple sugar strands with the wave of her finger. It wasn't a sugar rush that consumers would get but something far more pleasurable and intoxicating—strix. It was everywhere, glowing in one form or another and lingering like a storm cloud above the underground city.

Images of naked men and women were projected on some of the cement walls, advertising services found within. And there were smoke shops, gambling dens, fighting rings, Ability competitions, and animal racing.

But it wasn't only a place of carnal lust and debauchery. People entered the Shadow District to escape. It was a place where people came to numb their lives away. Or to feel alive again. Because there was one thing the underground city offered that people couldn't find anywhere else: freedom. Thieves, mercenaries, battle-broken soldiers, and entrepreneurs alike all had a place here in what was easily the richest district in the Corvo Kingdom. The royals just didn't know it.

I eyed a man smoking a pipe against a brick wall, barely hidden by the shadows. Then scanned the people who looked as if they were barely skin and bones curled on the streets—far more and far worse off than I'd seen before.

"Are they smoking strix like it's the new water or something?" Callon muttered. "I've never seen it this bad before."

He was right; it was getting bad, but I tried to stay focused on the task instead of on these people's plight.

We passed a food kiosk, and a man held out what looked like a fried alligator foot to Callon.

"Please tell me you're not looking for your fourth meal of the day already," Lyra whispered as Callon eyed it closely.

"Hell no," he said with a snort. "Even I'm not that desperate. I wouldn't trust anything I ate or drank down here. There's a reason everyone here looks high as a kite—they are." Callon nodded toward a man at a copper distillery, a blue, glowing liquid pouring from the spigot into a ceramic jug.

"It tastes good; don't get me wrong. But take my word for it. You'll regret it in the morning," he warned. Callon shook his head like he was shaking away a memory, and I snorted. "Don't drink or eat anything down here," he reiterated.

"I thought you said you hadn't been here before?" Lyra said, eyeing Callon closely. "You sure seem to know where you're going."

Callon smirked. "I said I hadn't been here on my own, which is true. I've only ever been here with Fin."

Lyra craned her neck to give me a reproachful look.

"We were here on business," Callon supplied. "Hence the favor we're going to collect."

Lyra eyed a scantily clad prostitute leaning against a wall. She winked in our direction, and Lyra's head snapped forward, looking straight ahead.

A one-legged man, propped up against the wall beside the prostitute, caught my eye. He was clearly a veteran of battle, his Medal of Honor all that held his tattered cloak in place. No matter which kingdom you fought for, that was how men and women were repaid for their service. Once they had served their purpose, there was no place for them in society. No place but down here.

We passed a fighting ring set up in one of the old animal enclosures, one I knew well, and made our way to the gaming sector.

"Stone should be in here," Callon said under his breath, and Lyra followed him into a gambling den lit with blinking red lights.

"What makes you think this is the place?" Lyra asked, her voice raised over the chanting, cheering, and dice rolling as bets were placed. "You said it's been nearly three years since you've seen him."

Callon laughed, just as I would have had I been walking beside them. "He's here. Trust me."

Lyra followed Callon inside, practically ducking under a cloud of smoke, a thick, rich scent of spicy tobacco mixed with strix wafting over us. There were gamblers everywhere, many looped out of their minds, with dark circles under their wide, bloodshot eyes. They hadn't slept in days. That much was obvious.

Gamblers looked at me, likely sensing I wasn't merely a ferret friend Lyra had dragged into the kingdom's underbelly but a *familiar*. I could feel the minds of a few animal Telepaths—strong ones, like me. But I pushed all of their minds away and searched the crowd for Stone instead.

I heard Stone's booming laughter before I saw him at the edge of the room, a long, rolled cigarette between his fingers and smoke billowing from his nostrils as he sat at a betting table. The moment he spotted Callon, his open expression faltered slightly, his gleaming eyes narrowed, and he straightened.

Callon and Lyra stopped by the wall and waited for Stone to join them.

Murmuring to his tablemates, he stood, his sweat-dampened, days old tunic stretched over his large belly.

"To what do I owe the pleasure?" Stone said with a hint of curiosity, despite the wariness in his eyes. He stood nearly a foot shorter than Callon, his blue eyes crisp and shrewd as he looked from him to Lyra, gauging their intentions.

When Stone's eyes lingered on Lyra for too long, Callon cleared his throat. "We've come to collect a favor," he told him.

"We?" It took only a second for Stone to comprehend Callon's meaning, and his gaze darted directly to me. "Fin," Stone grumbled in greeting. "I should have known you'd come to collect now that there's so much chatter about the outerlands."

"What do you know about the outerlands?" Lyra prodded.

Stone smirked and looked at Callon with a nod in her direction. "Is she new to the crew or something?"

"Or something," Callon said. "Trevor was killed during a trading trip last winter."

"I can't say I ever liked that guy, but if it's because of King Eduart, I'll offer my condolences. These days, it seems that bastard is taking more lives than those lost during the Turn." Stone took a puff from his cigarette, and a bluish smoke billowed from his nostrils once more. "So," he drawled. "Every second I'm standing here, I'm losing money. Out with it."

"You're always losing money, regardless," Callon volleyed with a grin. "But we're here about Maylar, ex-advisor to the Corvo queen—"

"*Dead* queen," Stone corrected. His sweaty brow lifted nonchalantly. "And so is Prince Alastor, I hear."

My pulse raced, though I shouldn't have been surprised he'd already heard about it. That's what Stone dealt in, rumors and secrets.

"Yeah?" Lyra tilted her head. "And what do you know about it?"

"Which part? That the greedy queen couldn't hack it without her elixir fix? Welcome to the real world. That's all I have to say about that."

"And the prince?" Lyra prompted.

Stone stared at her, his blond, bushy eyebrow arched. Even with the man's grizzled appearance and the lines around his eyes, he had a younger look about him. "I hear he had an interesting fall from a very high turret."

"What else did you hear?" Callon said as I silently urged them to keep Stone talking.

Stone glared at him. "Is that why you're here? To talk about a bunch of royals who got their dues?"

"Tell me," Callon demanded, not an ounce of amicability in his voice.

"There are a ton of speculations. Which one do you want to hear? The one about the princess sleeping with her bodyguard, who got jealous and offed the prince? The one where Alastor was what most princes are—a drunken, spoiled fool who thought he was invincible? Or the rumor that the scheming Sierra Kingdom is up to something nefarious again?" Stone shrugged. "The royals have wronged a lot of people to get the power they cling so desperately to. It's no surprise someone would murder Alastor, *if* that's, in fact, what happened."

He took another puff of his smoke. "None of it matters much. The result is the same: the Sierra Kingdom continues to grow as King Eduart continues to take. Meanwhile, the Corvo Kingdom continues to lose its power little by little." Stone shrugged. "If the new queen can't recover—and fast—chaos will ensue. It always does. But as the world crumbles, we'll all be down here, shoved away like they've wanted us to be, watching it all fall."

I didn't like the sound of that, and it was all I could do to remind myself I was in a ferret's head, and my only option was to listen.

"Why so curious about Corvo and the dead queen? You and your people are safe enough in the outerlands. So, what's it—" Stone's eyes widened, and he looked at me. "The prophecy," he realized.

It seemed the drugs hadn't dulled his senses as much as I'd assumed. With the way Stone looked at Callon then Lyra, I could tell he saw more than he should. More than was safe. Silently, I urged Callon to hurry the conversation along.

"And Maylar?" Lyra urged this time.

"*Maylar.* I haven't heard that name in a while."

Callon's eyes narrowed. "And by *a while,* you mean . . .?"

Stone glanced between them, taking his time to answer. "A few weeks."

"Tell us then," Callon pressed. "For Fin. And your debt will be paid."

Criminal that he was, Stone seemed to like the sound of that—anything to cut ties with someone like me, who knew where the only person Stone loved in the world lived—his only surviving daughter. If we gave her location to the authorities in any of the kingdoms in which he was a wanted man, they could use her to force him out of hiding. Because he would come out, only for her.

Stone cleared his throat. "Last I heard, that rat was slinking his way through Corvo."

"You're sure?" Callon deadpanned.

Stone peered down at the purse of coins in Callon's hand. "That depends. Is that for me?"

Callon gripped the purse tightly. "As you say, it *depends*. I want the truth—and don't skimp on me, Stone. You owe Fin for coming to your aid when you nearly got your thieving mercs slaughtered in Noctem. He has a hefty scar down his side to remind him of that debt every single day."

"There's talk Maylar's been in a few secret meetings, and he's been traveling through the realm. Last I heard, he was headed to Sierra. The *whys* aren't exactly clear. He's been seeing no one of direct importance, but some of the people he's met with have close ties with Eduart." Stone narrowed his eyes. "If it's this prophecy you're so concerned about, he's likely the man you want. He's always been obsessed with them. Then again, I've found it's the nature of intelligent men with too much power and time on their hands to seek ways in which they can twist words to benefit themselves."

"Then," Lyra said, "the question is, where is he now?"

Stone shrugged again and took another puff of his laced cigarette. "I could find out, but it will take a few days."

"Do it," Callon said without a second's hesitation. "And this purse, plus more, will be yours."

Though Stone tried to hide his surprise, he couldn't help but huff with shock. Callon and I both knew how much gambling Stone could get in with a clutch that heavy.

"You have two days," Callon amended. "And if you get the information sooner, consider the offer doubled."

Stone looked at my ferret form. "Fin, you know how long dredging up this stuff takes. Two days isn't realistic—"

Callon turned to leave.

"But I'll do my best," Stone offered. "I have a guy in Noctem who I heard mentioning Maylar last. Something about a Sierra guard he met who had an offhanded comment about the soon-to-be queen."

I felt Lyra's body stiffen at the mention of Del, and it was all I could do not to break the bond right now as unease filled me.

"I'll see what I can find out," Stone said, hooking his thumbs in his suspenders. "You have my word."

We all glared at him, knowing his word was useless without the promise of coin.

"Find out, Stone," Callon said coldly. "And do it fast."

The instant Stone agreed, I broke my connection with the ferret. I couldn't take it anymore. I was up on my feet and pacing the room before I was even fully cognizant in my own head. That Del's name had passed Maylar's lips at all unsettled me.

When pacing wasn't enough, I peered out at the sun lowering in the sky. I couldn't be seen on the streets, and I couldn't go to Del to warn her. There was nothing I could do but grit my teeth and wait for Callon and Lyra to return, yet I couldn't stew in the room a moment longer.

There was nothing I could do. Nothing to do but drink.

16

DEL

"You're sure this is the right inn?" I murmured over the lukewarm mead, tugging on my single, long braid, which I had pulled over my left shoulder.

The *Drunken Stag*'s barkeep had assured Garath the mead was the finest beverage they had available, which wasn't saying much. But watery mead was better than sour wine or bitter ale, so I sipped from my tankard and continued to scan the common room from our table tucked against the side wall. It was so rare for me to have the opportunity to observe my subjects anonymously that even if we were in the wrong place, I wouldn't have considered the past half hour of people-watching as wasted time.

Across the table from me, Garath nodded. "This is the place," he assured me and sat back in his chair, his arms crossed over his chest. His eyes never ceased their cautious scan of the tavern, his ale untouched on the table before him. He had exchanged his black guard leathers for brown leathers scarred with enough burn marks to make me suspect he had borrowed them from one of the castle blacksmiths. He looked like he belonged here.

I did not.

I had borrowed one of Ada's more casual dresses—soft, thin

wool in dove gray with simple white floral embroidery around the neckline, cuffs, and hem—and a plain, lightweight hooded cloak in a darker gray. In this part of town, however, I looked like I was wearing evening finery compared to the other patrons' garb.

I silently chastised myself. I should have listened to Garath and borrowed clothing from one of the female guards. The only other women wearing dresses in this establishment weren't wearing very much of them.

My cheeks heated as I watched a burly young man snag the wrist of one such woman. She yelped, then giggled as he pulled her down to his lap and palmed her nearly fully exposed breast. Garath had assured me this wasn't a brothel, which made me wonder what exactly went on in the actual brothels. Obviously, I *knew* what went on, but I assumed it all happened behind closed doors.

"There," Garath said, pitching his voice low. His attention locked on some point behind me.

I twisted in my chair and peered over my shoulder in time to watch Fin shut the door from the street. His eye caught on a woman wearing a belted violet tunic over dark gray leather leggings, perched on the edge of a table near the entrance. She was very pretty, with light brown skin, golden hair, and a faint smirk. It was no wonder she had drawn his attention.

He watched her with a guarded, curious expression as she slid off the table and approached him.

"We don't have time for this," Garath muttered, pushing his chair back and standing.

Fin glanced Garath's way as he closed in. And then Fin's focus shifted past Garath to me, and he blanched, his eyes widening. The woman in the purple tunic reached Fin before Garath and touched his arm, but Fin dismissed her with a few hushed words and a shake of his head, never taking his eyes off me. The woman glanced my way, her eyebrows raising. She mimed tipping her cap to me, then moved to another part of the tavern.

When Garath turned his back to Fin to return to our table, Fin only hesitated for a moment before following, a little unsteady on his feet. Garath switched seats, claiming the one adjacent to mine, which left only the chair on the opposite side of the table available for Fin.

I arched one eyebrow at Fin as he drew near. "Friend of yours?"

Fin pulled out the chair and eased down into it. "Who, Millie?" He glanced over his shoulder as though he was casually looking for the woman, then shrugged one shoulder. "I make friends everywhere." His slightly unfocused eyes met mine. Clearly, he had been drinking. I could hardly blame him after the events of the past two days.

"I'm sure you do," Garath muttered.

Fin's eyes narrowed slightly. "Her father owns this place, and keeping Millie happy keeps *him* happy. *And* it keeps them from asking too many questions about me—like why I arrived in Sierra military garb and now seem to be stuck in here, hiding." He crossed his arms over his chest, then glanced at Garath, who had already claimed that pose, and leaned forward to place his elbows on the table instead. "I thought you'd come by yesterday," Fin said, his voice carrying the faintest hint of accusation. "Or this morning, at least."

"I know," I said, leaning forward and mirroring his position. "We have a lot to talk about, and I wanted to come, but with Mother's death and then Alastor—" I held up one hand and shook my head. "No excuses. I *should* have come sooner, and I'm sorry I didn't."

Fin narrowed his glazed eyes, his jaw clenching and unclenching. He inhaled deeply, then released the breath in a sigh, much of the tension visibly leaving his body. "I can only imagine what it's been like for you these past few days," he said, his voice softening. "I'm glad you're here now."

I smiled, relieved. I cleared my throat and licked my lips. "I found something that I think might be important to both of us," I said, reaching into the cloak's concealed inner pocket to pull out my research notebook. "It's about the prophecy—or, well, the *prophecies*. There's more than one." I placed the thin leather-bound book on the table and flipped it open to the page where I had recorded each of the three relevant prophecies verbatim, turning the book so it was right side up for Fin. "There are actually three, all linked."

Fin scanned the lines I had copied, then blinked, studied them again, and looked at me once more. "Looks like two and a half to me."

"I know," I said, nodding. "That's the problem. The third prophecy is attributed to Becca, but it's only a fragment."

Fin's brow furrowed. "How do you know they're linked?"

"Well, *I* don't exactly." I paused, chewing on the inside of my cheek. "But Mother connected them. She has an entire book—an index of sorts—linking prophecies together. They're important, Fin." I tapped the third, fragmented prophecy.

When purity kills and the last raven falls, look to the dreamwalker for guidance. The cure will . . .

"Look," I said, nodding my encouragement for Fin to reread the third prophecy.

Even fragmented, it couldn't have been much clearer. Becca had seen something that related to the wasting sickness plaguing my kingdom. If I could just get my hands on the original, *complete* prophecy, I felt certain I could find a cure for the wasting sickness. It could very well turn the tide of war in our favor, strengthening my kingdom in the eyes of the other rulers enough for us to ally and rally against the Sierra Kingdom. King Eduart would have to back down.

Fin glanced at the open notebook again, then up at my face, down and up again. "I'm not sober enough for this," he muttered before scooting his chair back with the screech of chair legs over the worn wood floor. He stood and marched toward a nearby side door, yanking it open and stepping outside.

The scent of hay and manure wafting into the common room told me the door led to the inn's stable.

I exchanged a look with Garath, whose raised eyebrows and slight frown told me he was not impressed.

"Stop it," I hissed. "He's been through a lot."

"So have you."

"More than either of us knows," I said, ignoring his quip. "If you can't be nice, I'm sending you outside."

Garath's expression blanked, and he returned to staring at the open doorway.

Fin stepped into the inn a moment later, his hair dripping wet and plastered to his head. "All right," he said, dropping into his chair and scooting forward again. He planted his elbows on the table. "Let's talk prophecies."

I blinked, surprised by his sudden interest, and I tapped Becca's fragmented prophecy again. "There's not much to talk about," I admitted, offering him a sheepish smile. "I just need to ask Jake if he knows how and where she recorded her visions." I shrugged. "I *could* wander around the kingdom, checking every copy of her book of foretellings, but Mother's research was extensive. If *she* didn't find the complete prophecy, I doubt it's anywhere to be found in the Seven Kingdoms."

Fin sat back in his chair, the water dripping from his hair soaking the shoulders of his shirt. "So you didn't really come here to see me. You came here for Jake." He let out a short, bitter laugh and shook his head. "You're out of luck. I haven't seen him for months."

My heart plummeted. Jake was my best—and only—hope. "But —but—" My brows bunched together, and I opened and closed my mouth, floundering for words. "You must know where he is, at least? I can send trackers or a raven, or—"

Again, Fin shook his head. "I'm sorry. He's been distant since . . ." Fin pressed his lips together and raised his eyebrows. "Well, you know better than anyone what he went through."

I swallowed roughly and nodded.

What Mother *put* him through, he meant. While Jake had been Mother's prisoner during her last-ditch effort to tap into the Healers' gifts in search of a permanent cure for the wasting sickness, Mother had put him through extreme and intensive deep empathic interrogation. As a result, he retreated so deep into his own mind that Fin and I had barely been able to drag him back out.

"He was holding it together until we returned home after a trip to the north and saw the destruction—" Fin looked away, clenching his jaw. "When we found Autumn—" He cleared his throat. "After that, Jake stopped even pretending to be normal."

I wasn't like most Empaths, who could sense another's emotions by merely looking, but I didn't need to rely on psychic gifts to feel Fin's grief. His loneliness. Not when it was written across the hard lines of his face. Not when the ghosts of all the people he had lost haunted his eyes.

But he wasn't alone anymore. He had a son now—a son he deserved to know. And I wanted Liam to know his father.

"I'm so sorry, Fin," I said, reaching across the table to cover his hand with mine.

Fin pulled his hands off the table before I could touch him.

I froze, my stomach tangling in knots, then slowly retracted my arm. He didn't want my touch because, with me, it was never *just* a touch.

I set my jaw, refusing to let him see how much his physical retreat hurt, and inhaled a shaky breath. "You shouldn't be here," I told him, scanning the inn's bustling common room.

"Are you *commanding* me to leave your city?" Fin asked, his voice razor sharp.

"That's not what I said," I corrected him gently. He was on edge, his already raw emotions irritated by the alcohol. "You belong in the castle." I looked at Fin, meeting his shadowed stare. "With your son."

For long seconds, Fin didn't respond. He simply stared at me. "Does he know?"

"About you?" I asked, raising my eyebrows. "No. But I'll tell him tonight, and you and your people—" I paused and frowned. "You did mention someone was here with you, correct?"

"Two of my people are here," Fin confirmed.

"Well, then." I forced a smile. "The three of you should come to the castle tomorrow—to stay. I'll make sure rooms are prepared for you." I clasped my hands together, setting them on the edge of the table. "Once you're settled in, you can meet your son."

17

FIN

el wanted me to stay in the castle? With her and Liam? I wasn't sure why, but I looked at Garath, certain I would find him balking at the idea. But his expression was unreadable, and per usual, his eyes were on me.

I swallowed thickly. "Thank you," I said. Her offer surprised me. Not because I thought Del was heartless, but because whatever this was between us was complicated. And I'd been thinking about Liam nonstop since learning about him.

Now, Del was offering me exactly what I'd wished for: time with my son.

Not to mention, in all the years I'd given this city a wide berth, I never would have imagined I would be a welcome guest in the castle.

"But only until we've figured this mess out," I said as my momentary levity withered.

Del's brow furrowed. "Which mess are you referring to, exactly?" she asked carefully, and I wondered if she thought I referred to Liam.

"The prophecy. The desert—my people waiting for me," I explained. *This changes so much, and yet nothing at all. I don't know what happens next,* I wanted to tell her, but with Garath sitting there, the words wouldn't come.

The door to the inn opened, and I looked up to see Callon stride inside. Dark crescents shadowed his eyes as he scanned the tavern, and somehow, even his short black hair seemed slightly rumpled with exhaustion.

Lyra stepped inside behind him, her attention already locked on me. From the grave look on her face, I guessed she'd heard some of what we'd been discussing.

Lyra muttered something to Callon, and together, they walked over to our table. Both took in the sight of the princess and her stern-faced guardsman.

"Callon. Lyra," I said quietly and nodded to our *guests*. "This is Del and her . . . um, Garath."

Lyra nodded a greeting to both of them as Del rose to her feet.

Callon looked starstruck. "So you're the one Fin's been—"

"Callon," I grumbled so as not to draw unwanted attention to us, and I rubbed my pounding forehead. I wasn't even going to tell him we would be going to the castle as guests, afraid of what sort of ordeal he'd make out of it in front of all these people.

Remembering himself, Callon cleared his throat, and holding his hands up defensively, he bowed his head. "Apologies, your high—"

I cleared my throat in warning.

Callon closed his mouth and rested his palm on his chest. "It's an honor to finally meet you, is all," he amended. "I feel like I've known you for years."

Del bowed her head in return, her eyes darting to mine with curiosity. "It's good to meet you," she said. "I appreciate you accompanying Fin so far from your home."

"Ah, it's nothing," Callon said easily, his grin widening. He was clearly gobsmacked by the princess as he hooked his thumbs in his belt and rocked back on his heels. "We'd do anything for Fin—and you, of course."

Lyra rolled her eyes. "Patrons help me," she murmured. "I need a drink."

At the mention of alcohol, Callon's eyebrows popped up, and he leaned over to assess the two tankards on our table. "They've got you drinking this slosh?" He glanced at Del. "No wonder you all have long faces." Callon leaned into Del conspiratorially and glanced around the tavern. "Care to try the good stuff?"

"I, um—I was told this *was* the good stuff," she said, though her expression suggested she disagreed.

Callon reared back, his head tilting as he grinned. "Not even close." His attention snapped to me. "Fin, why didn't you get her the good stuff? It's the least we can do for the prin—" Callon caught himself this time and met my gaze.

"We've been a bit busy," I gritted out just as Del's stomach rumbled noisily. Her eyes widened, and her cheeks reddened.

Callon's eyes danced with glee. "And no food either?" He tsk-tsked at me. "Not to worry, Fin. I'll see to our guest." He held his hand out to Del. "My lady, would you allow me to get you the best lamb shank this side of the city? I like to pair it with an apple cider, which I'll admit is barely passable for *good*, but the meal will more than make up for it."

Del looked at me, considering the offer, and her eyes shifted to Garath next. While he seemed reluctant, I knew Callon would see to her every need.

"Callon knows the best food in this city," I admitted, shrugging my shoulder. "If you're hungry, I'd take his word for it."

Licking her lips, Del nodded primly and excused herself from the table to follow Callon to the counter, where Lyra already stood sipping on her ale.

Across from me, Garath seemed unsettled, and it was easy to imagine he very rarely brought Del into the city, knowing how dangerous it was for her, even if she didn't.

"If it's Callon you're worried about, don't be," I assured him. "I trust him with my life, and Lyra will be happy to keep him in check if he forgets himself."

That seemed to put the man at ease, though only slightly. He was more to Del than her personal guard. That much was obvious. The way she looked at him and stayed close—the way it seemed it was a chore for him to take his eyes off of her—proved he was far more than hired muscle to her.

"How is she really doing?" I asked, realizing if anyone knew what Del had been through the past ten years and how it affected her, this man would.

Garath's amber eyes met mine, lingering for a moment before they shifted back to Del on the other side of the room. "After you killed her husband, you mean?" he said.

"The man who was choking the life from her?" I replied in kind with equal sharpness. "Yes, but not just since that."

Garath's jaw clenched, and his hard gaze softened slightly. I saw regret in his eyes, though I wasn't sure why. Just like I saw anger in them too.

He cared for Del; that was painfully clear. I could easily assume Garath would have stopped Alastor from tormenting Del if he could, but hands tied or not, it was hard not to hold a slight grudge against him as I considered how long Del had lived like that.

Or maybe I begrudged Garath for taking care of Del and Liam when it should have been me. It was hard to tell which feeling was dominant, resentment or envy.

"She has sacrificed much over the years," Garath finally said. "To keep her secrets and her son safe. She is overjoyed that Alastor is dead, as are most at the castle. But the weight of her burden is not gone." Garath turned his untouched mug of ale around on the table. "I begged and pleaded with her not to marry him, but . . ."

"At least now, we have one less danger to worry about," I said.

"We?"

I raised my eyebrows. "You think I would leave now?"

Garath's head tilted slightly. "I thought you had a village to get back to in the desert lands?"

I smirked at that. *A village.* How quaint that sounded. "I do," I admitted. "But I have a son now, too. And I won't abandon him again. And I especially won't leave until I know he is safe—until I know they both are."

Lyra set a full pitcher of ale and an extra tankard for me on the table, her understanding gaze locking with mine. I nodded with gratitude. When she turned for the bar again, I glanced back at Del. She was smiling as Callon gestured wildly, regaling her with one adventure or another.

A smile. My chest ached at the sight. It had been so long since I'd seen that smile. I'd forgotten how mesmerizing it was.

Swallowing thickly, I turned back around to find Garath watching me. With the gravity of everything unknown and unspoken hanging between us, I poured myself a mugful of ale. After the decade I'd had, and the knot of nerves in my gut knowing I would finally meet Liam tomorrow, I figured another drink couldn't hurt.

The longer Garath watched me, though, the more I realized what he probably saw. Half sober and with damp hair hanging in my face, I was a mess. I'd give him that, but that wasn't all he saw. "You think I am reckless and dangerous."

"Aren't you?"

I huffed with amusement. "Not so much anymore. At least, I try not to be. I have people that rely on me—*many* people. Besides, I can't afford any more death on my conscience." I took a gulp of ale and rested my elbow on the table. "Whatever Del has told you —whatever you know . . ." I shook my head. "That's not who I am now. I haven't been that person in a very long time."

"Things would have been much different for her had you shown up at the solstice celebration."

I leaned back in my chair with a heavy exhale, wondering if the guy had any idea how guilty I already felt for staying away for so long.

Before my hackles could rise to bristling, Garath continued. "Despite all that's happened, and despite all that Del and Liam have been through, I can't say your coming back before now would've been for the better."

The crease in my brow deepened.

"Del and Liam would have left with you," Garath explained. "And then what? There are more dangers out there than we realized." This time, Garath stared at his warm ale as if he might actually take a drink, as if it pained him to admit such a thing. "Maylar, the traitor we think is behind this prophecy business," he said, spinning the mug around again instead. "We thought we were rid of him, but now—" The skin around his eyes tensed. "If she had left with you, she would have been far easier for him to get to. And after the queen tried to have him killed, I have no doubt he would have exacted his revenge, however possible. He's likely been planning it for years." Garath glanced toward our companions at the bar, his eyes softening when they landed on Del.

"And now the queen is gone," I mused and mulled his words over and over. Callon's laughter met my ears, and I hoped they would keep Del over there a little while longer. "About Maylar," I started, and Garath's eyes narrowed slightly.

He touched his index finger to his lips, suggesting silence on this topic.

I tipped my head toward my friends behind us. "There's nothing concrete yet," I admitted. "But we found his trail, and he's definitely been scheming. We just don't know to what end. Yet."

Garath pursed his lips, listening intently. "And how did you come by this information, exactly?"

I smirked at that. "You don't want to know, and it's not important. We should have more specifics within the next day or two. But there is one thing I do know for certain," I said, staring at him for a moment. "Del's name passed his lips a few weeks ago, and we both know that isn't good."

Garath's expression sharpened with rancor borne of fear and hatred, a look I imagined mirrored my own. Whatever distrust and dislike Garath and I had for one another, we both held Del and Liam's safety above all else.

"Can you trust everyone in the castle?" I asked, realizing danger could be closer than any of us thought.

"I don't trust *anyone*," Garath said. Loosening the grip on his mug, he sat back. "Which is why I think Del is right. You should stay within the castle walls."

I blinked at Garath. I expected him to have a number of opinions on the matter, but not that he would have agreed.

"Besides," he continued, "Eduart's troops are mobilizing. Whatever their next move, we need to keep Del and Liam safe."

With each clench of his jaw and flick of his gaze to me or Del, I knew Garath's thoughts churned as much as mine did. Still, it was obvious we'd just united in our hatred of Maylar and our fear for Del and Liam's safety.

"Then we'll stay in the castle," I said with a nod of agreement. My palms felt clammy at the thought of seeing Liam, not as a bird this time, and not when he was asleep by the fire, but in person. As father and son.

18

DEL

"Has not the count just told us that all human wisdom is summed up in two words: wait and hope."

I shut the book and set it on my lap, gripping the aged binding tightly in my hands. Liam lay in his bed, curled up on his side, his stare distant.

How perfect that Liam had picked *The Count of Monte Cristo* from Mother's collection. He had been sucked into the book, nearly completing it in barely a day. It was impossible not to see the parallels between the characters on the pages and our own lives. Mercedes de Morcerf, a woman who lost her love and had no choice but to move on. Edmond Dantes, a man who sought revenge for his shattered world. Albert de Morcerf, a boy who learned his father was a terrible person. I just hoped we came to a happier ending than so many of the characters in the book.

"*Do* kids inherit their parents' sins?" Liam asked quietly.

My chin trembled, my heart breaking for him. I drew in a deep breath, exhaling as I set the book on the nightstand and leaned forward, capturing Liam's hand and wrapping it up in both of mine. "Of course not," I murmured. I kissed the knuckle of his thumb, the only part of his hand that remained exposed, then inhaled, hesitating only a moment before speaking. "I need to tell you something."

Liam blinked, his red-rimmed eyes focusing on me.

I took a shuddering breath, bolstering my courage, then whispered my confession. "Alastor Windsor wasn't your father."

Liam's lips parted and his eyes widened.

"When I was younger," I told him, "I met someone and fell in love, but then he was gone, and I—" I sucked in a shaky breath. "When I discovered I was with child, the kingdom wasn't stable, and I felt like I *had* to marry Alastor to provide a legitimate heir." Of course, then Liam had been born a boy, when tradition dictated that the Corvo heir must be female to ensure the line continued unbroken. "It was a mistake," I told him, my voice wavering.

Hurt twisted Liam's sweet features.

"Not you," I said in a rush. "You are my greatest joy." I smiled, pouring my boundless love for him out though my gaze, letting him see how much I meant those words. "The mistake was marrying Alastor. It never should have been him, and I'm so sorry that we had him in our lives for so long."

Liam's eyes filled with tears but also with shimmering hope. "He's really not my father?" When I shook my head, Liam squeezed his eyes shut, his face scrunching. His relief flowed into me, overwhelming us both.

I shifted to the bed, sitting on the edge of the mattress, and gathered him into my arms. I held him as he cried, feeling what he felt as he released his pent-up worries and fears that he was doomed to end up a monster just like Alastor. I had been so preoccupied with trying to keep Liam safe that I had been blind to his inner torment.

"All will be well," I assured him, rocking him gently and rubbing his back. "All will be well."

Sniffling, Liam pulled away and wiped his face with his sleeve. "Who was he—my real father?"

His eyes were filled with longing, and his sorrow seeped into me. I had said his father was gone, and Liam had interpreted that to mean he was dead.

"He *is* a very good man. One of the best I have ever known." I watched realization dawn on Liam's face.

"He—he *lives*?"

Eyes stinging, I smiled. "He does. I only just found out." I paused, then asked, "Would you like to meet him?"

Liam nodded enthusiastically.

"Good." I smoothed down his mussed hair. "He's coming to stay at the castle. He'll be here tomorrow."

"To be your husband?"

My eyes bulged, and I choked on a laugh. "I don't know about that. Much has changed for us both in the years since we were together, but nothing will change the fact that he is your father." I pulled Liam in for another hug. "Let's take everything else one day at a time."

Liam was wired after the revelation about his true father. I lay beside him and answered every single one of his questions about Fin until his eyes drooped and his words slurred. Even after Liam was asleep, I continued to lie beside him, one of his hands grasped loosely in mine, and watched him. His mind filled with dreams of his father—the man he had yet to meet, not the man he had hated.

I was exhausted, but my mind wouldn't rest. Thoughts raced through my head—about Fin and Liam, about Jake and prophecies and the last raven falling, about the Sierra Kingdom and war and the wasting sickness and . . .

It was too much.

Mother would have known what to do. She would have been able to see all the possibilities laid out before her so clearly and picked a path forward that served the greater good. She wouldn't have waffled, torn between committing to military defense and seeking an alternative solution steeped in vague and cryptic visions of the future.

I was far too restless to sleep. Moving slowly and quietly, I released Liam's hand and scooted to the edge of his bed. I paused in the doorway and peered back at him, ensuring he was sound asleep. I had promised him I would stay with him through the night, but he had always been a sound sleeper, and it was unlikely he would wake before morning. So long as I returned within a few hours, he would never know I had left him at all.

I nodded to the guards posted in the corridor outside Liam's rooms, then wandered down the hallway to Mother's private chambers. I paused at her door, preparing myself for her absence in a space that had always been so full of her weighty presence. I hadn't been back to these rooms since her body was taken away. In my mind, she was still in there, lying on the bed, struggling for each breath.

I pulled the keyring from my belt, quickly found the right key, and unlocked the door. I pushed the door open before I could lose my nerve and stepped into the dark sitting room.

No lights were on, and no embers burned in the fireplace. The space felt more than empty. It felt like a void, vacuous and greedy.

I crossed the sitting room, slowly making my way to the doorway of the bedchamber. In the silver moonlight, I could see that Mother's bed was made, not even an indent on the pillows from her head. My chair had been moved back into the corner.

I started for the chair but realized halfway across the room that there was no need for the chair when the bed was unoccupied. Changing trajectory, I headed directly for the bed and hesitated only for a moment before easing down to sit on the edge of the mattress.

But compulsion gripped me, and I didn't stop there. I scooted back on the bed and lifted my legs, laying where Mother had spent most of the past few months. My eyes drifted shut, and I rested my hands on my chest, opening myself up to my empathic senses.

Most Empaths' gifts were fairly straightforward—they looked at someone and felt their target's emotions, often seeing some of their surface thoughts as well. Some Empaths, like Alastor, learned to weaponize their gift, using their connection to another's mind to hurt that person, like a psychic sucker punch. Others, like me, required touch to sense anything, but often that limitation came with unique advantages. I wasn't limited to human minds. I could also sense impressions from most animals, so long as I was touching them.

Sometimes the resonance was simply an emotion—a sense of dread or hope or longing. But other times, when an object was extremely significant to a person, it was as though they imbued the object with pieces of themselves. Then, entire scenes from another's life would flit through my mind, and for a short time, it would be as if I had *become* that person.

That was what I sought now. I wanted to feel what Mother had felt. I needed to be inside her head, just for a little while, to help me understand what she would have done in my shoes. Chase the prophecy, or make a stand. Cure the people, or prepare to fight the enemy. Or perhaps there was some other path forward—something I couldn't see but that would have been so obvious to her ruthless strategist's mind.

I sensed nothing of Mother as I lay on her deathbed, which struck me as odd. Usually, the things touching a person when they died held the strongest resonances, as if some of the deceased's essence soaked into those things when they passed. But not this time. Not with Mother.

Frustrated, I blew out a breath and opened my eyes. Maybe her clothes would work better? I pictured Mother in my mind's eye, recalling what she had been wearing when she drew her last breath.

I could see her so clearly, wrinkled and wasted, her sunken eyes closed and her lips parted. The fingers of one hand had been curled around her silver raven pendant, like always.

I sat bolt upright. The raven pendant. My gut told me it was significant.

I scooted off the bed and hurried out of Mother's rooms and nearly screamed when I opened the door from the sitting room to find Garath standing in the corridor, leaning back against the opposite wall, his arms crossed over his chest.

"Garath!" I stumbled backward a step and clutched my hands to my chest, like doing so might slow my racing heart. "You startled me!"

Garath appeared unperturbed by my admonition. "You promised to stay in Liam's rooms."

My shoulders slumped, and I lowered my hands. "I know, I just —" I shook my head, my brow furrowing. "I needed Mother's guidance."

"I see." He relaxed his arms and stepped away from the wall. "Did you find what you were looking for?"

I shook my head. "Come on." I passed through the doorway and started down the corridor, heading away from Liam's rooms. "I have an idea."

Garath followed me as I descended three flights of stairs to the ground floor of the castle and made my way into the throne room. I crossed to the dais at the back, bypassing the behemoth black granite throne for the heavy steel door concealed behind an enormous tapestry of the Patron Tree. Garath held the tapestry away from the wall as I unlocked the door and pulled it open, revealing a stairway. The stone steps descended into absolute darkness, and he handed me a lighter. I lit two lanterns hanging on hooks on the wall inside the dark stairwell and returned the lighter to Garath before passing him one of the lit lanterns.

It had been ages since I last visited the catacombs beneath the castle. I had forgotten how quiet it was down here. How still the air was.

Garath's footsteps shushed on the stone behind me as we started down the stairs. The descent always brought the illusion that the arched ceiling was closing in, and I hurried my steps to reach the bottom where the ceiling leveled out a little higher.

The catacombs had been carved out of the bedrock during the early stages of the castle's construction and consisted of a single tunnel, which spiraled outward from the bottom of the stairs. On alternating sides, dozens of burial chambers had been carved to house the bodies of the Corvo queens and their children—at least, the ones who didn't become a queen in their own right.

All Corvo queens who had come before me, save for the first queen and my namesake, Queen Delphinia, rested here. Queen Delphinia had been interred in a mausoleum located in the cemetery on the outer grounds, across the moat, where citizens were more welcome and could visit her.

Mother's burial chamber was the sixth on the left. I paused in the arched doorway.

Her body lay atop the undecorated lid of the sarcophagus. The black granite lid that would cover the sarcophagus once her body was interred was still being finished by the sculptors. She was dressed in a long, black gown decorated with feathers that had been saved from her first companion raven, Morigan, after the bird's death, long before I was born. Her silver hair had been fashioned in an elaborate braid that coiled around her head like a crown and was adorned with gleaming silver feathers.

Holding up the lantern, I stepped into the burial chamber and slowly approached Mother's body. The rich, slightly spicy smell of the incense and oils used during embalming scented the air.

I tilted my head to the side, studying Mother's face. Despite the extensive time and attention the embalmers had spent preparing her for her funeral, it didn't look quite right. Her mouth appeared stretched, her lips thinner and wider than they should have been, and her jowls were smoothed out. The effect of gravity on aged, anelastic skin, I supposed.

I shifted my attention down from her face to her neck and the high, feathered collar of her dress. A few inches of silver chain was barely visible over her collarbone. Setting the lantern on the corner of the sarcophagus, I reached for the chain to pull the pendant free from its concealment.

My fingertips brushed her cold flesh, and I jerked my hand back, sucking in a sharp breath. I glanced at Garath, who stood in the main passageway, keeping watch.

I made a fist, then stretched out my fingers and shook out my hand before trying again. This time, I didn't flinch when I touched her. I pulled the necklace out from under the collar of her dress, and the pendant clinked against the granite. I inched the chain around her neck until I found the clasp, and then I unfastened it and lifted the necklace.

Holding the necklace up by the chain, I studied the dangling silver pendant in the dim, golden light of the lantern. Mother had held the pendant concealed within her tight fist for so long that I had forgotten the finer details of the piece. The silver pendant of the nobly resting raven was tarnished in the creases, but the black diamond in the place of its eye sparkled in the lantern light.

My heart beat faster as I lowered the pendant toward my open, waiting palm. Grief poured into me the instant the silver raven made contact with my skin.

Memories from Mother's life flashed through my mind's eye. Through my heart.

Countless failed pregnancies. Three living children, none of which was *me*. One didn't live beyond infancy. One was male and must not have lived beyond the age of four or five because that was where Mother's memories of him stopped. The last, I recognized from portraits as my older sister, Calla, who had suffered from the wasting sickness but lived well into her teenage years, thanks to Mother force-feeding her the healing elixir. But Calla had figured out how it was made and ended up dying of the wasting sickness before she could be officially blessed as the Corvo heir.

I saw Mother speaking with Maylar in her study, discussing the infants born to other purebred Empath families throughout the kingdom and plotting to import strix to cover up the spread of the wasting sickness among the lowborn masses. Repeatedly, I watched her take bundled infants from their weeping mothers. I watched the fathers accept heavy coin purses in exchange for their babies. I heard Maylar's warning to the parents that telling a soul about the exchange would mean not only *their* deaths but also the deaths of their children.

I felt Mother's hope, which waned with each successive child. I felt her heartbreak as the adopted children fell to the wasting sickness, one by one. Each death was covered up as either an accident or an assassination. Mother raised a dozen adopted children to near adulthood, but none survived.

Until me.

I never got sick because I wasn't highborn. My family line wasn't pure and noble. She bought me from a poor family with too many children who lived in a village in the southern region of the kingdom. Three of their older children had been classified as Empaths, despite the parents having muddled gifts. There was a good chance that their newborn would express strong empathic Abilities as well. And none of their children showed any signs of the wasting sickness, which mattered because, even then, she had been aware that the disease impacted everyone in our kingdom, not only the purebred nobles.

Mother had been desperate for an heir. She had already been taking the healing elixir for long enough that the people of our kingdom were murmuring about her unnaturally long lifespan. She had stopped leaving the castle, so only those within the safety of the inner walls ever saw her too-young face.

If she wanted the Corvo Dynasty to survive, she had to find an heir.

My parents hadn't wanted to give me up, but they had needed the money. They had already been having difficulty feeding the seven children they already had. Seven children. Seven brothers or sisters could still be out there, somewhere. Probably in that same village.

The memories faded, the resonance ending with a whisper of Mother's voice.

I'm sorry . . .

I dragged in a breath as the resonance released me.

"Del!"

My knees gave out, and powerful arms caught me before I hit the stone floor.

Garath scooped me up, cradling me like I weighed nothing, and carried me out of the catacombs and back up to the royal living quarters while I quietly wept against his shoulder.

"Open the door," he ordered, and I raised my head enough to see that we had reached the door to my private rooms.

I glanced at the guards at my door, then at Garath. "Not here," I said, my voice small. "I need to be with Liam."

With my son. My family. The only blood relative I had ever known.

19

FIN

Callon and Lyra's chatter faded as I stood within the castle garden's stone walls watching the bees pollinating the lavender that filled one of the flowerbeds. I thought about Del, about that night in my room and the lavender scent of her hair that has stayed with me ever since. I had thought about Del every single day, and never once was a child involved.

It was safe to assume she'd thought of me frequently as well, but the circumstances were different. Del saw me when she looked at our son, but did she remember me with regret? She would never regret Liam, but did she regret he was the result of one night with me? Did she think of me with resentment, not knowing why I'd disappeared? I wasn't even sure how she felt now that I was back. I'd reappeared, and there'd been no time to talk about any of it.

"It's a nice place the princess has here," Callon mused, strolling closer. He bent over to sniff the honeysuckle vines winding up a trellis. Hands on his hips, he hummed with satisfaction as he assessed the bursts of white blossoms filling the perfectly manicured flowerbeds around it.

"It's a palace," Lyra muttered, meandering the mosaic pebble-stone path that etched its way through the garden. "What did you expect?" But despite her quip, even Lyra was mesmerized by the majesty of it. I could hear the awe in her voice. The pond and fountains, the birdhouses and grassy knolls with maple trees.

I was glad to see that everyone, even Tick, who was rolling around in a patch of sunlight on the grass, was soaking in the respite of the garden. I, on the other hand, couldn't stop glancing at the arched entrance, as if Del and Liam would suddenly be standing there . . . As if I could possibly miss their arrival.

When I saw the archway was still empty, I began to pace.

"You don't need to be worried, Fin," Lyra said, ambling her way over to me. "It's going to be fine."

"Is it? I barely remember my dad," I admitted, rubbing my forehead. "What if I'm shit at being one?"

"You won't be shit at it," Callon added. "You had Jake. Besides, you aren't shit at anything—well," he backpedaled. "I mean, you aren't shit at *most* things. You could work on your underwater basket weaving a bit. You're definitely shit at that."

I huffed a laugh, earning a triumphant grin from Callon.

"But seriously, Fin," he said, plopping down on a wooden bench by the rose garden. "You'll be fine." He rested his elbows on his knees. "You said he's an animal Telepath, like you. So you already have something in common. You just have to find common ground and ease into it, you know?"

"Yeah," I said, licking my lips with sudden confidence. "Yeah, that's a good idea." I sat beside him, exhaling a deep breath just as Tick's head shot up, her ears shifting as she listened.

As they drew closer to the garden, I felt Liam's mind and jolted to my feet. "They're here," I breathed, my eyes glued to the arched entrance.

Callon stood as well. "I guess that's our cue." He grabbed my shoulder, squeezing it affectionately. "You got this, Fin."

While my friends seemed certain I wouldn't screw this up, my palms were sweating, and my heart was galloping in my chest. I'd never felt more inadequate or unprepared.

"Good luck," Lyra whispered, and she nudged Callon, leading him out the other side of the garden.

Garath stepped through the archway first, and when he saw me, he moved to the side for Del and Liam to walk through. My gaze fixed instantly on Liam. I had to see his expression, to know if he was afraid or dreading this, especially after losing the man he'd always thought was his father, until now.

Del leaned in and whispered something to him. Then, squeezing his hand, she led him closer. Liam looked curious and maybe anxious but not uneasy, and I took a few steps forward to meet them.

Tick trotted over to Liam immediately, her tail wagging as she sniffed every inch of him, taking in his smell and feeling his mind. *I* could feel his mind. It was open. Searching. Sussing out and feeling mine, the same as I was doing to him.

Liam smiled at Tick and stroked the coyote's head. He scratched the spot she loved most behind her ears, making me smile. "I've never seen a coyote before," he said, eyes trained on her back leg as it began to twitch.

"Her name is Tick," I told him and chuckled as her leg twitched faster. "For obvious reasons. She's been with me for almost six years." When I looked at Del, she was watching me. Her features were soft, but I knew that look in her eyes; she was as nervous as I was, but I wasn't sure why.

"Are there a lot of coyotes where you're from?" Liam asked.

I looked at him. "There are packs of them in the desert and lands surrounding it, but there's only one like Tick."

Liam understood my meaning—my connection to the canine— and he glanced at me with a knowing glint in his green eyes.

In that moment, I saw myself in him, and while I'd thought the reality of having a son had already sunk in, tears filled my eyes, and a lump formed in my throat. The more Liam lathered Tick with attention, the more his smile grew, and the more my heart felt like it might explode.

"So," Del started and cleared her throat. She ran her fingers through Liam's auburn waves, and I wondered if she even knew she was doing it. "I was thinking we could have a picnic here in the garden for lunch?"

It struck me that there Del stood, giving Liam and me this time together when I knew she had a hundred other tasks to complete in preparation for the coronation.

When Liam nodded at the idea, Del's umber eyes met mine again. I held them, willing her to know how much I appreciated this because there were no words. "I'd like that," I said.

Her lips pursed and curved into a watery smile. "Then I'll go let the kitchen know," she offered, and I knew this was her gift to me —time alone with Liam.

"I'll be right back, okay?" she said, barely having to look down at him; it wouldn't be long before Liam was as tall as she was.

When he met her gaze, I saw strength in him. With quiet stoicism, Liam wordlessly reassured his mother that everything would be all right, and I nearly smiled with pride at that.

Pride for what, I wasn't sure. I hadn't raised him. I hadn't been around for a single moment of his life, and as grateful as I was to be there with him after years apart, that reality still stung.

"All right then," Del breathed. She looked at me again. "I'll be right back."

I dipped my head, and she made her way back to Garath. I'd never wanted time to slow down as much as I did at that moment, knowing being here with Del and Liam would pass far too quickly. But I refused to think of that right now.

"It was you a couple of days ago," Liam said, drawing my attention back to him. "In the crow's mind," he clarified.

"It was," I said, following him to the birdhouses. Finches chirped and hopped from the feeder to the bath. "Does that bother you?"

Liam shook his head. "No. I'm glad it was you."

I exhaled a breath I hadn't realized I'd been holding. "You are?"

Liam nodded and held his finger out to a finch that hopped onto it. "Your mind feels . . . right," he explained.

"So does yours," I admitted. "I've never felt that with a person before—that sort of connectedness."

Liam looked at me with a hint of a smile. "Me either."

Tick trotted by, returning to the sun patch in the grass to roll around again. "Where is your raven friend from the other day?" I asked him.

"Nyx? Probably harassing Cook in the kitchen with Sid." A grin engulfed Liam's face, and I couldn't help a smile of my own.

"Yes," I said with a chuckle. "I remember how she felt about animals in the kitchen last time I was here. I would've loved to have seen her face when she woke the next morning to find the remnants of Beast's lamb shank."

"Beast?"

"My companion at the time—a cougar I'd had since I was your age. Cook should have been grateful, really. We made sure he licked the water pot impeccably clean when he finished it."

Liam laughed, and the finch on his finger flitted back with the others.

"You look like your mother," I thought aloud, which earned me a confused look.

"Everyone thinks I look like you."

My brow lifted as I studied his features, seeing so much of Del in him, even if he couldn't. "You have your mother's nose and smile. And something tells me you have her strength too."

Liam seemed to appreciate that, but his expression sobered as he scuffed his shoe on the pavement. "I asked her about you, you know."

Flexing my hands, I watched him from the corner of my eye and cleared my throat. "You did?"

Liam's head bobbed slightly, but it was hesitant.

"And what did she tell you?"

He shrugged as he stepped onto the grass. "That she loved

you," he admitted. "But you were gone when she found out she was going to have me."

My stomach dropped twice in the span of a single second. "Liam, I didn't know—"

"I know," he reassured me and plopped down next to Tick. "But I wish it had been you my mother married instead of . . . *him*."

I sat down a few inches from Liam. I wasn't sure if my heart was soaring or breaking, hearing him utter such words, and I swallowed the emotion that lodged in my throat as I forced my heartbeat to steady. "I wish things had been different too, Liam. I wish you knew how much." I didn't care that my voice was strained. I only hoped he understood how true the words were. "And I'm sorry things have been so bad." My jaw clenched. "I wish I'd known."

Liam stared at the ground as he picked at a blade of grass. "You're here now," he said, his voice quiet and wavering, and he bit the inside of his cheek.

"Yeah," I said, wiping the escaped tear on my cheek. "I'm here now."

Liam met my gaze before studying my face. I didn't know if he was gauging my sincerity or not, but finally, he nodded.

20

DEL

"We'll start the day in the throne room for the funeral," Marta, the castle's event coordinator, said from beside me, launching into her review of the schedule for Friday. Was the equinox really only two days away?

With one hand, I gripped Mother's silver raven pendant, which I now wore around my neck, while the fingers of the other were curled around the bronze railing of the viewing balcony overlooking the throne room.

The vernal equinox, as one of the Temple's four major holidays, along with the autumnal equinox and the two solstices, was always a big deal throughout the Seven Kingdoms. But this year, it was tenfold the production with the weekly sabbath, Mother's funeral, *and* the coronation all happening on the same day.

I watched the servants rushing around on the polished black granite floor below to place tables, chairs, and other decor. The floral arrangements—all living plants to symbolize rebirth, renewal, and the promise of Spring—would be added the morning of the celebration, but at least the furniture helped me to picture how the room would look for Mother's funeral.

"Then," Marta continued, "we will move everyone out to the

gardens for brunch and the regular equinox celebration—the egg painting and egg hunts, the seed planting and seedling exchanges, the group devotional . . . " In my periphery, I saw her peer down at the schedule on her clipboard. "We'll bring out a late lunch around 4 p.m."

"Without spirits, correct?" I clarified, glancing at the tall, lithe woman sidelong.

She gave a brusque nod. "No alcohol will be served until after the coronation."

"Good," I said, relieved.

We wanted everything to go as smoothly as possible, and while it was tradition for the castle to provide libations as well as food during the quarterly holiday celebrations, Garath and Hills agreed it was best to hold off until *after* the coronation. Especially with the cryptic line in Becca's prophecy about the *last raven* falling. Garath and Hills considered *me* the last raven, even though both were now aware of Mother's terrible secret—that I wasn't a true, biological heir—and were doubly cautious of anything that could cause that prophesied fall.

But I wasn't so sure it *was* talking about me.

What if the *last raven* was actually Mother? Technically, she was the last of the Corvo bloodline, *and* she had fallen. If I was right, then the two qualifying pieces of the prophecy were in place. Purity *was* killing—Class purity exponentially increased a person's chances of developing the wasting sickness—and the last raven *had* fallen when Mother died. The time was right for the prophecy to be fulfilled. I just needed to find the dreamwalker, whoever that was, and the rest of the prophecy, and so much of this suffering could come to an end.

Ever since I touched the pendant and discovered Mother's secret, the impending war with the Sierra Kingdom had felt remote, like it wasn't truly my problem. Logically, I knew it should have been my top priority, but the prophecies were all I could think about. More and more people were falling sick and dying every day. Mother's memories had made it clear—the wasting sickness *was* impacting people throughout the kingdom, pure and mixed-Class alike. Strix saturation and a more varied gene pool made the wasting sickness take longer to become apparent among the lowborn, but it was there. It had been there since before I was born.

I needed to find Jake and figure out the missing piece of Becca's prophecy. That was what would best serve the people, not sending them to fight and die in a fruitless war. At this rate, we were all doomed eventually.

My gut knotted. Did I still need to go through with the coronation? I didn't deserve the crown, and I didn't belong on the throne. I *wasn't* of the Corvo line. The dynasty Mother had fought so hard to preserve had died with her. But what mattered more—I didn't *want* to rule the Corvo Kingdom. Of course, I wanted to help the people, but did I need a crown to do that?

Part of me felt like I had always known I didn't truly belong in the role of Corvo heir. I wasn't like Mother. I didn't see the people as game pieces on a board, waiting to be moved to where they were needed or sacrificed when necessary. I couldn't ignore the suffering of individuals to focus instead on the greater good.

"Attendees will be escorted back into the throne room at half-past six," Marta said, continuing her recitation of the schedule. "And the coronation ceremony will begin promptly at seven, with the goal of setting the crown on your head and having you light the vernal flame at the exact moment the sun vanishes behind the horizon. The equinox feast will be ready in the onyx ballroom by the time the coronation ends, and the bonfire will be lit in the courtyard at nine."

I turned to face her, one hand still gripping the railing. "It's a lot for one day." I glanced at Garath, standing watch at the doorway to the balcony.

His eyes met mine, just for a moment, then flitted away to scan the floor of the ballroom below. Could he sense my doubts? Could he tell I was seriously considering walking away from all of it—the crown, the throne, the crushing responsibility?

I turned my attention back to Marta. "Are you sure the staff can handle all the preparation and the transitions—even without bringing in extra help?"

Gauges would be nulling the crowd, but tradition dictated that we couldn't shut the public out during a coronation. Come Friday, *anyone* could enter the outer castle grounds and even cross the bridge to the castle proper.

"I have the best staff in the Seven Kingdoms," Marta said, raising her chin. "Trust me, Your Highness. We can handle it."

I bowed my head in thanks. "Then I'll leave you to it," I said before turning and approaching Garath. "Are they still in the gardens?"

Fin and Liam had really hit it off during our picnic earlier, so I had given Liam the option to skip his usual afternoon lessons and stay with his father for a few more hours. Liam had jumped at the chance, and thankfully, Fin hadn't looked too terrified. Garath had been maintaining a connection to Sid, who was still with them, even while he guarded my back, just to make sure all was well.

"They are," Garath said, falling in step beside me as I started down the corridor.

I tucked the raven pendant into the collar of my tunic as we descended the stairs to the ground floor. I still didn't fully understand how Mother had concealed the truth of my birth from me, but I suspected it had everything to do with the pendant. Or rather, Mother subconsciously tied those memories and the related emotions to the pendant in a way that allowed her to hide them from me during our weekly empathic communions over the past decade. I hadn't known such a thing was possible, but I imagined it had taken incredible focus and an iron will—two of Mother's trademark characteristics. She had lived a long time, far longer than was natural for anyone but a Healer, and I could only imagine all the empathic tricks she had learned.

I wondered if she had intended for me to find out or if she had truly wished to take this secret to the grave. She had known me well enough to guess how deeply this would shake me. She had to have known my discovery of the truth would threaten the entire kingdom.

But she had also suggested I take Liam and run. Abandon the kingdom. The people. Her legacy. Why? Because she didn't think I could handle it? Because she didn't think I deserved it? Or because she loved me—and Liam—and genuinely wanted what was best for us both?

Garath and I stopped by the kitchen to check in with Cook on the food preparations and to confirm with Fillip, the head butler, that under no uncertain terms was the cellar to be unlocked or *any* alcohol be distributed until the feast *after* the coronation ceremony.

"I want to check in with Liam and Fin before we head out to the barracks," I told Garath as we passed through the door to the kitchen garden.

The top of Fin's and Liam's heads bobbed into and out of view on the upper terrace lawn as they ran back and forth, and a peel of joyous laughter reached my ears. Despite Alastor's menacing presence, Liam had always been a happy child, but I hadn't heard his laugh for days. He had been serious and somber since Mother slipped into a coma.

A faint smile curved my lips. I hurried up the stone steps to the upper terrace. Sid and Nyx swooped above Liam and Fin in what appeared to be some form of team keep-away, with Liam and Nyx making up one team while Sid and Fin made up the other. I spotted Callon sitting with Ada on the bench at the edge of the lawn, her poorly concealed grin and shaking shoulders telling me Callon was likely regaling her with some of the same tales he had entertained me with the previous afternoon.

I stopped at the top of the steps and raised a hand to shield my eyes from the drooping afternoon sun while I caught my breath from the quick climb. My knees felt a little shaky, and suddenly dark spots danced along the edges of my vision.

"Whoa," Garath said, gripping my elbow firmly as I swayed from side to side. "Why don't you sit for a few minutes?" He gestured to a nearby stone bench.

I shook my head, my brow furrowing. "Hills is waiting for us, and—"

"I'll let Hills know to expect us in an hour," Garath said, guiding me toward the bench. "She'll understand."

I leaned on him more and more with each step, so much so that I didn't argue further. Gratefully, I sank to the bench and released a relieved sigh as I relaxed against the hard backrest.

Garath stepped in front of me, fists on his hips, his broad form blocking the sun. "You didn't touch the food at the picnic. When was the last time you ate anything?"

I shrugged weakly. "I don't know," I said, and I meant it. I honestly couldn't remember the last thing I ate. Maybe a scone at breakfast? Or had that been the previous morning?

"Del . . . " Garath reached out, tipping my chin upward with gentle fingers. "You spend so much time worrying about Liam and the kingdom—everyone but yourself. You need to take care of yourself, too. Without you, there is no more Corvo Kingdom."

My chest shook with a weak, defeated laugh. "That's not true, and you know it."

"It *is* true," he countered. "You are the future of this kingdom. I know it to be true, as did your mother. Regardless of your bloodline, *you* are the queen we need *right now*."

"And if you're wrong?" I asked, raising my eyebrows.

Garath pulled his hand back and flashed me a roguish smile. "I'm never wrong."

21

FIN

I dreamed of grit and sand and my hovel in the stones. Of burnt orange sunrises and the arid desert wind that sent both a wave of heat and chills over my skin in a single gust. I dreamed of familiar faces. Some were smiling, some were streaked with tears, but all looked to my team to save them from the enemy —an army driven by a prophecy that, for all I knew, might be their doom.

And just like most nights back home, I woke in a rush of anxious breaths and night sweats, my heart pounding and my head full of worry.

I blinked into the dawn pouring through the windows onto my goose-down bed. Tick whimpered at my bedside, her head tilted as she watched me, waiting for the haze of night to drift away.

"I'm all right," I rasped, scratching under her chin. My throat was as dry as the desert, and I took a sip from the water on my bedside table. "I'm all right," I murmured again. I gripped my forehead, exhaled a deep, grounding breath, and reminded myself where I was: the castle.

Tick licked my hand reassuringly, and I sat up, the bed

creaking under my weight, though it felt like I was lying on clouds. It was so foreign, I'd had a difficult time falling asleep.

I peered around my guest room. It wasn't a suite, like Callon and Lyra's, but it was grand all the same. A single room with a luxurious bed big enough for two, a hearth devoid of flame because it wasn't cold enough for a fire, and a stately—empty—chest of drawers. I'd pulled off my clothes before bed and discarded them on the floor. I hadn't come to Corvo planning on staying as a guest in the castle, and I looked as out of place as I felt.

As predictable as ever, the door to my room flung open and Callon strode in. "Oh, good!" he sang. "Lyra said you were awake."

I groaned and fell back against my pillow. "Don't you ever sleep?" I groaned and scrubbed my hands over my face.

"Aye. I've never slept like such a baby, actually," he mused, picking a grape from the fruit bowl on the table. He plopped it into his mouth. "And now, I'm hungry. And you, sir, haven't eaten since your picnic yesterday, so it's time to get some breakfast in ya. Plus, I don't like to eat alone."

"Since when?"

"Since Lyra threw me out of our suite." He nodded to the rooms next door. "She said she refused to spend another morning alone with me and that I should come bother you."

"Of course she did." Ever his chipper self, Callon smirked and tossed another grape into the air, catching it in his mouth.

A servant hustled down the hall, which meant the castle was already awake. "Do I at least get some privacy?" I said, motioning to the open door.

"That depends." The grape popped between his teeth. "Are you going back to sleep the moment I step outside and close the door?" Callon crossed his arms over his chest, his arms flexing as he settled in to wait for my answer.

"As if that were an option," I muttered.

Callon nodded. "Touché."

Yawning, I sat up and ran my fingers through my mop of hair.

"You need a woman, Cal," I said, flinging the covers back. And then it dawned on me. "*That's* why you're so . . . awake." I bent down and snagged my pants from the floor.

"What do you mean? I'm always like this in the morning."

"Annoying? Yes, I know." The ground was cool under my feet as I tugged my trousers on.

"No," he deadpanned. "It's called being *chipper*, but I know you're unfamiliar with the term. I'm sure Del has a dictionary of some sort in this palace," he said, making a show of looking around for one. "I can look up the term and define it for you, if you'd like?"

I ignored him and smiled. "You want to see Ada at breakfast," I drawled ruefully.

"This has nothing to do with *Ada*—"

"Yes, it does!" Lyra called, her voice drifting down the hallway.

"I figured," I said with a chuckle, enjoying Callon's stuttering response as he tried to deny it. But as Del, Hills, and her coronation liaison walked past my room, our laughter faded, and my easiness all but vanished.

Del paused, her eyes meeting mine as I snagged my shirt off the floor.

"Good morning, Your Highness," Callon said, turning to face her. He bowed his head.

Del smiled, if a bit weakly, as she tore her gaze from me and looked at him. "Good morning, Callon." But her eyes quickly met mine again. "Good morning, Fin."

"Good morning," I said, tugging my shirt over my head. Despite having my pants on, I felt strangely naked, rumpled in my bare feet.

Del uttered something to her companions, and leaving them to wait for her farther down the hall, she stepped into the doorway. "I trust you all slept well?" She looked at Callon. "Your suite is comfortable?"

Callon nodded. "It's perfect. I was able to shut Lyra's door when she started snoring."

I could practically hear Lyra rolling her eyes from the other room.

Del smiled despite herself. "I'm glad." She fingered the parchment in her hand as she glanced around my room, but there was nothing to see. Nothing in it was mine, save for the boots discarded at the end of the bed and jacket draped over one of the chairs.

She looked at me, taking in my attire. "I'll—uh—send someone in with fresh clothes for you while yours are laundered. I'm sorry, I hadn't thought of it until now."

This stiltedness between us was foreign to me, yet it felt apt after all that had happened and all the time we'd been apart.

I cleared my throat. "You've got enough to worry about," I said and waved her concern away.

"I'll send someone," she insisted, more adamant this time. "And there's breakfast in the dining room if you're hungry." With another tight-lipped smile, Del turned to leave.

"Thank you, Your Highness," Callon said with another slight bow. Del glanced back at him, another look of uncertainty in her expression before she joined her companions.

Something was wrong, though it wasn't the time to ask. Nor was I certain it was my place. So, I glared at Callon because it was easier.

He shrugged. "What?"

"Why do you always make it weird?"

He blanched. "Weird? How? She *is* the queen regent. She's being crowned tomorrow. I'm not about to get on her bad side."

I rolled my eyes. "Just give me a minute, would you?"

Palms up in surrender, Callon muttered his acquiescence and stepped outside.

"And close the door," I called.

"As you wish, *sir*," he called back, shutting the door behind him.

I stared at it for the longest time. Is this how it would be between Del and me? This uncomfortable tension between us? It felt like we were strangers, and yet we had a son together.

The answer was yes. Of course, it would be like this. In a day, she would be the queen of an entire kingdom. And who the hell was I?

Getting a grip on myself, I washed my face and cleaned my teeth with what had been left for me at the wash bin, then Tick and I joined Callon and Lyra in the hall of portraits.

Though animal companions were allowed at most taverns because of Telepaths like me, I never brought Tick into any town or establishment, too worried that if something happened to me, she'd be at someone else's mercy. But here in the castle, where Liam was an animal Telepath protected by the most well-honed Ability wielders and trained guards in the kingdom, I hadn't thought twice about having Tick by my side.

She trotted around, sniffing corners and exploring as we meandered one side of the grand hall. Light poured through the windows on the other side, illuminating the portraits of queens and princesses that glinted in their gilded frames along the wall. My eyes lingered on only one, though. Princess Delphinia, donning a black and crimson gown fit for a queen. As striking as she looked, she didn't look like . . . Del. She looked stoic and uncomfortable, not expressive and fiery, like the girl I used to know.

"You'd think the royal family could have found *something* to smile about over the centuries," Callon muttered as we made our way through the room.

"You think they should all be smiling buffoons like you?" Lyra tossed his way, and Callon's exaggerated smile widened.

"Couldn't hurt," he countered. "It might liven the place up a bit." They continued to banter until we got to a grand staircase, then Callon jogged down the steps and took the lead.

"You know where the dining room is?" I clarified. Having never eaten a sanctioned meal in the castle before, I had no idea.

Callon winked. "I already scoped the place out."

Lyra and I looked at one another. His predictability was too entertaining not to hedge a slight smile.

As we made our way down another corridor, it registered that I'd walked the halls of Castle Corvo a time or two, but it had always been in the dead of night, scurrying between one secret passage in the wall to another. Being in the castle in the daylight, without having to hide in the shadows, felt surreal, like even now I was doing something nefarious.

Don't get used to it, I reminded myself, because I wasn't staying. While I was basking in my time with Liam, all was not well back home. Plus, I had a prophecy to avert and King Eduart's army to stop, even if I didn't know how I was going to do it or when Eduart would make his move.

"When do we meet up with Stone again?" I asked.

Callon sobered, looking at Lyra. "Tomorrow, at the docks," he said. "Midnight."

"He swore he'd be there," Lyra added, but she seemed hesitant to believe it.

"Good," I said quietly, taking a deep breath. "Too much time is passing. It's making me anxious."

"Aye, same." Callon ran his hand up the back of his head. "Is it weird to say I trust Stone, though?"

"Yes," Lyra muttered as I said, "No."

Her head whipped to me. "You trust him?" Lyra scoffed, shoving her hands into her back pockets. "That's surprising."

"Perhaps trust isn't the right word," Callon mused.

"He's predictable," I amended. "He wants his secrets kept and to collect the coin he's been promised. He'll do whatever he can to earn both. *That* is what I trust."

Lyra lifted her chin in understanding.

I was about to tell her she'd get the hang of making deals with the underbelly of society when my eyes lingered on a painting of the Patrons circled around the Patron Tree. Jake was among them. Though it was only his back, it was obviously him, holding hands with raven-haired Zoe.

Lyra, Callon, and I exchanged an uneasy look. "It's so weird seeing paintings of him around the castle," Lyra said.

"You have no idea," I muttered, and as we continued walking, I felt Liam's mind.

Hearing his footsteps coming down the hall behind us, I looked over my shoulder to find he and Ada were heading to breakfast, too. I smiled. "Good morning," I said, my voice carrying through the corridor.

A smile lit Liam's face as he jogged closer. His raven ruffled as she bounced on his shoulder, but she was probably used to it. Liam's hair was damp, as if Ada had run a wet comb through it, and he was dressed in his princely clothes—a fresh, tailored tunic and pants—ready for the day.

"Morning," Liam answered and fell into step beside me. Our fists pounded lightly in greeting. After our game of keep-away yesterday, it officially became our high-five, hello, and goodbye gesture. That it made Liam smile, chased any anxieties I'd woken up with away.

Liam scratched Tick on the top of the head, and I watched as the coyote and raven eyed one another with cocked heads and curiosity. It wasn't the first time they'd met, but I figured they were coming to some sort of mutual agreement that they would be seeing a lot of each other moving forward.

"Good morning," Ada said when she finally caught up, her eyes meeting mine quickly before a shy smile curved her lips. Callon held out his arm to escort her onward, and Lyra, Liam, and I continued down the hall.

"You look well rested, Your Highness," Lyra said, and her eyes sparkled as she smiled at Liam. They'd formed a kinship teasing Callon yesterday, and it made my heart happy to see Lyra smiling more around him. She was always so closed off, though I understood why. And if I had to venture a guess, I would say she took a shining to Liam because he was the same age her brother would be now, had he survived the slaver attack when her family had fled the Crescent Kingdom.

"How did you sleep?" I asked him, wishing I had as much pep in my step as he did this morning. My muscles ached a little from all of our running, jumping, and tumbling yesterday.

"Really good," he said, absently stroking Nyx's feathered breast with the crook of his finger.

I grinned. "I thought you might."

"Yesterday was really fun," he said, green eyes brightening. "Can we play again?"

I glanced at Ada for confirmation, but she was chatting with Callon, oblivious.

"We'll see what your mother says," I told him. I didn't want to step on Del's toes and upend their routines more than I already had since arriving. "I'm sure you have lessons or something you can't neglect. But definitely afterward," I promised.

That seemed to appease him as we neared a set of double doors. "Are you coming this way for breakfast?"

I snorted a laugh. "Of course. Callon would never let me hear the end of it if we missed a meal."

Liam was familiar enough with Callon by now to know he was always hungry. "Good." He leaned in conspiratorially. "Don't eat the blood pudding, though," he told me. "It's disgusting."

"Noted," I said with a chuckle. A bundle of barely restrained excitement, he leaped for the double doors and hauled one open. I grabbed the top to help him, and we stepped into the dining room.

"Oh, my Patrons. I'm salivating," Callon said behind us as the scent of maple ham filled the air.

"I hear the blood pudding is delicious," I told him, giving Liam a wink. His shoulders shuddered with a laugh, and we shared a secret smile.

Glancing around, the dining room was as I'd expected it would be. It was sumptuous, with mirrors and more gilt framed paintings lining the walls. Wrought iron sconces were mounted between them to match the chandelier that must have held three dozen bulbs hanging over the center of a long oak table.

Del stood at the coffee bar on the other side of the room, talking with Garath as she poured them both a cup of tea from the pot.

"Is he ever *not* around?" Callon whispered in my ear. "I mean, he's nice enough to look at, but really, Fin. I'm beginning to think you have some competition here."

I wanted to tell Callon it didn't matter. I wasn't here to woo Del, yet, I couldn't deny the way my stomach fell a little whenever I saw them together. "None of this is easy," I said instead. "For any of us. As long as she's safe, that's all that matters."

"Aye," he agreed and took a step back, but the sympathetic look on my friend's face lingered before he finally walked toward the buffet. I knew Callon was worried about me after all that had happened and all that I'd learned since returning. And I couldn't fault him for that.

"Down here!" Liam called, pulling out a chair for me by his mother. "You can sit with us."

For now, there was nothing for Callon to worry about unless it was my having to leave Liam behind one day soon and the affect it would have on me. Even if it was just temporarily.

For today, though, I would relish my first official breakfast with my son.

22

DEL

I stood concealed by shadows in the doorway to the balcony and watched the throne room fill. My lungs strained against the constriction of my bodice, and the blood seemed to hum in my veins. My stomach had been tied in a perpetual knot for days. I didn't want this. I didn't want to be queen.

Liam stood with Hills and Pythia Salma on the dais at the front of the throne room, Nyx perched on his shoulder. The head of the Oracle Class had always been the highest religious authority in the Seven Kingdoms. As such, Pythia Salma was the one who would guide the coronation ceremony.

Ada, Fin, Lyra, and Callon stood in the front row of the growing audience, the latter three dressed as members of my personal guard. Dozens more castle guards cut an aisle through the center of the crowd, lining my pathway to the Corvo crown, the wreath of delicate silver branches and black diamonds resting on the seat of the throne. A gleaming silver raven stand stood to the right of the throne, and a polished black granite pillar was placed to the left, proudly displaying the multicolored vernal votive.

Everything was in place.

I smoothed down the front of my coronation gown. Tiny black feathers covered the entire dress, soft against my fingertips.

Sid rustled his wings on my shoulder, his talons clacking against the silver filigree decorating the black leather pauldrons.

Ada had helped me tame my curls into an intricately braided knot at the base of my skull, leaving room for the Corvo crown atop my head. My fingers itched to yank out the pins and free my hair. Now that the coronation was imminent, I wanted nothing more than to tear off this gown and run. To take Liam from this place that had only ever offered either of us lies and torment disguised as luxury and power.

"It's time," Garath said, his voice a hushed rumble in the dark corridor behind me.

I stepped back from the doorway and turned to face him, wringing my hands. "Is this a mistake?" I asked, my brows bunching together as I studied his stony features, the angles of his face sharpened by the deep shadows.

Garath's expression softened. "You already know what I think," he said, hesitating for a moment before adding, "I pledged my life to *you*, Del, not your position, so stay or go, rule or run, I will be at your side."

I swallowed the rising emotion swelling up from my chest and nodded mutely. And then I stepped past him and started down the corridor, making my way toward the stairs that led to the arched doorway of the throne room.

At least I could be certain no Empaths could sense my unsteady emotions, my wavering resolve. Fin and Ada were just two of the many Gauges stationed strategically throughout the castle to ensure a seamless nulling field suppressed the gifts of every attendee, regardless of Class or strength.

I felt as though I were floating through a dream as I glided toward the entrance to the throne room. Copper light from the setting sun poured in through the huge stained-glass window filling the top half of the wall behind the throne's dais.

I stopped in the doorway, and a hush fell over the buzzing crowd. All eyes were on me. There was no turning back now.

With a caw, Sid launched himself from my shoulder and swooped under the vaulted ceiling toward the empty raven stand awaiting him on the dais.

As I took my first step into the room, a lone drumbeat began. By my fourth step, a second drum joined in. By my eighth, two more merged seamlessly into the processional beat, forming a primal rhythm. As I approached the dais, more drummers joined in, filling the throne room with their pulsing tempo. And as I ascended the three steps to the throne, the chorus of drums reached a crescendo.

And then the drummers stopped, silence ringing throughout the room.

Breaths were held. Anticipation filled the space, the crowd generating palpable energy. My people. Their expectation, excitement, and hope all rested on my shoulders.

I stood in front of Pythia Salma, my heart hammering, my knees unsteady.

Pythia Salma reached out her hands, palms up. When I didn't move, she offered me a slight but encouraging smile.

Taking a shaky breath, I placed my hands in hers. Her grip was cool and steady, reassuring, and her trained mind was a vault, sealed shut against me.

"Princess Delphinia," she said, her resonant voice echoing through the cavernous space. "You have come to ask the Patrons' blessing on your claim to the Corvo throne. Do you truly believe you are worthy to wear the crown?"

Despite the verbiage being tradition, her question cut deep, and I hesitated before answering.

A faint crease appeared between the Pythia's brows, and she squeezed my hands gently.

I cleared my throat and straightened my spine. "I do."

"I do *not*," a familiar, weaselly voice said from the far end of the throne room.

The crowd gasped, and there was a rustle of clothing and shuffling feet as everyone, myself included, turned to see the man who had interrupted the ceremony.

Maylar stood in the doorway to the throne room, his pinched features more heavily lined than they had been when I last saw him a little over nine years ago, but the cruel glint in his eyes was exactly the same.

"Princess Delphinia is unfit to sit on the Corvo throne," Maylar said, his heels clicking on the granite floor as he strode up the aisle.

Mother had known his true nature. He was like a cancer to this kingdom. So long as there was breath in his body, he would always come back to wreak havoc within our borders. No wonder she had ordered the hit on him. Too bad she had failed.

Two more, larger figures darkened the doorway behind Maylar, following him into the throne room. They appeared to be father and son, both tall and lanky, with dark hair and rich brown skin. Their steps formed an arrhythmic beat as they made their way to the dais.

I heard a name whispered through the crowd: *Reyes*. That had been Father's name. Except, as I now knew, he wasn't my father after all.

I kept my expression guarded as I studied the face of Maylar's older companion. I had been too young to remember Mother's consort when he had supposedly died, but there were portraits of him scattered around the castle, and even I could see the resemblance between this man and the one I was told was my father.

Garath shifted to stand in front of me on the steps, shielding me with his body, and Fin eased away from the front row, sliding into place in front of Liam. Lyra, Callon, Ada, the guards—everyone armed—had a hand on their weapon and were ready to draw.

"What are you doing here, *Maylar*?" I hissed, moving out from behind Garath.

Maylar stopped shy of reaching the bottom step, his mysterious entourage of two flanking him. His stare locked with mine, his mouth twisting into a sneer, and then he turned his back to me, ignoring me completely. The younger of his companions caught my eye, his lip curling haughtily.

My stomach lurched. Such contempt. Such masculine intimidation. How many times had I seen a nearly identical expression on Alastor's face? This man looked nothing like my dead husband, but he exuded the same sense of entitlement and oppressive dominance.

"*Princess* Delphinia is unfit to sit on the Corvo throne," Maylar repeated, his voice booming. "Because she is *not* a princess at all."

My heart skipped a beat.

"She is not even of the Corvo line," Maylar continued. "Queen Corisande was unable to bear a female heir who survived to adulthood. Not even the venerated Corvo line has been spared from the worst effects of the cursed wasting sickness plaguing our kingdom."

My breaths came faster, and I pressed my palm to my stomach. *How* did he know?

I swallowed my panic, pushing away the irrational thoughts.

Of course, he knew. He had assisted Mother in acquiring the infants. In acquiring *me*.

"*Delphinia* was born to a poor, mixed-Class family from the southern village of Monterey," Maylar went on. "She is not elevated by blood but by luck and circumstance. She is *no true Corvo heir*."

Garath backed up a step and gripped my upper arm. "We need to get you out of here," he murmured, angling his face toward me but not taking his eyes off the newcomers.

A quick glance over my shoulder told me Fin was already hustling Liam away, Callon, Lyra, and Ada alongside him. Hills descended the stairs to stand defensively at the bottom, another body between the intruders and me. Only Pythia Salma remained on the dais, and the enraged stare she cast in Maylar's direction made me think she had already been aware of all of this.

"How?" I asked Garath, my jaw clenched and lips barely moving. "Everyone is watching us."

"*But,*" Maylar exclaimed, gesturing toward the younger of his companions with a confident sweep of his arm. "Queen Corisande *did* bear a healthy *male* child who lived to adulthood." Maylar pushed his bony shoulders back, reminding me of a preening bird. "I present to you, Prince Nolan, son of Queen Corisande, and her banished consort—" He swept his hand toward the older man. "—High Lord Reyes."

Tense silence filled the throne room. None dared to speak.

"I recognize many faces in this crowd," Reyes said, nodding to a few people. "You know me. Queen Corisande attempted to have me assassinated for daring to disagree with her plot to deceive you. I barely escaped the city with our young son, Nolan, the last remaining descendant of the Corvo bloodline and your true king."

Whispers exploded throughout the throne room.

"Blasphemy!" Salma declared, stepping to stand beside me at the edge of the dais. "The Corvo Kingdom has *never* had a king."

There was a *twang* followed by a *hiss*, and an arrow struck the vernal votive close behind Salma, impaling the thick, multicolored candle and sending it flying off the stand.

Salma gasped, her eyes wide, and she touched her hand to the side of her neck. Her fingertips came away red. The arrow had just nicked her skin.

The throne room filled with a suffocating quiet.

"The next one goes in your throat," Nolan told her matter-of-factly, turning his back to the crowd and climbing the dais. He stopped one step below the platform.

I stood my ground, refusing to back down to this usurper,

Mother's *supposed* son. Garath sidestepped, angling his shoulder between us.

"You can still be queen," Nolan said, his voice cast so low that it only reached my ears—and Garath's. The corner of Nolan's mouth twitched. "*If* you become my wife. You have the people's love— their loyalty. I could use that." His eyes narrowed to wicked, challenging slits. "Or, you can be charged with murdering the queen —*my* mother—by withholding the healing elixir from her, and you will be publicly executed." His lips curved into a sly smile. "The choice is yours."

Throughout the audience, attendees shed their colorful equinox tunics and robes, revealing pale-gray leather armor emblazoned with the crest of a black circle surrounding a single black feather, no doubt symbolizing the lone member of the Corvo royal bloodline. And he was the man standing before me threatening to take my life.

Maylar and his pet heir had quietly packed the throne room with their supporters. They outnumbered my guards two to one, at least. If they were here in the throne room, I had little doubt they had also infiltrated the rest of the castle and were tracking down as many of the Gauges as they could to bring down the nulling field suppressing everyone's gifts.

My mind raced, flipping through all the options. I could run, but then Maylar and the usurper's clearly formidable manpower would be focused on a manhunt. They would likely track me down and capture me. They would capture Liam as well.

I could surrender. I could let them imprison me. I could give up, comforted by the hope that Fin had escorted Liam out of the city. That he would take Liam far away from here, where he could live a full, *free* life. I might never get to see him grow up, but at least he *would* grow up.

Or, I could agree—for now—to be this man's queen. My chest clenched at the idea of willingly stepping back into the cage from which I had only just escaped because there wasn't a doubt in my mind that Nolan was the same kind of man as Alastor. Intolerant. Tyrannical. Cruel.

Between the wasting sickness and the increasing threat from the Sierra Kingdom, the Corvo people had already suffered so much. I wasn't fool enough to believe I would have any sway over the new Corvo king as his queen. I would be a prisoner as surely as if I had been thrown in the Tower of Solitude, but the possibility that I could potentially influence policy, no matter how minutely, left me with no choice.

I balled my hands into fists and held my head high. "I will be your wife."

Nolan's cheeks tensed with a smile that didn't touch his eyes. "Command your people to stand down. I would hate to spoil this joyous occasion with bloodshed."

I swallowed roughly and caught Garath's eye. "Take the guards and leave," I commanded.

Garath set his jaw, standing a little straighter. "I will not—"

"Take the guards and leave *now*," I repeated, my voice harder and razor edged.

His throat bobbed, his eyes filling with a plea to not make him do this. To not make him leave me.

Finally, he turned and barked a command to the guards lining the aisle and posted around the edges of the throne room. They hesitated—only for a moment, but long enough to prove to all here that I truly held their loyalty. I hoped Garath could get them across the moat and beyond the outer walls before Maylar realized his mistake in letting them live.

I waited until Garath and Hills followed the last guards out of the throne room. Garath paused in the doorway, turning partway and holding my stare for a long moment before continuing on his way.

I returned my attention to Nolan. "There," I said coolly. "It is done."

Maylar weaseled closer to Nolan, hands wringing, and cleared his throat. "I would not trust her, my king. Her last husband suffered an unfortunate accident within these very castle walls, and she *is* responsible for your mother's death. I fear your fate will be similar should she be allowed to walk free."

Nolan's eyes narrowed on me. "Are you the black widow Maylar believes you to be?" he murmured. "Is your value worth the risk?" He stared at me for a long time, but finally, he glanced at one of the gray-armored soldiers who had made his way into the aisle. "Lock her up in the tower."

I stared in shock but refused to react as the soldier approached. He quickly secured handcuffs around my wrists and, grip firm on my arm, tugged me down the dais stairs.

"You're a snake, Maylar," I hissed, digging in my heels as I passed him. "Soon enough, everyone will see you for what you really are—poison to this kingdom—and they will *finally* end you."

A muscle under Maylar's eye twitched, and he inhaled to respond.

Before he could get a word out, I spat on his pinched face.

"Get her out of here," Nolan barked.

"He's been working with the Sierra Kingdom!" I shouted to Nolan as I was yanked away. "He's been feeding Eduart state secrets. He wants this kingdom to fall. You *can't* trust him!"

My only consolation was that I could see the fear in Maylar's eyes as Nolan turned to face him a moment before I was dragged through the doorway and away from the throne room. Away from the crown.

As it turned out, I wouldn't have to be queen after all.

23

FIN

T he sky was a darkening blue as Callon, Lyra, Liam, and I followed Ada through the garden, getting as far away from the throne room as we could to regroup without leaving the castle walls and Del behind. Though it went unsaid, none of us were willing to leave the compound until we understood what was going to happen to Del.

Unsure which Ability-amped minds might have zeroed-in on us, Ada and I continued to null outsiders who would be looking for us, or more specifically, looking for the prince.

As fast as we needed to move to get Liam to safety, I had to stop frequently so I could use Sid and Nyx to see what was happening in the throne room after we fled.

"They're taking Del to the tower," I rasped so only Lyra could hear. She looked at me, as concerned as I was at the sound of that. "She sent Garath away, and now she is their prisoner."

As the others disappeared through a dense wall of juniper, we ran to catch up. Lyra and I popped out into a hidden gardening corner with an array of discarded tools scattered around a large shed. Huddled in the center of the cobblestone, we all seemed to take a collective breath.

Liam was trembling, and I rested my hand on his shoulder and pulled him into me. "It's okay," I breathed. "It will be okay."

Lyra looked at Ada. "What the hell happened in there?"

I ran my free hand through my hair, grappling with how very, very wrong this was. I knew something had been bothering Del, and now I couldn't help but wonder if she'd known Maylar was close and had said nothing. Had Garath known? Were they aware she wasn't really the princess? I had no idea if there was any truth to it, but my gut told me Del wasn't completely surprised by Maylar's claims.

"So, Del *isn't* the princess?" Lyra clarified.

Ada paced. "I—I don't know," she said shakily. I knew she was as well-trained to fight as Del was, but dressed in her black and silver procession gown, Ada looked more like a maiden than a warrior. "I mean, yes, Del's the princess. But—" She shook her head. "I don't know what's happening. I should've stayed in there with Garath and Hills—"

"Why?" Callon said softly, his eyes locking with hers. "So you could be locked in the tower with her?" He spoke quietly, his gaze shifting to Liam as he shook his head. "You know Del would want you to stay with the prince."

The rising moon illuminated the tears in Liam's eyes. "My mother—"

"Will be fine," I promised, bending down to him. "We'll make sure of it." I peered into his wide, worried gaze. Aptly, Nyx flew over the garden walls, landing deftly on Liam's shoulder. "I saw where the guards took her," I told him. "She is not hurt, and you know Garath won't let anything happen to her. *I* won't let anything happen." I gently squeezed his shoulders.

Liam searched my face for certainty, or perhaps it was for a sliver of doubt. Whatever he found, he seemed to relax ever so slightly. But I could feel his confusion and fear as much as I could see it on his crumpled face, and I looked at Lyra. Her hands rested on her hips as she paced, each step coiled with battle-ready adrenaline.

When she met my gaze, I nodded to my son. "Hey, Liam, why don't you sit with Lyra for a minute, okay? Let me talk with Ada and Callon, and we'll get it sorted."

Liam hesitated, his chin trembling until, finally, he straightened a little, nodded, and let Lyra guide him to a stack of burlap sacks against the shed.

I turned to Ada and Callon, and he inhaled a deep breath. "Maylar seems . . . fun," he muttered. "I guess we don't need Stone anymore."

"We might," I told him and looked at Ada. "Will Garath know where to—"

I heard the rush of footsteps, and my head snapped to Lyra. "Hills and Garath," she supplied, and I realized Garath had likely used Nyx to find us.

Before I could ask Lyra if anyone else was with them, Garath and Hills rushed into the clearing. Alone. I'd never been happier to see Del's guard, and Liam wasted no time running into Garath's arms. The sight was endearing, even if it stung a little.

"They're taking her to the tower," I told them, knowing Garath had already left the throne room when Nolan turned on her.

He glared toward the castle as Lyra came to collect Liam again. "I would expect nothing less from Maylar." Garath's jaw clenched, and he shook his head. He was the epitome of calm, but I knew his mind and heart were racing. They had to be. Del wasn't at his side. He could not protect her like this.

"What don't we know?" I demanded. My focus, accusatory as it was, shifted between him and Hills. "Was that guy for real?"

Garath was expressionless, which meant he knew exactly what was going on. He knew the truth about Del. And by the lack of surprise on Hills's face, she did too.

Ada gasped. "You both knew?" she whispered. I wasn't sure if it was only shock in her voice or if there was hurt too.

"Only recently. Del has had little time to process it." Hills shook her head, vehement, and held up her hand. "But none of that matters now. We need to get Del out of that tower. Nolan and Reyes are just pawns in this. There's no telling what schemes Maylar still has to play." Breath ragged, she looked from Garath to me. "And whatever Del thought she was protecting by agreeing to marry Nolan is for naught," she said more quietly.

Garath nodded, but my hands fisted at my sides. Once again, Del was willing to sacrifice herself—to marry another monster—for a kingdom I wasn't sure deserved her.

"Del's the princess of Corvo. No matter her bloodline, the people love her. She's far too dangerous for them to keep her alive."

"Lucky for us," Hills offered, "I saw the way Nolan was looking at her. It will take some convincing on Maylar's part to kill her, which buys us a little time."

"Very little," Garath echoed.

I glanced over at Liam as Lyra did her best to distract him, chatting about his raven and how she'd never had an animal friend of her own.

"Which is why we need to get into the tower," Ada said, and as her lips pursed, I could tell a plan was forming. "Garath knows it inside and out, and if I can get in, I can amplify Del's Ability so that she can sneak out the same way she used to sneak *in*."

I nodded, glad they had a plan because I felt lost and useless when it came to the inner workings of the castle. "I don't know the tower, but I have a way out of the city. If you can get Del, I can get her and Liam away from this place," I told them.

"How?" Garath asked, and I wasn't sure if it was distrust in his voice as much as fear.

"We have a man waiting for us at the docks," Callon offered.

"And once we're away from the city," I said, "I can take her home with me." I looked Garath in the eyes, promising him. "I can protect her there."

His jaw tightened again, this time in consideration. "And this man you know at the docks?"

"We were supposed to meet him at midnight to exchange information about Maylar," Callon explained. He looked at me, both of us fully aware of how poorly that panned out.

"Information about Maylar? That worked out well," Hills muttered with exasperation. "Are you sure this man of yours is even still alive?"

I nodded. "Stone is one of the slipperiest men I know. He's alive."

"Ethan Stone?" she said, and when I nodded again, she narrowed her eyes in consideration. "I knew him—once. If he *is* there, are you sure he can be trusted?"

"We don't have much choice at this point," I retorted. "But yes, I trust him. He's not in on this scheme any more than I am. He fought two wars for this kingdom as a captain in Her Majesty's Royal Navy and was cast aside when his nightmares got too bad and they deemed him useless. Needless to say, he hates the aristocracy—doesn't trust any of them. He would *never* help Maylar or those other two." Of that, I was certain.

"But would he help Del?" Garath asked, his voice thick with unease.

I'd wondered the same thing. "He will," I said, "if there's something in it for him."

"Which would be what, exactly?" Callon asked.

I glanced at Ada, Callon, Garath, and Hills, all of them staring at me, waiting for an answer. "Let me worry about that. And," I added, "if his ship is not at the docks, I'll commandeer one myself and get us the hell out of here."

Garath seemed appeased by that idea, knowing he had few other options at this point.

"And you're sure you can get into the tower?" I clarified, knowing this was all for nothing if they couldn't get Del out.

Garath's gaze snapped to Ada.

"Yes, we can get her out of the tower," she said, though her tone was far more confident than she looked. Ada and Garath exchanged a few drawn-out moments of silent understanding, as if they knew what needed to be done.

Finally, Garath looked at Callon, then at me. "But if something happens," he added, a grave, reluctant expression darkening his features, "if we're not at the docks by dawn, you get Liam out of here—get him to safety."

"You know I will," I said without hesitation.

"Hills," Garath continued without skipping a beat. He was back in planning mode.

She was already looking at him, a grim expression on her face, like she knew what he was going to say. "Go with Fin into the city. Gather as many loyalists as you can find. We are the resistance, and Del will be queen. We need to work quickly and quietly to maintain our foothold in the city."

"Long live the queen," she said with a nod, but they stared at one another, a few silent moments passing between them.

"We have to hurry," Ada urged.

With a final nod, Hills glanced between Del's most loyal lady's maid and her fiercest protector. "Be careful. Both of you."

Ada squeezed Hills's hand. "You as well."

Garath watched Liam and Lyra at the gardening shed for a moment, then looked at me. "We'll meet you at the docks as soon as we can."

I nodded in promise. "We'll be waiting."

With a final, silent *good luck* exchanged between us, Garath and Ada disappeared through the juniper to rescue their uncrowned queen.

As I peered up at the tower in the distance, an idea formed.

24

DEL

I stared at the electrified bars holding me prisoner. I hadn't been inside the Tower of Solitude since Jake was held prisoner here all those years ago, and at that time, *he* had been the one in the cage. Now, it was me sitting on this cot, forlornly reflecting on the events that had led to me being here, fretting about my loved ones.

Sid hopped closer to my perch on the edge of the cot and nuzzled his beak against the back of my hand. I raised my index finger, and he nipped gingerly at the back of my bent knuckle.

"You don't have to stay with me," I murmured, knowing full well the raven couldn't understand me, not like he would have been able to with Liam, Garath, or Fin.

Sid shook his head suddenly and rustled his wings, then cawed, "Tough stuff!"

I pulled my hand away, cocked my head to the side, and narrowed my eyes. As a raven, Sid could mimic human speech. I had taught him every word and phrase he knew, and I definitely hadn't taught him to say *tough stuff*. In fact, I hadn't heard *anyone* say that since . . . Since Fin called me *tough stuff* during our adventures together a decade ago. It had been his nickname for me when he believed me to be merely a castle servant out running an errand for her masters.

"Fin?" I breathed, glancing at the usurper's guard in pale-gray leathers standing at the glassless window beyond the electrified bars of my cell. The gap between the bars was just large enough for Sid to have threaded without frying his feathers.

The guard was an Elemental, his presence keeping the bars of my cage electrified. I wasn't sure what he found so fascinating about the view of the moonlit castle, but at the moment, I didn't really care, so long as his attention wasn't focused on me or Sid, and the man I suspected was attempting to communicate with me through the raven.

I hunched my back, leaning closer to Sid, and searched his beady black eyes. "Is that you, Fin?"

The raven cawed again, bobbing his beak up and down.

The guard glanced my way.

Tears welling in my eyes, I slid off the cot to kneel before Sid—Fin—the stiff, feathered skirt of my coronation gown mounding up around me. I touched my index finger to my lips, signaling for him to remain nonverbal, before folding my hands together on the cot like I was praying.

"Liam?" I whispered. "Is he with you? Did you all get out?"

Again, the raven's head bobbed in what I assumed was assent, and he hopped back and forth on the edge of the cot.

A sob burst from my chest, and I clapped my hands over my mouth. "Oh, thank the Patrons," I mouthed. I sucked in a shuddering breath and sniffled, hastily wiping under my eyes. "Whatever happens to me, you have to protect him." I leaned in closer, and the raven cocked his head to the side, watching me through one eye. "Promise me, Fin. Promise me you'll keep him safe."

He bobbed his head again, then hopped closer, resting the side of his feathered face against my cheek.

I squeezed my eyes shut and bowed my head, my face screwing up as tears streamed down my cheeks.

The clang of metal echoed up the winding stone stairway, and my head snapped up. Someone was unlocking the door at the base of the tower.

The Elemental turned away from the window and strode over to the stairs as the screech of hinges in need of greasing announced that the door was now open.

I stood slowly and faced the stair landing, my hands gripping the heavy skirt of my gown.

"What does *she* want?" the Elemental barked down to whoever had opened the door, hands planted on his hips.

"She has a change of clothes for the prisoner," another man called up the stairs. "She worked in the castle and wants to put the impostor in her place—to make her look like the commoner she truly is."

"Did you search her?" the Elemental asked.

"Fuck you, Brax."

The Elemental let out a cruel chuckle, glanced back at me over his shoulder, and sneered. "You ready to strip down, sweetheart?" He smirked. "Give us a little show?"

I didn't respond. I didn't even react with a change in my expression. I merely stared at him, imagining all the ways I could kill him.

His lip curled. "Bitch," he muttered and turned away from me once more. "Send her up. I'm going to enjoy this." He backed away from the landing at the top of the stairs just enough to let the newcomer pass.

I nearly sagged with relief when I saw who it was. Ada. Her pale hair gleamed like spun silver in the moonlight streaming through the tower windows.

The Elemental followed close behind Ada as she approached the bars of my cell, a packed leather satchel strung across her body. Her gaze roved over me like she was searching for injuries, but all of my wounds were the invisible kind.

"What are you doing here?" I asked, careful to keep my voice cool, my expression stony. We weren't supposed to be friends. Inside, adrenaline surged, making my blood feel like it was humming in my veins.

Ada flashed me a tight-lipped smile, side-eyeing the guard lurking behind her. "Are you deaf as well as stupid?" she asked snidely. "Take off that gown. It doesn't belong to you." She rolled her eyes at me, then smiled sweetly at the guard over her shoulder. "We're going to burn it at the equinox bonfire to celebrate the start of a new era under King Nolan's rule."

She turned back to me. "Strip, impostor," she ordered.

"I can't," I said, speaking the truth. But then, she knew that. She had been the one who helped me into the impossible gown in the first place.

"Strip," the guard said, repeating Ada's command.

The corners of Ada's mouth tensed in a suppressed smile, like this was all playing out exactly how she wanted. Her smug expression finally tipped me off to her plan.

"I can't get out of this dress on my own," I said, speaking the words as if the admission was being dragged out of me.

The guard's low chuckle was like raw sewage sliding over my skin. "I think I can help with that." He stepped around Ada and approached the cell door. "Turn around, sweetheart," he said, fitting the key into the lock, not remotely hurt by the lethal current of electricity charging the cage. "I'll get you out of that dress in no time."

Behind him, Ada mimed gagging. I stifled a highly inappropriate laugh and turned my back to the guard. My eyes locked with Sid's, and I wondered if Fin was still in the raven's head, watching this all play out. Assuming he was, I flashed him a quick, reassuring smile, though it was more for myself than for him. If this didn't work, I would surely be killed. Ada, too.

Which meant it *had* to work.

I stood stiffly while the guard skimmed his fingers over my neck and shoulders, making my skin crawl. He took his time with the tiny buttons running in a line from my nape to my tailbone. I gritted my teeth, cringing every time he caressed the exposed skin of my upper back.

He was almost to my hips when Ada finally struck.

His hands fell away, and I spun around to see him scratching at the thin leather belt Ada had wrapped around his neck. Her pretty features were contorted into a ferocious snarl. I had thought it many times before: people *always* underestimated Lady Adasia, with her gentle smiles and soft curves. It was what made her so dangerous, and part of why I had chosen her to be Liam's primary guardian when I wasn't around.

"He's an Elemental," I blurted. "He's electrifying the cell!"

"Not anymore," Ada gasped.

Only then did I realize the incessant hum of electricity was gone. She was nulling him.

The guard stumbled backward, ramming Ada's back into the cell bars, but she held fast, raising one leg and digging her knee into his spine to increase the pressure on his neck that much more.

It didn't take long for the loss of blood flow to his brain to knock him out. His eyes rolled back in his head, and his knees gave out. Ada grunted as she dropped to the floor with the unconscious guard.

She didn't let up for another couple of minutes to ensure he was out for good, not merely unconscious. She blew out a breath, releasing the pressure on the belt, and slumped sideways. Her chest heaved as she struggled to squirm free from where she was pinned against the cell bars by the guard's body.

I rushed forward, gripping his shoulders to pull him away from her, and she scrambled free. "Ugh, why are men so disgustingly predictable?" she grumbled, climbing to her feet.

I stifled a laugh. "If they weren't, this might not have worked," I reminded her, turning my back to her so she could finish what the guard had started. She gripped either side of the gaping gown and tugged, popping buttons clean off and sending them clinking against the bars.

I shoved the sleeves away from my arms and pushed the stifling gown down until I stood only in the black silk slip I had worn underneath the dress. I hastily stripped the slip off over my head and turned back to Ada.

She already had the satchel open and tossed me a pair of black leather leggings.

"Who's with you?" I asked, pulling on the pants.

She handed me a bra next. "Just Garath. He's rounding up the loyal guards scattered throughout the grounds and getting them out into the city. He'll meet us at the hedge maze. The others are waiting at the harbor." She handed me a dark gray tunic, leather patches hand sewn—likely by Ada herself—onto the shoulders to protect me from Sid's talons.

Once I was dressed, I reached for her hands. "Thank you, Ada. I don't deserve you."

She gave my hands a squeeze and flashed me a cheeky smile. "Nobody does."

I returned her grin. In a matter of seconds, I had sifted through her surface thoughts to absorb the details of the plan she and Garath had concocted together.

She intended to boost my empathic gifts, allowing me to remotely create an illusion—something I could never have done on my own. Once the two guards stationed at the base of the tower were essentially blind and deaf to us, believing nothing out of sorts was going on in their immediate vicinity, we would leave the tower, with them none the wiser. Then, we would row Ada's little boat across the moat and meet up with Garath. After, we would sneak to the secret entrance of the western escape tunnel to flee the castle grounds. It was beautifully simple.

"Are you ready?" she asked.

I took a deep breath, then nodded and closed my eyes, focusing on constructing my illusion. I cast out the mental mirage like a net and held my breath. If it hadn't worked, if they noticed someone was tampering with their senses of perception, we would know in a matter of seconds when the other guards burst into the tower. Or in a few minutes, when we found a slew of them lining up for us on the outer edge of the moat.

Nothing happened. No creak of rusty hinges. No clang of the lock.

I blew out the breath and opened my eyes, smiling at Ada and shaking my head. "I cannot believe you did this." I pulled her in for a tight hug. Tears threatened *again*, but this was no time to fall apart. "Thank you, Ada. *Truly*."

She squeezed me back, then gripped my shoulders and pushed me away. "We must go. Let us hurry."

I nodded vehemently, eager to reunite with Liam. The blood rush on top of the massive effort I had expended in using my gifts to cast the illusion made my head spin and my limbs tremble.

"Are you all right?" Ada asked, her brows pinched together. She gripped my elbow to steady me.

I nodded. "I'll be fine. Wiped out, but fine."

Her lips twitched into a quick, unconvinced smile, but she returned my nod anyway. "Come on, then."

Sid launched off the cot, swooped out through the open cell door, glided a full circuit around the tower interior while Ada and I hurried from the cell, then landed on my proffered arm, shuffling up to perch in his usual place on my shoulder. I wondered if Fin was still in there, my cheeks heating and heart beating even faster at the thought of him having watched me strip out of my dress and slip just a moment ago. It had been years since I cared one way or another about another person seeing my unclothed body, but suddenly, something that shouldn't have mattered compared to everything else going on *did* matter to me. Very much so.

Ada and I raced down the stairs and exited the tower without a hitch, the guards apparently oblivious to our escape, and quickly settled in the rowboat. Under cover of darkness, we crossed the moat. Ada rowed, sticking close to the shadows cloaking the edges of the Tower of Solitude from the moonlight until we reached the back end of the island, while I downed the bread and cheese she had stashed in a second, smaller satchel in the boat. With the food, some of my energy returned. My Empathy was still mostly spent, but at least the worst of the fatigue left my muscles, and the shaking ceased.

When we reached land, Sid launched into the air to scout our way from above while Ada and I scrambled out of the boat and hurried across the gravel road encircling the moat, to the thicker cover of the trees lining the opposite shoulder. I crouched beside Ada, waiting for her to catch her breath after all that rowing.

The entrance to the western escape tunnel wasn't far, just a couple hundred yards away, hidden at a dead-end branch of the hedge maze near the wall. We were in the last stretch now, and we needed to be quick and stealthy.

The fruit trees, with their branches covered in fluffy blooms, provided plenty of cover, and we reached the hedge maze without issue. We plunged into a break between the tall hedges, retreating deeper into the shadows beyond the immediate entrance.

"Garath?" I whisper-shouted, searching the impenetrable darkness. My heart leaped into my throat when he stepped out of the shadows, his eyes scanning over me endlessly. I raced forward and flung myself into his arms.

He squeezed me tightly but only for a moment. "You caught a tail," he hissed, pulling away and gripping my elbow to drag me farther into the labyrinth. "We have to get to the tunnel."

I didn't argue.

Ada ran ahead, leading the way around the bends.

"Our guards?" I asked between panting breaths. In the distance, dogs barked and people shouted. My stomach lurched. Garath was right. We were being hunted.

"Already out," Garath said. "They'll be waiting for you on the other side."

Ada reached the end of the maze first, where the hedge itself concealed the tunnel's entrance that only the Corvo queens, their heirs, and their most trusted guards and advisors had known about for nearly two centuries. As soon as she saw us barrel around the corner, she slipped into the hedge, vanishing completely.

Garath pushed me through the hedge ahead of him, following close behind me. The tunnel was narrow, the ceiling low enough that Garath needed to duck, and the air carried the thick scent of mildew, but I could breathe easier knowing we were concealed. We were safe.

Ada was a dozen paces ahead, an Elemental-charged electric torch in hand to light the way.

Garath caught my wrist before I could delve deeper into the narrow tunnel. "Del, wait."

I turned back to him, my eyebrows raised.

"You may not have been born the Corvo heir, but you *are* the Corvo queen," he said, his voice hushed but his hurried words impassioned. He stepped closer to me, gripping my shoulders. "The kingdom needs you. The *people* need you. Promise me you'll remember that?"

"What are you talking about?" I asked, shaking my head as I searched his face in the electric torchlight. "What are you—"

His words from a moment earlier finally registered. *They'll be waiting for you on the other side.*

They'll be waiting for you . . .

My leaden heart sank into my stomach.

"You're not coming?" I said, my voice thready.

"They have dogs," Garath said. "I can sense them closing in. I can sway some of them to turn on their masters, but most are loyal. They'll find the entrance to this tunnel, and they will follow us. They will track us to the harbor, and they will catch you, Del. They will catch you and Liam unless one of us stays behind to slow them down."

"You can't—" My chin trembled, and I shook my head more vehemently. "We might make it."

"Might," he said, laughing hollowly, "isn't good enough. You *have* to make it. For Liam. For the kingdom."

"Garath—" My voice broke, tears welling and spilling over instantly. "Please don't do this. Please don't leave me."

He offered me a grim smile, but his shadowed eyes were filled with devotion. "I believe in you, Del," he whispered, cradling my face in his hands. He leaned in, pressing his lips to my forehead, then pulled away and gave me a gentle push deeper into the tunnel. "Now, go."

My stomach knotted, my rib cage constricting around my lungs. This couldn't be happening. Garath had always been there, one of the few constants in my life. I couldn't do this without him.

I stumbled backward until I reached Ada, who gripped my arm and dragged me deeper into the tunnel. Every few steps, I glanced over my shoulder, watching Garath grow fainter and fainter in the distant shadows as he prepared to make his last stand. And then he was gone, and there was nothing but darkness behind and ahead, Ada's electric torch the only thing lighting our way.

The first crack of gunfire echoed down the tunnel a moment before we emerged from the exit, stumbling through a mausoleum and out into the cemetery.

"Highness," Saira said, rushing forward to meet us.

My feet felt leaden, my heart stuck at the other end of the tunnel where Garath was giving his life so I could be free. My legs refused to move. I couldn't stop staring back at the mausoleum concealing the tunnel's exit.

Saira grabbed my arm and helped Ada drag me between and around grave markers. "Let's get you out of here," she said. More dark figures emerged from the shadows to guard the way ahead and behind. "The others are waiting."

I dug in my heels as a burst of gunfire echoed out of the tunnel, followed by muffled shouting and growling dogs.

A sharp slap to the side of my face made my ears ring. I blinked, surprised to see Ada's delicate features mere inches from mine. "Garath's sacrifice is a gift, Del. Do not waste it. We must go —*now*."

Too stunned to argue, I let Ada and Saira lead me away.

25

FIN

My mind was a storm cloud. A chaotic churn of tumultuous emotion as images flicked through my head. Images of that guard's filthy hands on Del. Of that snakelike look in eyes I would have gladly removed from their sockets if I could have. And the irrefutable truth that Garath had just given his life to save Del. As Sid, I'd felt his familiar mind fade to nothing.

"Fin," Liam said, his voice quiet as it stirred me from a daze.

I stopped absently stroking Tick's ear and blinked the bay back into focus. The whitecaps crested to the staccato of my heart. I pushed off the mast. "Yeah, bud," I said, swallowing thickly. I looked down at him, into his big green eyes that housed far more worries than any nine-year-old should have to bear.

How did I tell him Garath was gone? That the man who had been so loyally at his side his entire life, protecting him from shadows, was dead?

Liam stroked Tick's head too, sensing she was afraid of the water. "Do you know when my mother's getting here?"

Clearing my throat, I offered him a reassuring smile. "Soon.

She'll be here soon." I feared what state she would arrive in, though.

"Hey, Liam," Lyra said, calling him over to her with a wave. "Stone said you can help the crew ready the ship to set sail."

That seemed to distract him enough for now, and he hurried over to her, his auburn hair catching the gleam of the swaying lantern light as he passed. The water was growing choppier by the minute.

"What is it?" Callon said quietly. He came up beside me and crossed his arms over his chest, his stance widening as he prepared himself for whatever I had to report.

I watched Lyra and Liam helping one of the crewmen untie some of the ropes. "Garath is dead."

On the other side of the ship, Lyra froze, hearing every word. Straightening, she quickly recovered and answered something Liam asked with a forced smile.

"He held out as long as he could," I told them.

"And Del?" Callon said thickly. "And Ada?"

I nodded, peering down the dock, hoping they were close. Without Sid's eyes, I couldn't be certain, but my head was heavy from so much mindwalking, and I needed the rest of my strength for whatever the night still had in store for us. "Garath kept the dogs from following them. They were at the edge of the city the last I saw them. They'll be here soon—"

"You're talking about your friends, I hope." Stone's baritone met my ears as he strode closer. Smoke from his cigarette swirled for only a moment before it was carried away by the breeze. Thumbs hooked on his suspenders, he stopped a few feet away, his blue eyes glittering in the moonlight. They shifted between Callon and me, impatient. "Because these men are still waiting to get paid."

"For what?" I practically growled. "Your intel came far too late."

Stone's eyes narrowed on me. "Careful, Fin. I have a ship for you, do I not? And a crew to take you south. It's a pivot in the plan, that is all—"

"A pivot?" Callon echoed.

Stone looked at Liam and shrugged. "You're welcome to disembark *Lady Liberty* if you'd like."

I tore my gaze from him, knowing he was more bluster than anything else, because he would do whatever I needed him to do—he still owed me.

"Look," he said, running his hand through his long, thinning hair with a sigh. "I did what I could, Fin. I know it wasn't in time, but at least you know where your enemies are now." He peered toward the castle, gleaming in the distance. "And we'll get the kid to safety. But we have to leave soon. These rough waters are going to slow us down as it is, and I'm assuming we're going to need as quick an exit as we can manage."

Heaving out a breath of my own, I rubbed my hands over my head. "I know. They'll be here—"

"They *are* here," Lyra said, hurrying over with Liam in tow.

Hills appeared from inside the ship, and she and I disembarked, rushing down the pier straight for Del. Three guards came into view. I recognized two of them as being the unconscious guards outside Del's chambers the night I killed Alastor. They flanked Ada as she ushered Del closer.

There was no Garath. Even if I knew he would not be there, his absence still felt unfathomable, even to me.

"Hills," I called as we jogged closer. "Get the guards on the ship. We have to leave immediately."

I didn't wait for a response as I slowed, meeting Ada's gaze first. Though her expression was set with determination, her eyes gleamed with sadness. I nodded, letting her know I knew everything. Or perhaps I was confirming it had happened; I couldn't be certain.

She slowed in front of me, and Del wavered, her chest heaving as they came to a stop. Her gaze was almost blank, and my heart tore open at the sight of her in utter ruin.

"Del," I said softly, leaning in to peer into her eyes. Hills's commands to the guards faded to nothing as I used the crook of my finger to tilt Del's face up to look at me. "Hey, tough stuff," I softly urged. "Look at me . . ."

Her chin trembled. "He's gone, isn't he?" It wasn't a question, not really, but I dipped my head ever so slightly.

I could tell she wanted to fall apart right there. To break into a million pieces, but there was Liam to think about. He wasn't safe yet. We needed to get both of them the hell out of there.

"I'm so sorry," I whispered, and while I wished I could comfort her more, assuming she even wanted me to, we didn't have time.

But then Del fell into me like her legs were giving up, and her body shook as she wrapped her arms around me to stay upright. She didn't cry. It was worse. She kept it all bottled in.

"Del," I breathed, unable to stand it. Squeezing my eyes shut, I held onto her, barely able to keep my tears in check. "I know," I whispered, resting my cheek against the top of her head as she trembled, silently unhinged.

I didn't tell Del it would be okay because I knew it wouldn't, not for a very long time. And I didn't repeat my sentiments from earlier and tell her I was sorry because it helped nothing. Instead, I held her for as long as I dared before I heard Callon in my mind.

"Fin, we have *to go."*

Nodding as if he could see, I lifted my head and gently pulled away from Del. I helped her to stand, worried if I let go she might fall again. "Come on, tough stuff," I whispered. "Liam is waiting for you." I gestured toward the ship, her attention snapping to our son instantly.

"Liam," she breathed, wiping the silent tears from her cheeks. She took a deep, steady breath as best she could, and I watched as her determination and strength bolted back into place. "Does he know?" she whispered, eyes locked on him.

I shook my head.

Del looked at me as she wiped a final escaping tear, and she reached for my face, cupping my cheek with her other hand. "Thank you for getting him here safely."

"Of course," I breathed. "You don't have to thank me for that—"

"And for in the tower," she added. "With Sid."

My frown eased, and with a tight-lipped smile, I nodded. "Of course," I repeated.

Clearing her throat, Del looked back toward an anxiously waiting, wide-eyed Liam barely restrained on the boat with Ada and Hills. With a final deep breath, she hurried toward *Lady Liberty*, and Hills helped her climb aboard.

I made my way back as Del took Liam in her arms, the sound of the crewmen readying the ship suddenly blaring in the still night air.

Instinctively, everyone gave them a wide berth, me included, and I went to ensure Stone's crew was ready.

When I found Stone at the bow, his head was tilted in my direction, his expression narrowed. "You know I'm an addict, right? Not an idiot," he said coolly. The ember of his cigarette burned red in the night shadows, and he pointed toward Del in her commoner clothes. "Your *friend* right there is the princess. The impostor. *That* is General Hills over there, and if I'm not mistaken, those three there are Corvo guards."

I eyed Stone carefully, knowing full well he had no love for the royals. "Is that what *you* think? That Del is an impostor?"

Stone eyed me closely, no doubt dissecting my familiarity with her, and he shrugged. "I don't much care about court politics," he said. "I care about coin." Stone might have sounded careless, but I knew that wasn't entirely true. Coin was a crutch, just like his addiction, but at the core of it all was abandonment by the Crown, and he was angry.

"And coin you will have," I told him for the hundredth time.

"But that's not what I'm asking about. Is *this* going to be a problem for you and your crew?"

Stone stared at Del and Liam as she embraced him so tight, I wondered if she would ever let go. Both of them cried, and it was all I could do to stand on the periphery, useless.

"Interesting how he looks just like you," Stone mused aloud. I wasn't sure if that was an unspoken threat or him simply stating he knew more than I was letting on.

When I finally met his knowing gaze, Stone shrugged again. "She looks like a palace servant to me," he said, and a plume of smoke filled the air between us. "Better get them inside. It's about to get a hell of a lot colder up here."

And with that, Stone took another puff of his cigarette, glanced once more at Del and Liam, and I felt the ship angle away from the pier.

I watched the dock shrink as we sailed farther and farther away, praying Dusty and the other horses would make the journey back to the desert safely on their own since we couldn't take them. Then I sighed with relief. By the afternoon, we'd be in Morro City, far from this place. And Del and Liam were here and safe. For now.

26

DEL

Thunder rumbled in the distance, and choppy whitecaps filled the bay. A golden glow cut through the thinner parts of the cloud cover near the eastern horizon, period- ically illuminated by streaks of lightning as dawn gave way to sunrise and my first day in a world without Garath by my side.

I sat with my back propped against the foremast, Liam snug- gled in against my side, his cloak wrapped tightly around him, seeking refuge from the icy wind. We would have to go below deck soon, but I couldn't bring myself to stand just yet. Up here, I could fool myself into thinking that Garath was still with us, but as soon as I went below deck with the others, his absence would feel all too real.

I held Liam close, one arm curled around his lanky body and my cheek resting atop his head. A deep ache had settled in my chest, and my face felt swollen from the constant threat of tears. Tears I had managed to hold in, for the most part, because I needed to be strong for my son.

Liam whimpered, and I lifted my head to peer down at him. His eyes were shut. His hand twitched, and he let out another whimper. Asleep, finally, and dreaming. About Garath? About

Alastor? About the crashed coronation and terrifying events that had followed? Because I felt certain all of those would haunt *my* dreams the next time *I* slept.

I pressed a kiss to Liam's forehead.

I was so tired of being strong. Of holding in my pain. It was not a healthy way to cope with emotions, as Garath had so often reminded me. But I had been doing it for so long that I didn't know how to let myself unravel. Garath had always been my safe place to fall apart. He was the one who held me together when the burdens of existence became too much.

At least, he used to be.

A tear streaked down my cheek, instantly chilled by the frigid wind.

Lightning forked through the sky as the bow of the ship sailed for the storm clouds darkening the western horizon. The stone wall surrounding the castle, its copper roofs, bell tower, and open turrets were barely visible anymore to the south.

Would I ever return to Castle Corvo? To Corvo City?

A flask appeared before me, tarnished silver wrapped in worn brown leather. The hand holding the flask was large and sturdy, with thick fingers, blunt nails, and protruding veins. The hand of someone who worked hard for their living.

My eyes widened when I followed the line of the arm connected to that hand up to broad shoulders and the face that had haunted my most heartbreaking dreams over the years.

"Thought you might need a drink," Fin murmured, a deep crease between his brows. He crouched, elbows on his thighs. The rocking motion of the ship forced him to plant one knee on the deck for stability.

I accepted the offered flask but couldn't figure out a way to unscrew the cap without disturbing Liam.

"Here," Fin said, taking the flask back for a moment to open it, then handing it to me once more.

I flashed him a wan smile and brought the mouth of the flask to my lips. The rum within burned going down, but at least it eroded some of the choking lump in my throat.

"Thanks," I said, my voice hoarse from disuse. I cleared my throat.

Fin squinted slightly, the first rays of the rising sun glinting off his eyes, turning his irises a brilliant emerald. "I'm sorry," he said, his voice gruff. "I know Garath meant a lot to you."

Something that was equal parts a laugh and a sob clawed its way up my throat. I took another, longer drink, pretending for a moment that the stinging in my eyes was from the burn of the alcohol and the bite of the wind, not from the grief of losing my best friend. I stared out at the roiling storm clouds. Another streak of lightning cut across the sky. We would have to get below deck soon.

"You know, he wanted me to run away," I said, my voice hushed, so it didn't disturb Liam. I glanced at Fin, just for a moment. "Before . . ."

The corner of Fin's mouth twitched. "Before I snuck into your castle and killed your husband?" He raised his eyebrows. "Could that be what you're referring to?"

I let out a hollow laugh. "Yeah, before that." Had it really only been a couple of weeks since that conversation with Garath? *Everything* had changed since then. "We all knew how much worse things would get with Alastor once Mother was gone and I was queen. Garath kept badgering me to let him kill Alastor, even knowing he was the only thing keeping Eduart from invading."

I swallowed my rising grief. My overwhelming regret. I should have listened—then Garath might still have been alive.

"He wanted me to take Liam out of Corvo City," I said remotely, lost in the memory. "To run away."

"With him?" Fin asked, the words seeming to have been dragged out of him.

I knew why he was asking and glanced at him sidelong. Garath and I were close. Fin wouldn't have been the first person to assume there was more than friendship and loyalty between us. Maybe there could have been, but that possibility had vanished the moment Fin exploded back into my life.

"To *you*," I told Fin, holding his stare for a long moment before returning to gaze out into the storm.

Rain had broken free of the clouds in the open ocean farther out, blurring the view. The deluge would reach us soon. Or, I supposed, we would reach it.

"Except," I said, "we didn't know where you were—or if you were even alive."

"Del . . . " Fin raised a hand, reaching for my face.

I flinched involuntarily before he could touch me. It was an automatic response born of years of Alastor's unique brand of *affection*.

Fin curled his fingers into a fist and lowered his hand.

I considered apologizing for my reaction, but at the moment, I didn't have the energy to explain myself to Fin, not when everything in me was focusing on holding myself together.

Another conversation with Garath flitted through my mind, one that had included complicated schemes and talks of a baby. "Have you ever had someone in your life who you knew—you *knew*—would do anything for you?"

Out of the corner of my eye, I watched Fin bow his head, and I wondered who he was thinking of—his devoted sister, Autumn, or Beast, the cougar who had been utterly loyal to him? Or maybe he was thinking of Callon or Lyra or someone else, someone I didn't know. I could have reached out and touched him, straining my exhausted empathy to find out, but he deserved his privacy.

Fin shifted to sit beside me, one knee raised and an arm wrapped around his leg to hold him steady against the rocking motion of the ship as it raced forward, cutting through the swells. "I know it's not the same. I'm not him," Fin said. "But I *am* here for you—for you and Liam, both. Whatever you need."

I flashed him a weak smile. "You may come to regret those words."

Fin shook his head. "Never," he breathed.

His earnestness gave me pause, and the ache in my heart eased just a little.

The bow of the ship angled more southward, heading for Noctem, the realm bordering the kingdom on Corvo's southern edge.

"Are you sure it's safe to travel through Noctem?" I asked, anxiety for the future rising as the raw memories faded into the past. Garath had sacrificed his life so Liam and I might live. I refused to waste that gift.

"Someone there owes me a favor," Fin said. "They're well connected. We'll be safe."

I glanced over my shoulder, watching the ship's crew move about. I would have had to be blind not to have noticed the suspicious glances they cast my way. "And here?" I looked at Fin. "Are we safe *here*, on this ship?"

Fin's jaw clenched, telling me my concerns were not unfounded. "Stone and his crew won't touch you," he vowed. "They'll get us to Morro City."

I exhaled a sigh, fatigue settling into my bones. Acting on impulse, I tilted my head to the side, resting it on Fin's shoulder.

He stiffened, his breath catching. A heartbeat later, he relaxed, his arm curling around my back. As we sailed away from everything I had ever known, the three of us huddled together—Fin, Liam, and me. My first true family.

27

FIN

While Ada and Lyra stayed with Liam, the three Corvo guards, and some of Stone's men on the ship, Callon, Del, Hills, and I made our way into Morro City with Stone strangely vigilant at our side.

Morro City wasn't a gleaming capital built on the peninsula like Corvo, with stone and moats and towering ramparts, but the seaside capital of Noctem housed towns and villages along the coastline, and the Menagerie—the palace complex surrounded by metal-framed walls of glass—glinted from the cliffs above.

The landscape itself was awe-inspiring, riddled with crevices and craggy caves, and the lush forest-covered mountains met jagged cliffs along the coastline. But Noctem wasn't the most dangerous kingdom of the seven for nothing. Its natural beauty offered a plethora of hiding places to its criminal inhabitants—mercs, pirates, and thieves seeking refuge from all around the world, which was why I hadn't balked at Stone's offer to keep some of his crew back on the ship.

Still, it was impressive. Every building in Morro City was lined with solar panels, reimagined remnants from the world before, converting the sun's rays into energy to power the city. Windmills that stood taller than any redwood I'd ever seen lined the cliffs, using the coastal winds as additional energy sources, making Noctem the only kingdom with a fully functional electrical infrastructure without the constant use of people's Abilities to power.

As the nine of us wove our way up the dirt path, winding through the heavy foot traffic leading to and from the city center, the Menagerie glinted in the sunlight upon the cliff.

A woman's shoulder knocked into mine, and I glared reflexively at her as she stumbled passed. When my eyes met hers, red-rimmed and glassy, she offered me a weak wave of apology and continued on. Though Pyra took good care of her people, I couldn't help noticing that quite a few looked unwell, especially in the afternoon heat. Then again, it was hard to say where most people came from and what they'd been through. Noctem was a melting pot of scavengers, outliers, and criminals. They came here when they were restless, lawless, or had no place else to go.

But as I watched the people as we passed, I could feel their gazes on us as well. I glanced at Del, walking a few paces behind me, and wondered if it was obvious to any of them who she was under her gray cloak.

Hearing the scratch of a match and the sound of a flaring flame, I looked at Stone beside me as he lit up another strix-laced cigarette. A single hit visibly calmed his nerves, and I wondered how much physical pain he was in from his time in the navy. He'd been in ships blown to smithereens and lost countless men during the Santa Cruz Siege, when Queen Corisande's fleets fought to maintain control of her trading ports against the foreign kingdoms, years before I was born. Trading ports that made Corvo and Noctem the wealthiest kingdoms when it came to importing and commerce.

Or was Stone's pain and restlessness only caused by the marks it left on his mind?

I'd paid him when we'd arrived at the docks, just as I said I would. And while I'd expected him to scoot us along, glad to be rid of the hassle and danger Del's very presence presented, Stone had surprised me by keeping some of his crew members on the ship to ensure Liam's safety with the others.

That wasn't part of our deal, and I wasn't sure if Stone had business inside the Menagerie, or if there was another reason he was accompanying us, but I didn't ask questions about that either. Stone knew things I didn't about everyone and everything. No matter how fleeting his loyalty could be at times, he was a useful person to have around. Usually.

"Is walking into the Menagerie with you going to bite me in the ass?" I asked, giving him a sideways glance. Stone might've had connections everywhere, but that didn't mean they would all be welcoming.

A blue plume of smoke wafted around him as he exhaled. "Kalliope will see us if Pyra won't," he muttered, matching my stride. I stared at him, curious what he meant by that, exactly, because Kalliope would see me too, but I had a feeling it was for an entirely different reason.

"Fin," Del said, hurrying up behind me. She could barely take her eyes off the glinting glass archway we were about to walk through. "What's the plan?"

It was easy to forget Del hadn't been to many places. To the Sierra Kingdom with her husband, perhaps, but I doubted there were many reasons for her to explore any place else in the past ten years.

"Best case," I started, stepping through the giant entrance to the city. "We speak with Pyra and ask her to ally with us against King Eduart."

Del's gaze bore into the side of my face. I was well aware it was a tall order, but we needed it to work. "And the worst case?" she asked carefully.

I scratched my stubbled jaw. "They grant us safe passage and the horses and supplies we need to return to the desert without hassle."

"And you two," she said, looking between Stone and me. "You're just going to walk in there and ask Pyra for all of this?"

I nodded. "I helped her three years ago and lost many good people in the process. That's when I met Stone," I explained. My gaze flicked to him, remembering the blade scar running up my side. "Pyra owes me the respect of an audience, if nothing else. Besides," I added, knowing Pyra had eyes and ears everywhere. "I have a feeling they're expecting us."

Del didn't have time to ask any more questions because a familiar face greeted us in the courtyard. Pyra's sister, Kalliope, stood against a cypress tree, arms crossed over her chest. Her leather ensemble hugged every curve, and her boots, tied to her knees, made her look every part of the assassin-pirate she was.

A smirk curved Kalliope's lips as we drew closer, and her brown eyes lined with kohl drank me in, up and down, before a full grin engulfed her bronze face. After spending a few nights together the last time I was in Noctem, I knew where her mind had likely wandered.

"My, my," she purred. "Look what the cat dragged in." She sauntered closer, acting all too delighted to see me, even if it was mostly to get a reaction.

I could feel Del's attention too, but I straightened my shoulders as we met Kalliope on the cobblestone walkway.

Stone took another puff of his cigarette, and she looked at him, her long black ponytail falling over her shoulder as she tilted her head. "I can't say I expected I'd ever see the two of you walking in together. Not after the bloody heap you left Fin in." Kalliope's eyes narrowed on him. "And you still owe me money from your last visit." Her delicate brow arched expectantly.

Kalliope was Pyra's right hand, the head of the guard and as lethal as she was beautiful. More than that, she was Pyra's younger, very protective sister.

Stone tapped his pocket. Some of the coins I'd given him jangled inside. "All in good time," he promised, taking a long drag of his cigarette with the other hand.

It started to make sense why Stone needed to ensure he got his money from me if he was bringing us to Noctem. For as rich as he was in the secrets he kept, Stone always seemed to be in debt. "There's some business that needs tending to first," he prompted, pointing at me.

I glanced at the glinting, domed ceiling of the Glass Palace. "Will she see me?" I asked, looking Kalliope in her smoky-painted eyes. My tone was as exhausted and impatient as I was beginning to feel.

The catlike smirk on her face fell a little. "Already back to business, then?" she said with a small pout, and tearing her gaze from me, she scanned the entourage surrounding me, studying Hills first, casting an appreciative gaze on Callon next, then her eyes lingered on Del. "Hmm."

Finally, with another slight arch of her eyebrow, Kalliope nodded reluctantly. "Of course, Pyra will see you." With one more look at me, Kalliope motioned for us to follow her.

Taking a deep breath, I readied myself for whatever happened on the other side of the tinted glass walls of the complex. We received a few curious looks as we made our way through the city, but I knew it was because Kalliope was our escort and had nothing to do with Del. Kalliope wasn't a woman to mingle with the commoners. She was too busy being a badass and rarely meandered the city without a small army at her back.

Flashing a reassuring smile at Del, I continued behind our hostess, taking in the oasis within the Menagerie walls. Fruit and shade trees adorned the interior, as did ponds and flower gardens. Despite its ruffians and scallywags, Morro City felt more like a refuge, and I knew Pyra was responsible for that.

This was the hub where the city grew its food and tended to its community gardens, where the solar power generated electricity and kept the lights glowing at night so that Abilities didn't have to. And it was where the walls kept the wind at bay and wells dredged water up through the purification centers to provide fresh water for the villages below.

A set of glass doors opened with the flick of Kalliope's wrist, revealing two guards standing sentry inside the Glass Palace, the glinting birdcage Pyra called home. They didn't look anything like the Corvo guards with regimented black leather armor, but what they lacked in uniform, they made up for in weapons. Laser batons and tasers were holstered on their hips, and large, semi-automatic firearms were clutched in their hands and strapped to their backs.

"No one comes in," Kalliope murmured to the muscled, stout man at the entrance to Pyra's quarters. "And no weapons," Kalliope tossed over her shoulder.

I'd expected as much and looked at Hills, nodding for her to do as Kalliope said. I unsheathed my own knives, strapped to my belt and hidden inside both of my boots, and handed over my shotgun holstered on my back.

"Pyra doesn't like weapons," I explained.

Del frowned, looking at the guards adorned in them.

"*I'm* the one who likes weapons," Kalliope said. She winked at Del.

Del handed over the pistol and knife she wore on the belt slung around her hips, and Hills went about disarming herself, which took a bit longer. Kalliope watched the petite older woman with interest, and once she was satisfied we'd given up all our goods, she continued walking.

The moment we stepped into Pyra's chambers, I heard a collective gasp behind me. I smiled at Del and Hills. "It isn't what you'd expected, is it?"

Both of them shook their heads, peering around the atrium. It was half greenhouse, half arboretum, and everything was lit with natural light pouring over the foliage that burst to life from every planter box and garden area. Water trickled somewhere off in the distance, and the chirping of birds and fluttering wings stirred as we made our way down the tiled walkway that cut in and around the garden beds.

Del gasped. "This place is . . ."

"Dangerous," Kalliope said over her shoulder, and glancing back at us, she smirked. "Careful of the bird shit."

Del's brow lifted, and on cue, a black bird fluttered overhead. Even Callon flinched, and I chuckled softly despite myself.

"You'll be fine," I told them. "They mostly keep to the trees."

"Speak for yourself," Callon said. "Last time, there were some pretty close calls."

My smile faltered as we rounded an elephant ear plant taller than me, and Pyra, bent over her desk, came into view. Her throne room wasn't only an aviary of sorts; it was more like her house, with meeting rooms and coffee nooks nestled around the place. She was the most even-keeled ruler I'd ever met, making her meditative, strategic, and very frightening when she wanted to be.

Our footsteps echoed as we drew closer, and Pyra peered up from the glass table strewn with papers. "Ah, Fin," she said, her voice almost melodic and her accent reminiscent of her home country.

I leaned into Del. "Hang back with the others, for now," I whispered. Her big brown eyes met mine. Whatever thoughts churned behind her expressive gaze, she seemed to agree it was for the best. Biting her bottom lip, Del nodded.

Clasping her hands, Pyra rested her elbows on her desk. And just like her sister often did, Pyra tilted her head, her eyes widening slightly. "I was wondering when you would arrive."

The sisters were known for their beauty but, more than that, for their ruthlessness. They came from a very long line of assassins feared throughout the foreign kingdoms across the sea. Here, they lived like queens. There, they lived like outlaws, and what better place to hide and rule than among others just like them?

While Kalliope could cut a man in half before he even realized she was in the room, Pyra had a coldness about her, a cunning callousness that instilled fear in the bravest warriors.

"Pyra," I said, knowing she cared nothing for titles or pleasantries.

She gestured for me to sit in a high-back chair across from her desk.

Stone stayed with the others, lingering behind. I exhaled as Pyra assessed me, just like I watched her. Both of us wondered who had the leg up and knew more.

"I appreciate your seeing me," I said, earning me a beautiful smile. A *dangerous* smile.

"Yes, well, I have heard the prophecy, and my little birds tell me you're smack dab in the middle of whatever Eduart wants."

I nodded. "Unfortunately, your little birds are right. But the prophecy—I'm not here about that, exactly."

Her eyebrow lifted with intrigue. "No?"

I shook my head. "I've come to make you an offer."

She leaned back in her chair. "This should be good. I'm not sure you have much I want at the moment, Fin."

I shrugged, sitting back in my chair as well. "Perhaps, but I wouldn't be too hasty." Kalliope went to stand beside her. Good. With them both present, we would come to an agreement much faster. "There's a Corvo usurper, and even if Eduart isn't involved, which I highly doubt, we know his troops are mobilizing within Corvo as we speak. And I propose we stop Eduart once and for all."

Pyra smiled, glancing at my guests behind me. "Oh? Why would I do that? I have no love for the Corvo Kingdom. Eduart can take it if he wants it."

"So you say," I replied. "But I don't believe you are as indifferent as that."

Pyra was smart. She knew as well as I did that Eduart was a threat to everyone. Perhaps she knew it more than most. She just needed a bit more convincing.

"Now that Prince Alastor is dead, King Eduart has no puppet in place to take what he's always wanted—the wealth of the Corvo Kingdom. The very harbor your own traders frequent and make pit stops at from all around the world," I reminded her. "If Eduart controls that harbor, you and I know your business here is screwed. You also know it's only a matter of time before he takes Noctem, too. Because King Eduart is coming to the desert lands next. I've heard the city boasts as much, and if my people can't suppress his armies, they will take it, and you will be surrounded by three kingdoms controlled by the man you loathe most in this world. And you will lose your power, Pyra. You know you will. It's only a matter of time."

"And you are going to help me keep Eduart at bay?" she said, only mildly scoffing at the idea. "What about this *true son* of the queen I hear is holed up in Castle Corvo? I know the princess has fled, Fin. Who will rule the Corvo Kingdom if we get rid of this new king? Because I know what civil unrest does to countries, and I will not incite a war for a ruined, falling kingdom like Corvo. For all I know, the princess is dead. Corvo will not ally with me, nor do I want them to."

Kalliope took the seat beside her sister, suddenly interested in our conversation.

"Don't worry about the princess," I told them and rose to my feet. Their skeptical expressions sharpened.

"Why not?" Kalliope asked carefully.

"Because she is alive," I said. "And I know where she is."

They both looked at Stone. "This is where you come in, I take it?" Kalliope deadpanned.

"No," Del said, taking a step forward. "This is where *I* come in." She removed her hood, letting it fall around her shoulders. "I am Delphinia Corvo, heir to the Corvo throne. And if you help us—if you help my people by removing the usurper—I promise you, those loyal to me will be with you. They will stand with Noctem against King Eduart."

Both women's eyes glittered with intrigue and surprise, though their expressions gave little away.

Pyra scrutinized Del up and down. "Princess Delphinia," she drawled, shaking her head. I moved to stand protectively beside Del. "You've caused quite a commotion lately." Pyra rose to her feet, as did her sister. Both of them stood on the other side of the desk, and Pyra looked from Del to me and back to Del again.

"How do you fit into this picture, Fin?" Kalliope asked, but I could tell she had assumptions already because the look in her eyes was unsettling.

"None of that matters," I told them both. "Only that all our people are in trouble, and we can help one another."

Pyra walked to a small table and poured herself a glass of water, nodding to a servant I hadn't noticed through the foliage to get some for the rest of us. No wonder her *birdies* were so good at getting information. They hid themselves well.

"Princess Delphinia," Pyra said, then took a sip of water. She licked her lips. "You just lost your husband in that terrible accident. Eduart's youngest son. Do you grieve him?"

Del swallowed thickly. "There was no love lost between us," she said flatly.

"No," Pyra mused. "I imagine not. I know what Alastor was like." Pyra's gaze shot to me, and a slight smile curved her lips. "You wouldn't have had anything to do with his sudden death, would you, Fin?" Pyra waved her question away and refocused on Del. "Never mind. What matters is that your people are dying. Your kingdom is riddled with the wasting sickness. It's why you've been so vulnerable. Your kingdom is falling to ruin, and I'm not convinced—"

"There's a solution," Del blurted. "To the wasting sickness. I just need time to confirm it."

"A solution." Pyra parroted. "To the wasting sickness?"

"Yes. I'm so close to getting it figured out. I would have already, only . . ."

Del's voice trailed off, and I knew she was considering all that had happened in the past two weeks—even just in the past two days. My hand moved to her lower back, uncertain of what else to do other than offer her my strength. The motion didn't go unnoticed by Pyra or Kalliope.

"I'm taking her to the desert," I told them. "Where she will be protected. But when the time comes—"

"*If* the time comes," Kalliope interjected.

"When," I said more firmly. "Can we count on you, Pyra?" I looked at Kalliope. "On both of you?" It was Kalliope I was more worried about.

After a few pulse-pounding moments, Kalliope looked at her sister and shrugged. "I've been itching for a good fight. And I've been wanting to put King Eduart in his place since the day we arrived on this continent."

With a barely there smile, Pyra looked Del in the eyes. Ruler to ruler. "You better hurry and find your *solution*. Because time is the one thing we are grossly short of."

28

DEL

Working by the flickering light of the campfire, I sat hunched on a fallen log on the border of the redwood forest, frantically scribbling words onto the pages of the soft leather-bound notebook Fin found for me at the market. Fin and Farris, our Noctem addition, sat quietly chatting around the fire with Saira and Ada. Liam was already asleep on the bedroll laid out beside mine, directly behind my perch.

My gaze lingered on the Noctem emissary, Kalliope's most powerful Telepath, wondering why he had joined us this morning only to keep to himself, talking to us only when addressed directly. Otherwise, the spindly blue-eyed, black-haired man remained quietly watchful, frequently moving to the periphery of our group.

I shouldn't have been surprised Pyra's man was reclusive, just as I imagined Pyra was, spinning her web while she waited to strike. It wasn't that I didn't trust her, because I trusted that Fin would have warned me if there was something I needed to worry about with her, but I wasn't entirely comfortable in Farris's presence. I couldn't shake the suspicion that he was really only with us to observe and report back to his mistress when we were finished with our journey. At the same time, now that Noctem was invested in what might turn into an ugly fight for power, I could understand why the sisters wanted an emissary with us on the journey.

Sighing, I returned my attention to my notebook. Unfortunately, the copy of Becca's book of foretellings found in the Glass Palace was just as fragmented as Mother's, which meant my quest to uncover the rest of the prophecy still hinged on finding Jake and learning whatever he knew about how and where Becca had recorded her prophecies.

And now, the only chance I had to reclaim a crown many would argue I had no right to—that I wasn't even sure I wanted—was to prove to Pyra that the Corvo Kingdom was still strong by finding a cure for the wasting sickness.

Why had I opened my mouth in the meeting with Pyra and Kalliope? Why had I hinted at solutions I wasn't even sure existed? Prophecies from the distant past. Vague references to a cure. For the first time in my life, I was out of the game—a game I had never wanted to play. So why was I scheming to get myself back in?

Because of Garath. Because of a promise I hadn't actually made but that he had requested all the same. Because he had believed in me, and that belief had cost him his life.

My pen scratched on the paper as I crossed out the last few lines. I had recalled and recreated the single page from Mother's prophecy index relating to our current situation and the associated prophecies perfectly, but I was second-guessing myself about everything else. What about the notes Mother had scrawled in the margins of the associated books of foretellings? What about all those file folders in the bottom drawer? Had I seen anything potentially relevant stored there?

I turned the page in the notebook and started fresh, attempting to list the labels I had seen on the files. But there had been *so many*. For minutes, I stared at the blank page, but I couldn't recall anything specific.

"Ugh!" I growled, snapping the notebook shut with the pen marking my page and tossing it onto the ground beside my log.

This was useless. I rubbed my temples and dug my fingers into my hair. *I* was useless. And my skin was caked in salt from the sea spray, and my hair was tangled and greasy. Even tied back in a braid, it was driving me crazy. I hadn't bathed in days, since before donning my coronation dress, and I couldn't stand being filthy a moment longer.

I stood and rounded the end of the fallen log, then crouched by my pack at the head of Liam's and my bedrolls. For a long moment, I stared at Liam, watching the steady rise and fall of his chest and taking in his relaxed features, so different from the masks of grief and fear he alternated between while awake.

Protecting him was my number one priority, but it seemed like there was no path stretching out ahead that could guarantee his safety. Every territory within the Seven Kingdoms was dangerous in its own way, but the wildlands were worse. The Ferals. The bandits. The reclusive mountain folk. Maybe one of the foreign lands could offer safe refuge instead. The emissaries from both the Evergreen Nation and Yellowstone had been friendly enough when they had stayed at Castle Corvo, but that was years ago.

But to reach the Evergreen Nation, I would have to cross three of our kingdoms or travel the open sea, and to reach Yellowstone, I would have to cross a vast desert larger than all the land in the Seven Kingdoms combined. Even if we survived the perilous journey, the Evergreen Nation could very well turn us away, as our gifts —all Abilities—were outlawed there.

Regardless, in either place, I would be powerless and at the whims of those in charge.

But, if we stayed and fought, if I attempted to reclaim the Corvo throne and succeeded, I would have more control over the situation. I could build a world that was safe for Liam.

I found the spare shirt Ada had packed for me, wishing there was a towel and a bar of soap in my pack as well, then stood and walked deeper into the shadowed woods bordering our camp. When we first made camp hours ago, I should have taken Ada up on her offer to stand watch while I bathed, but I had been too focused on getting all that valuable information out of my head and down on paper. I didn't even know where the soap was stored. Not in my pack, that much was certain.

A creek trickled nearby, and I spotted Hills standing watch on the outskirts of camp on my way down to the rocky bank.

She glanced at me as I approached, her lips curving into a half-hearted smile. "Can't sleep?"

I barked a laugh. "I haven't even tried," I admitted. I paused beside her and held up my folded shirt. "I just want to wash up. Is it safe to go down to the creek alone, or do I need an escort?"

"I can see the creek from here," she said, leaning her shoulder against a tree trunk.

I squinted down the dark slope. *I* couldn't see the creek, but I didn't have the enhanced sight of a Super like Hills. Thanks to her gifts, she was stronger, faster, and could hear and see better than anyone I had ever met, except for Lyra.

"Go on," she said, nodding toward the trickling water. "I'll keep an eye on you."

A vice clenched around my heart, and I pressed my hand against my chest. Garath would have demanded he escort me to the creek.

"It *will* get easier," Hills said softly, and I wondered if she heard a change in the rhythm of my heartbeat that clued her in to the morose direction of my thoughts. "In time."

I nodded and flashed her a weak smile, then started down the slope. When I reached the edge of the creek, I unfastened my cloak, laid it out on the ground, did the same with my weapons belt, and set the clean tunic on top of the small pile. I pulled my worn tunic off over my head and crouched to soak it in the running water before scrubbing it over my face. I wiped my upper body down as best as I could without soap, warm water, or a clean towel. It was a lame attempt at bathing, but at least the frigid water gave me something else to think about for a few minutes. When I was as clean as I was going to get, I rang out the wet tunic and exchanged it for the clean, dry top.

Feeling a little more like myself—whoever she was—I sat on a large rock by the creek and picked up a small stone to toss into the water. Had Mother known Nolan was alive? What would she have thought of her son returning and claiming the throne out from under me? I pulled the raven pendant out from under the collar of my tunic and curled my fingers around it.

I could walk away from the Corvo Kingdom, from Nolan, from Mother's ghost—from all of it. I *could* do it.

Garath's last words to me whispered through my mind.

The kingdom needs you. The people *need you.*

Did they really? Garath had believed so. But *why*? What did I have to offer the people that Nolan couldn't give them?

I tossed another stone into the creek. *Plunk.*

I was nobody, just a girl from a southern village who happened to have been raised as the queen's daughter. Just a mother looking out for her son. Just a woman mourning her best friend.

Plunk. Another stone. *Plunk.* Another.

Where had it all gone wrong? When Fin killed Alastor? When I refused to run away with Garath? When I chose Alastor to be my husband? When I demanded Mother release the captive Healers and cut off the mass production of healing elixir? When I sat and waited for Fin at the solstice celebration? When he didn't show up?

A twig snapped behind me, and I twisted on my rock, my heart suddenly hammering as I squinted up the dark hillside. Fin coalesced out of the darkness but paused, his hands raised defensively as he slowed his approach.

Only then did I realize I was holding up a stone as if I would throw it at him.

"Why didn't you come to the solstice celebration?" I asked quietly, standing and turning to face him. I dropped the rock.

"I—" Fin lowered his hands, but his explanation seemed to catch in his throat just as his feet seemed to be rooted to the ground.

"I waited for you." I took a step toward him. "I was going to tell you about the baby." Another step. "I would have run away with you," I said, taking another step. "We could have been a family, and everything would have been different." With another step, I reached him. My nostrils flared, and my chin trembled. "Everything would have been *better.*"

"You don't know that," Fin said, his voice hushed.

My hands balled into fists, and I searched his shadowed features. "Why didn't you come?"

Fin let out a bitter laugh and shouldered past me to approach the creek. "I wanted to," he said, his back to me. "I had planned on it, but when Jake and I returned to a slaughtered village . . . things changed." His voice broke, and he bowed his head.

I hadn't realized the attack was right before the solstice.

"And you thought it was Mother who ordered the attack," I remembered aloud.

My gut knotted. Had he thought I was in on it too? All these years, had I been pining after a man who believed me capable of such an atrocity? I had to know—not merely hear him admit it, but to truly *know* if he had believed me to be a monster.

I approached behind Fin and took his hand, but he snapped his head to the side and jerked his hand away before I could get a read on him. Pressing my lips together, I grabbed his hand again, gripping it in both of mine before he could pull away. He stared down at me, his eyes narrowed to a glare that conflicted with the tsunami of regret I sensed within him.

In his mind, I saw him with his people in the desert. I saw Callon, Lyra, and so many others, all working together to survive in a place where the land itself seemed to want them dead. I saw his people looking to him for guidance and felt him brace against that heavy burden. I saw him fighting alongside his people against

Ferals and bandits and soldiers alike. I saw him lose friend after friend, human *and* animal, only to drown his mounting turmoil in drink and a long string of nameless, faceless women.

I felt his pain as he returned to his village all those years ago, only to find that Autumn had been killed. I felt his rage at Mother. His hurt and confusion. His agony at being alone in the world. Even surrounded by his people in the desert, he lived in solitude, keeping his heart isolated.

I felt the sinkhole of regret that had formed in his chest the moment he learned about Liam. About Alastor and the true nature of my marriage. About what *I* had been forced to do to survive. About not meeting me at the solstice celebration.

And I sensed his relief at being with me once more after years of wondering. Of longing. He hadn't forgotten about me, and he certainly hadn't hated me. He *had not* believed me to be a monster.

I pulled out of Fin's mind, tears streaming down my cheeks, and released his hand. My breath hitched when Fin reached out, threading his fingers through mine.

"When we got back to the village, I was just going to stop at my cabin to get cleaned up and pack fresh clothes," he said, his voice rough. "I was planning on meeting you, but—" His throat bobbed, and he closed his eyes.

"I'm so sorry, Fin." I stepped closer, reaching up to touch the side of his face. His stubble scratched against my palm as he leaned into my hand.

"So am I." He turned his head, pressing his lips against the heel of my hand.

My heart skipped a beat, and warmth blossomed in my chest. I stepped closer and angled my face up toward his, a silent offering.

Fin slid a hand behind my neck, cradling the back of my head. His lips hovered in front of mine. "I wish," he breathed. "I wish things had been different. I wish I had come."

"You're here now," I whispered and pressed my lips against his.

The kiss started sweet and gentle. Tentative. But as my arms wound around Fin's neck, his fingers tangled in my hair and he slid an arm around my back, pulling my body flush against his, and the kiss morphed into something else. Something more. An apology. A penance. A promise.

I pushed Fin's coat off his shoulders, and his hand slid under my tunic to settle on the curve of my hip, his touch possessive. So much had happened since the last time we were together—we were entirely different people now—but the spark between us remained. And with each ragged breath, with each beat of our pounding hearts, that spark burned hotter, spreading to an inferno.

"Your mom is down at the creek, washing up," Hills said, her voice raised, obviously for my and Fin's benefit. Liam must have awakened and gone searching for me.

Gasping, I broke away from Fin, my chest rising and falling with each exaggerated breath as we clung to one another. Eyes locked with his, I licked my lips and cleared my throat. "I'm almost done," I called up to Hills and Liam.

Fin traced my jawline with the pad of his thumb. "This isn't over," he swore.

I pressed my lips to his, lingering there, savoring his kiss. And then I backed out of his embrace and reclaimed my cloak, weapons belt, and soaked tunic while Fin put on his coat. Anticipation charged the air between us as we climbed back up the slope.

Despite everything else going on, hope swelled within me. I had given up on Fin long ago, but he was right. This thing between us wasn't over.

It had only just begun.

29

FIN

My black-maned steed plodded along the animal trails worn throughout the giant sequoia forest, staying off the main road and out of sight as much as possible. Because many of us were doubled up on our borrowed horses, Liam rode with me while our animal friends scouted for danger. Nyx took to the sky with Sid while Tick scoured the forest floor, nose to the earth as she forged ahead.

Callon and Lyra led our procession through the trees while Hills, the Corvo guards, and Farris, ever quiet and watchful, brought up the rear. Stone, however, stayed behind, though I was certain we hadn't seen the last of him.

We might've been a ragtag band of misfits, but with Del, me, and her closest confidants, we were a well-honed party of a dozen heading toward our next stop, where we would rest again for the night.

I glanced at Del on the white horse she and Ada rode a few paces behind us. The afternoon sunlight filtered through the towering canopy, illuminating Del's brown eyes when she looked at me.

Warmth, as equally exciting as it was comforting, unfurled

through me as I recalled the feel of her lips from last night's kiss at the creek. I hadn't expected that, and I couldn't get it out of my head. I couldn't get *Del* out of my head. Then again, I'd never been able to before, either. I was desperate to kiss her again. To prove to myself that it wasn't a dream.

When Del realized I was staring, she blushed a little, and her mouth twitched at the corner as if she knew exactly where my mind had drifted.

"Fin," Liam said, stirring my thoughts. He craned his neck to peer up at me, his auburn head of hair coming just below my chin.

"Yeah, bud?" I said, clearing my throat.

His mind was so similar to mine, the last thing I wanted him to do was somehow glean what I was thinking about regarding his mother—to sense the carnal thoughts in my mind. So, I focused on the scent of sun-washed redwood needles, the cones that littered the ground, and the sound as they crunched beneath horses' hooves.

"Why are some of the trees black, like they've been burned?" Liam pointed to one as we passed.

I gazed around the generations of forest, charred trunks centuries old and foliage freshly sprouted. "Because the sequoias have stood for thousands of years," I explained. "Many of them have withstood many wildfires."

"Then how are they still standing?"

I thought of Jake and our many walks through this very forest over the years. "Someone once told me that their bark is so thick and so special, the trees are flame resistant, and that's why some of them can live for 3,000 years."

"Really? Is that why they are so big? Because they are so old?"

I nodded. "They never stop growing."

"They're the biggest trees I've ever seen," Liam said with awe in his voice. "You could live inside them." I remembered the first time I saw the forest of giants and the exposed roots of the toppled trunks gnarled and reaching like giant monster fingers.

"I slept inside one, once," I told him.

"You did?"

I nodded as my thoughts drifted to the storm Jake, Beast, and I were caught in once, years ago. I was young, and it was my first trip away from the village and my sister. The rain was pelting, unrelenting for nearly a day as we holed ourselves away. But it never felt scary, only like an adventure, one of my first and favorites.

"Who taught you about the trees?" Liam asked. He idly picked at a seam in my tunic sleeve, wrapped around him where I gripped the reins. Having him this close, him fidgeting and his head constantly shifting around as he took in the world around him, was the most surreal experience. I had a son. He was right here with me, blood of my blood and flesh of my flesh, asking me questions. He didn't hate me. He didn't resent me for not being around. He was curious and beautiful and perfect.

"Was it your father?" Liam prompted.

"Who?"

"That taught you about the trees?"

I smiled, if a little sadly. "You could call him that. His name is Jake."

"*The* Jake? Patron of Healers?"

I grinned. "Yes. He raised me and taught me many things because he has lived for many, many years. He knows a little about everything. At least," I added, "he likes to think so, anyway."

Liam peered up at me again, his big green eyes blinking. "Will I get to meet him where we are going?"

"Yeah, Liam," I said with another grin. I knew without a doubt my son would meet Jake, even if I wasn't sure when. I still had no idea where he was or when he was coming back.

"What else did Jake teach you?" Liam asked.

"Let's see . . . " I perused the random bits of knowledge I had. "Did you know that black bears can be brown? We might even see some while we're in the forest. Or that these trees are the tallest in the world?"

"Really?"

"Yeah, really. And it's said that they are as old as the dinosaurs." I paused, realizing I had a very different upbringing, being raised with Jake—a man with hundreds of years of knowledge—to guide me and teach me things. "Do you even know what a dinosaur is?" I had no idea what other children were taught about the old world before.

Liam shook his head.

"No? Oh man, then I'll tell you all about them. I used to love hearing stories about dinosaurs when I was younger—giant animals as big as these trees roaming the earth. Imagine mind-walking with one of *those*."

"Wow," Liam said with a burst of laughter. "That would be so cool."

"Yeah, it would." I chuckled as we lost ourselves in thoughts. I imagined Liam five years from now. Ten years. Fifteen. And I tried to think of what sort of man he would be. A prince? A king? A ghost, living on the outskirts of society, like I did, simply trying to survive this world? I told myself that would not be his fate. Whatever happened with Corvo and Del and her place on the throne, I would do everything I could to give Liam a life worth living.

"Fin?" His voice was soft in our silence.

The horses' hooves clacked on the rocks as we maneuvered through a dried-up creek bed.

"Yeah, bud?"

"When Mother gets her crown back," he began tentatively. "Are you going to leave again?"

I stopped breathing for the briefest moment. "No, Liam," I said quickly before he could feel the stutter and stop of my heart. But I realized the instant I said it that it wasn't a promise I could make to him. "Even if we are separated for a while, I will always come back to see you," I amended. "Always. But I have others who need me, people who don't live in the Corvo Kingdom, and even if I never want to leave you and your mother again—*ever*—I can't abandon them either." I leaned over to look into his eyes. They were green and sparkling and full of unspoken questions and worries. "Does that make sense?"

Liam licked his lips and nodded. "Is that where you're taking us? To see your people because we aren't safe at home anymore?"

My heart sank a little more, hating that Liam had to ask such questions—that he had to worry about any of this at all. That he had to be a prince, not just a boy, and that he didn't have a home, not right now. Not anymore.

Only for now, I told myself, and I forced a smile for Liam's sake. "Yes. In a few days, we'll be in the desert—in my home, where you might make some new friends for a little while."

"Is that where Lyra and Callon are from, too?"

I nodded. "That's where they live, yes. Lyra and Callon help me keep everyone safe. Their families will be very happy to see them come home."

That made Liam pause for a moment, and he chewed on his bottom lip. "Do you have family there, too?"

I wasn't sure why I hesitated, only that it was a sucker punch to the gut to realize the answer was no. I had no one, and yet, it was a relief as well. I had no previous ties to complicate what Del, Liam, and I might share.

"No, Liam," I breathed, my heart in my throat. "I've been waiting . . . for you."

30

DEL

"I want to show you something," Fin said, pine cones crunching and twigs snapping under his boots as he approached.

"Oh?" I glanced back at him and bent to pick up a few more sticks to add to my slowly growing pile. I would have expected firewood to be more readily available when camping in the woods, but these ancient giants seemed reluctant to shed reasonably sized branches, and I was left to scrounge the very perimeter of our camp for anything remotely usable in the campfire.

Having grown up in the castle as the Corvo heir, my lessons had been focused on things that would help me rule—history, philosophy, political theory, the Temple's teachings, and both large-scale battle strategy and personal combat tactics. I didn't have many practical skills applicable to camping and long journeys, so I was making myself useful any way I could, like hunting for firewood.

Fin gathered my hoard of sticks in a sweeping scoop of his arms and hugged it close to his body. "Come on," he said, heading back toward the heart of camp with the lion's share of my stash.

Sid swooped down from his perch high up in one of the giant redwoods and glided to a branch directly over our camp.

I hurried to catch up with Fin, shifting the last few sticks into one hand and admiring his backside as I followed him. The years since we last saw each other had been difficult for him—physically demanding as well as emotionally taxing—and I hated that his life seemed to be one struggle after another. But that didn't mean I couldn't appreciate the effect of that struggle on his honed physique. He moved like a wildcat, the muscles of his backside flexing visibly through his leather trousers with each step.

Fin dropped his burden on the stack gathered by a few others and turned to face me. "So, what do you say? Should we go take a look?"

I blinked, opening and closing my mouth, at a complete loss for words because I had absolutely no idea what he had been saying while I had been ogling his backside. Heat crept up my neck and cheeks. "I'm sorry, I—" I shook my head and cleared my throat. "What did you say?"

Fin's lips curved into a lopsided grin that seemed to turn back time, reverting him to the young man I had known so well, if for such a brief time. Long enough for him to sear his claim on my heart. He pulled the last few sticks from my grasp, set them on the pile of firewood, and stepped closer to me.

"The fire lookout." He glanced up at the peak jutting into the sky, the top quarter of the mountain a solid mass of gray rock topped by an ancient-looking structure. We had been climbing all day; I almost couldn't believe there was any more *up* to go. "It won't take more than an hour to climb to the peak and half as much time to get back down. We'll be back before sundown with plenty of time to spare."

I peered around the camp, searching for Liam. He wasn't with Ada, as I had expected, who was assisting Callon with the horses. Instead, I found him with Lyra, helping her prep dinner, and I couldn't help but smile. He had taken a real shine to her, and she to him. She wasn't the same as Garath, though she seemed to have a similar, slightly surly disposition, but it was good for Liam to make room in his heart for new friends. I silently reminded myself that I needed to do the same.

"She had a brother," Fin said, following my line of sight. "Pretty sure Liam reminds her of him."

"Had?" I asked, my eyebrows raising as I looked at Fin, sympathy for the loss I already suspected sprouting in my chest.

Fin pressed his lips together and shook his head. "Slavers."

"Oh," I breathed. I couldn't even imagine it.

"I'm heading up there to scout." Fin rubbed the back of his neck and stared up at the rocky slope. "I, uh, already checked with Lyra. She's happy to watch Liam for a few hours if you want to come with me." His eyes returned to mine. "It would give us some time alone to talk."

"To *talk*?" I asked, the corners of my mouth tensing. My heart beat faster at the unspoken implication.

Mischief danced in his green irises. "Did you have something else in mind?"

I chuckled, glanced at Liam once more, then grabbed Fin's hand and turned away from camp, marching straight for the steep slope. He didn't even flinch or try to pull away, and his comfort with my touch was a balm to my aching heart.

Fin's slower steps halted my forward movement. "Hang on, tough stuff," he said, amusement in his voice. He pulled his hand free and jogged to his bedroll to retrieve a small pack, then returned to me, reclaiming my hand and pulling me toward a different part of the slope. "The trailhead is this way."

It felt so strange to hold Fin's hand while we walked. In recent memory, I had only ever held my son's hand, and though Liam was growing rapidly, his hand was still smaller than mine. Fin's hand was the opposite; it engulfed mine. The skin on his palm and the undersides of his fingers was rough with calluses, whereas mine were smooth and soft. I felt small and fragile compared to him but somehow safe with him by my side. So different from how I had felt with Alastor's painful grip on my wrist or arm.

I was tempted to lower my guard and peek into Fin's mind to see if his surface thoughts were as scandalous as mine, but I found the mystery of not knowing—the anticipation of being surprised— far more exciting. I wondered if he expected me to look into his head again or was trusting me to stay out. Did he even care? I couldn't know without snooping, and I was determined to respect his privacy—this time, especially after I had forced my way into his mind by the creek.

Fin released my hand when we reached the trailhead, hanging back so I could walk in front since the trail was too narrow for us to walk side by side.

"I take it you've been here before?" I asked him over my shoulder.

"I have," he said. "There are lookouts all over these mountains. We have them all mapped out—which ones are still safe, which ones are compromised . . ."

"By the Sierra Kingdom?"

"And by bandits and Ferals," he said. "This one used to be well outside Sierra's territory, but they've been slowly, quietly expanding east. We're right on the border now."

"But—" I frowned. "Isn't the lookout *theirs*?"

"Theirs?"

"Didn't they build it?" I clarified.

"No," Fin said. "It's leftover from before the Ending—the Turn, I mean. They used towers like this one to watch for forest fires and monitor the danger they posed as they spread."

Fin was filled with knowledge about the old world—the time of abundance and extravagance before the Turn. His people had held that knowledge close, aided by Jake, one of the few people— possibly even *the only* person—left alive from those ancient times.

"*I* should know that." I shook my head, frustrated by the useless knowledge filling my head about made-up traditions, while the true history of the land and people who had made us into what and who we were remained unknown to me. "*My people* should know that." I laughed under my breath and grumbled, "Not that they're really *my* people anymore."

"Maybe you should let them decide that," Fin suggested. "Seems to me the people in the Seven Kingdoms have lived for far too long under the rule of leaders who *claimed* their power. People like Eduart and Nolan, and even your mother. Why not try something new—like letting the people decide who's in charge?"

"A democracy? In the Seven Kingdoms?" My brow furrowed. "None of the other leaders would go for that."

"Who says they have any say in the matter?" Fin countered. "Without the support of the people within the Corvo Kingdom, neither you nor Nolan have any power. And without *his* people's support, King Eduart is powerless too. If you can keep the people's loyalty, you can keep a kingdom, and the person who *wants* the power becomes irrelevant."

"Huh." I peeked back at Fin over my shoulder, wondering when he had found the time to read up on political philosophy during all the chaos and strife of the past decade.

"What?" he asked, his eyes narrowing.

I faced forward, returning my attention to the trail ahead, appreciation curving the corners of my mouth upward. He was different from how I remembered him. He was *more*. "Nothing," I said, keeping my thoughts about him to myself.

Fin snorted softly. "Whatever you say, tough stuff."

The final third of the trail was completely exposed, climbing a wandering path up the only passable route to the top of the rocky peak. The higher we climbed, the windier it became. But all of that was forgotten when I saw the view. It was incredible, with evergreen forests and craggy mountains for as far as the eye could see.

It was so different from the wooded hills, sprawling fields, and endless ocean I was used to from the castle windows.

The lookout structure was a simple, one-room hut perched on a raised platform about thirty feet above the top of the peak, with a decaying deck wrapping around the building. It was in surprisingly good shape for a three-hundred-year-old building, likely thanks to the boarded-up windows and the patched roof.

"Did your people do the repairs?" I asked Fin as we ascended the wooden stairs. The boards were sturdy and appeared relatively new.

"A few years back, yeah," Fin said from close behind me. "We travel this route a lot when trading with Noctem." He paused, then added, "At least, we used to."

A narrow catwalk of newer boards laid atop the older, rotted platform allowed us to walk around the deck safely, and my breath caught at the staggering view. We were so high, and the sides of the peak were *so* sheer. I had never considered myself afraid of heights, but then, I had never been this high. Up here, with the wind tugging at my hair and pulling at my clothes, and with what appeared to be the entire world stretched out below, I seriously reconsidered my stance on heights.

"It's breathtaking." I inched backward, away from the unprotected edge and closer to the hut's exterior wall, except it wasn't the wall that stopped me but Fin's body.

His hand settled on my hip, and his nose brushed against my ear. "It is," he whispered.

I craned my neck to look at him, but his focus wasn't on the view. It was locked on me.

His hair whipped wildly around his face as he leaned in, and my breath caught. "Do you want to see inside?" he asked, his lips grazing my cheek as he spoke.

My heart hammered, and my voice lodged in my throat. I licked my lips and nodded.

Fin claimed my hand and pulled me back the way we had

come, to a boarded-up door on the same side of the lookout hut as the stairs. He wedged his knife between the wide board and the exterior wall. Nails creaked in the wood as he pried the board away. It was a smart, if rudimentary, way to detect if anyone had disturbed the lookout in his people's absence.

As soon as the board was free, Fin tossed it aside and tugged the door open.

I followed him in, my pulse pounding in my ears, fear battling with excitement within me. The kiss the previous night had been one thing when unwieldy emotions had ruled me, but now, while my rational mind prevailed, memories of another man pushed their way to the forefront of my mind. A man whose touch had never been kind.

The wind caught the door, slamming it shut, and Fin and I were ensconced in instant darkness, almost no light filtering in through the boarded-up windows. Fin was little more than a shadowy figure, his outline suddenly looming.

It was so easy for my mind to play tricks on me. For me to believe he was someone else. Someone who had only ever hurt me.

"Fin?" I said, my voice high and tight. My chin trembled, my heart racing. I reached for him with shaking hands, and he pressed his lips to my palm. "Do you have a light?"

"Yeah," he said, and lowering my hand, I heard him drop his pack onto the floor and removed his shotgun from his back holster. "Why? Are you afraid of the dark?" he teased. Fin unclipped his bag.

"Will you still call me tough stuff if I say yes?" I was barely able to keep my voice steady as panic gripped my chest.

He laughed softly. "Always," he said. A dozen tense heartbeats later, a light bloomed in a small solar-powered lantern, illuminating the space. There was nothing here but us and a few large canvas packs set against one wall, which I assumed contained the supplies Fin's people kept stashed here.

Fin stood, his focus latching onto the lone tear that streaked down my cheek. His brows bunched together, and he searched my eyes. "I didn't realize—" He shook his head, raising one hand to brush away the tear with the pad of his thumb. "I didn't mean to laugh at you."

I closed my eyes and swallowed roughly. "*He* preferred the dark," I said, hoping Fin wouldn't need any more of an explanation than that. Even saying that much about Alastor dredged horrible memories closer to the surface, and I didn't want even that much of him here with us.

"Del, we don't have to—"

My eyelids flew open. "I *want* to," I said, speaking over Fin. "I *need* to." I inhaled shakily, attempting to steady my breathing on my exhale, even as tears welled anew. "Will you help me remember what it feels like to be loved?"

Fin's jaw clenched, and his nostrils flared. Rage burned in his eyes, but then his expression softened. "Del . . . " He leaned in, pressing his forehead against mine. "You have always been loved," he whispered. "You have no idea how much." And then his lips were on mine, and I was drowning in his kiss. In *him.*

It was a slow but desperate kiss. Passionate but gentle. A kiss that roused every fiber of my being—parts of myself I hadn't acknowledged in years were suddenly brimming with need.

"Fin," I breathed, the ghosts of my past all but forgotten.

"Hmm?" His lips were featherlight against the sensitive skin beneath my ear, and his fingertips trailed down the column of my neck, brushing a loose curl from my face.

"More," I breathed. "Please."

Fin stilled long enough to pull back and meet my gaze in the lantern light. His eyes danced like mischievous green flames, and he was all too happy to hear the plea in my voice, but his smirk faded as he stared into my eyes. Maybe, like me, he couldn't believe we were here. That this was us. Together. Finally.

This time, when Fin's lips touched mine, his kiss wasn't gentle. It was ravenous. It was ten years of wanting and waiting. His lips and hands were greedy, sending us both into an impassioned frenzy as he backed me against the wall.

Without breaking the kiss, I pushed his coat off his shoulders, letting it fall to the floor, and he did the same with mine. He tugged at my tunic, but it was trapped under the weapons belt slung around my hips. I hastily unfastened the buckle and dropped the belt with its pistol and knife to the floor.

Unhindered, Fin drew my tunic up my torso, and I broke the kiss just long enough for him to drag it over my head. I twisted my arms behind me to unfasten my bra while he pulled off his own shirt, and those clothing items quickly joined the rest of our discarded things on the floor.

Fin trailed the lightest of kisses down my neck and along my collarbone as his fingers teased the laces at the waist of my leather leggings. His lips blazed a path down the centerline of my body, moving between my breasts, which rose and fell with each shaky breath, and down my belly. I leaned back against the wall, my legs suddenly unsteady.

I wondered if he could feel the stretch marks etched into my skin from my pregnancy with Liam. They had faded a little over the years, and I had at first found them ugly, but over time, I had come to love them. They were the only marks Fin had ever left on my body, however inadvertently, scars of love rather than those Alastor had branded into my skin.

My heart skittered when Fin hooked his thumbs into the waistline of my pants, and my breath hitched as he dragged them down over my hips, pulling my underwear along with them. He unlaced and pulled off my boots, then guided my leggings down over first one of my feet, then the other, and tossed the rest of my clothing away.

His hands glided up the outsides of my thighs, settling on the curve of my hips, and he leaned in, bringing his face closer to the core of my being.

Fin gazed up at me, his stare molten. "Let me help you remember, princess." He trailed the pads of his thumbs along the crease at the tops of my thighs, using gentle pressure when he reached my sex, opening me up for him.

I didn't stop him when he leaned in the rest of the way. My fingers tangled in his hair, and I gasped at the first touch of his lips against my most sensitive flesh, at the first sweep of his tongue. Blissful warmth flooded through me, soothing all the aching parts of me. I couldn't remember ever feeling anything so wickedly delightful. With each stroke of his tongue and press of his fingers, my legs trembled, my knees quaked, and I gripped his hair tighter. "Fin . . ."

He chuckled, low and rough, the sound filled with knowing promise. "Yeah, tough stuff?" he rasped.

But I couldn't answer him. All I could do was squeeze my eyes shut and hold on to him as his tongue moved faster. As he held me tighter. As his mouth worshipped me.

"Fin—"

He groaned, kissing my inner thigh, and his hands fell away from my hips and dropped to his belt buckle. "I swear I will finish what I started," he rasped. "I swear it. But—" He rose onto his feet, pushing his trousers down and freeing himself, his desperate need for me more than evident. "You're making it impossible to wait any longer." His hands returned to my hips, and he pinned me against the wall, his body pressed against mine as he buried his face in my hair. "I *need* you, Del."

I groaned as his erection nudged my belly, and suddenly *I* was the one who couldn't wait any longer. I wrapped my arms around his neck, my legs around his hips, and shifted forward, sinking onto him.

Fin hissed in a breath, his hands clutching my backside, his entire body going rigid.

And just like that, we were back in Fin's bedroom, ten years younger and filled with idealistic hope. I had given myself to him then, knowing we had little chance of a future. And yet, here we were, ten years later. Together.

"Show me, Fin." I rocked against him, watching his face with each slow shift of my hips. "Show me how much you need me."

Once again, he gripped my hips, guiding my movements, taking me harder and faster. He shifted his right hand, his thumb dipping to press against the point of aching need at the crest of my sex, and I moaned, my eyelids fluttering shut.

"Yes," I breathed, my pleasure building.

This was what I needed. *He* was what I needed. What I had always needed. I clutched his hair, pulling his face to mine, savoring every touch, every stroke, every thrust, as Fin thoroughly reminded me what it felt like to be loved.

We stood together on the lookout deck after having reluctantly dressed, finally doing our job of scouting the surrounding area in the fading daylight. Fin's body, I'd learned, was a tapestry of scars I both wanted to and was afraid to ask him about, and I couldn't get it out of my mind.

I was about to ask him about it when a glint of light flashed in the dense forest on the opposite side of the peak from our camp. "Did you see that?" I asked, glancing at Fin.

"No," he said, moving in to stand close behind me and pressing his scruffy cheek against mine so he could see what I saw. "What was it?"

"I don't know." I narrowed my eyes, scanning the woods below.

It happened again, like a blink of light.

"Shit," Fin hissed, dragging me backward around to the far side of the lookout. "That was the glint of light off glass. Likely binoculars or a spyglass."

"What does that mean?" I asked, panic rising, desperate to understand.

"I'm not sure," Fin said, flexing and relaxing his hand. "Nothing good."

He crouched by his pack near the lookout hut's door and reached inside, digging around for a moment before pulling out a pair of binoculars. He stood and peeked around the corner of the hut, focusing on the area where we had seen the glint.

"Shit," he repeated. He lowered the binoculars and ducked back behind the building with me. "It's Sierra soldiers." He kicked the wall of the hut, his foot almost breaking through the frail siding. "Fuck," he rasped, running his hands through his hair. "We have to stay here tonight."

"What?" I shook my head as his stare grew unfocused, which I assumed meant he was using his telepathy.

Sid cawed, swooping lower from where he had been soaring high overhead.

Fin blinked and looked at me, his focus sharpening. "Sid will get word to Liam. Hills, Callon—they'll know to pack up and move camp farther away," he said, his words rushed. "I sent Tick to scout the Sierra camp."

I was already shaking my head, my heart sinking.

"We'll meet up with the others as soon as the soldiers move on at first light."

"*Tomorrow?*" I blurted, my eyes opening wider. "I can't leave Liam overnight!"

"We won't make it back down the trail without them spotting us," Fin said. "We need to sit tight. We'll make our way down as soon as we can. Our people will be able to put distance between themselves and the other camp regardless of whether we're there."

"I can't—" I shook my head, despondent. "Liam . . . " What if something happened to him while I was stuck up here? This was a mistake. I couldn't believe I had been so reckless. I never should have left him.

Fin took my hands in his, holding them tight. His eyes held mine as he waited for me to catch my breath. "We'll be putting

Liam in greater danger if we descend now," he said carefully. "The enemy could follow us back to our camp." He squeezed my fingers. "Besides, he's surrounded by people who will do everything they can to protect him. If we stay put—for now—he has a better chance of remaining safe." Fin pulled me in closer and wrapped his arms around me. "As do you."

31

FIN

Waiting for dawn to crest with Del in my arms was something I never thought would happen again. And having already checked in with Nyx a few hours ago at camp to ensure the move in the night had gone smoothly, I was able to bask in the afterglow of last night a little.

I was still nulling us from any Sierra soldiers who would most definitely be searching for close human minds while the troops slept, but despite my surmounting exhaustion, I was in my own little bubble of heaven.

Unlike when we were younger, Del and I—us together—felt real this time. Not like an orphaned kid from the outskirts of the forest and a princess having a stolen night together. Not a fleeting night we knew would end. It felt possible to hope that there would be many mornings like it to come.

I frowned a little, remembering the pain in Del's voice last night. The nightmare that was her life seeping back into our reality. I would've given anything to never hear that fear in her voice again. Knowing getting back to Liam would alleviate some of her anxieties, I let my nulling guard down and cleared my mind. I reached out for Tick's a few klicks east. Through her senses, I felt the distant vibrations of a mass of footsteps and heard faraway voices as Tick lingered behind the Sierra troop, finally moving away from us. Finally, we could make our way to the new camp.

Kissing Del's forehead, I squeezed her tighter to my chest and inhaled the scent of her hair. Yep, it was still there, just barely—lavender. But as much as I wished we could have lain there all morning—that I could've let Del sleep a little longer after being up most of the night, anxious about Liam, I had to force the haze of delirium from my mind and stir her awake.

"Del," I whispered, pressing my lips to her forehead. Sid stirred from sleep on his perch near the window ledge. His feathers ruffled as he stretched his leg.

Slowly, Del's lashes flitted open, her gaze darting around a little before she seemed to realize where she was. Then her big, brown eyes landed on me. She sat up, and her cheeks reddened a little.

"Good morning, beautiful," I whispered, unable to help my smirk as I tamed her hair, a little unruly from sleep.

"Morning." Her voice was hoarse from disuse. "I finally fell asleep."

"Yeah, you did." I grinned, tucking a final wayward strand behind her ear.

"Have you been up all this time?"

I nodded. "I didn't want to give our location away to any curious minds below," I explained. "And don't worry. The troops are finally heading the opposite way, and I already checked in with Nyx, and everything is fine at the new camp."

"That's a relief," Del breathed, and I watched the tension leave her body.

That made me happy, and sitting up, I rubbed my hand over my face and through my hair, only for it to flop into my eye again. "Shall I get our provisions for the morning so we can get on our way, then?" I climbed to my feet, and after a euphoric stretch, I walked to the door and opened it to let in some fresh air.

Sid flapped his wings eagerly, and with a squawk, he launched out the door to enjoy the morning.

"Provisions, huh?" Del blinked around the decrepit watch tower, her eyes adjusting to the muted pre-dawn pouring in through the open doorway.

I reached down by my feet to grab my pack. "Jerky for breakfast, followed by a sprig of mint to freshen up after."

Del smiled, her head tilting slightly. "And you just happen to have all of this with you?" she asked skeptically.

I handed her a piece of jerky. "I always have both in my pack," I explained. "You never know if something like last night might happen."

When Del was quiet, I looked at her. "Something like last night? Which part, exactly?" There was humor in her voice, but it was forced, and I could feel the air in the room shift with her discomfort.

I knew what Del had likely seen in my mind the other day when she dove into my memories. The women, among many things. And I could only imagine what she was thinking of me right now. "Getting stuck in situations like this," I told her honestly. "Stuck. *Alone*," I added. "It's happened more times than I can count. So, I've learned to be prepared. But," I added with a grin. "I would be lying if I said I didn't ensure I had some in my pack this time before leaving camp." I shrugged. "Just in case."

That got me a cute curve of an easy smile, and to see Del's face brighten, especially after last night, when she'd been so desperate to erase the shadows of her past, was a gift I hadn't expected. Like *just maybe* we could really get past the lives we'd led before now and make this thing work between us.

Our eyes lingered on one another, and Del tore a bite of jerky between her teeth.

Being alone with her like this wasn't something that would happen very often, and though I wanted to savor it a little while longer, I knew everyone was likely worried about Del, and we had to get a move on. "It's still early," I mused, chewing a hunk of jerky. "With any luck, we'll reach the new camp before Liam even wakes."

Smiling at the idea, Del rose to her feet. She inhaled the morning air, long and deep, and sighed as she peered out at the soft gray glow of the forest. "It's beautiful here," she whispered. At least for now, it seemed Del had forgotten about the prophecies and her kingdom. She was at peace.

I wrapped my arm around her waist, pulling her into my side. "I'm glad you like it." I kissed her temple. "Come on. I know you're anxious to get back. Let's go."

Del nodded, flashing a grateful, relieved smile, and I stepped inside to grab my pack. Within the hour, we would be back at camp with the others, packing up to head out again into the desert lands.

I felt nervous for some inexplicable reason, bringing Del and Liam into my part of the world. I didn't know what they would think of our settlement outside Shoshone, but it was all I could offer them right now.

"Fin," Del murmured as I slung my pack over my shoulder. When I turned around, she was leaning against the doorframe, her eyes glittering in the early morning light.

I handed her a bit of mint and put a leaf into my mouth. "If you're going to ask if I always look this radiant in the morning, the answer is yes. Yes, I do," I said and winked at her. That earned me a cute little laugh.

Sincerity filled her eyes. "Thank you for this. For last night," she said. "For making me feel special again."

My pulse leapt, my heart dropped, and I shook my head as I stepped closer. "You've always been special, Del," I said, willing her to understand. Taking her chin between my fingers, I pressed a kiss to her lips, long and lingering. "You will always *be* special." I couldn't help it. I grinned. "But when you need another reminder, I'm happy to oblige—"

She smacked my arm, laughing as she pulled me in for another quick kiss. "Come on." She shook her head, a knowing look glinting in her eyes. "Let's go see our son."

Butterflies took flight in my chest, and I stepped out onto the platform with her. "I'm not sure I'll ever get used to hearing you say things like that."

"Just wait," Del started, and her eyes flicked to me, "soon Liam will start talking about girls or wanting to go off on his own—"

"Hey, now. I just learned I *have* a son. Let's not rush it."

She chuckled softly in reply.

After closing the door, I knocked the boards barring the door back into place, and with one final connection to Tick's mind, I knew which direction we needed to go.

We walked around the platform to the ladder. "Tick found the trail to the new camp—she'll show me the way," I said and gestured down the steps. "After you, tough stuff."

I loved the way Del's eyes glittered whenever I called her that. Like maybe it was a part of her past she'd always held onto, and if I could do nothing else today, tomorrow, and every day after, I would want to keep that look in her eyes that made her quintessentially Del, despite the bullshit she'd had to deal with over the years.

We ruminated in our thoughts for a while as we kept up a brisk walk, drawing closer to Tick and the new camp. We'd been walking for almost an hour when Tick's panic filled my chest, and I froze mid-step.

"Fin?" I could hear Del's voice somewhere behind me, but all I could smell was the scent of strangers clinging to the earth as Tick sniffed her way into camp. There were so many scents, and she had a hard time following them.

I blinked myself back to focus. "Something's not right." I was already running before I could finish.

"Fin, what's going on?" Del asked through a ragged breath.

"I don't know, but we have to hurry."

"Liam?" Del rasped, and we kept running, our strides eating up the forest floor in leaps and bounds.

"I don't know," I admitted, and I ran so hard, my chest was on fire, and my eyes blurred from the cool morning air.

We ran until both Del and I were heaving for breath, and our night of bliss was entirely forgotten.

"The Sierra soldiers?" Del asked as our people's tents came into view through the trees.

We halted at the campfire of dying embers, staring at nothing but an abandoned camp, and I shook my head. "No," I rasped, bending down to study the fresh wagon wheel tracks that were not part of our caravan.

Dread seeped through me, sucking out all the warmth. "This wasn't soldiers." I looked up at her, feeling sick to my stomach. "Not bandits or Ferals, either. There would've been a fight. There would be bodies."

Del's face drained of color. "Then who—what the hell happened, Fin?"

I shook my head, my mind racing. I didn't want to say the word out loud. "Liam is not here," I said instead. "If there are no bodies—it means he's likely still alive. All of them might be." I shut my eyes, trying to focus on Liam's mind, praying I could find him.

When I couldn't, and there was no trace of his cerebral signature anywhere near us, my blood ran cold.

"Fin," Del croaked. Her voice was barely a breath as she looked frantically around. "Where is Liam?" she demanded more hysterically, and her wide, fear-filled eyes met mine. "Where is my son?"

32

DEL

Numbly, I walked around the deserted camp. Sid circled above, crying out for Nyx while Fin and Tick searched the perimeter for clues. Everyone was gone, the horses and tack, too. It was as though our people had just picked up and ridden away without any of their things. Like they had simply vanished.

My feet dragged as I approached Liam's abandoned bedroll. The tangle of knots in my gut tightened, and each beat of my heart whooshed in my ears. My awareness tunneled to my son's discarded blanket. To his pack. To his boots, set neatly at the foot of his sleeping mat.

My rib cage constricted, and my breaths came faster. I pressed one hand against my chest, the other against my belly, and fought for air. A guttural moan clawed up my throat and leaked from between my lips. I dropped to my knees and gathered Liam's blanket, hugging it to my chest.

Where *was* he? Where was my boy? My baby?

I closed my eyes, focusing on the blanket, seeking a resonance to help me understand what had happened and where he had gone.

But there was nothing, only the faint scent of my son on the wool. I hugged the blanket tighter, breathing him in as tears streamed down my cheeks.

I jumped when Fin rested his hand on my shoulder, my eyelids snapping open. I jerked my head to the right to look up at him.

"Tick found one of our people on the perimeter," Fin said, his voice hushed and a grim set to his features.

Tick stood with her shoulder pressed against Fin's leg, her eyes alert and searching.

"It's Macy," Fin added. "Her throat was cut."

My heart dropped into my stomach, and images of Liam with his throat slit flitted through my mind's eye, but even through the dread and panic, an idea formed in my head. The minds of the dead might not be completely out of my reach. I had never tried to skim the mind of a dead person, not even Mother, when I had visited her in the catacombs. I didn't even know if it was possible, but I had to try.

I gripped Fin's wrist. "Show me," I said, the two words a command, and used his arm for leverage to pull myself to my feet.

Fin lowered his chin in silent assent.

I dropped the blanket and followed Fin and Tick to the edge of camp where Macy lay sprawled on the ground, the forest floor beneath her saturated with her blood. My senses of the world muffled as I knelt beside my guard and gathered her cool hand in both of mine. I hadn't known her well, but I had genuinely liked her, and Garath had trusted her.

"May you find peace in the next life," I murmured, bowing my head.

I closed my eyes, focusing on the wispy threads of *something* I felt within Macy. A chaotic jumble of images ghosted through my mind, but everything was warped and fractured, tainted by the last remnants of her desperation to live. I couldn't make sense of any of it.

Pressing my lips together, I released Macy's hand. If she had seen who attacked our camp, she took that information to the grave.

Blowing out a breath in frustration, I sat back on my heels and scrubbed my hands over my face.

"Come on," Fin said, gripping my elbow. "Let's get to cover so I can search telepathically."

I glared as I rose to my feet. "You haven't done that already?" I snapped.

Fin narrowed his eyes right back at me. "I searched for Liam when we first arrived, but I can't protect you if my focus is elsewhere."

"I don't care about myself!" I stared at him, dumbfounded that I had to explain this. "I care about Liam. We *have* to find him."

Fin pulled me closer, his grip on my arm tightening. "And how are you going to find him if you're dead, Del? Tell me that."

My mouth opened, but the retort caught in my throat. My chin trembled, my rage evaporating. "He must have been so scared," I said, choking on a sob. "And I wasn't here." The tears flowed freely, guilt consuming me from the inside, and I sucked in a shaky breath. "He needed me, and I—I wasn't here."

"Shh," Fin murmured, pulling me close to his body and engulfing me in an unyielding embrace. "We'll find him." Fin pulled back enough that he could see my face and meet my eyes. "We *will* find him. I promise," he repeated, speaking the words with such conviction that I had to believe him. It was that or give up right now. Just collapse onto the ground and lose my will to go on.

Fin blinked, his focus shifting to the trees. He released me and claimed my hand, pulling me back into the heart of the abandoned camp.

Tick stood near the dying campfire, her hackles raised and a low growl rumbling within her as she stared at something on the ground. It looked like a small metal can.

"Stay here." Fin released my hand and jogged ahead, crouching near the object but not touching it.

I sniffled, hugging my middle. "What is it?"

"A gas grenade." Fin narrowed his eyes and scanned the camp again. "I knew it," he muttered. "Slavers use them to incapacitate their targets so they can take captives with minimal loss of life."

I covered my mouth with one hand. "*Slavers?*"

"This is a good thing," Fin said, standing. "Better than Ferals or bandits."

I shook my head, my brow furrowing. "*How?*" I squeaked. The single word was all I could manage while holding in the sobs.

Finishing his scan of the camp, Fin turned his face to me, his expression grim. "Slavers are predictable. Without *living* captives, they have nothing to sell. Their priority is to capture. Their second priority is to keep their *merchandise* alive." He reclaimed my hand, his hold gentle, and bent his neck to bring his face closer to my eye level. "We will find him," he said again and pointed to the wagon wheel tracks in the earth. "We have their trail."

My thoughts spun, spiraling out of control. Images of Liam in a cage, of him hurt and dying, flashed through my mind.

"Del?"

My breaths came faster, my heart suddenly racing.

In my mind, I could hear Liam calling out for me. Crying. Screaming. His face was bloody. His skull was caved in. His throat was cut. He was crushed. Drowned. Burned. Suffocated. Flayed. He died over and over again in my head, dozens of different ways, and each time he was scared, crying out for me, and I wasn't there to comfort him.

I couldn't catch my breath.

Here was my greatest fear come to life right in front of me. My son was in grave danger, and *I wasn't there.*

"Del . . . " Fin cradled my jaw in his hands, his face filling my vision. "You need to take deep breaths, or you're going to pass out."

"I can't," I gasped, clutching my chest like I might tear my ribcage open and relieve the crushing pressure. Spots glittered around the edges of my awareness. "I can't breathe!"

Fin's eyes were wild, the green so vivid it appeared electrified. He crushed his lips against mine, and I froze, momentarily stunned. He broke away, leaving me breathless—but in an entirely different way than before. Stunned rather than panicked.

My chest heaved as I stared at him. "Thanks," I gasped, my lungs still pulling in deep breaths but slower than before.

Fin kissed me again, quickly, gently, then pulled away. "Any time." He slid a hand down my arm, threading our fingers. "Let's get out of the open. I need to do a more thorough telepathic search of the area to see what else we can discover, and we need to take stock of what we have. *Then* we'll go after him."

I nodded and followed him, my stomach twisting with regret. "I'm sorry," I said as we made our way to the denser woods at the edge of camp. "I shouldn't have lashed out at you like that before. It wasn't fair, and I'm sorry."

"You're scared," he said, giving my hand a squeeze. "You're not the only one. I get it. I am too. And I'm sorry."

"Don't," I said, tugging him to a halt. "This isn't your fault."

Fin nodded but said nothing, dragging his gaze away from me as he ran his hand over his face.

We crouched in a hollow formed of two giant redwoods, settling side by side against a massive, gnarled root rising from the ground. Tick laid down like a sphinx at the mouth of the hollow, blocking the opening to the rest of the woods.

"Guns out, tough stuff," Fin said, glancing down at the holster belted at my hip. "If something happens—if someone finds us—I might not hear it."

I licked my lips and nodded, drawing my pistol. I understood exactly what Fin meant. I had seen Liam fully immerse himself into animal minds before, leaving him completely unresponsive to what was happening around him.

Fin inhaled deeply, closing his eyes before slowly releasing the breath. He went completely still, the shallow rise and fall of his chest the only movement of his body.

I watched him, listening for all I was worth to the surrounding forest. Minutes passed. Tick perked up a few times, trotting off to investigate this or that, but she never stayed away for longer than a minute.

Finally, Fin sucked in a deep breath and opened his eyes. "Callon and Ada are coming."

I clutched his forearm. "But did you sense Liam?"

Fin's brow furrowed, and he shook his head. "It doesn't mean anything, though," he said quickly. "Just that the slavers have surrounded themselves with a defensive nulling field. It's clever, actually." He tilted his head to the side, a reluctant nod of respect. "Combining a sedative gas with a nulling field would minimize struggle and loss of life on both sides during a capture."

"So you're saying *smart* slavers have captured our son?" I said. "That doesn't make me feel any better."

Fin glanced at me sidelong. "Better to know what we'll be walking into, right?"

I huffed out a humorless laugh. "I suppose so."

Tick perked up again, trotting deeper into the woods. Not long after, the faint sound of footsteps crunching through the under-brush reached my ears.

"It's Callon," Fin said, standing. He reached down a hand to pull me up.

Callon appeared between the thick trunks of a couple of redwoods a dozen paces away, Ada trailing behind him, her skirt gathered up and draped over one arm to keep it from snagging on the shrubbery.

I rushed forward to meet Ada, overtaking Fin and brushing past Callon. I threw my arms around her, and she clutched me tightly. "You're all right! Thank the Patrons!" I pulled back, scanning her features. "How did you escape?"

Ada averted her gaze, a rosy blush creeping up her cheeks. "I, um . . . " She cleared her throat. "We went for a walk."

I glanced over my shoulder at Callon, who had his hands stuffed into his pockets and was staring at the ground.

"A walk?" I repeated back to her. "At *dawn*?"

Her blush burned redder.

"By the time we realized what was happening, it was too late for us to do anything but hide," Callon said, coming to Ada's defense. He moved closer to stand at her side. "I tried to reach you, Fin."

Fin threw his arms up. "I've been hiding us from a Sierra regiment." He ran his hands through his hair, exasperated.

"None of that matters now," Ada cut in. "They had a device. It created the most potent nulling field I have ever felt."

My eyebrows rose. "An *artificial* nulling field?" I looked at Fin. "Have you encountered such a thing before?"

Fin shook his head. "Not in person, but I've heard of people selling them in the Shadow District before." Fin took a steadying breath, focusing on Callon. "Please tell me you at least saw how many slavers there are, so we know what we're up against. So we can get Liam back."

Callon took a step back, raising his hands in placation. "We can do you one better," he said, his expression serious for once. "We followed their tracks until we caught up with them."

Ada nodded. "And I think I figured out how the nulling field generator works."

33

FIN

The four of us followed two sets of wagon tracks through the forest, using Tick's senses and Sid's aerial view whenever there was confusion in the path so we could keep up. Time was against us because the slavers were a solid two hours ahead.

Del and Ada's footsteps crunched loudly behind Callon and me. I would've been worried about the tracks we were leaving in our haste, but I was too focused on finding Liam. On not berating myself for leaving camp when I knew there were dangers, because there were *always* dangers.

I hooked my thumbs in my pack straps and tried to concentrate. To be strong for Del. She was unhinged on the inside and far too quiet. I knew she was trying to rein herself in as best she could.

So, I stayed vigilant, keeping my senses open for as long as I could.

I kept looking toward the sky, hoping to find Nyx up there, like maybe she might be looking for us. But only Sid flew ahead, in and out of sight, through the towering trees. We assumed Nyx was keeping close to Liam since I couldn't sense her mind either, shrouded by the nulling field.

Eventually, the wagon path led us out of the dense forest and onto an old concrete road that weaved its way out of the trees. A paved road meant we were headed toward an old town, likely overgrown and left in ruins. Still, I knew it would be some place in the open, where the forest could no longer protect us, and without the cover of trees, there would be fewer places to hide.

"If this device really does null via an electromagnetic field," Callon wondered aloud. "We're—"

"It does," Ada said. "It *must*."

"Well," Callon continued, "it couldn't possibly be selective enough to tell the difference between who the prisoners are and the slavers, so everyone should be nulled, right?"

"If they have such an intricate contraption," Del started, and I could hear the fear in her voice as the wheels turned, "couldn't they also have blockers or something so the device doesn't affect them?" I'd thought about that too and hoped the slavers weren't *that* smart.

"I doubt it," Ada said. "Or they would've known we were following them earlier. There were a dozen slavers, probably some mercs too, which means someone's Ability would've sensed us."

We all looked at each other and seemed to visibly relax, but only minutely. If Ada was right, that was one less thing we had to worry about.

"At least we have the element of surprise," Callon said, his voice ragged as we continued along the road, sticking to the thick foliage that grew up around it to stay out of sight.

"Assuming this even works," I muttered.

"The mylar blanket will block *some* of the electromagnetic waves," Ada said, her voice labored and words rushed. "But we won't know how well it will work until we've actually covered the device."

Ada was adamant that smashing the device could cause a devastating explosion, so all we could do was hope the mylar blanket I pulled from my emergency pack would block the effect of it well enough.

I looked over my shoulder at her, and her eyes locked with mine. "Access to our Abilities could be spotty," she added. "We must both be ready to null them."

"Understood," I said with a nod and glanced at Callon. "While I'm covering the contraption, you're going to look for those goddamn gas grenades—and some gas masks. Because whether it's now or later, I have a feeling we're going to need them."

Callon agreed, grinning at the thought of a new toy to play with.

"Don't you have to figure out where it is first?" Del asked. "The device—it could be anywhere."

"They must keep it in one of the wagons," Ada explained, holding up her skirt as she stepped over a log in the path. "Before I lost access to my gifts, I could feel it—the source of the nulling field."

I glanced at Callon. "How close could you get?"

"I'd say forty-fifty yards or so," he guessed.

"Then we can get relatively close," Del mused, and I could hear the relief in her voice. It was slight, but it was there nonetheless.

As soon as Sid's mind blinked to nothing, I knew we were near the slavers. Even Tick and I were out of cerebral contact, which felt strange since she was trotting alongside us.

"This is it," I told them, slowing as I peered through the break in the trees. Everyone came to a stop behind me as we caught our breaths.

A shrubby meadow spread out around an old church in the distance, stone ruins from long before the Turn. But it wasn't the crumbling white church that held my attention. At first, it was the two men on the opposite side of the churchyard patrolling the old road. Then, it was the additional wagons and all the horses tied up in the field.

"Looks like our slavers were meeting some friends," Callon muttered.

Del grabbed my hand, her arm brushing mine as she came in close beside me, her focus on the cages. "I don't see him," she whispered in a panic.

"I don't either, but he's there," I reassured her.

There were four wagon cages, and from this angle, it was difficult to tell how many and who were in each.

Callon stiffened. "Are those—"

"Ferals," I said, gritting my teeth. It was a much larger operation than I'd hoped it would be.

"Over there—" Ada pointed to an old mausoleum that was little more than rubble. "We should get closer."

I squeezed Del's hand, and we hurried along the tree line, stopping between shadows and sporadic redwoods, edging our way closer to the churchyard. It was noon, and the sun was high in the sky and hot on my face as we dashed through the clearing as fast as we could, racing toward the crypt.

The closer we got, the more the cage bars glinted in the sun, blinding us as we crouched behind a pile of granite stone. There were heaps of church rubble littered around the premises as well. The slavers had done some cleaning, which meant they used the outpost often . . . Which also meant they knew it inside and out, and they were likely prepared for just about anything.

Inhaling a deep breath, I glanced at Del and then at Callon and Ada. All of us braced ourselves as we peeked over the rubble, uncertain of what sort of state we would find our friends.

Del gasped. Her hands flew to her mouth the instant she saw Liam inside one of the other cages, wrapped protectively in Hills's arms. "Fin—"

"I know," I breathed, bracing her shoulder. I squeezed reassuringly, but my heart stopped and stuttered, equal parts relieved to see Liam and enraged that he was in a cage like an animal. As much as I wanted to hate myself at that moment for allowing something like this to happen to my son, the tracker in me—the logical part of my brain—knew we would not be able to get him out if we were in the cage with him.

His eyes were closed, and I couldn't tell if he was crying or unconscious, possibly just lethargic from the gas. Zion, Lyra, Hills, and Liam were in one wagon, while Saira and Farris were in the other. Either way, our people were all partially dressed, having been stirred so early in the morning, and baking in the hot sun; their skin glistened with sweat. I knew the slavers wouldn't leave their captives outside in the afternoon heat for very long. Not if they needed them healthy for purchase. We didn't have much time.

Crouching down again, I slung the pack off my back and pulled out the folded mylar blanket. "The guards could loop back this way any moment," I muttered. I glanced around, wishing I could use Tick's senses to see where they were. "We don't have much time." The foil-like material rustled as I shoved it under my shirt. I didn't want it glinting in the sunlight, catching the attention of anyone who might be watching.

I looked at Del and Ada. "You have your guns," I told them. "Use them if you have to." The weapons we left camp with were all we had since the slavers had pilfered everything.

"You should take one of the pistols," Del said, grabbing the hilt of her gun.

I shook my head. "I have my shotgun and my knives."

"Fin, a pistol is easier—"

"I won't leave you with a giant shotgun to lug around if you have to run," I told her, refusing to argue about it. I glanced at Ada. She dipped her head as if swearing that, whatever happened, she would keep Del safe.

I looked at all of them. "I doubt there are two devices. They don't need one for the Ferals."

"Still," Callon said. "I'll check the Feral wagons, just in case." He and I took a collective breath. There was too much unknown not to be afraid of whatever came next.

"We've got this," Ada said, her eyes fixed on mine. She was referring to our nulling capabilities. "It will work, Fin. Just find that device and get our people out of there." She looked at Callon, offering him a weak smile.

Both of us nodded, knowing we couldn't fail them—couldn't fail *any* of them.

When I met Del's gaze, she squeezed my hand so tight, I worried she might not let go. "Be careful," she breathed as her eyes scoured mine.

I didn't want to leave Del, but getting Liam out mattered more. "I'll be quick," I told her, squeezing her hand back.

Del blinked. Her nostrils flared, and she pursed her lips. "Go," she whispered. "Get our son back."

With a brusque nod, I let go of her hand, and together, Callon and I darted toward the only headstones exposed in the cemetery —a tall pillar and a life-size, crumbling angel.

That close, we could see the wagons more clearly. They were rudimentary, which I'd hoped for, and the metal cages on top of them were rusted in places from being out in the elements. Old and rusted meant there would be weak areas should we have to break into them.

With no movement, save for the people in the cages, Callon and I locked eyes, a silent plan forming. On three, we would separate. He would look for devices on the other wagons, and I would get to our people. With a nod toward the captives, Callon and I crouched down and ran for them.

I pressed my finger to my lips as I drew closer to Zion's and Hills's gaping, relieved faces, hoping the Ferals would stay quiet. I'd seen evidence they could be clever and organized, but I couldn't be certain it wasn't a secluded incident, that we hadn't gotten very, very lucky before.

"Fin," Hills whispered. Her face was smudged with dust, but she looked okay, and Liam stirred in her arms, his dirty, sock-covered feet curled under him. When his eyes opened, his lethargy from the lingering gas effects seemed to vanish, and he straightened. The green depths of his eyes welled with tears, and though I wanted nothing more than to go to him, I pressed my finger to my lips again, willing him to be strong and to remain quiet.

Liam's chin trembled, but he nodded and let Hills pull him back into her arms.

I met Farris and Saira's cloudy but relieved gazes, nodding a promise that I would get them out as soon as I could. Farris's eyes leveled on me, and he nodded toward the perimeter where I knew the slaver guards paced, as if he was promising he'd keep an eye out for them. I nodded in thanks.

"Fin." Lyra hissed my name as she sat up, blinking her eyes to focus. Like Hills and Liam, she looked sweaty and tousled, likely from being dragged or falling from the gas, but she was not beaten or harmed in any other way I could see. "The device," she started, her voice hoarse as she beckoned me closer.

She nodded to the driver's bench of the other wagon, caging Saira and Farris. "It's under the seat," she whispered. Her lips were chapped, and I could tell the gas and sun were taking their toll.

"There's only one?" I asked.

"That we saw."

I nodded and took a step toward the other wagon.

"Fin."

My eyes snapped to Lyra.

"There's about thirty of them now," she warned, swallowing thickly. "They're eating in there." She glanced at the crumbling church. "But they'll be out soon. They said they had to be at Charlotte Lake before nightfall."

Flashing her a look of grateful understanding, I hurried to the front of the second wagon. The horses craned their necks to look at me, and what I wouldn't have given to have been able to communicate with them right then. To tell them to flee with our friends.

I could hear the distant rumble of slaver voices inside the church but pushed the distraction away as I bent to look under the driver's seat, finding a small wooden box. My pulse leapt as I pulled it out, praying the contraption was inside and that I was not going to fuck this up.

Lifting the lid, I stared at an electronic gadget from another era, and before I could consider anything else, I pulled the folded mylar blanket out from under my shirt. The thin, silvery fabric rustled as I slowly, carefully unfolded it, but when Farris forced a cough so loudly the Ferals stirred, I knew we were out of time.

34

DEL

"Hurry up, Fin," I muttered, crouching with Ada behind the ruins of the mausoleum. "Hurry . . . "

Fin paused beside the wagon containing Liam, Hills, Lyra, and Zion to exchange hushed words with our people. Beyond the cluster of cages on wheels, Callon searched the supply crates stacked along the pitted stone wall of what had once been an old-world church but now appeared to be some sort of outpost for a collective of slavers.

Fin snuck along the side of the wagon and crossed to the other, the cage containing Saira and Farris, but he didn't pause to speak with them at all. He headed straight to the front of the wagon and searched under the driving bench.

"Del!" Ada hissed, gripping my forearm. "Look!" She pointed toward the line of horses at the far side of the churchyard clearing, beyond the cluster of wagon cages, our stolen mounts among them.

Alarm widened my eyes. One of the slavers who had been standing guard around the perimeter of the wagons was approaching Fin's location. The guy was big all over, with arms like tree trunks, and he carried a shotgun, a strap loaded with extra shells draped over his shoulder and strung across his body.

I quickly scanned the area for the other two guards. They still meandered along the outskirts of the churchyard, their attention focused outward on the woods and hillside. But the third guard was closing in on Fin. He had reached the back end of the neighboring wagon—one filled with at least a dozen unexpectedly quiet Ferals.

Panic rising, I glanced at Fin. A moment later, he pulled out the mylar blanket and carefully started to unfold the crinkly fabric. He *must* have found the device, but he was moving too slowly. The guard was going to find Fin before he could finish his task and escape.

My heart lurched, already preparing to grieve another person. The formidable guard was going to find Fin and capture him, too. Or worse, kill him.

Fin must have heard the slaver's approaching footsteps because he froze, the mylar blanket partially unfolded.

Without thinking, I scrambled over the pile of concealing rubble and hurried into the churchyard. I didn't have a plan beyond distracting the guard. Fin *had* to cover the nulling device. He *had* to free Liam. He *had* to survive.

They both had to make it out of this alive, or there was no future for me. Not without them.

I ran toward the packed cages. "Hey," I said, my voice raised but not shouting. I wanted to capture *this* guard's attention, not draw the notice of the other two watching the perimeter of the churchyard.

"Mom?" It was Liam. Hills and Lyra shifted so he could move to the edge of their cage and curl his slim fingers around the rusted bars. His eyes were wild with fear. "Mom, no!"

"I've been looking for you," I said once I had caught the guard's attention.

The guard narrowed his beady eyes at me from the far side of one of the Ferals' cages, then stomped around the back end of the wagon.

I glanced at Fin, a quick flick of my eyes. He had resumed carefully unfolding the shiny silver blanket, trying to avoid sudden movements or loud noises that might draw the guard's attention toward him. I slowed to a walk as I neared the beast of a man.

"Oh, yeah?" He scanned me, his attention hitching on my sheathed knife and holstered pistol, and narrowed his eyes to a suspicious glare. "Why?"

"Because you stuck my son in a cage, you asshole."

His lip curled, his cheek twitching. "I'd be glad to reunite you two." He grabbed my arm at the exact moment that Fin draped the mylar blanket over the nulling device.

My empathic senses flared to life, and I smacked my hand against the slaver's throat, curling my fingers around his thick neck. His grip on my arm tightened painfully, and I gritted my teeth.

His confusion flooded me, and I skimmed his surface thoughts in a single heartbeat. He didn't understand why I hadn't come in with my weapons out. He didn't realize there were more of us and that I was merely a distraction, just buying Fin time. Firing my gun —or appearing remotely threatening, even with my knife—might have encouraged *him* to fire his shotgun, and I didn't want to draw the attention of the slavers guarding the perimeter or those gathered inside the ancient church.

He gripped my wrist. "Listen, bitch—"

I cast an illusion of pain over his mind. Of fire and burning flesh. My gifts flickered out, the nulling device momentarily breaking through the imperfect shield of the blanket, and I held my breath as I stared at the guard's face with unblinking eyes. Had it worked? Was it enough?

The guard released me, sucked in a breath, and let out a scream of pure agony.

"Shit!" I hissed, watching him run away, his arms flailing and his shriek neverending. I hadn't thought that through. Every slaver in the area was sure to hear him.

Acting on instinct, I drew my pistol and fired twice. The first shot only grazed his shoulder, but the second struck him through the chest, and he dropped, his scream fading to a wet gurgle.

I ducked down, slinking toward one of the cage wagons filled with eerily quiet Ferals, and looked toward the former church. The commotion was bound to draw the attention of the slavers within, no matter how raucous the gathering. I spotted Callon rushing toward the double doors at the front, a shovel in hand. If I could get back to Ada, she could boost my gifts to make me strong enough to cast an illusion over this entire cesspool.

I heard hurried, crunching footsteps and spun around. It was one of the other guards who had been patrolling the perimeter. He stomped toward the cluster of cage wagons, a rifle at the ready, searching for the source of the gunshots.

I crept around the wagon to get out of his line of sight. When I straightened enough to peer over the wooden lip surrounding the cage, I found myself staring directly into the vivid blue eyes of a middle-aged Feral woman.

I gulped and raised my index finger to my lips, silently begging her—and the others with her—to remain quiet.

She stared back, no acknowledgment that she understood. But she didn't make a sound to alert the guard, either.

I spotted the small silver canister tucked into a loop on the guard's gun belt at the same moment as he found his dying companion. It looked like one of the gas grenades that knocked out our people back at our camp.

The guard stopped and turned in a slow circle, scanning the area with his eyes and the nozzle of his rifle.

I glanced at the church. It was an enclosed space, and most of the doors and windows were boarded up. Callon had slid the shovel through the front door handles, effectively locking the slavers packed in there inside, for now.

People banged on the doors from within. The shovel's wooden handle wouldn't hold forever.

Emboldened by desperation, I darted out from my hiding spot and rushed the guard while his back was to me. I unsnapped the leather loop holding the grenade canister and backed away, but not fast enough.

He spun toward me with his rifle, and I dropped the gas grenade, catching the barrel of his rifle in both hands and shoving it over my head a fraction of a second before he pulled the trigger. The explosive shot made my ears ring.

He released the rifle and reached for my neck.

Fin crashed into the guard, tackling him to the ground. I stumbled backward, scrambling for the gas grenade and clutching it to my chest.

For several heartbeats, all I could do was watch Fin pummel the guy he held pinned beneath him on the ground.

"Mom!" Liam shouted, his voice knocking me back to my senses. We may have gained the upper hand—for the moment— but that would evaporate the instant the slavers broke through the church doors.

I spun around and sprinted toward one of the boarded-up windows on the side of the church, this one missing one of the lower boards. I fumbled with the grenade's pin as I closed the final few steps to the side of the building.

I had a narrow view of abandoned tables topped with playing cards, dice, bowls of stew, and bottles of booze. People were scattered, searching for another exit or clustered toward the front of the former church, trying to get out. If they focused their efforts, they would be able to break through.

I finally pulled the grenade's pin free and tossed it into the church through the narrow opening, then I backed away toward the wagons behind me. Wisps of cloudy white gas escaped through the opening in the window boards, but thankfully, that was the only thing that got out.

I yelped when hands gripped my arms, and bucked against the restraining hold.

"It's me," Fin said, gathering me into his arms. "It's just me."

I let out a sob of relief and relaxed against him. The shouts and banging from within the church were quieting, the gas making quick work of the captive slavers.

"I'll go check the door I barred in the back," Callon said, rushing around the corner of the church, and I felt Fin nod.

I turned around. Fin's face was smeared with crimson, and my brows bunched as I searched every part of him I could see for an injury.

"It's not my blood," he told me. "Mostly."

My chin quivered, and I pressed trembling fingers to his scruffy cheek. "I thought I was going to lose you."

His eyes sparked defiantly. "Never," he said, pressing a hard kiss to my lips. "You're stuck with me, now."

35

FIN

"The third guard!" Lyra warned from inside the cage. Del and I spun around just as he lifted his pistol, aiming at us from across the clearing. He didn't get a chance to pull the trigger, though.

A rifle fired. The horses spooked and tugged at their ties, and a bullet went straight through the guard's head. He blinked, dropped his unfired pistol, and fell to his knees before careening face-first into the dirt.

Callon lowered his rifle from where he stood at one of the hitching posts. His shoulders hunched, and his chest heaved with relief. "That was close," he said, dripping with exhaustion.

"Too close," I told him. "Thank you." I stared into my best friend's eyes. It wasn't the first time he'd saved my life.

Ada rushed out from behind the mausoleum to Callon to ensure he was okay, placing a hand on his arm as their eyes met.

The horses nickered anxiously, and Del and I let out a collective sigh as the wagons shifted with anxious bodies.

"Liam," Del breathed.

"Mom!" he croaked. She ran to the cage our son was locked in.

Though it tore at me to watch Liam reach through iron bars to grasp hold of Del, I exhaled my relief now that he was safe and ran my hand through my hair.

"I'll figure out how to turn the device off," Ada offered.

"Don't destroy it," I said, turning to her. "We might need it."

She agreed, but hearing quiet whimpers, I turned back to Del.

"It's all right," she promised Liam. Gripping the bars with one hand, she wiped a stray tear from his cheek with the other. "We'll get you out of there—all of you." Her gaze swept the weary, dirt-streaked faces peering out from the cages.

"Everyone get back," Hills said, jiggling the rusty cage door to check its integrity.

Del looked at her, nodding as she put space between herself and the wagon.

Liam, Lyra, and Zion crowded to the back, and the entire wagon shook with Hills's unbound strength now that she was no longer subdued. In one swift kick, the gate smashed open, torn from its hinges, and the iron clattered to the ground.

Since everyone who had been gassed was a bit unsteady on their feet, Callon and Ada helped them climb out of the cage. They murmured with anxious relief as they stretched and reveled in their sudden freedom.

Hills made her way to the second cage with Farris and Saira, and I went to my son.

"You were so brave," Del murmured, holding him tight against her. She squeezed her eyes shut, likely thanking her Patrons that, once again, Liam was safe.

I wasn't sure how much more of this Del could take. How much *I* could. First, Alastor and King Eduart, then Maylar and the usurper. Now, this?

Liam peered up at me with a different sort of fear in his eyes. "I saw them," he said, his voice reedy. "When they snuck into camp, but it was too late. I tried to send Nyx, but I couldn't—"

"Hey," I told him, crouching to take his hand. The disappointment in Liam's voice was soul-crushing. "There was nothing you could've done. That device of theirs made certain you couldn't have." I held my son's shoulders, staring into his eyes, praying he saw the pride I felt for him. "You were very brave, Liam. Much braver than I was when I was captured."

His brow furrowed—even Del seemed to stiffen hearing that—and Liam licked his lips, his head tilting slightly. "You were caught by slavers?"

I nodded, only allowing myself to think about those three days now that Liam was no longer in danger. "My sister and I were. I was eight, and it was the first time I met Jake—he came to get us out, just like your mother and I will always come for you. No matter what."

After that day, Jake started coming around more and staying longer each time, until one year, he decided not to leave at all. "You were far braver than me."

Liam nodded, and my heart nearly burst as he wrapped his arms around me.

I held him tightly, squeezing my eyes shut. "I'm proud of you."

"Here," Lyra said, coming up to us with a canteen. "Water." She handed it to Liam. All the captives looked parched and drained from the beating sun, desperate for shade and water. But it was Lyra I was worried about.

I stared into her eyes. "Are you okay?" It wasn't her thirst or bruises that concerned me but the old wounds likely reopened. Her second run-in with slavers in recent years.

Lyra nodded and looked down at Liam, her eyes gleaming slightly, but I left her alone. "Drink up," she told him. "There's plenty more."

Liam gulped a few long pulls down, gasping for a breath when he was finished.

"Hey, Liam," I said carefully, knowing he was exhausted, but I had little choice. He wiped his mouth dry with the back of his hand. "We need to make sure there are no more slavers." I glanced at Del, watching us with red-rimmed eyes.

I stood, looking between Liam and the ravens who had flown over from the forest at some point and landed on the metal cage. "Will you help Nyx and Sid check the roads?" Tick was already sniffing around the back of the churchyard, looking for any unseen danger. "I need my attention focused here."

"Yeah," he said, nodding as he licked his lips.

"Come on," Del said, curving her arm protectively around Liam's shoulders. "Let's sit in the shade and get you out of the sun." She gave me a tight-lipped smile and led Liam over to a fallen headstone in the shade of a poplar tree.

While Callon and Ada helped distribute water to the others, I focused on the cart horses and the few tied to the wagon the slavers had collected along the way. The animals were still restless and reeling from all the commotion, tugging and pulling against their ties and tack, desperate to get away.

"Shh," I breathed, drawing closer. Callon was busy retrieving gas grenades from where they had been stashed under the benches in each of the wagons, but I hardly noticed as I tried to soothe all the horses, my mind extending to theirs in supplication. Slowly, I reached out to the closest one and pressed my palm to his face as I closed my eyes. *Friends.*

There was a moment when I felt the shift. A moment when not only the horse understood, but I felt a calm overcome me as well, and the adrenaline coursing through me subsided enough to feel the ground under my feet, the breeze against my skin, and the air in my lungs as I drew a breath in and out. I felt grounded again.

Rarely had I been completely cut off from my powers, and it was a strange sensation, like part of me was missing. I breathed with the horse, relishing the feeling of connection again.

There was something else on the periphery of my mind. A tingling sensation that I'd felt before but couldn't quite place, and I nudged it, uncertain what it was.

"Fin," Callon said quietly at my side. My eyes popped open, refocused, and I looked at him.

He nodded behind him to where the others sat under the shade of an old oak tree, hydrating as they tried to gather themselves after such a taxing ordeal. They weren't looking at me but at the caged Ferals.

I scanned the Ferals' faces, just as browbeaten and slicked with sweat as our people were. Nearly a dozen of them watched us with as much anger as they had apprehension and desperation. Then I saw her.

Shrewd blue eyes. Long, coal-black hair. The woman from the forest. The Feral who had led the attack on the Mantis envoy and had let me take the Sierra soldiers' uniforms. Her eyes were locked on me. I saw the recognition gleaming back at me. I saw the uncertainty as much as I saw her curiosity, the same as I felt.

Hers was the mind I could feel. Or perhaps all of theirs—a gentle nudge against my consciousness.

I stepped over to the cage.

"Fin," Callon warned, but I couldn't hear him. Not really. I was lost in the Feral woman's eyes. Unable to stop reaching for her mind.

Ferals running. Being corralled and bludgeoned. Children screaming and running to get away. The gas. The shooting. I saw flickers of their home in the hills somewhere to the south. I saw crude dwellings and campfires. I saw her on her horse. The horse I'd just calmed.

For all the memories the woman showed me, all I could offer her were the images of the Feral slaves I'd seen digging in Death Valley. And I knew when she'd felt them because I sensed her rage like it was my own. I sensed the loss of someone dear to her. I sensed her fear.

Slavers. Bodies in the church. It was the only consolation I could give her, other than her freedom.

"Let them out," I told Hills, her quickly recovering super-strength allowing her to shed the effects of the gas much faster than the others.

"I don't think—"

I looked at her. "I said let them out. Please."

Hills stared at me, her expression hard.

The Ferals glanced anxiously between all of us, permanent scowls on their faces. They didn't trust our people, the same as mine lacked trust in them.

"They have helped us before," I explained, trying to keep my voice steady. "Let them out."

Hills looked at Del, who must have nodded because Hills finally relented. Though Hills clearly didn't like the idea, she went to the cage, attention fixed on the keen-eyed Feral woman. The other Ferals looked at one another, bracing themselves and readying to lunge at Hills if needed. I flexed my hand, readying myself, just in case.

Their leader hummed something. It was almost inaudible, but the sound commanded the attention of everyone in the cage with her. Their focus locked on her, waiting for another command, but the woman's gaze remained on me.

Reluctantly, and after a heavy sigh, Hills tore the cage door off.

The Ferals grumbled, and finally, their leader looked at them, dipping her head before she said what sounded a lot like *friends*.

My eyes widened. For centuries, the Ferals had been consumed by their most primal instincts, a side effect of the Turn that no one truly understood. The more I saw them, and the more I interacted, the more I realized they were so much more than we believed.

"Nobody hurts them," I warned, eyes shifting over Hills and the Corvo guards.

Slowly, the Ferals climbed out, skittish and ready to pounce at the slightest threat. Hills pulled the last cage open, moving aside as the rest stepped out into freedom.

"Let them take what they want," I told everyone. "We take the device, weapons, and only what the slavers took from us. The rest is theirs."

"What about the slavers?" Callon asked, his voice wary as he nodded toward the church. "They won't sleep forever."

"We leave them to their fates," I said, glancing at the Feral leader as she walked carefully over to her horse. "Let these people decide what they will do with them. They've more than earned it."

36

DEL

I rode as close beside Fin's horse as I could without knocking the black mare off course. The rest of our people plodded ahead and behind us on their own mounts, Callon and Ada leading the way a good distance ahead.

I had originally demanded that Liam ride with me, so I could be as close to him as possible, but Fin and Hills had pressured me to reconsider. Now that I watched Liam droop sleepily on the back of Fin's horse, Fin's sturdy arms the only thing keeping him from toppling to the ground, I was grateful for their clearheaded foresight.

All of our people who had been captured still suffered from the lingering effects of the sedative expelled by the gas grenades, but they could all at least stay awake enough to ride. Likely because of his smaller size, Liam seemed the most affected. He had been drifting in and out of consciousness, lulled by the steady, rocking motion of the horse.

Dust swirled above the dry, cracked earth. The towering redwoods had given way to increasingly scrawny pines as we crossed the mountains dividing the verdant land of the Sierra Kingdom from the unclaimed desert lands east of the Seven Kingdoms. Cacti and scraggly shrubs had replaced the pines as we descended from the mountains, but now there was only a flat expanse of parched ground dotted by sagebrush for as far as the eye could see. Fin's people supposedly had a manned outpost set up on the edge of the desert lands, stocked with supplies to ease the journey, but I had yet to see any sign of such a place.

I twisted in my saddle and peered up at the sun hanging in the clear, blue sky, baking our backs. I wanted to get Liam somewhere shady to rest. This heat couldn't be good for his already taxed body.

"We're almost there," Fin said, and I turned my attention back to him.

"Am I that transparent?"

His cheeks tensed with the hint of a smile, and he shook his head. "It's that hot." He laughed dryly. "Been living out here for years, and I still haven't grown accustomed to the dry heat."

My wrung-out heart ached for Fin and his many losses, not least among them his home on the coast.

"We're close. Look," he said, pointing to the way ahead.

A dark strip cut through the sun-bleached ground from one horizon to the other. At the front of our train of horses, Callon veered left to travel parallel to the dark strip.

I squinted. "Is that *a road*?" I looked at Fin. "Out here?"

"It was a highway from before the Turn," he said, nodding slowly as he gazed at it. Heatwaves rose off the ancient asphalt, distorting the air.

"People *lived* out here?" I raised my eyebrows. "Voluntarily?"

"Not many," Fin said, glancing at me sidelong. "But the desert's not as forbidding as it looks. It has its own unique kind of allure."

I studied him out of the corner of my eye, wondering if he meant that or if he was just saying that to make the best of an unpleasant situation.

"And there's the Pearsonville outpost," Fin said, his attention focused on the way ahead.

I followed his line of sight, spotting the boxy outline of a small building beyond the gradual rise of a low slope stretching out from the foothills we had just left behind. A short string of even smaller structures came into view as we drew closer, leaning precariously. I couldn't make sense of what I was seeing. The whole place looked like it was about to collapse in on itself.

"*This* is the outpost?" I asked, raising my eyebrows.

The corner of Fin's mouth twitched. "Doesn't look like much, does it?"

I snorted a laugh.

"That's the point," he said. "We reinforced the main building from within but preserved the original exterior for camouflage. Anything that *appeared* sturdier would have drawn unwanted attention."

I frowned, studying the cluster of buildings as we approached, noting a third structure, nearest us, fallen to the pressures of time. It lay in a heap of rotted wood, broken glass, and rusted metal. A half dozen decrepit ancient vehicles lined one side of the collapsed building. Another structure appeared to be one strong gust away from joining the other on the ground.

Signs were intermittently nailed along the top of buildings: *Hotel, Barber Shop, General Store.*

My brow furrowed. "Was this a town?"

"At one point," Fin said. "I think, in the end, it was an Old West museum."

I looked at him and shook my head. "I don't know what that means. What is *Old West*?"

"It was what our ancestors called this area centuries before the Turn." He pointed to the narrow, precariously leaning structures. "That's a ghost town." He shrugged. "It's what the early settlements out here looked like before the big cities like San Francisco and Seattle rose up."

I was very familiar with San Francisco, of course. Its ruins were the bones lying beneath Corvo City, after all. But I had only ever read of the ancient city called *Seattle*, though I was fairly familiar with the settlement that had risen there since the Turn, the Evergreen Nation, thanks to the emissaries from that strange land who had visited Castle Corvo.

"We turned that into a stable," Fin went on, speaking of the long "ghost town" structure. "We needed a hidden place for horses. Wouldn't do us much good to work so hard to conceal the outpost if we left the horses out in the open."

We were close enough that, now that he had mentioned the longer structure was used as a stable, I could make out the shadow of a horse's head moving through one of the broken windows.

Fin pointed to the larger, boxy building, maybe fifty yards ahead. "That's where we'll actually be staying."

At the head of our group, Callon stopped his horse and raised a hand to his mouth, whistling a complex combination of tones that was clearly a signal.

I glanced at Fin, my eyebrows rising.

"We always station a null here to hide the mind signatures from any who venture nearby," Fin explained. Which meant Callon hadn't been able to telepathically communicate with the people posted here. Our arrival would be a complete surprise to them. "Callon is letting them know we're friendlies."

On cue, a door on the side of the larger building opened, and three people emerged—a shrewd-eyed, middle-aged woman, a hawkish man of around the same age, and a slim, androgynous teenager with dark, close-cropped hair. I figured the latter was the null. Otherwise, I couldn't imagine why Fin's people would allow a relative child to take up what was undoubtedly a dangerous post.

The woman's hard features softened when her eyes landed on Callon, and her lips spread into a broad grin. He had that effect on pretty much everyone.

Callon slid down from his saddle and wrapped his arms around the woman, lifting her off the ground. Her coarse, booming laugh reached us, and I couldn't help but smile. Callon greeted the man much the same way, then chucked the teen under the chin.

Hills, Lyra, Saira, and Zion dismounted, everyone but Hills sagging against their horses. Hills seemed to have recovered the quickest from the lingering effects of the sedative gas.

Farris stayed atop his mount, peering around as Hills approached Fin's horse and helped Liam down from the saddle.

Liam blinked and peered around groggily.

With an exhausted groan, Fin dropped down as well, then reached up to help Ada dismount from our shared mount, then me. The gesture was unnecessary but sweet all the same. I swung my leg over the rear of my horse and accepted his support as I lowered to the ground. My knees ached from so long in the saddle, and my leg muscles were a little shaky.

Fin and I headed for Callon and the trio stationed at the outpost, Hills following close behind with Liam. The strangers' good-humored laughter transitioned into protests from the woman and crossed arms from the man.

"I'm sorry, Callon," the woman said, shaking her head. "A group of ten just arrived. I don't know if we have the rations or space—"

The man noticed Fin first. "Joya," he said, his stare tracking our approach. The man stepped forward, placing a hand on the woman's shoulder.

When the woman—Joya, apparently—spotted Fin, her eyes widened. "Finlay," she said, bowing her head. The man and teen already had their faces angled toward the ground.

Intrigued, I hung back with Hills and Liam, curling my arm around Liam's back as I watched the interaction between Fin and the others with interest. I had known Fin felt a lot of responsibility where his people were concerned, but this level of respect and deference was unexpected.

"I didn't realize you were here," Joya said, raising her head and meeting Fin's eyes.

"I'm sorry for the trouble, Joya, but we need to stay the night," Fin said, stopping in front of her. "We'll sleep wherever there's room. No need to fuss over us," he assured her. "We'll head for the settlement at first light, take these people with us, and send more provision to you as soon as possible."

Joya bowed her head again. "Of course." She straightened. "No trouble at all. Mikail, Sacha," she said, glancing at her companions. "Help them get their horses situated." She returned her attention to Fin. "Follow me. It'll be cramped in there, but we'll make it work."

Fin turned, his attention locking onto me, and he waved us forward. "Let's get Liam inside."

Hills, Liam, and I followed Joya and Fin to the larger building, the others trailing behind us, feet dragging, while Callon and Ada hung back with Farris to unload the horses.

Joya pushed the back door open and toed a wooden wedge underneath it to keep it from shutting. "Are these people unwell?" she asked, scanning our group.

"Not exactly," Fin said and stepped to the side to stand with Joya, letting Hills and me usher Liam through the doorway and into the cooler indoor space.

The reinforcements Fin's people had made to the structure— sturdy new posts and beams—were glaringly obvious inside the room. It reminded me of a warehouse of sorts. Barrels and crates were stacked up along one wall. The supplies and provisions Fin had mentioned. About a dozen cots were spread out through the space, long, unmoving lumps filling them, telling me people were currently slumbering there.

Hills and I stood with Liam in the middle of the room, unsure where to go. Liam's eyelids drooped. Even Hills, with her enhanced constitution, appeared worn out.

"He can use my cot," Sacha said, apparently shirking Joya's command to see to the horses and walking ahead of us to the semi-private nook. "Let me just tidy up." The teen gathered books from the cot and hugged them to their chest as they sidestepped out of the way.

"Thank you," I told Sacha, hoping my weariness didn't completely mask my genuine gratitude.

Hills and I guided Liam forward, Hills settling him on the cot while I unlaced and pulled off boots I'd brought with a few of the things the slavers had left at our camp. I tucked Liam's shoes under the cot, and he was already asleep by the time I knelt near his head.

I combed my fingers through his unruly curls, closing my eyes and reaching out with my empathic senses to double-check that his sleepy state was still just a side effect of the sedative gas and not caused by something more serious, like a head injury. His mind was foggy with the drugged haze, and he felt unwell, but I didn't sense the disjointed confusion characteristic of a concussion.

Sighing, I opened my eyes and sat back on my feet.

Hills rested a hand on my shoulder. "I'll stay with him," she offered, lowering herself to the floor beside me. "I'm sure they could use another pair of hands attached to someone who can actually think straight out there." She indicated the back door with a raise of her chin.

I didn't want to leave Liam, but my skim of his mind had assured me he wouldn't be waking soon, and helping to get the horses settled and resting up for the remainder of the journey would be more useful than hovering over Liam and fretting. I covered Hills's hand with mine and flashed her a small smile filled with gratitude. "Thank you."

She pulled her hand away and leaned against the edge of the cot. "You showed true bravery back there and handled yourself well," she murmured, laying her head on her curled arms. "Garath would have been proud."

Her mention of Garath caught me off guard, knocking me temporarily breathless, and I shook my head. My chin trembled, and tears welled in my eyes. I couldn't believe I had any left to cry. "He would have been so mad," I told her.

"No," Hills said with a sleepy smile. "He only would have pretended to be mad."

Heart aching, I stood and headed back for the door, passing the others getting settled on the floor. Fin was still speaking with Joya immediately outside the door, and I grasped his hand, giving his fingers a quick squeeze as I passed him.

I saw Callon disappear behind the camouflaged stable while Ada and Farris remained with the horses still milling out in the open, methodically removing their saddlebags and piling them up to the side.

I headed for Ada and the cluster of horses, nodding to her before gathering a couple of sets of reins and leading two of the animals toward the end of the stable, following Callon's trail. I found a wide, open doorway on the backside of the long building, near one end, and could hear Callon's voice within. The horses plodded along behind me amiably as I guided them into the enclosure.

Within, sunlight filtered through the broken windows, revealing a long line of stalls, most of which were already occupied by horses. I found Callon within the third stall from the door, unsaddling a palomino mare. Mikail and Sacha fed the horses in stalls farther in.

"Glad for the help, princess," Callon said, exhaustion only mildly tempering his good humor.

I released the reins on one of my charges and lured the other into the first vacant stall, glancing past Callon to Mikail and Sacha. Despite Sacha's kindness to Liam, they were strangers to me, and I was uneasy about them learning who I really was.

Callon peeked over his shoulder. "Ah. Sorry." He mimed zipping his lips. "I'll be more careful."

The corners of my mouth twitched. "I thought your lips were zipped?" I set to work on the saddle cinches.

Callon grinned at me over the mare. "Like that would ever hold."

Laughing under my breath, I shook my head.

Mikail made his way down the stable aisle, nodding to me as he passed.

I watched him leave, gripping the horn and seat of the saddle, prepared to haul it off the horse's back, then looked at Callon. "They really respect Fin, don't they?"

"Of course they do," Callon said offhand. "He's our leader. It would be weird if they didn't respect him."

I stared at him, dumbfounded. The bulky saddle slid off the horse, heavy in my grip as I took a staggering step backward. "Do you mean, like, *the* leader of your people?" I shook my head, heaving the saddle over the rail.

I had seen how the others acted around him, but I had thought his role among his people was more of leadership in the general sense, not that he was *the leader.* I removed the saddle blanket from the horse's back and draped it over the saddle, then stepped out to the aisle, shut the stall door, and approached Callon's stall. "What do you mean?"

Callon's ever-present smile slipped, and he narrowed his eyes at me. "What do you mean, *what do I mean?*"

"I mean . . . what, exactly, do you mean?"

Callon frowned. "You don't know?"

Again, I shook my head, rolling my eyes. "Know *what,* exactly?"

Callon lifted the saddle off the mare much more smoothly than I had and carried it out of the stall. "You've heard of the Ghost King?" He set the saddle down on the floor. "You must have. The name is whispered all over the Seven Kingdoms."

I scoffed a laugh and crossed my arms over my chest. "Yeah, but the Ghost King is just a rumor." There was always the name of some mythical foreign ruler on the lips of the people, either sowing fear in their blood or hope in their hearts. The Ghost King was only the latest, around for four or five years, rumored to be amassing a vast army of renegades and outlaws.

"Is he a rumor?" Callon said, narrowing his eyes and tilting his head to the side. "Is he really?"

I studied Callon's features, reading his implied meaning. "You're saying *Fin* is the Ghost King?" My brow furrowed. "But I didn't see anything about that in his mind."

That gave Callon pause, and I realized how that might've sounded to him. "Well," he continued, "Fin doesn't think of himself as a king, and I certainly wouldn't recommend calling him the *Ghost King* to his face."

"But—but—" Again, I shook my head. "Are you *sure*?"

Callon flashed me an apologetic smile and gave my shoulder a squeeze. "Maybe you should be having this conversation with Fin," he said and stepped past me. "Seems to me you two have a lot to talk about."

I turned, watching him leave. And then I followed him out and marched straight for Fin.

37

FIN

"They came just a few hours ago," Joya explained, nodding to the ten newcomers passed out on the cots inside. "They didn't eat or anything but went directly to sleep. When they wake up, they'll be ravenous." She sighed sadly and crossed her arms over her chest. Her slightly graying brown hair was pulled into a ponytail at the base of her neck. "They said they lost two people on the way here from Zenia. Two run-ins with bandits between here and there."

"How many soldier sightings?" I asked, wondering if there were any signs of Eduart mobilizing his army to invade our lands yet.

Joya shrugged. "They didn't mention soldiers. But it seems the slavers have quite the enterprise in that part of the country now."

I shook my head, wondering if the world would ever get better. "We'll make sure we get them to the settlement tomorrow when we leave at first light," I promised her. "In the meantime, thank you for accommodating us. I know you weren't expecting more mouths to feed or bodies to house."

Joya smiled sadly. "I'm never expecting anyone, and yet they keep coming. Everyone looking for a safe place." Her gaze was distant for a moment, fixed somewhere beyond me, then she licked her lips and nodded inside. "It's a tight fit, but at least we can help everyone. It looks like you've all been through a lot." Her gaze lingered on Zion and Saira. "Those are Corvo guards," she noted. Even if they'd dressed down from their normal garb, their weapons were etched with the Corvo seal.

I realized Joya was watching me, waiting for a response.

"You forget I lived in Corvo City for twelve years," she said, and glanced at Liam, sleeping on the cot inside, Hills at his bedside. "And if I didn't know any better, that is the young prince."

Joya eyed me closely, more curious than anything, and I inhaled a deep breath. I knew we couldn't keep the secret of who Del and Liam were for very long—I didn't want to. These people deserved to know what trouble might come their way. But I hadn't thought I would have to address it quite so soon.

"There's plenty to tell," I confessed, scrubbing the side of my face. "But for now, we need to keep these people safe. We'll address everyone when we're ready."

Joya's brown eyes softened, and I knew she would remain quiet. "I'll have Sacha help me get some food together for every-one. And some water."

"Thank—" I looked past Joya to see Del marching toward me. There was a strange look on her face, one I hadn't seen before, and the last of my easiness vanished. She looked . . . angry.

"Can I talk to you for a minute?" she asked, coming to a halt in front of me. It sounded more insistent than a mere request.

Joya's gaze shifted between Del and me, and if I didn't know better, I would have said she looked rather intrigued. I cleared my throat. "Let me know if there are any issues with the supplies. Or with the feed for the horses."

"Of course." Joya bowed her head, which I had told her a dozen times to stop doing, and she left me alone with a fierce-eyed Del.

I was almost afraid to speak, but I turned to face her, bracing myself. "What's wrong?"

Del clenched her hands on her hips and tilted her head quizzically. "It's funny how, in all our conversations over the past week, you failed to mention that you're the *Ghost King*," she said in a rushed whisper, and my cheeks flushed red.

I glanced around to ensure we weren't the center of attention, then took Del's hand. I led her toward the shade of the old General Store that wasn't much more than boards hardly standing.

"First of all," I started. "It's not like we've had a ton of time to talk." I wasn't sure why I was feeling defensive. Or maybe it was that I didn't like talking about this kingly business. Ever. "Second, it's *just* a name—"

"Just a name?" Del gaped at me. "I've been receiving weekly reports on the rumored Ghost King and his supposed amassed army *for years*. And you're telling me it's you—it's been you this whole time?"

"No. Well, yes, I guess, but that's what the Ghost King is. A rumor. I am no king, Del. You know that as well as anyone." I rubbed my temple. "Are we really arguing about this?"

"No, I just—I see these people looking at you as if you are everything to them . . . " She scowled, her annoyance obvious. "I didn't realize."

I peered around the abandoned town, at this world so different from any Del's ever known. One of strife and loss and constant movement. An existence that hinged on hope and camaraderie. Whatever misgivings Del might've had, and whatever it was that she'd heard, when she looked at me, I didn't want her to see anyone but me. Not a rival or a king, even an outcast one.

"These people came out here with nothing, Del. They were either forced away from their homes, or they fled from them in fear. So no, it's not a kingdom, and I am no king. But it is a refuge, and it's all they have left. All *I* have left." Her eyes shadowed with regret, and my mind wandered back to Fallen Wood and my life with my sister, Jake, and my friends. We lived on the outskirts of existence because our lineage was connected to a dangerous past that threatened the core beliefs tying the Seven Kingdoms together.

"You know I come from a long line of *Ghosts*," I told her. "It's what your people have always called me and mine. Only now, the nickname has taken on a life of its own. As the raids and displacement worsen, people use the name to rally survivors together. To bring them here."

I took Del's hands, peering into her thoughtful brown eyes as she absorbed words I'd never spoken. Not to anyone. "I'm not amassing a vast army. And we don't want to fight—many already have just to be here, with us. But my people will fight if they have to. So will I."

"I guess it makes sense now," she muttered and huffed an exasperated laugh.

"What does?"

"All the people you know. I mean, you were granted an immediate audience with the *assassin twins,* of all people."

I chuckled at the moniker and lifted Del's hand. "I guess there are perks to being a nomadic outlaw," I teased and brushed my lips across her knuckles. My eyes didn't leave hers as I said, "I rescued a princess along the way."

Del smiled, a real, heart-stopping smile, and the uneasiness or shock she had was gone for now.

"And," I continued, "she's had my heart ever since."

Del practically snorted and rolled her eyes. "Wow. What a line—"

"It's the truth," I promised, neither of our smiles wavering.

Del took her hand back and lifted an expectant brow. "Yeah? I bet you say things like that to all the ladies."

"No, no lines."

"Why? Because you're so suave that you don't need them? Women swoon the second you step into a room?"

Though I knew Del was teasing, there was a hint of something more in her voice that I didn't like, and I shook my head. I wanted to tell Del that no one compared to her. That no one else had ever mattered because it was always her . . . But she would think it was another line, so I took her hand instead. I placed it on my chest, splaying my fingers over hers.

My heart was pounding as I opened my mind to her. Whatever she saw, if she wanted to glean anything at all, she couldn't unsee. But it would be worth it if she finally knew how much she meant to me. Truly knew it and felt it in her bones the way I did.

"It's only ever been you, Del," I told her, and the moment she realized what I was offering her, her brow furrowed with uncertainty.

Her touch was so intimate and terrifying, yet, I'd never wanted Del to see me more than I did standing there with her. In that moment. I lifted my other hand and stroked the side of her face.

Del's eyes flitted shut, and I showered her with the memories that had kept me up each night and had absorbed me for the past ten years. I held nothing back because I wanted her to see me. To feel what I felt for her with every memory, no matter how much they changed throughout the years. I wanted Del to know Fin, the man, not the boy. I wanted her to feel and see it all.

The seconds passed painstakingly slowly, and my heart continued to race as I considered how very dangerous this might be, but still, I waited.

When Del's eyes finally opened, the amber flecks in those brown depths glowed in the dying sunlight, and it wasn't discomfort or misery or regret shining back at me. It was something indescribable, something that made me feel as if every unspeakable thing we'd gone through over the years had been worth it. Had brought us to this moment.

"I've missed you too," she breathed, and seeing the relief in Del's eyes, I couldn't help myself. In the heat of the setting sun, I wrapped my arms around Del and kissed her for what felt like the first time in days.

It was only as I heard Callon clear his throat that I begrudgingly opened my eyes and broke our kiss.

Callon grinned as he passed, his arms stacked with blankets to shield our people against the cool desert night. Glancing around, I realized we did have a few onlookers, some curious, others confused and intrigued.

I cleared my throat. "I should be helping them," I said, but when I looked at Del, at her kiss-swollen lips and flushed cheeks, I knew so much would change when we reached Shoshone, and I wasn't ready for that yet. "Can I show you something?" I asked.

Del huffed a laugh and tucked a loose strand of hair behind her ear. "Last time you said that, things didn't end well."

That was a sucker punch to the gut, but I knew she was only teasing. "We don't even have to leave camp," I promised.

She smiled, a soft, pretty curve of her lips that awakened every male part of me. "Of course, you can show me."

"Hey, Callon!" I called, and he looked over his shoulder. I beckoned him to me, and he took a few steps backward. "We'll be on Birdy if you need anything." I jogged over and snagged one of the blankets off the stack in his arms.

He nodded with a trademark grin. "Have fun."

Del grinned as I jogged back to her. "We'll be on *Birdy?*" she clarified.

"She's my favorite."

"Your favorite *what?*" Del asked as I led her over to the rusted semi-truck trailer I'd spent many nights on over the years. "Should I be scared?"

"Not at all." I winked and helped Del climb to the top.

"What are we doing up here, exactly?"

"The sun is about to set," I told her and plopped down on the roof. "The desert is famous for its sunset."

"Oh, really?" She smiled and sat down beside me, easily leaning back into my arms. I pulled her against my chest and reveled in the moment. There was something about having Del out in the desert I now called home, with the people I trusted, that made everything feel strangely right, and I wanted to show her every secret, special thing about this place.

"You know what else the desert is known for?" I asked, voice low in her ear.

Del craned her neck to look at me. "What's that?"

"Its sunrise."

A knowing smirk curved her perfect lips. "Oh?" Her eyes sparkled in the setting sun, and I wanted more than anything to have Del by my side forever. But if for now was all I got, I would take it a thousand times over. "And what is there to do out here until sunrise?" she asked with a smile in her voice.

I brushed my lips against her ear. "I can think of a few things."

Del giggled, my breath tickling her neck, and leaning in, I kissed her like tomorrow didn't matter. Like she was just Del, and I was just Fin, and there were no kingdoms and no prophecies. I kissed her the way a man worships the woman he loves, with every breath and brush of my lips, because Del was the part of me I'd lost for so long. And I finally had her back.

38

DEL

T he slog across the desert took two days and was hard and exhausting. Now that we had the refugees from the outpost with us, Callon, Lyra, and Fin seemed to fall into a different rhythm—more serious and attentive. I imagined that's how they were out here, in the desert they called home, where they were responsible for others. Still, as well adapted as Fin and his friends seemed, I didn't understand how anyone could live out in this barren wasteland, where the world was painted in shades of muted brown.

We stopped near a hidden freshwater spring to make camp for one night, moving on at first light. Now that we were so close, Fin was eager to return to his people.

By midafternoon on the second day in the desert, when the sun hovered high in the sky like it was resisting its inevitable descent and my clothing was soaked with sweat, the cracked, patchy road we had been traveling alongside since early that morning met with the vestiges of another ancient highway. A rusted green sign on the right side of the new road declared that we would reach some old-world place called *Shoshone* in one mile.

Had there really been a town out here, nestled between the

craggy mountains to the east and the barren hillsides to the west? I couldn't imagine *why* anyone would have settled out in this wasteland, especially during those ancient times of convenience and plenty. Perhaps overcrowding drove them away from the cities.

"I'll let them know to prepare for the group," Callon told Fin, and he trotted ahead. We were getting close.

Perhaps Fin and his people had settled atop the ancient ruins of this *Shoshone*. I glanced at Fin, riding on my left at the front of our group, but he seemed deep in thought and didn't notice my attention. On my right, Liam had the glazed look of someone who had spent hours upon hours on horseback.

As we veered south, following the new highway, spots of vibrant green appeared here and there on either side of the road. At first, there were just a few bushy shrubs, larger and of a more vibrant green than the scraggly sagebrush that littered the desert floor. But soon, patches of tall grass swayed in the warm breeze. Those patches gradually merged, becoming a legitimate field.

"Look, Mom!" Liam said from his mount beside me as we passed through a gap the highway cut into a low slope in the hillside. He pointed farther up the road. "Palm trees!"

My eyes widened. About a quarter of a mile ahead, squat palm trees clustered along the shoulder of the highway. Beyond them, I could just make out the outlines of dozens of small huts, some wooden, some adobe. It was hard to tell for sure through the distorting heat waves rising off the road, but I thought I could see people moving around among the structures.

"Not quite what you were expecting?" Fin said from my other side.

I glanced at him sidelong, unable to tear my attention fully from the settlement ahead.

"There was a town here—before," Fin explained. "We've been able to repair enough of their wells to make them functional for our numbers. Plus, there's a spring-fed creek we use—sparingly—for irrigation. Just enough to get by without running it dry."

I frowned, my eyebrows rising. Of all I had seen in Fin's mind, nothing had prepared me for such a well-established settlement. I had been picturing a glorified camp filled with people scrounging to get by. But since he mentioned irrigation, I could see the patches of green on the ground along the edge of the settlement that had to be their gardens and small agricultural fields.

"You can grow enough food to feed everyone?"

Fin shook his head. "We forage a bit, too—pine nuts, mostly— but hunting is the real staple. Bighorn sheep and deer when we can find them, jackrabbits and tortoises when we can't."

I suppressed a grimace, not loving the idea of eating a tortoise.

"There's not much wood to smoke the meat, but there's plenty of salt, so . . ."

As we drew closer to the settlement, I attempted to count the dwellings but gave up when I passed twenty-five. There had to be well over a hundred huts, with tents scattered around the outskirts of the more permanent structures.

"How many people do you have out here?" I asked, looking at Fin fully.

"We had just passed a thousand before I left." He lifted one shoulder. "But new people are always trickling in—more and more of late, as you have seen." He nodded to the new folks riding on horseback behind us. "What, with the unrest in the Seven Kingdoms." He clenched and unclenched his jaw. "I imagine we'll see a big influx soon from the Corvo Kingdom, now that you're no longer in power."

I pressed my lips together, not so sure.

"You don't think your people care who rules them?"

I shrugged. I didn't think they cared if *I* ruled them. I was nobody special, and now the world knew. *My people* knew.

Fin let out a dry chuckle. "You're wrong, Del."

Unsure how to respond, I flashed him a halfhearted smile.

"You're wrong," he repeated. "You'll see."

At the sound of approaching hoofbeats, we looked up to see a figure on horseback galloping toward us from the settlement. I recognized the paint horse as Callon's, but the rider was someone else entirely—someone I hadn't seen in over a decade. The very same man I needed to find. Jake.

"He's back," Fin whispered. He nudged his horse ahead at a trot.

Fin met Jake a hundred yards ahead, both stopping and reaching out from atop their horses to grasp hands in greeting. They exchanged a few words, and Fin glanced back at us. Jake's stare weighed a thousand pounds as it settled on me. Fin wheeled his mount around and trotted back toward me, Jake following alongside him.

My mare slowed, then stopped as the pair approached, either by choice or at Fin's telepathic request.

"Princess," Jake said, nodding his head in my direction. His borrowed mount came to a stop beside Fin's horse, and his focus shifted to Liam. He scanned my son's face, almost certainly looking for physical similarities to Fin, then bowed his head to Liam as well, and his attention returned to me. "A lot has changed since I last saw you."

I laughed under my breath. "Like the fact that I'm no longer a princess?"

"Leadership has little to do with bloodlines. Just look at Fin here." Jake glanced at Fin, pride shining in his eyes. "I was sorry to hear about the unrest in Corvo City, but I'm glad to see you escaped."

"When did you hear?" Fin asked. "I'm surprised the news has already reached all the way out here."

"I heard when I was in the mountains and brought the news here myself." Jake flashed Fin a halfhearted grin. "I figured you would want to rescue Del and came to offer help, but I see you've already done it. Next thing I know, you'll be putting me out to pasture."

Fin smirked, but the shadows in Jake's eyes made me wonder if there was something more behind the statement. Something darker.

"Let's keep moving," Fin said. "I want to get Del and the others settled in. And I promised Joya we'd send her provisions. There'll be plenty of time for catching up this evening." Fin guided his horse to turn around again, and Jake's mount fell in step beside Fin's as they led us into their settlement.

It was even more impressive up close. The fields of crops were lush, if compact, the tents were large, sturdy canvas and leather structures, and I mentally upgraded the huts to cabins. A cluster of larger adobe structures with obvious purposes—blacksmith, tanner, butcher, bakery, trading post—formed something of a town center at the heart of the settlement.

Callon and a few others joined us in the pseudo town square, and Fin dismounted to greet them. His quiet confidence shone brighter when he was around the people who looked to him for guidance. I had seen sparks of his knack for leadership back at the outpost, but watching him delegate so deftly, I couldn't help but admire him. He was a natural. Born to lead.

I glanced at Jake, understanding what he had meant about bloodlines.

"Sorry about that," Fin said after dispatching the last of his people to help our group settle in. "I know you're exhausted." He approached my horse and gathered up Liam's and my reins, guiding us on our mounts away from the others toward a break in the buildings. "We're just through here."

It took me a moment to make sense of what I was seeing behind the adobe structures. Sturdy wooden doors set about ten feet apart, rested against the face of a low cliff that curved around the backside of the buildings.

I squinted, studying the doors. They weren't resting *against* the cliff face. They were set *into* the cliff. Doors to something dug into the cliff.

The words of the first prophecy whispered through my mind.

The same prophecy being used as propaganda all over the Sierra Kingdom to unite the people and bulk up their army. To rile them up.

Uncover and destroy the destructive force hidden under the earth in Death Valley.

"Patrons preserve me," I breathed. "Fin, I think I know what the first prophecy is about."

He glanced back at me as we approached the centermost door. "Oh, yeah?"

"It's you," I said, my voice barely audible. "Your people. Your settlement. The destructive force Eduart is so desperate to get his hands on *is you.*"

39

FIN

“It’s you,” Del said breathily. “Your people. Your settlement. The destructive force King Eduart is so desperate to get his hands on *is you*.”

I stared at Del, my stomach churning at the implications of that. “If you’re right, then they were here digging up the land, searching for something they would never find.”

Del blinked at me. “They don’t know,” she added. “They’re searching blind. They have no idea what they’re looking for.”

“Eventually, they’ll figure it out, and when they do, they’ll want to annihilate us,” I thought aloud. Prophecies were poison, and though I knew King Eduart having his sights set on us would be bad, if Del was right, we wouldn’t be fighting over land and whatever lay buried beneath our home, we would be fighting for our right to live.

My pulse quickened. My palms began to sweat. I looked up at Liam in the saddle, his tired gaze glancing worriedly between us.

“Let’s get you settled in,” I said, clearing my throat. “Then we can discuss this.” Part of me felt horrible that my quarters weren’t a suite like at the castle, more of a hovel carved into stone than anything. But the cliffs were the coolest dwellings in the settlement, and Liam was already struggling in the heat.

I stopped the horses in front of the door to my quarters. "This is us. There's a cot you can share." I nodded toward the door in the cliff face. "Make yourselves at home—whatever you or Liam need, just let me or Callon know."

Del seemed reluctant to let the topic drop in the middle of such a big unveiling, but Liam was more important than the looming future right now. "Callon's bringing water for you both to clean up with," I told them. We were all sunbaked and dusty.

"Thank you," Del said, sliding down from her horse. She reached for my arm and gave it a squeeze, then lifted on tiptoes to press a kiss to my lips, letting it linger a brief second. She unfastened the saddlebags, and when I pulled the door open, she guided Liam inside.

Sighing with relief that we were finally here, I peered out at the settlement, the cabins and the tents filled with people who were counting on us, more than they realized yet.

Jake walked alongside Callon, both carrying large waterskins our way, and Jake met my gaze. A mixture of exhaustion, frustration, and resentment bubbled inside me as Jake approached. Callon offered water to the refugees dismounting their horses, and I looked directly at Jake.

"Where have you been?" I asked him.

"Searching," Jake said cryptically, handing his waterskin to a woman in the group. Then he came to stand with me.

Farris, who I had forgotten about, eyed us closely before he scanned the settlement, taking it all in. It was far too easy to forget Farris was around most of the time. He was so quiet, which was one of many reasons Pyra and Kalliope chose him to accompany us. Farris was here to observe, that much was clear. And there was no doubt in my mind he would have a list of observations to report back to Pyra by the time he returned to Noctem. He met my gaze before he nudged his horse toward the stable.

Once he was gone, I gave Jake a sideways look. "Searching for what? I woke up one day, and you were gone." I knew that's how Jake used to be, always wandering around the continent, but most of my life, he'd been present, and I thought his nomadic days were over.

"I was searching for answers." His reply was short and unapologetic, and while I was used to Jake, both the haunted look in his eyes and the distance in his voice, I'd needed him with me. I'd needed his help and guidance more than ever, and for months, he hadn't been here. The little boy in me was angry at him for that.

"We could've used you here," I told him. "We have people coming in droves every week. We have a new threat every day to the people that came to us to protect them. And you just . . . vanished."

"There will always be trouble, Fin. There will always be someone in need and hard decisions to be made—"

"I know, and I thought we were in this together."

"This is *your* path, Finlay," he snapped at me, and I felt myself stiffen. Once the words were out, regret filled his amber gaze. "I'm sorry," he said, rubbing his hand over his face. "Like you, I've just arrived, and I'm exhausted." He placed his hand on my borrowed horse's face, his thumb brushing her nose absently. "It wasn't my intention to abandon you, especially now with so much unrest. But this is what leadership is," he said. "You will always be up against something—there will always be a fight or a war to be waged. It is the way people are." He peered out at the horizon like it had a beauty only he could see after so many centuries walking toward it.

I wanted to know where his heart was because it wasn't here with us. Not like before. "I might not always be here."

Knowing Jake's regenerative Ability would not let him die, I wondered what he was implying, exactly. "Are you leaving again?" I asked, my heart inching its way into my throat.

All issues with King Eduart faded away as I watched Jake. He stared at me with those emotion-filled eyes that held lifetimes of unrest.

I was beginning to feel the toll even one lifetime took . . . I could barely fathom centuries of them.

A little dust tornado whipped by, sending my hair blowing into my face. "Look, Jake. I know you don't like to talk about what troubles you," I told him, lowering my voice. "And I didn't mean to project my shortcomings onto you. It's just—it's been a long couple weeks, and every time I wanted to ask for your guidance, you weren't there."

Jake turned to me, resting his hand on my shoulder. "And yet here you are," he said with a proud smile. "You saved the princess and have come home to us. To your people. Whatever your adventures have been this time, Fin, you are a leader now. You lead these people, not because of me, but because it is who you are. It's you they are drawn to. I'm just . . ." Jake shrugged with a soft chuckle. "I'm just the crazy uncle everyone knows about, but no one understands."

I laughed at that. "You *are* an uncle, now, you know?"

Tick trotted up, her tongue lulling from her mouth and her tail wagging as if she couldn't be happier to be home.

Jake looked to the doorway as Callon emerged. Del and Liam stood inside, wiping off the dust from the journey. "Or," I amended. "Maybe a grandfather?" I shrugged. "I guess you get to pick." It was a strange reality to consider, given he looked no more than forty years old, at most.

Jake's eyebrows popped up. "Grandfather?" he mused. "I haven't been one of those in a very long time." Another memory from long ago clouded his gaze, painful if the sudden lines around his eyes were any indication, but also pleasant as his mouth quirked slightly. But Liam—I grinned at the thought of him. He would make Jake smile, despite himself.

I scratched Tick's head a final time before she meandered her way back into the square, soliciting all the attention she could get now that there were so many people to lavish her with it.

"Would you like to formally meet my son?" I asked Jake. He had seen Liam when we arrived, but they hadn't truly met. I wasn't sure why, but I held my breath, waiting for disappointment or censure to cross Jake's face from my reckless boyhood decisions. But none ever came.

Instead, Jake tilted his head ever so slightly, and his eyes began to shimmer. "I would be honored."

I exhaled, relief creeping between my lips as I smiled and waved Jake to follow me. "Hey, Liam," I said, leaning outside the doorway.

Liam and Del both stopped scrubbing their arms clean and looked at us.

"Remember the old man I told you about, the one who thinks he knows everything?"

Jake chuckled behind me, and I felt a little lighter at the sound.

Liam nodded with gusto. "*The* Jake?"

"Yes. This," I said, glancing at the only father figure I'd really ever known, "is *the* Jake."

Del whispered something to Liam, and he trundled over, his eyes wide with excitement, even though exhaustion weighed heavy on him. "You're a Patron," he started and studied Jake carefully as he looked him up and down.

"I've been called worse, I guess," Jake muttered.

"And really old," Liam mused. "But, like, *how* old exactly?"

"*Very*," Jake answered with a slight grin.

"Can I guess?" Liam asked.

"Do you think you can beat Fin's record of guesses?" Jake lowered his chin, patiently waiting. I remembered playing this same game when I was younger.

Liam considered it and shrugged. "How many guesses do I have to get it right?"

"Seven—"

"Six," I corrected. "Don't skimp out on me now, old man," I told him.

Liam grinned. "I bet I can," he beamed.

"Good, then you can guess while we unpack some of the stuff I brought back for you guys on my travels."

Liam gaped at him. "You knew we were coming?"

"Of course," Jake said. "It's just like Fin said—I know every-thing," he joked, and Liam fell into step beside *the* Jake as they made their way to his cliff quarters two doors down.

I huffed a laugh as Del hummed contentedly, looping her arm through mine. But when I looked at her, she sobered a little. "We should get some rest," she said. *Because we have a lot to figure out* went unsaid.

I leaned in and kissed her temple, peering out at the bustling settlement surrounding us, filled with people depending on me to keep them safe. I wanted to say there was no time to rest, but I knew Del was right. Whatever came next, we would need clear heads to face it.

40

DEL

Kneeling beside Liam's cot, I tucked the blanket under his chin and leaned over to kiss his forehead. "I'll be in shortly," I murmured.

"Where are you going?" he asked, the hint of a whine in his voice. He didn't whine much anymore, but after all we had been through in the past few weeks, he was hesitant to let me out of his sight.

"Outside—just on the other side of that door." I glanced at the heavy wood door, which was cracked open, letting the deep murmur of Fin's and Jake's voices drift into the cave. They had stepped out after Jake returned with Liam, so I could get Liam settled into bed. "I need to talk to Fin and Jake about something. I won't be long." My jaw cracked with a yawn. "I'm as eager to rest as you are."

Liam nodded, putting on a brave face, but worry still shadowed his eyes. He inhaled to respond but coughed instead. He had been weak and complained of being light-headed several times throughout the day, but he had seemed well enough when we arrived. I pressed my hand to his forehead and frowned, wondering if he truly felt warm or if it was all in my head.

It was impossible not to think of the wasting sickness when it was present at the forefront of my mind so much recently. But this was likely just a cold, some bug Liam picked up during the journey. I tried and failed not to consider any lasting effects the gas might've had on him.

Even so, the need for a wasting sickness cure felt more urgent now than ever.

I removed my hand and pressed another kiss to Liam's forehead. "I'll only be a moment," I reassured him and stood, gathering my notebook off the floor. I turned to the door, the notebook hugged to my chest. The muted voices grew clearer as I approached.

". . . heard about the digging?" Jake asked.

Heat slammed into me the instant I pulled the door open. It was amazing how much cooler the temperature was in this man-made cavern dug into the cliffside than it was outside. Based on the aged appearance of the door, the dwelling had been here a while. I wondered just how long.

Fin nodded, glancing at me as I crossed the threshold. "That's originally why I left. I wanted to find out what they were looking for—to see if we need to be worried."

I pulled the door shut to block our voices from reaching Liam and quietly moved closer to Fin.

"Did you find any answers?" Jake asked.

"Not exactly," Fin said. "There's a prophecy that seems to be at the root of the excavations. It's being used as some sort of propaganda by Eduart. I can't remember the exact wording." He shook his head and peered over his shoulder at me. "You have it memorized, don't you?"

"Oh, um . . ." I cleared my throat. "'Uncover and destroy the destructive force hidden under the earth in Death Valley,'" I recited. "I'm pretty sure it's talking about you guys—your people." I glanced back at the door to the man-made cavern. "Since Fin here is technically living *under* ground."

"Could be," Jake grumbled and blew out his breath. "Damn prophecies—vague and cryptic, as usual."

"Speaking of that prophecy," I said, relaxing my hold on the notebook so I could open it to the page listing the prophecies I had scrawled from memory. I turned the book around to face Jake. "I think there's more to it. I stumbled across these when I was going through my mother's desk."

Jake clenched his jaw at the mention of Mother. Not surprising, considering all the physical and mental torture she had put him through.

"She's gone—dead," I told him, hoping that knowledge would ease his mind some, even if it troubled mine. I hastily pushed onward, tapping the tip of my index finger against the page listing the three prophecies verbatim, starting with the one about the destructive force that *had* to be Fin's people.

Jake's eyes moved from side to side as he read the lines.

Uncover and destroy the destructive force hidden under the earth in Death Valley.

One by one, the seven will fall until only one remains.

When purity kills and the last raven falls, look to the dreamwalker for guidance. The cure will . . .

When Jake reached the end, he looked at me. "Very ominous," he said, his voice a low rumble. "Why are you showing *me* this?"

"The third prophecy is attributed to Becca," I explained. "And the same fragment appears in every copy I've seen of her book of foretellings." I met Jake's cautious stare. "I think we need the original."

"Then you're out of luck," Jake said, shaking his head. "There is no *original*. Becca didn't record most of her own prophecies—especially not near the end." He cleared his throat, his focus drifting past me. "She wasn't well." His throat bobbed. "Zoe recorded what she could." The corner of his mouth twitched, and again he shook his head. "But then, she wrote down *everything*. She always had multiple notebooks going. They were stashed all over the farm, so she would always have one close at hand when she needed it."

He was talking about the Patrons' original homestead in Hope Valley.

Jake blinked and refocused on me. "That's probably why Becca's 'book of foretellings' is so spotty. We had bookshelves filled with Zoe's notebooks at one point, but if you ask me, they should all have been burned."

My eyes widened with terror. "Did you burn them?"

Jake looked at me and rubbed the back of his neck as he reluctantly shook his head. "No, Zoe wouldn't let me. But we couldn't bring them all when we abandoned the farm, either. We hid what we could, but I'm sure we missed a few. The fragmented prophecies that have been reprinted are probably from the notebooks we left behind."

I searched his eyes, my heart beating faster. "Does that mean you know where the rest of Zoe's notebooks are? The ones you hid?"

Jake narrowed his eyes. "Assuming they're still there, yeah."

"Where?" I asked, closing the book and once again hugging it to my chest.

Jake glanced at Fin, then returned his attention to me. "How badly do you need this prophecy?"

I laughed halfheartedly, my shoulders hitching higher. "The wasting sickness is destroying my kingdom, and every attempt to create a synthetic healing elixir fails. These prophecies are the only hope we have of a cure."

"That's not entirely true, is it?" Jake said pointedly, crossing his arms over his broad chest.

"I'm not like my mother," I snapped. "I won't imprison Healers and harvest their blood."

Jake eyed me, his stare assessing. And then he sighed, his shoulders sagging as he looked to the sky. "Will I never be free of these damn prophecies?" he asked nobody in particular.

I reached out, resting my hand on Jake's forearm. "Where are the notebooks?" I asked, hoping to skim the location from his mind. But there was nothing concrete. No images of places or flashes of memory. His mind was a vault, sealed tighter than ever.

I did, however, sense a hint of something dark. He was so weary. It settled around me, heavy and suffocating. It pushed the air from my lungs, and I locked my knees to keep them from buckling under the weight of his misery. How was he walking around with this leaden heart? How was he still walking around at all, talking to us like everything was okay?

Jake looked down at my hand, then raised a glare to my face and took a deliberate step backward, moving out of arm's reach.

Once I was no longer touching him, I could finally draw in a breath.

"Del?" Fin asked, his hand settling on my back. "Are you all right?" He looked back and forth between Jake and me, knowing something serious had passed between us.

But before he could ask more, Jake said, "Looks like you're going back to where it all started, kid."

"What?" Fin asked, surprise driving away the concern tensing his features. "What do you mean?"

"Zoe's notebooks," Jake said. "I stashed them in a chest with some other things we couldn't bring with us but didn't want to leave out in the open and buried it at the base of the tree on the farm." He looked at me. "As much as I hate the thought of going back there, if you really want to find the rest of that prophecy, you'll need to go there and dig up the notebooks."

It was clear that all the talk of Becca's prophecies scared Jake. How could it not? Her prophecies had upended his life repeatedly, eventually forcing him and the rest of the Patrons into hiding. He didn't want to unearth them, but that didn't mean he *wouldn't* do it.

"Wait, are you talking about the Patron Tree?" I shook my head, my brow furrowing. "But that's going to be impossible to get to unnoticed."

The Patron Tree had been created by Camille, the Patron of the Movers, at the Patrons' original homestead on the first anniversary of the Turn. It was a huge metal tree, the leaves of which were engraved with the names of all the Patrons' loved ones who fell to the virus and the turmoil after.

The farm was located in Hope Valley in Zenia, the kingdom immediately to the north of Corvo Kingdom, and the entire site was a holy place for people throughout the Seven Kingdoms. Tens of thousands of people went on pilgrimages yearly, and the surrounding land was supposedly *always* crowded with visitors' tents. How would we ever be able to dig up a chest buried at the base of the holy site's focal point?

Jake looked from me to Fin and back. "I've lived long enough to know that *nothing* is impossible."

41

FIN

"Leave for Hope Valley? *Now*?" I frowned and led Jake and Del farther away from the door to my quarters, not wanting to disturb Liam's rest. For the first time since reuniting with Del, I felt the future I'd dared not hope for with her wavering around me like it could crumble at any moment.

"Del," I said carefully. "We just got you and Liam here where it's safe." Dread slithered its way in because if Del and Liam left, I couldn't go with them. Not this time. Not when the people here needed me more.

"I know it's not ideal, Fin—"

"Ideal? King Eduart could have his army here within the week."

"Or maybe months," she countered. "It could be ages—a year— before he makes his move. He has to figure out that *you're* the danger first. Besides, his troops are scattered all along the borders right now."

"And if he attacks the settlement and we're not here?" I said, glancing at Jake. "What happens to all of these people?" I glared at him. I knew the settlement wasn't his priority, but it was mine. "I won't leave them to fend for themselves."

"Then you should stay," Del said, resolved. The words were reluctant, but they were true. I *should* stay. I knew I should. "Hills and Ada," she continued, "they'll go with Liam and me. Jake, too." She glanced at him, waiting.

He nodded reluctantly.

"We'll figure it out with Jake's help, and you can stay here and prepare for what comes next. But this is important to—"

"To the Corvo Kingdom. Yeah, I get that, but those aren't my people. Corvo and the rest of the kingdoms turned their backs on me and everyone else here. I *won't* do the same to these people. Look—" I took Del's hands in mine, willing her to understand what a risk she'd be taking. "I know you don't want your people to suffer the same fate as your mother, but right now, you aren't even their princess. You aren't their queen. You'd be risking your life to find a cure for people who stood by while you were imprisoned. Don't forget, all those people at the coronation turned their backs on you." My words were desperate, but I grasped for them all the same. "You've already given so much to them, and now there is a bounty on your head. You realize that, right?" I hated the way her expression shadowed, hearing such truths, but Del knew she might be dead right now if we hadn't gotten her out of her precious kingdom.

I saw the indecision in her eyes. The resolve mixed with the questions neither of us could answer. "I don't care," she said. "My people are dying, Fin, and I might be able to do something about it. And just like you, I won't turn my back on them."

"You mean the wealthy aristocrats who doomed themselves?" The words were snide, but I didn't care. Knowing Del had sacrificed her happiness and safety for the past ten years to keep both Liam and her kingdom safe, and was yet again considering risking her life for people who were completely unaware of the sacrifices she had already made for them, made me sick to my stomach.

Del glanced between me and Jake. "I know you both resent the nobles of Corvo Kingdom for what was done to the Healers, but that was all Mother and Maylar. And it's no longer only the pure-bred nobility who are getting sick. There have been countless other cases—people whose ancestors crossed Class lines and whose gene pools should be so diluted, a hereditary, congenital illness like the wasting sickness *shouldn't* affect them at the numbers it is. But *it is*."

I stared at Del, hardly hearing her because I already knew there was nothing I could do to change her mind. And there was nothing that would change mine, either. She would not stop until she knew if the cure mentioned in Becca's prophecy was real, and I would not abandon my people to search for a cure for Del's. Not when real, tangible lives were at stake here. And more than that, I wouldn't continue to risk my life for people who didn't deserve it, not when I had a son's future to think about now, among all the others.

"Then I guess we know where our paths lead us next," I said, and squeezing Del's hands once more, I let go of them.

Del's eyes watered as she peered up at me. "I have to try, Fin," she whispered, pleading with me to understand. But I already did.

I nodded. "That's because, crown or not, you're the Corvo queen. You were born to lead them, Del, even if they don't know it yet." I wrapped my arms around her and inhaled the scent of her hair, faint lavender and pine from the forest. I knew it might only be hours or days before she and Liam walked away again, and I wasn't certain they would ever be back.

"When will you leave?" I breathed, meeting Jake's gaze over her head. None of us wanted this, and for the first time, I thought I knew the loss Jake had felt before—far too many times to count.

"I don't know. Soon, I guess," Del murmured.

I squeezed my eyes shut. "It's not fair," the little boy in me said. "I just got you back."

"I know," she whispered into my chest.

I met Jake's regretful gaze again. "How many times have you

had to do this?" I asked. "Had to leave—to flee because some prophecy told you to?"

Jake didn't answer because I knew it was an unanswerable question. In over three hundred years, it must have been countless. His sister, family, and friends—as originals, they were at the heart of so many of the prophecies.

At the crunch of footsteps, I glanced over my shoulder to see Callon and Ada approaching, Callon carrying a large cast-iron pot by its handle and Ada a stack of bowls, with spoons and napkins resting on top. "We brought stew," Callon said, holding it up. His gaze roved over us, likely noting the tension clouding the air. "We'll just put this all on the table inside."

I nodded my thanks and hadn't fully turned back to Del when Ada's voice rang in the air. "Something's wrong!"

The three of us spun around as Ada rushed into my quarters, Callon standing at the doorway, pot in hand and fixed in place.

Del ran into the room, and I followed to find Liam leaning over the cot, his face red, his breathing shallow—too shallow. His eyes were glassy with fever in the candlelight, and a sheen of sweat glistened on his skin.

"Liam, sweetie—" Del knelt on the floor by the cot and ran her fingers through his hair, pressing her other hand against his forehead.

"Fever," Del breathed.

Crouching beside them, I offered Liam a cup of water from the table.

"Fin," Callon said. "He looks just like Dylon."

"Who's Dylon?" Ada asked, hovering by Del's shoulder.

"A little boy in camp who's been sick with a fever too." I shook my head. "But this can't be the same thing. We only just arrived. Liam couldn't have caught it already."

Tears clouded Del's eyes. "Have Dylon's hands been trembling?" she asked, swallowing thickly. The gravity in her voice made my stomach lurch.

"I don't know," I admitted, and though I dreaded her reply, I needed to know the answer to my next question. "Why do you ask?"

Del closed her eyes, and a tear dripped down her cheek as she lifted Liam's hand. His fingers twitched in a way that seemed unnatural. "It's the wasting sickness," she breathed, only barely. She rose to sit on the edge of the cot and pulled Liam into her arms. Her chin quivered as she murmured reassurances to him.

When I looked at Ada, there was horror in her eyes. And then I remembered the ill and intoxicated people outside the Menagerie and the crowded streets of the Shadow District. The look of fever. The tremors. I'd thought it had been strix, but was it *all* the wasting sickness?

The world shattered as I peered down at my son.

I thought I'd known terror. That I'd been afraid before, but never had I felt the claws of panic inching their way up my throat or this insurmountable weight of absolute dread. Liam was just a boy. An innocent. He wasn't one of the purebred elites who had damned themselves with inbreeding—he came from Del and me, and we were perfectly fine. We were nobodies.

"How can this be?" I asked Jake, suddenly desperate for him to have the answers. "What do we do?"

Jake's expression wasn't one of surprise or despondency as he shook his head. It was one of sympathy. Of resignation. Because this was how life was—this was the life he'd been living for centuries.

I fell to my knees beside Del and Liam, pulling them into my arms. "It's okay," I said, desperate for it to be true. "We will find the cure," I told Del, more adamant. I looked into her tear-filled eyes. "We'll find the cure. I promise. And we'll do it together."

THE END

Del and Fin's adventures continue in *The Ghost King*, book two in The Ending Legacy series, releasing in late 2023.

In the meantime…

If you haven't read *World After*, the prequel story where Fin and Del's adventures began, you can purchase it at all book retailers.

The series that started it all…
Follow Jake and fellow Patrons during the first year of the great Turn in *After The Ending*, book one of The Ending Series.

And be sure to check out the Savage North Chronicles, another Ending World Series, written by Lindsey Pogue.

More Books by the Lindseys

ABOUT LINDSEY POGUE

Lindsey Pogue is a genre-bending fiction author, best known for her soul-stirring, post-apocalyptic survival series, Savage North Chronicles and Forgotten Lands. As an avid romance reader with a master's in history and culture, Lindsey's adventures cross genres and push boundaries, weaving  together facts, fantasy, and timeless love stories of epic proportions. When Lindsey's not chatting with readers, plotting her next storyline, or dreaming up new, brooding characters, she's generally wrapped in blankets watching her favorite action flicks with her own leading man. They live in Northern California with their rescue cats, Beast and little girl Blue.

Access VIP Exclusive Content & Newsletter
www.lindseypogue.com/newsletter

About Lindsey Sparks

Lindsey Sparks lives her life with one foot in a book—so long as that book transports her to a magical world or bends the rules of science. Her novels, from Post-apocalyptic (writing as Lindsey Fairleigh) to Time Travel Romance, always offer up a hearty dose of unreality, along with plenty of history, intrigue, adventure, and romance.

When she's not working on her next novel, Lindsey spends her time hanging out with her two little boys, working in her garden, or playing board games with her husband. She lives in the Pacific Northwest with her family and their small pack of cats and dogs.
www.authorlindseysparks.com

MAIN SOCIAL MEDIA
Instagram: @authorlindseysparks
YouTube: Author Lindsey Sparks
Discord: discord.gg/smTeDHQBhT

OTHER SOCIAL MEDIA
TikTok: @authorlindseysparks
Pinterest: @authorlindseysparks
PATREON: https://www.patreon.com/lindseysparks
www.authorlindseysparks.com/join-newsletter